"Lay down your w̶ ̶ ̶ ̶ ̶ ̶ ̶ ̶ ̶u are surrounded and outnumbered!" shouted the lead soldier, stepping forward.

Before he could utter another word, Ezio had sprung from his stance, energy returning to his weary limbs. The lead guard had no time to react, not expecting his opponent to be so bold in the face of such overwhelming odds. Ezio's sword arm circled in a blur, the blade whistling as it sliced through the air—the guard tried in vain to raise his sword to parry, but Ezio's movement was simply too quick. The Assassin's sword hit its mark with unfaltering accuracy, slicing into the guard's exposed neck—a plume of blood following its impact. The three remaining guards stood motionless—astonished at the speed of the Assassin, and idiotic in the face of such a skilled foe. This delay was their death. Ezio's blade had barely finished its first lethal arc as he raised his left hand, the mechanism of his hidden-blade clicking as the lethal spike revealed itself from his sleeve.

It pierced the second guard between the eyes before he could even twitch a muscle in defense.

Ace titles by Oliver Bowden

ASSASSIN'S
C R E E D ®
BROTHERHOOD

OLIVER BOWDEN

ACE BOOKS, NEW YORK

THE BERKLEY PUBLISHING GROUP
Published by the Penguin Group
Penguin Group (USA) Inc.
375 Hudson Street, New York, New York 10014, USA

USA / Canada / UK / Ireland / Australia / New Zealand / India / South Africa / China

Penguin Books Ltd., Registered Offices: 80 Strand, London WC2R 0RL, England
For more information about the Penguin Group, visit penguin.com.

ASSASSIN'S CREED® BROTHERHOOD

An Ace Book / published by arrangement with Penguin Books Ltd.
and Ubisoft Entertainment Ltd.

Ace Books are published by The Berkley Publishing Group.
ACE and the "A" design are trademarks of Penguin Group (USA) Inc.

For information, address: The Berkley Publishing Group,
a division of Penguin Group (USA) Inc.,
375 Hudson Street, New York, New York 10014.

ISBN: 978-0-441-02057-7

PUBLISHING HISTORY
Ace premium edition / December 2010

PRINTED IN THE UNITED STATES OF AMERICA

14   13

Interior text design by Kristin del Rosario.

Special thanks to Yves Guillemot, Jean Guesdon, Jeffrey Yohalem, Corey May, Ethan Petty,
Matt Turner. And also Alain Corre, Laurent Detoc, Sebastien Puel, Geoffroy Sardin,
Sophie Ferre-Pidoux, Xavier Guilbert, Tommy François, Cecile Russeil, Christele Jalady,
The Ubisoft Legal Department, Charlie Patterson, Chris Marcus, Eric Gallant,
Maria Loreto, Guillaume Carmona.

AUTHOR'S NOTE

Most of the translations from foreign languages in the text are my own, but for the quotation from Machiavelli's *The Prince* and the quotation from Virgil's *The Eclogues* (though I have adapted the latter very slightly). I am indebted to the late scholars George Bull (1929–2001) and E. V. Rieu (1887–1972), respectively.

—OLIVER BOWDEN, PARIS, 2010

PROLOGUE

The events of the past extraordinary fifteen minutes—which might have been fifteen hours, even days, so long had they seemed—ran through Ezio's head once more as he stumbled, his brain reeling, from the Vault beneath the Sistine Chapel.

He remembered, though it seemed like a dream, that in the depths of the Vault he had seen a vast sarcophagus made of what looked like granite. As he'd approached it, it had begun to glow, but with a light that was welcoming.

He touched its lid, and it had opened as if it were light as a feather. From it a warm yellow light glowed, and from within that glow arose a figure whose features Ezio could not make out, although he knew he was looking at a woman. A woman of unnatural stature, who wore a helmet, and on whose right shoulder sat a tawny owl.

The light surrounding her was blinding.

"Greetings, O Prophet," she said—calling him by the name that had been mysteriously assigned to him. "I have been waiting for you for ten thousand seasons."

Ezio dared not look up.

"Show me the Apple."

Humbly, Ezio proffered it.

"Ah." Her hand caressed the air over it but she did not touch it. It glowed and pulsated. Her eyes bore into him. "We must speak." She tilted her head, as if considering something. Ezio, raising his head, thought he could see the trace of a smile on the iridescent face.

"Who are you?"

"Oh—many names have I. When I . . . died, it was Minerva."

Ezio recognized the name. "Goddess of Wisdom! The owl on your shoulder. The helmet. Of course." He bowed his head.

"We are gone now. The gods your forefathers worshipped. Juno, queen of the gods, and my father, Jupiter, its king, who brought me forth to life through his forehead. I was the daughter, not of his loins, but of his brain!"

Ezio was transfixed. He looked at the statues ranged around the walls. Venus. Mercury. Vulcan. Mars . . .

There was a noise like glass breaking in the distance, or the sound a falling star might make—it was her laughter. "No—not gods. We simply came before. Even when we walked the world, Humankind struggled to understand our existence. We were just more advanced in Time." She paused. "But, although you may not comprehend us, you must take note of our Warning."

"I do not understand!"

"Don't be frightened. I wish to speak to you but also *through* you. You are the Chosen One for your Time. The *Prophet*."

Ezio felt a mother's warmth embrace all his weariness.

Minerva raised her arms above her and the roof of the Vault became the Firmament. Her glittering face bore an expression of inexpressible sadness.

"Listen! And see!"

Ezio could hardly bear the memory: He had seen the whole Earth and the heavens surrounding it as far as the Milky Way, the galaxy, and his mind could barely comprehend his vision. He saw a world—his world— destroyed by Man, and a windswept plain. But then he saw people—broken, ephemeral, but undismayed.

"We gave you Eden," said Minerva. "But it became Hades. The world burned until naught remained but ash. But we created you in our image, and we created you, whatever you did, however much cancerous evil was in you, by choice, because we gave you choice, to survive! And we rebuilt. After the devastation, we rebuilt the world and it has become, after eons, the world you know and inhabit. We endeavored to ensure that such a tragedy would never again be repeated."

Ezio looked at the sky again. A horizon. On it, temples and shapes, carvings in stone like writing, libraries full of scrolls, and ships, and cities, and music and dancing.

Shapes and forms from ancient civilizations he didn't know, but recognized as the work of his fellow beings.

"But now my people are dying," Minerva was saying. "And Time will work against us . . . Truth will be turned into myth and legend. But, Ezio, Prophet and Leader, though you have the physical force of a mere human, your Will ranks with ours, and in you my words shall be preserved—"

Ezio gazed at her, entranced.

"Let my words also bring hope," Minerva continued. "But you must be quick, for time grows short. Guard against the Borgia. Guard against the Templar Cross."

The Vault darkened. Minerva and Ezio were alone in it, bathed in a fading glow of warm light.

"My people must now leave this world. But the Message is delivered. It is up to you now. We can do no more."

And then there was darkness and silence, and the Vault became a mere underground cellar again, with nothing in it at all.

And yet . . .

Ezio made his way out, glancing at the writhing body of Rodrigo Borgia, the Spaniard, Pope Alexander VI, Leader of the Templar faction—bloody in his apparent death agonies; but Ezio could not bring himself, now, to deliver a *coup de grâce*. The man seemed to be dying by his own hand. From the look of him, Rodrigo had taken poison, no doubt the same canterella he had administered to so many of his enemies. Well, let him find his own way to the *Inferno*. Ezio would not give him the mercy of an easy death.

He made his way out of the gloom of the Sistine Chapel. Out—into the sunshine. Once on the portico, he could see his friends and fellow Assassins—members of the Brotherhood, at whose side he had lived so many adventures and survived so many dangers—waiting for him.

PART I

It cannot be called prowess to kill fellow-citizens, to betray friends, to be treacherous, pitiless, irreligious. These ways can win a prince power, but not glory.

—NICCOLÒ MACHIAVELLI, *THE PRINCE*

ONE

Ezio stood for a moment, dazed and disoriented. Where was he, what was this place? As he slowly regained his senses, he saw his uncle Mario detach himself from a crowd of people and approach him, taking his arm.

"Ezio, are you all right?"

"Th-th-there was a fight—with the Pope, with Rodrigo Borgia. I left him for dead."

Ezio trembled violently. He could not help himself. Could it be real? Seconds earlier—though it seemed like one hundred years ago—he had been involved in a life-and-death struggle with the man he most hated and feared—the leader of the Templars, the vicious organization bent to the last on the destruction of the world Ezio and his friends in the Brotherhood of the Assassins had fought so hard to protect.

But he had beaten them. He had used the great powers of the mysterious artifact, the Apple, the sacred Piece of Eden vouchsafed by the old gods to him to ensure that their investment in humanity did not vanish in bloodshed and iniquity. And he had emerged triumphant!

Or had he?

What had he said? *I left him for dead*? And Rodrigo Borgia, the vile old man who had clawed his way to the head of the Church and ruled it as Pope, had indeed seemed to be dying. He had taken poison.

But now a hideous doubt gripped Ezio. In showing mercy, mercy that was at the core of the Assassin's Creed and which should, he knew, be granted to all but those whose life would endanger the rest of mankind, had he in fact been *weak*?

If he had, he would never let his doubt show—not even to his uncle Mario, leader of the Brotherhood. He squared his shoulders. He had left the old man to die by his own hand. He had left him with time to pray. He had not stabbed him through the heart to make sure of him.

A cold hand closed over his heart as a clear voice in his mind said: *You should have killed him.*

He shook himself to rid himself of his demons as a dog shakes itself to throw off water after a swim. But still his thoughts dwelled on his mystifying experience in the strange Vault beneath the Sistine Chapel in the Vatican in Rome. The building from which he had just emerged, blinking into the unfamiliar sunlight. Everything around him seemed strangely calm and normal—the buildings of the Vatican standing just as they always had, still resplendent in the bright light.

The memory of what had just passed in the Vault came back to him, great surges of recollection overwhelming his consciousness. There had been a vision, an encounter with a strange goddess—for there was no other way of describing the being—whom he now knew as Minerva—the Roman goddess of Wisdom. She had shown him both the distant past and the far future in such a way as to make him loathe the responsibility that the knowledge he had gained had placed on his shoulders.

And whom could he share it with? How could he explain *any* of it? It all seemed so unreal.

All he knew for sure after his experience—better call it an ordeal—was that the fight was not yet over. Perhaps one day there would be a time when he could return to his hometown of Florence and settle down with his books, drinking with his friends in winter and hunting with them in autumn, chasing girls in spring, and overseeing the harvests on his estates in summer.

But this was not it.

In his heart he knew that the Templars and all the evil they represented were not finished. In them he was pitted against a monster with more heads than the Hydra and, like that beast, which had taken no less a man than Hercules to slay, all but immortal.

* * *

"Ezio!"

His uncle's voice was harsh, but served to snap him out of the reverie that had him in its clutches. He had to get a grip. He had to think clearly.

There was a fire raging in Ezio's head. He said his name to himself, as a kind of reassurance: *I am Ezio Auditore da Firenze. Strong, a master of the traditions of the Assassin.*

He went over the ground again: He didn't know whether or not he'd been dreaming. The teaching and the revelations of the strange goddess in the Vault had shaken his beliefs and assumptions to the core. It was as if Time itself had been stood on its head. Emerging from the Sistine Chapel, where he had left the evil Pope, Alexander VI, *apparently* dying, he squinted again in the harsh sunlight. There were his friends, his fellow Assassins, gathered around, their faces grave and set with grim determination.

The thought pursued him still: *Should* he have killed Rodrigo—made *sure* of him? He had elected not to—and the man had indeed seemed bent on taking his own life, having failed in his final goal.

But that clear voice still rang in Ezio's mind.

And there was more: A baffling force now seemed to be drawing him back to the chapel—and he sensed that there was something left undone.

Not Rodrigo. Not *just* Rodrigo. Though he would finish him now!

Something *else!*

"What is it?" Mario asked.

"I must return—" Ezio said, realizing afresh, and with a lurching stomach, that the game *wasn't* over, and that the Apple should *not yet pass from his hands.* As the thought struck him, he was seized with an overwhelming sense of urgency. Tearing himself free of his uncle's sheltering arms, he hurried back into the gloom. Mario, bidding the others to stay where they were and to keep watch, followed.

Ezio quickly reached the place where he'd left the dying Rodrigo Borgia—but the man *wasn't there!* A richly decorated papal damask cope lay in a heap on the floor, flecked with gore; but its owner was gone. Once again the hand, clad in an icy steel gauntlet, closed over Ezio's heart and seemed to crush it.

The hidden door to the Vault was, to all intents and purposes, closed, almost invisible indeed, but, as Ezio approached the point where he remembered it to have been, he found that it swung open gently at his touch. He turned to his uncle and was surprised to see fear on Mario's face.

"What's in there?" said the older man, fighting to keep his voice steady.

"The Mystery," Ezio replied.

Leaving Mario on the threshold, he walked down the dimly lit passage, hoping he was not too late, that Minerva would have foreseen this, and would show mercy. Surely Rodrigo would not have been allowed entry here. Nevertheless, Ezio kept his hidden-blade, the blade his father had bequeathed him, at the ready.

In the Vault, the great *human*, yet, at the same time, *superhuman* figures—but were they statues?—still stood, holding the Staff.

One of the Pieces of Eden.

The Staff was apparently welded to the figure that held it, and indeed as Ezio tried to pry it loose, the figure seemed to tighten its grip, glowing, as did the Runic inscriptions on the walls of the Vault.

Ezio had remembered that no human hand should ever touch the Apple unprotected. The figures then turned away and sank into the ground, leaving the Vault void of anything save the great sarcophagus and its surrounding statues.

Ezio stepped back, looking around briefly and hesitating before taking what he instinctively knew would be his final leave of this place. What was he expecting? Was he hoping that Minerva would once again manifest herself to him? But hadn't she told him all there was to tell—or at least all there was that it was safe for him to know? The Apple had been vouchsafed him. In combination with the Apple, the other Pieces of Eden would have accorded the supremacy Rodrigo craved, and Ezio understood in the fullness of his years that such united power was too dangerous for the hands of Man.

"All right?" Mario's voice, still untypically nervous, floated down to him.

"All's well," replied Ezio, making his way back to the light with a curious reluctance.

Once reunited with his uncle, Ezio wordlessly showed him the Apple.

"And the Staff?"

Ezio shook his head.

"Better in the hands of the Earth than in the hands of Man," said Mario, with immediate understanding. "But you don't need me to tell you that." He shuddered visibly. "Come on! We can't linger."

"What's the hurry?"

"Everything's the hurry. Do you think Rodrigo is just going to sit back and let us stroll out of here?"

"I left him for dead."

"Not quite the same as leaving him *good* and dead, is it? Come *on!*"

They made their way out of the Vault then, as quickly as they could; and a cold wind seemed to follow them as they did so.

TWO

"Where did the others go?" Ezio, his mind still reeling from his recent experiences, asked Mario as they made their way back to the great nave of the Sistine Chapel. The gathered Assassins were no longer there.

"I told them to go. Paola has returned to Florence. Teodora and Antonio, to Venice. We need to keep ourselves covered in all Italy. The Templars are broken but not destroyed. They will regroup if our Assassins' Brotherhood is not vigilant. Eternally vigilant. The rest of our company have gone ahead and will await us at our headquarters in Monteriggioni."

"They were keeping watch."

"So they were. But they knew when their duty was

done. Ezio, there is no time to waste. We all know that."
Mario's face was earnest.

"I should have made sure of Rodrigo Borgia."

"Did he harm you in the fight?"

"My armor protected me."

Mario clapped his nephew on the back. "I spoke hastily before. I think you were right to decide not to kill needlessly. I have always advised moderation. You thought him as good as dead, by his own hand. Who knows? Perhaps he was faking—or perhaps he genuinely failed to give himself a fatal dose of poison. Either way, we must deal with the situation as it is now and not waste energy pondering what we might have done. In any case, we sent you—one man against an entire army of Templars. You've done more than your part. And I am still your old uncle, and I've been worried about you. Come on, Ezio. We have to get out of here. We have work to do, and the last thing we need is to get cornered by Borgia guards."

"You wouldn't believe the things I've seen, Uncle."

"Just be sure to stay alive, then, that I may hear of them. Listen: I've stabled some horses just beyond Saint Peter's, outside the precincts of the Vatican. Once we reach them, we'll be able to make our way safely from here."

"The Borgia will try to stop us, I expect."

Mario flashed a broad grin. "Of course they will— and *I* expect the Borgia to mourn the loss of many lives tonight!"

In the chapel, Ezio and his uncle were surprised to

find themselves faced with a number of priests, who had returned to complete the Mass interrupted by Ezio's confrontation with the Pope, as he and Rodrigo had battled for control of the Pieces of Eden they had discovered.

The priests confronted them angrily, surrounding them and clamoring:

"*Che cosa fate qui?*—What are you doing here?" They yelled. "You have desecrated the sanctity of this holy place!" And: "*Assassini!* God will see that you pay for your crimes!"

As Mario and Ezio pushed their way through the angry throng, the bells of Saint Peter's began to ring the alarm.

"You condemn what you do not understand," said Ezio to a priest who was trying to bar their way. The softness of the man's body repelled him. He shoved him aside as gently as possible.

"We must go, Ezio," said Mario urgently. *"Now!"*

"His is the voice of the Devil!" another priest's voice rang out.

And another: "Turn away from them!"

Ezio and Mario pushed their way through the mob and out into the great courtyard of the church. There, they were confronted by a sea of red robes. It seemed that the entire College of Cardinals was assembled, confused, but still under the dominion of Pope Alexander VI—the Spaniard, as he was known—and also as Rodrigo Borgia, captain of the Order of the Templars.

"For we wrestle not against flesh and blood," the

cardinals were chanting, "but against Principalities, against Powers, against the Rulers of the Darkness of this world, against spiritual wickedness in high places. Wherefore take unto you the whole armor of God, and the shield of Faith, wherewith you shall be able to quench all the fiery darts of the Wicked."

"What's the matter with them?" Ezio asked.

"They are confused. They seek guidance," Mario replied grimly. "Come on. We must get away before the Borgia guards take notice of our presence." He looked back toward the Vatican. There was a glitter of armor in the sunlight.

"Too late. Here they come. Hurry!"

THREE

The sea of red, the billowing vestments of the cardinals, parted as four Borgia guards pushed through in pursuit of Ezio and Mario. Panic took over the crowd as the cardinals started shouting in fear and alarm. Ezio and his uncle found themselves encircled by a human arena—the cardinals, not knowing where to turn, had inadvertently formed a barrier; perhaps their courage had been unconsciously bolstered by the arrival of the heavily armored guards, breastplates gleaming in the sunlight. The four Borgia soldiers had unsheathed their swords and stepped into the circle to face Ezio and Mario, who in turn had drawn their own blades.

"Lay down your weapons and surrender, Assassins. You are surrounded and outnumbered!" shouted the lead soldier, stepping forward.

Before he could utter another word, Ezio had sprung from his stance, energy returning to his weary limbs. The lead guard had no time to react, not expecting his opponent to be so bold in the face of such overwhelming odds. Ezio's sword arm circled in a blur, the blade whistling as it sliced through the air—the guard tried in vain to raise his sword to parry, but Ezio's movement was simply too quick. The Assassin's sword hit its mark with unfaltering accuracy, slicing into the guard's exposed neck—a plume of blood following its impact. The three remaining guards stood motionless—astonished at the speed of the Assassin and idiotic in the face of such a skilled foe. This delay was their death. Ezio's blade had barely finished its first lethal arc as he raised his left hand, the mechanism of his hidden-blade clicking as the lethal spike revealed itself from his sleeve. It pierced the second guard between the eyes before he could even twitch a muscle in defense.

Meanwhile Mario, unnoticed, had taken two steps sideways, closing the angle of attack on the two remaining guards—their attention still entirely drawn to the shocking display of violence unfolding before them. Two steps more, he closed in and heaved his sword under the breastplate of the nearest guard—the point rising up sickeningly into the man's torso. The guard's face contorted with confused agony. Horror shone in the eyes of the one man left and he turned as if to flee—but too late. Ezio's blade struck his right flank as Mario's sword sliced into his thigh. The man fell to his knees with a grunt. Mario kicked him over.

The two Assassins looked around—the blood of the guards spread across the paved ground, soaking into the scarlet hems of the cardinals' vestments.

"Let's go—before more of the Borgia's men reach us." They brandished their swords at the now-terrified cardinals—who quickly fled the Assassins—a path clearing that would lead them from the Vatican. They heard the sound of approaching horses, no doubt more soldiers. They pushed their way forcefully toward the southeast, running at full speed across the expanse of the plaza, away from the Vatican and in the direction of the Tiber. The horses Mario had organized for their escape were tethered just outside the purlieus of the Holy See. But they had to turn to those papal guards who had followed on horseback and were bearing down on them fast. The thundering of hooves echoed on the cobbles. Using their falchions, Ezio and Mario managed to strike away the halberds the guards were thrusting at them.

Mario cut one guard down just as he was about to stab Ezio from behind with his spear.

"Not bad for an old man," Ezio cried gratefully.

"I expect you to return the favor," replied his uncle. "And not so much of your 'old man'!"

"I haven't forgotten everything you taught me."

"I should hope not! Look out!" And Ezio whirled around just in time to slice the legs of a horse from under a guard who'd galloped up wielding a vicious-looking mace.

"*Buona questa!*" shouted Mario. "Good one!"

Ezio leapt sideways, avoiding two more of his pursuers,

and managed to unsaddle them as they careered past, carried forward by their own momentum. Mario, heavier and older, preferred to stand his ground and cut at his enemies before leaping out of their reach. But once they had gained the edge of the broad square that faced the great cathedral church of Saint Peter, the two Assassins quickly clambered to the safety of the rooftops, scaling the crumbling house walls as nimbly as geckos, and scampered across them, leaping over the gaps where the streets between them made canyons. It wasn't always easy, and at one point Mario nearly didn't make it, his fingers scrabbling for the gutters as he fell just short. Panting hard, Ezio doubled back to pull him clear, succeeding just as the crossbow bolts fired by their pursuers rattled uselessly past them into the sky.

But their going was far faster than that of the guards, who, more heavily armored and lacking the skills of the Assassins' Brotherhood, tried in vain to keep up by running though the pathways beneath. They gradually fell back. The two men clattered to a halt on a roof overlooking a small square on the edge of Trastevere. Two large, tough-looking chestnut horses were saddled and ready outside a lowly-looking inn, its battered sign bearing the image of a sleeping fox. Watching over the horses was a walleyed hunchback with a bushy mustache.

"Gianni!" hissed Mario.

The man looked up and immediately undid the reins by which the horses were tethered to a huge iron ring set into the wall of the inn. Mario instantly leapt down from the rooftop, landing in a crouch, and from there sprang into the saddle of the nearer, and larger, of the two horses. It whinnied and trod the earth in nervous anticipation.

"Shh, Campione," said Mario to the animal, and then, looking up to where Ezio still stood on the parapet, he yelled: "Come on! What are you waiting for?"

"Just a minute, *Zio*," said Ezio, turning to face two Borgia guards who had managed after all to struggle up to the roof and were now facing him with—to his astonishment—cocked pistols of a type that was new to him. Where the hell had they got those from? But this was no time for questions. He whirled through the air at them, unleashing his hidden-blade and slicing each neatly through the jugular before they could even fire.

"Impressive," said Mario, reining in his impatient horse. "Now, get a move on! *Cosa diavolo aspetti?*"

Ezio threw himself off the roof to land close by the second horse, held firmly by the hunchback, and rebounded off the ground to spring into the animal's saddle. It reared excitedly under his weight but he immediately had it under control and wheeled it around to follow his uncle as he rode fast toward the Tiber. At the same time Gianni disappeared into the inn, and a detachment of Borgia cavalry tore around the corner, into the square. Digging his heels into the horse's flanks, Ezio sped after his uncle as they made their way at breakneck speed through the broken-down streets of Rome toward the dirty, sluggish river. At their backs they could hear the shouts of the mounted Borgia guards—cursing

their prey as Mario and Ezio galloped through the maze
of ancient streets, slowly pulling farther away.

Having reached Tiber Island they crossed the river
by a rickety bridge that trembled beneath their horses'
hooves, and then they doubled back, turning north to
ride up the main street leading out of the squalid little town that had once been the capital of the civilized
world. They did not stop until they were in the depths
of the countryside and had assured themselves that they
were out of the reach of their pursuers.

Near the settlement of Sette Bagni, in the shade of a
massive elm tree by the side of the dusty road that ran
alongside the river, they reined their horses in and took
time to draw breath.

"That was too close, Uncle."

The older man shrugged and smiled, a little painfully.
From a saddlebag Mario produced a leather flagon of
rough red wine and proffered it to his nephew.

"Here," he said, slowly catching his breath. "Good for
you."

Ezio drank, then grimaced. "Where did you get this?"

"It's the best they can do at the Sleeping Fox," said
Mario, grinning broadly. "But once we get to Monteriggioni you'll fare better."

Ezio, grinning, too, passed the flask back to his uncle.
But then his features became troubled.

"What is it?" asked Mario, in gentler tones.

Slowly Ezio produced the Apple from the pouch in which he'd stowed it. "This. What am I to do with it?"

Mario looked grave. "It is a heavy responsibility. But it is one you must shoulder alone."

"How can I?"

"What does you heart tell you?"

"My heart tells me to be rid of it. But my brain . . ."

"It was vouchsafed you . . . by whatever Powers you encountered in the Vault," said Mario solemnly. "They would not have given it back to mortals if there was not a purpose devised for it."

"It is too dangerous. If it fell into the wrong hands again . . ." Ezio looked ominously at the slothful river flowing nearby. Mario watched him expectantly.

Ezio hefted the Apple in his gloved right hand. But still he hesitated. He knew, he couldn't throw such a great treasure away, and his uncle's words had swayed him. Surely Minerva would not have allowed him to take back the Apple without reason.

"The decision must be yours alone," said Mario. "But if you feel unhappy at having custody of it now, give it to *me* for safekeeping. You can take it back later, when your mind is calmer."

Ezio hesitated still, but then they both heard, in the distance, the sound of thundering hooves and the baying of hounds.

"Those bastards don't give up easily," said Mario through gritted teeth. "Come, give it to me."

Ezio sighed but replaced the Apple in its leather

pouch and swung it over to Mario, who quickly stowed it in his saddlebag.

"And now," said Mario, "we must jump these nags into the river and swim them across. That'll put the damned dogs off our scent, and even if they're bright enough to ford the Tiber themselves, we'll be able to lose them in the woods over there. Come on. I want to be in Monteriggioni by this time tomorrow."

"How hard do you expect to ride?"

Mario dug his heels into his mount's flanks. The beast reared, foam at the corners of its mouth.

"Very hard," he said. "Because from now on we don't simply have Rodrigo to contend with. His son and his daughter are with him—Cesare and Lucrezia."

"And they are . . . ?"

"The most dangerous people you are ever likely to meet."

FOUR

It was the afternoon of the following day when the little walled town of Monteriggioni, dominated by Mario's *rocca*, appeared on its hill on the horizon. They had made better time than they'd expected and had now eased their pace to spare the horses.

". . . and then Minerva told me about the sun," Ezio was saying. "She told of a disaster that happened long ago, and foretold of another which is to come . . ."

"But not for some time in the future, *vero?*" said Mario. "Then we need not fret about it."

"*Sì,*" Ezio replied. "I wonder how much more work we have to do." He paused reflectively. "Perhaps it will soon be finished."

"Would that be so bad?"

Ezio was about to reply when he was interrupted by the sound of an explosion—cannon fire, from the direction of the town. He drew his sword, rising in his saddle to scan the ramparts.

"Don't worry," said Mario, laughing heartily. "It's only exercises. We've upgraded the arsenal here and installed new cannon all along the battlements. We have training sessions daily."

"As long as they aren't aiming at us."

"Don't worry," said Mario again. "It's true that the men still need to get their eye in, but they have enough sense not to fire at the boss!"

A short while later they were riding through the open principal gate of the town and up the broad main thoroughfare, which led to the citadel. As they did so, crowds gathered to line the street, looking at Ezio with a mixture of respect, admiration, and affection.

"Welcome back, Ezio!" one woman called.

"Grazie, Madonna." Ezio smiled back, inclining his head slightly.

"Three cheers for Ezio!" a child's voice rang out.

"Buon giorno, fratellino," Ezio said to him. Turning to Mario, he added, "It's good to be home."

"I think they're more pleased to see you than to see me," said Mario, but he was smiling as he spoke, and in fact much of the cheering, especially from the older townsmen, was for him.

"I'm looking forward to seeing the old family seat again," said Ezio. "It's been a while."

"It has indeed, and there are a couple of people there who'll be looking forward to seeing you."

"Who?"

"Can't you guess? You can't be that preoccupied with your duties to the Brotherhood."

"Of course—you mean my mother and my sister! How are they?"

"Well. Your sister was very unhappy when her husband died, but time heals most things, and I think she's much better now. In fact, there she is."

They had ridden into the courtyard of Mario's fortified residence now, and as they dismounted, Ezio's sister, Claudia, appeared at the top of the marble staircase that led up to the main entrance, flew down it, and ran into her brother's arms.

"Brother!" she cried, hugging him. "Your return home is the best birthday present I could have wished for!"

"Claudia, my dearest," said Ezio, holding her close. "It is good to be back. How is our mother?"

"Well, thanks be to God. She's dying to see you—we've been on tenterhooks ever since the news reached us that you were returning. And your fame goes before you!"

"Let's go in," said Mario.

"There's someone else who'll be glad to see you," continued Claudia, taking his arm and escorting him up the staircase. "The Countess of Forlì."

"Caterina? Here?" Ezio tried to keep the excitement out of his voice.

"We did not know when exactly you would arrive. She and Mother are with the abbess, but they will be here by sunset."

"Business first," said Mario, knowingly. "I am calling a meeting of the Council of the Brotherhood here tonight. Machiavelli, I know, is especially keen to talk to you."

"Is it finished, then?" asked Claudia intently. "Is the Spaniard truly dead?"

Ezio's grey eyes hardened. "I will explain everything at the meeting this evening," he told her.

"Very well," replied Claudia, but her own eyes were troubled as she took her leave.

"And please give my greetings to the countess when she returns," Ezio called after her. "I will see her, and Mother, this evening. First I have business to attend to with Mario that will not wait."

Once they were alone, Mario's tone became serious. "You must prepare well for tonight, Ezio. Machiavelli will be here by sunset and I know he has many questions for you. We will discuss matters now, and then I advise you to take some time off—it won't hurt you to get to know the town again a little."

After a session of deep conversation with Mario in his study, Ezio made his way back into Monteriggioni. The question of the Pope's survival hung heavily over him, and he sought distraction from it. Mario had suggested he visit his tailor to order some new clothes to replace his travel-stained ones, and first he made his way to the man's shop, where he found him sitting cross-legged on his workbench, sewing a brocade cloak of a rich emerald green.

Ezio liked the tailor, a good-natured fellow a little older than Ezio was himself. The tailor greeted him warmly.

"To what do I owe the honor?" he asked.

"I think I'm due some new clothes," said Ezio a little ruefully. "Tell me what you think. Be honest!"

"Even if it were not my job to sell you clothes, *signore*, I would have to advise you that a new suit would be the making of you."

"I thought as much! Very well!"

"I'll measure you now. Then you can pick out the colors you'd like."

Ezio submitted himself to the tailor's ministrations and chose a discreet dark grey velvet for the doublet, with matching hose in wool.

"Can it be ready by tonight?"

The tailor smiled. "Not if you want me to do a good job on it, *signore*. But we can try for a fitting toward midday tomorrow."

"Very well," replied Ezio, hoping that the meeting he was to attend that evening would not result in his having to leave Monteriggioni immediately.

He was making his way across the main square of the town when he noticed an attractive woman who was struggling with an unwieldy box of red and yellow flowers—clearly too heavy for her to lift. At that time of day there were few people around, and Ezio had always found it difficult to resist a damsel in distress.

"Can I lend you a hand?" he asked, coming up to her.

She smiled at him. "Yes, you're just the man I need. My gardener was supposed to pick these up for me but his wife's sick so he had to go home and as I was passing this way in any case I said I'd fetch them—but this box is far too heavy for me. Do you think you could—?"

"Of course." Ezio stooped and hefted the box onto his shoulder. "So many flowers! You're a lucky woman."

"Even luckier now that I've run into you."

There was no doubt that she was flirting with him. "You could have asked your husband to fetch them for you—or one of your other servants," he said.

"I only have one other servant and she isn't half as strong as I am," replied the woman. "And as for a husband—I have none."

"I see."

"I ordered these flowers for Claudia Auditore's birthday." The woman looked at him.

"That sounds like fun."

"It will be." She paused. "In fact, if you'd like to help me out some more, I am rather looking for someone with a bit of class to escort me to it."

"Do you think I have enough class?"

She was bolder now. "Yes! No one in this entire town walks with greater bearing than you, sir. I am sure Claudia's brother, Ezio himself, would be impressed."

Ezio smiled. "You flatter me. But what do you know of this Ezio?"

"Claudia—who is a particular friend of mine—thinks the world of him. But he rarely visits her, and from what I can gather, he's rather distant."

Ezio decided it was time to come clean. "It's true, alas—I have been . . . distant."

The woman gasped. "Oh, no! *You* are Ezio! I don't believe it. Claudia did say you were expected back. The party's supposed to be a surprise for her. Promise you won't say a word."

"You'd better tell me who you are now."

"Oh, of course. I am Angelina Ceresa. Now promise!"

"What will you do to keep me quiet?"

She looked at him archly. "Oh, I am sure I can think of several things."

"I'm longing to hear what they are."

They had reached the door of Angelina's house by this time. Angelina's elderly housekeeper opened it to them and Ezio placed the box of flowers on a stone bench in the courtyard. He faced Angelina and smiled.

"Now are you going to tell me?"

"Later."

"Why not now?"

"*Signore*, I assure you it will be worth the wait."

Little did either of them know that events would overtake them and they would not meet again.

Ezio took his leave and, seeing that the day was drawing in, directed his walk back toward the citadel. As he was approaching the stables, he noticed a child—a little girl—wandering down the middle of the street, apparently alone. He was about to speak to her when he was interrupted by the sound of frantic shouting and the thunder of a horse's hooves. Quicker than thought, he snatched up the child and moved her to the shelter of a doorway. He'd been in the nick of time. Around the corner a powerful warhorse came at a gallop, fully harnessed but riderless. In less than hot pursuit, and on foot, came Mario's stable-master, an elderly man called Federico, whom Ezio recognized.

"Torna qui, maledetto cavallo!" yelled Federico helplessly after the disappearing horse. Seeing Ezio, he said, "Can you help me, please, sir? It's your uncle's favorite steed. I was just about to unsaddle and groom him— something must have scared him—he's highly strung as it is."

"Don't worry, father—I'll try and get him back for you."

"Thank you—thank you." Federico mopped his brow. "I'm getting too old for this."

"Don't worry. Just stay here and keep an eye on this child—I think she's lost."

"Surely."

Ezio raced off after the horse, which he found without difficulty. It had calmed down and was even grazing some hay that was loaded onto a parked wagon. It balked slightly when Ezio approached, but then recognized him and did not run. He laid a comforting hand on its neck and patted it reassuringly before taking its bridle and leading it gently back the way they had come.

On the way, he had the opportunity to do another good deed. He encountered a young woman, frantic

with anxiety, who turned out to be the mother of the
lost child. Ezio explained what had happened, taking care to tone down the degree of danger the little
girl had actually been in. Once he'd told her where the
girl was, she ran ahead of him, calling out her child's
name—"Sofia! Sofia!"—and Ezio heard an answering
cry of "Mamma!" Minutes later he had rejoined the little group and handed the reins over to Federico, who,
thanking him again, begged him not to say anything to
Mario. Ezio promised not to, and Federico led the horse
back to the stables.

The mother was still waiting with her daughter. Ezio
turned to them with a smile.

"She wants to say a thank-you," said the mother.

"Thank you," said Sofia dutifully, looking up at him
with a mixture of awe and trepidation.

"Stay with your mother in future," said Ezio kindly.
"Don't leave her alone like that, *capisci*?"

The little girl nodded mutely.

"We'd be lost without you and your family to watch
over us, *signore*," said the mother.

"We do what we can," Ezio said, but his thoughts
were troubled as he entered the citadel. Even though he
was pretty sure he could stand his ground, he was not
looking forward to his encounter with Machiavelli.

But there was still time enough before the meeting, and
to avoid brooding on the course it might take, but also
from natural curiosity, Ezio first climbed the ramparts to

have a closer look at the new cannon Mario had installed and was so proud of. There were several of them, each with a pile of iron cannonballs neatly stacked by their wheels, beautifully chased in cast bronze. The biggest had barrels ten feet long, and Mario had told him that these weighed as much as twenty thousand pounds, but there were also lighter and more easily maneuverable culverins interspersed with them. In the towers that punctuated the walls were saker cannon on cast-iron mounts and lightweight falconets on wooden trolleys.

Ezio approached a group of gunners clustered around one of the bigger guns.

"Handsome beasts," he said, running a hand over the elaborately chased decoration around the touchhole.

"Indeed they are, *Messer* Ezio," said the leader of the group, a rough-hewn master-sergeant whom Ezio remembered from his first visit to Monteriggioni as a young man.

"I heard you practicing earlier. May I try firing one of these?"

"You could indeed, but we were firing the smaller cannon earlier. These big 'uns are brand-new. We don't seem to have got the trick of loading 'em yet and the master-armorer who's supposed to be installing them seems to have taken off."

"Have you got people looking for him?"

"Indeed we have, sir, but no luck so far."

"I'll have a look around, too—after all, these things aren't here for decoration and you never know how soon we'll need them."

Ezio set off, continuing his rounds of the ramparts. He hadn't gone more than another twenty or thirty yards when he heard a loud grunting from a wooden shed that had been erected on the top of one of the towers. Near it, outside, lay a box of tools. As he approached, the grunts resolved themselves into snores.

It was dark and hot inside the shed and smelled appallingly of stale wine. As his eyes grew accustomed to the dim light, Ezio quickly made out the form of a large man in his none-too-clean shirtsleeves spread-eagled on a pile of straw. He gave the man a gentle kick, but its only effect was for the man to splutter, half awake, and then turn over with his face to the wall.

"Salve, Messere," Ezio said, jostling the man again, less gently this time, with the toe of his boot.

This time the man twisted his head around to look at him and opened one eye. "What is it, friend?"

"We need you to fix the new cannon on the battlements."

"Not today, chum. First thing."

"Are you too drunk to do your job? I don't think Captain Mario would be very happy if he got wind of that."

"No more work today."

"But it's not that late. Do you know what time it is?"

"No. Don't care, either. Make cannon, not clocks."

Ezio had squatted down to speak to the man, who in turn had pulled himself into a sitting position and was treating Ezio to a gale of his breath, pungent with garlic and cheap Montalcino, as he belched luxuriously. Ezio drew himself to his feet.

"We need those cannon ready to be fired, and we need them ready now," he said. "Do you want me to find someone else who's more capable than you?"

The man scrambled to his feet. "Not so fast, friend—no other man's going to lay hands on my guns." He leaned on Ezio as he got his breath back. "You don't know what it's like—some of these soldiers, they got no respect for artillery. Newfangled stuff for a lot of 'em, of course, grant you that—but I ask you! They expect a gun to work like magic, just like that! No sense of coaxing a good performance out of 'em."

"Can we talk as we walk?" said Ezio. "Time isn't standing still, you know."

"Mind you," the master-armorer continued, "these things we've got here, and I mean they're in a class of their own—nothing but the best for Captain Mario—but they're still pretty simple. I've got hold of a French design for a handheld gun. They call it a 'wrought-iron murderer.' Very clever. Just think—handheld cannon. That's the future, chum."

By now they were approaching the group around the cannon.

"You can call off the hunt," said Ezio cheerfully. "Here he is."

The master-sergeant eyed the armorer narrowly. "Up to it, is he?"

"I may be a little the worse for wear," retorted the armorer, "but I am a peaceful man at heart. In these times, encouraging the sleeping warrior in my gut is the only way to stay alive. Therefore, it is my duty to drink."

He pushed the sergeant aside. "Let's see what we've got here . . ."

After examining the cannon for a few moments, however, he rounded on the soldiers. "What have you been doing? You've been tampering with them, haven't you? Thank God you didn't fire one—you could have got us all killed. They're not ready yet. Got to give the bores a good clean first."

"Perhaps with you around we won't need cannon after all," the sergeant told him. "We'll just get you to breathe on the enemy!"

But the armorer was busy with a cleaning rod and wads of coarse, oily cotton. When he'd finished, he stood up, easing his back.

"There, that's done it," he said. Turning to Ezio, he went on, "Just get these fellows to load her—that's something they can do, though God knows it took 'em long enough to learn—and you can have a go. Look, over there on the hill. We set some targets up there on a level with this gun. Start by aiming at something on the same level; that way, if the cannon explodes, at least it won't take your head off with it."

"Sounds reassuring," said Ezio.

"Just try it, *Messere*. Here's the fuse."

Ezio placed the slow match on the touchhole. For a long moment, nothing happened, then he sprang back as the cannon bucked and roared. Looking across to the targets, he could see that his ball had shattered one of them.

"Well done," said the armorer. "*Perfetto!* At least one person here apart from me knows how to shoot."

Ezio had the men reload and fired again. But this time he missed.

"Can't win 'em all," said the armorer. "But come back at dawn. We'll be practicing again then and it'll give you a chance to get your eye in."

"I will," said Ezio, little realizing that when he next fired a cannon, it would be in deadly earnest.

FIVE

When Ezio entered the great hall of Mario's citadel, the shadows of evening were already gathering, and servants were beginning to light torches and candles to dispel the gloom. The gloom accorded with Ezio's increasingly somber mood as the hour of the meeting approached.

So wrapped up in his own thoughts was he that he did not at first notice the person hovering by the massive fireplace, her slight but strong figure dwarfed by the giant caryatids that flanked the chimney, and so was startled when the woman approached him, touching his arm. Immediately he recognized her, and his features softened into an expression of pure pleasure.

"*Buona sera*, Ezio," she said—for her, a little shyly, he thought.

"*Buona sera*, Caterina," he replied, bowing to the Countess of Forlì. Their former intimacy was some way in the past, though neither of them had forgotten it, and when she had touched his arm, both—Ezio thought— had felt the chemistry of the moment. "Claudia told me you were here, and I have been looking forward to seeing you. But"—he hesitated—"Monteriggioni is far from Forlì, and—"

"You needn't flatter yourself that I have come all this way just on your account," she said with a trace of her former sharpness, though he could see by her smile that she was not entirely serious, and, for himself, he knew that he was still drawn to this fiercely independent and dangerous woman.

"I am always willing to be of service to you, Madonna— in any way I can." He meant it.

"Some ways are harder than others," she countered, and now there was a tough note in her voice.

"What is it?"

"It is not a simple matter," continued Caterina Sforza. "I come in search of an alliance."

"Tell me more."

"I am afraid your work is not over yet, Ezio. The papal armies are marching on Forlì. My dominion is small, but fortunately or unfortunately for me it lies in an area of the utmost strategic importance to whoever controls it."

"And you desire my help?"

"My forces on their own are weak—your *condottieri* would be a great asset to my cause."

"This is something I will have to discuss with Mario."

"He will not refuse me."

"And nor will I."

"By helping me, you will not just be doing me a good deed. You will be taking a stand against the forces of evil we have always been united against."

As they spoke, Mario appeared. "Ezio, *Contessa*, we are gathered and await you," he said, his face unusually serious.

"We will talk more of this," Ezio told her. "I am bidden to a meeting that my uncle has convened. I am expected to explain myself, I think. But afterward—let us arrange to see each other afterward."

"The meeting concerns me, too," said Caterina. "Shall we go in?"

SIX

The room was very familiar to Ezio. There, on the now-exposed inner wall, the pages of the Great Codex were arranged in order. The desk, usually littered with maps, was cleared and around it, on severe straight-backed chairs of dark wood, sat those members of the Assassins' Brotherhood who had gathered at Monteriggioni, together with those of the Auditore family who were privy to its cause. Mario sat behind his desk, and at one end sat a sober, dark-suited man, still young-looking, though with deep lines of thought now etched into his forehead, who had become one of Ezio's closest associates, but also one of his most unremitting critics—Niccolò Machiavelli. The two men nodded guardedly at each other as Ezio went over to greet Claudia and his mother, Maria

Auditore, matriarch of the family since his father's death. Maria hugged her only surviving son hard, as if her life depended on it, and looked at him with shining eyes as he broke free and took a seat near Caterina and opposite Machiavelli, who now rose and looked questioningly at him. Clearly there was going to be no polite prologue to the matter at hand.

"First, perhaps, I owe you an apology," began Machiavelli. "I was not present in the Vault and urgent business took me to Florence before I could truly analyze what happened there. Mario has given us his account, but yours alone can be the full one."

Ezio rose in his turn and spoke simply and directly. "I entered the Vatican and encountered Rodrigo Borgia, Pope Alexander VI, and confronted him. He was in possession of one of the Pieces of Eden, the Staff, and used it against me. I managed to defeat him and, using the combined powers of the Apple and the Staff, gained access to the Secret Vault, leaving him outside. He was in despair and begged me to kill him. I would not." Ezio paused.

"What then?" prompted Machiavelli, as the others watched silently.

"Within the Vault were many strange things—things not dreamed of in our world." Visibly moved, Ezio forced himself to continue in level tones. "A vision of the goddess Minerva appeared to me. She told of a terrible tragedy that would befall mankind at some future time. But she also spoke of lost temples that may, when found, lead us to a kind of redemption and aid us. She appeared to invoke a phantom that had some close connection with me, but what that was, I cannot tell. And after her warning and her predictions, she vanished. I emerged to see the Pope dying—or so it seemed; he told me he appeared to have taken poison. But then something compelled me to return. I seized the Apple, but the Staff and a great Sword, which may have been another Piece of Eden, were swallowed up by the earth, and I am glad of it. The Apple alone, which I have given in custody to Mario, is already more than I personally wish to have responsibility for."

"Amazing!" cried Caterina.

"I cannot imagine such wonders," added Claudia.

"So—the Vault did not house the terrible weapon we feared—or at any rate, the Templars did not gain control of it. This at least is good news," said Machiavelli evenly.

"What of this goddess—Minerva?" Claudia asked. "Did she appear—like us?"

"Her appearance was human, and also superhuman," Ezio said. "Her words proved that she belonged to a race far older and greater than ours. The rest of her kind died many centuries ago. She'd been waiting for that moment all that time. I wish I had the words to describe the magic she performed."

"What are these temples she spoke of?" put in Mario.

"I know not."

"Did she say we should search for them? How do we know what to look for?"

"Perhaps we should—perhaps the quest will show us the way."

"The quest must be undertaken," said Machiavelli crisply. "But we must clear the path for it first. Tell us of the Pope. He did not die, you say?"

"When I returned, his cope lay on the chapel floor. He himself had disappeared."

"Had he made any promises? Had he shown repentance?"

"Neither. He was bent on gaining the power. When he saw he was not going to get it, he collapsed."

"And you left him to die."

"I would not be the one to kill him."

"You should have done so."

"I am not here to debate the past. I stand by my decision. Now we should discuss the future. What we are to do."

"What we are to do is made all the more urgent by your failure to finish off the Templar leader when you had the chance." Machiavelli breathed hard, but then relaxed a little. "All right, Ezio. You know in what high esteem we all hold you. We would not have got anything like this far without the twenty years of devotion you have shown to the Assassins' Brotherhood and to our Creed. And a part of me applauds you for not having killed when you deemed it unnecessary to do so. That is also in keeping with our code of honor. But you misjudged, my friend, and that means we have an immediate and dangerous task ahead of us." He paused, scanning the assembled company with eagle eyes. "Our spies in Rome report that Rodrigo is indeed a reduced threat. He is at least somewhat broken in spirit. There is a saying that it is less dangerous to do battle with a lion's whelp than with an old, dying lion; but in the case of the Borgia the position is quite otherwise. Rodrigo's son, Cesare, is the man we must match ourselves against now. Armed with the vast fortune the Borgia have amassed by fair means and foul—but mostly foul"—Machiavelli allowed himself a wry smile—"he heads a large army of highly trained troops and with it he intends to take over all Italy—the whole peninsula—and he does not intend to stop at the borders of the Kingdom of Naples."

"He would never dare—he could never do it!" Mario roared.

"He would and he could," snapped Machiavelli. "He is evil through and through, and as dedicated a Templar as his father the Pope ever was, but he is also a fine though utterly ruthless soldier. He always wanted to be a soldier, even after his father made him Cardinal of Valencia when he was only seventeen years old! But as we all know, he resigned from that post—the first cardinal in the Church's history to do so! The Borgia treat our country and the Vatican as if they were their own private fiefdom! Cesare's plan now is to crush the North first, to subdue the Romagna and isolate Venice. He also intends to extirpate and destroy all of us remaining Assassins, since he knows that in the end we are the only people who can stop him. *Aut Caesar, aut nihil*—that's his motto—'Either you're with me or you're dead.' And do you know, I think the madman actually believes it."

"My uncle mentioned a sister," Ezio began.

Machiavelli turned to him. "Yes. Lucrezia. She and

Cesare are . . . how shall I say? Very close. They are a very close-knit family; when they are not killing those other brothers and sisters, husbands and wives, whom they find inconvenient to them, they are . . . coupling with each other."

Maria Auditore could not suppress a cry of disgust.

"We must approach them with all the caution we would use to approach a nest of vipers," Machiavelli concluded. "And God knows where and how soon they will next strike." He paused and drank half a glass of wine. "And now, Mario, I leave you. Ezio, we will soon meet again, I trust."

"You're leaving this evening?"

"Time is of the essence, good Mario. I ride for Rome tonight. Farewell!"

The room was silent after Machiavelli left. After a long pause, Ezio said bitterly, "He blames me for not killing Rodrigo when I had the chance." He looked around at them. "You all do!"

"Any of us might have made the decision you made," said his mother. "You were sure he was dying."

Mario came and put an arm around his shoulders. "Machiavelli knows your value—we all do. And even with the Pope out of the way, we'd still have had to deal with his brood—"

"But if I had cut off the head, could the body have survived?"

"We must deal with the situation as it is, good Ezio, not with it as it might have been." Mario clapped him on the back. "And now, as we are in for a busy day tomorrow, I suggest we dine and then prepare for an early night!"

Caterina's eyes met Ezio's. Did he imagine it, or was there a flicker of the old lust there? He shrugged inwardly. Perhaps he'd just imagined it.

SEVEN

Ezio ate lightly—just *pollo ripieno* with roasted vegetables; and he drank his Chianti cut half-and-half with water. There was little conversation at dinner, and he answered his mother's string of questions politely but laconically. After all the tension that had mounted in anticipation of the meeting, and which had now melted away, he was very tired. He had barely had a chance to rest since leaving Rome, and it looked now as if it would be a long time still before he could realize a long-cherished ambition of spending some time back in his old home in Florence, reading and walking in the surrounding gentle hills.

As soon as he decently could, he made his excuses to the company and set off for his bedroom, a large, quiet, dimly lit space on one of the upper floors, with a view across the countryside rather than the town. Once he'd reached it and dismissed the servant, he let go of the steeliness that had supported him throughout the day, and his very body slumped, his shoulders sagged, and his walk eased. His movements were slow and deliberate. He moved across the room to where the servant had already drawn him a bath. He approached it, tugging at his boots and taking off his clothes as he did so, and, naked, stood for a moment, his clothes bundled in his hands, before a full-length mirror on a stand near the copper tub. He looked at his reflection with weary eyes. Where had the four long decades gone? He straightened. He was older, stronger even, certainly wiser; but he could not deny the profound fatigue he felt.

He threw his clothes onto the bed. Under it, in a locked elm chest, were the secret Codex weapons Leonardo da Vinci had once fashioned for him. He would check them over first thing in the morning, after the council of war he'd be holding with his uncle. The original hidden-blade never left him except when he was naked, and then it was always within arm's reach. He wore it always; it had become part of his body.

Sighing with relief, Ezio slipped into the bath. Immersed to his neck in the hot water, breathing in the gently scented steam, he closed his eyes and let out a long, slow breath of relief. Peace at last. And he had better make the most of the few short hours he had of it.

He had dozed off and begun to dream when the softest of noises, the door opening and closing behind its heavy tapestry hanging, caused him to awake, instantly alert, like a wild animal. Silently his hand sought the blade and with a practiced movement he attached it to his wrist. Then, in one fluid motion he turned and stood upright in the tub, poised for action and looking in the direction of the door.

"Well," said Caterina, grinning as she approached, "you certainly haven't lost any inches with the years."

"You have the advantage of me, *Contessa*." Ezio smiled. "You are fully clothed."

"I expect we could arrange something to change that. But I am waiting."

"Waiting for what?"

"For you to say that you don't really need to see for yourself. For you to say that you are sure, even without seeing my naked body, that Nature has been as kind to me, if not kinder, as she has been to you." Her grin broadened at Ezio's confusion. "But I remember you were never as good at paying compliments as you were at ridding the world of Templars."

"Come here!"

He drew her to him, pulling at the girdle of her skirt as her fingers flew first at the blade, detaching it, and then at the laces of her bodice. Seconds later he had lifted her into the bath with him, their lips glued to one another's and their naked limbs entwined.

They did not linger in the bath long, but soon got out, drying each other on the rough linen towels the servant had left. Caterina had brought a vial of scented massage oil with her and drew it from a pocket of her dress.

"Now, lie on the bed," she said. "I want to make sure you are good and ready for me."

"Surely you can see that I am."

"Indulge me. Indulge yourself."

Ezio smiled. This was better than sleep. Sleep could wait.

Sleep, Ezio found, was obliged to wait three hours. Then she curled up in his arms. She fell asleep before him and he watched her for a while. Nature had indeed been kind to her. Her slender yet curvaceous body, with its narrow hips, broad shoulders, and small but perfect breasts, was still that of a twenty-year-old, and her cloud of fine, fine light red hair that tickled his chest as she laid her head on it carried the same scent that had driven him wild all those years ago. Once or twice in the depths of the night, he woke to find he had rolled away from her, and when he took her in his arms again, she nestled up to him with a tiny sigh of joy and closed her hand round his forearm; but she did not wake. Ezio wondered later if this hadn't been the best night of love of his life.

They overslept, of course, but Ezio was not about to forgo another bout in favor of cannon practice, though a part of his mind reproved him for this. Meanwhile, he could distantly hear the sounds of marching men— clattering men moving at a *running* march—and shouted orders, and then, the boom of cannon.

"Target practice with the new cannon," said Ezio,

when for a moment Caterina stopped him and looked at him quizzically. "Maneuvers. Mario's a hard taskmaster."

The heavy brocade curtains across the windows shut out most of the light and the room remained cocooned in comfortable dimness; and no servant came to disturb them. Soon, Caterina's moans of pleasure drowned out any other noise to his ear. His hands tightened around her strong buttocks—she was pulling him up urgently toward her, when their lovemaking was interrupted by more than just the roar of cannon.

Suddenly, the peace and the softness of the big room was shattered. The windows blew away with a mighty roar, taking a part of the stone outer wall with them, as a gigantic cannonball smashed in and landed, searing hot, inches from the bed. The floor sagged under its weight.

Ezio had thrown himself protectively and instinctively over Caterina at the first instant of danger, and in that moment the lovers transformed themselves into professionals and colleagues—after all, if they were to *remain* lovers, they first had to *survive*.

They leapt from the bed, throwing on their clothes. Ezio noticed that apart from the delicious vial of oil, Caterina had concealed a very useful jagged-edged dagger beneath her skirts.

"What the hell—?" Ezio cried.

"Go and find Mario," said Caterina urgently.

Another ball flew in, shattering the beams over their recently vacated bed and smashing it to pieces.

"My troops are in the main courtyard," said Caterina. "I'll find them and get them around the back of the citadel and see if we can't outflank them there. Tell Mario that's what I've decided."

"Thank you," said Ezio. "Stay out of sight."

"I wish I'd had time to change," she said, laughing. "We'd better book into an *albergo* next time, eh?"

"Let's make damned sure there *is* a next time," rejoined Ezio, laughing, too, but nervously, and strapping on his sword.

"You bet! *Arrivederci!*" cried Caterina, rushing from the room without forgetting to blow him a kiss.

He looked at the ruins of the bed. The Codex weapons—the double-blade, the poison-blade, the pistol— were buried under it, in all probability destroyed. At least he still had his hidden-blade. Even in *extremis* he would never forget that. His murdered father's last bequest.

EIGHT

Ezio had no idea what time it was, but sense told him attacks usually began at dawn, when the victims were still confused and wiping the sleep out of their eyes. He was lucky that his training had bestowed on him, even after he'd reached the age of forty, the alertness and agility of a wildcat.

Once outside and on the battlements, he scanned the landscape around the little town. The town itself, now below him as he skirted around, was in flames in many quarters. He saw where the tailor's shop was burning and Angelina's house, too.

There would be no birthday party for poor Claudia tonight.

He ducked as another cannonball smashed into the

ramparts. For God's love, what guns were their attackers bringing to bear? How could they reload and fire so fast? Who was behind this?

Through the smoke and dust he made out Mario, dodging toward him through crumbling masonry. Ezio leapt off the ramparts to land in a crouch near Mario and ran to join him.

"Uncle! *Che diavolo . . .* ?"

Mario spat. "They've caught us on our back foot. It's the Borgia!"

"Fottere!"

"We underestimated Cesare. They must have massed to the east during the night."

"What must we do?"

"The main thing is to get all the townspeople clear— those who haven't already been killed. We've got to hold them off until we've done that. If they take the town with the people still inside it, they'll kill them all— everyone in Monteriggioni is either an Assassin or an Assassin's abettor, in their eyes."

"I know the route out. Leave it to me."

"Good man. I'll muster our defenders and give them everything we've got." Mario paused. "Look. Let's take them on first. You go and command the cannon on the ramparts."

"And you?"

"I'll lead a frontal assault. Take the battle to the bastards."

"Caterina is going to try to take her forces around the flank."

"Good. Then we are in with a chance. Now *hurry!*"

"Wait!"

"What is it?"

Ezio lowered his voice. "Where is the Apple?" He did not tell his uncle that the Codex weapons had been destroyed by one of the first cannonades. Inwardly he prayed that, by some miracle, his path would cross with Leonardo's again, for he did not doubt that the master of all the arts and sciences would help him reconstruct them, in case of need. In the meantime, he had the hidden-blade still, and he was a past master himself in the use of conventional weapons.

"The Apple is safe," Mario reassured him. "Now go. And if you see that the Borgia show the *slightest* chance of breaching the walls, shift your attention to evacuating the town. Do you understand?"

"Sì, zio mio."

Mario placed his hands on Ezio's shoulders and looked at him gravely for a long moment. "Our fate is only partially in our own hands. There is only a certain amount of it that we can control. But never forget, *never* forget, nephew—that whatever happens to you, or to me, this day, there is never a feather lost by a sparrow that is not brushed away by the finger of God."

"I understand, *Capitano.*"

There was a brief moment of silence between them. Then Mario extended his hand.

"Insieme per la vittoria!"

Ezio took his uncle's hand in his and wrung it fervently. *"Insieme!"*

Mario turned to go.

Ezio said, "*Capitano*—be careful!"

Mario nodded grimly. "I'll do my best! And you—take my best horse and get to the outer walls as fast as you can!" He drew his sword and, with his great war cry rallying his men, ran toward the foe.

Ezio watched him briefly and then ran himself toward the stable, where the old groom whose runaway horse he'd saved only the day before was waiting. The huge chestnut was saddled and ready.

"Maestro Mario had already sent orders," the old man said. "I may be past my prime, but no one could ever accuse me of being inefficient. *Ma attenzione!* This horse is full of spirit!"

"I brought him to heel yesterday. He'll know me today."

"True enough! *Buona fortuna!* We all depend on you!"

Ezio swung himself into the saddle and urged the eager horse toward the outer walls.

He rode through the already devastated town. The tailor, dead and mutilated in front of his shop. What harm had he ever done anyone? And Angelina, weeping in front of her burned-down house; what was the point of not showing her pity?

War—that was all. Brutalizing and cruel. Vicious and infantile. Ezio's gorge rose at it.

Freedom and Mercy. And Love. These were the only things worth fighting for, worth killing for—and these were the prime elements of the Assassin's Creed. Of the Brotherhood.

* * *

Ezio, as he rode forth, encountered scenes of terrible desolation. Devastation and chaos surrounded him as his horse carried him through the burning town.

"My children! Where are my children?" a young mother screamed as he passed, helplessly.

"Just pack what you can and let's get out of here!" cried out a man's voice.

"My leg! My leg's been shot away!" yelled a townsman.

"How can we escape?" shrieked several people, rushing around in panic.

"I can't find my mother! Mamma! Mamma!" rang out the voice of a little child.

Ezio had to steel his heart. He could not go to the rescue of individuals. There was no time. But if he could organize the defense properly, more people would be saved than lost.

"Aiuto! Aiuto!" a teenaged girl, mobbed by Borgia troops, cried out as they forced her down.

Ezio rode grimly on. He would kill them. Kill them all, if he could. Who was this heartless Cesare Borgia? Could he be actually worse than the Pope? Could there ever be a more evil Templar?

"Water! Water! Bring water!" a man's voice bellowed despairingly. "Everything is burning!"

"Where are you, please, oh, God! Where are you, Marcello?" a woman's voice sang out.

Ezio rode on, his mouth set. But the cries for help still rang in his ears: *"Come usciamo di qui?"*

"Run! Run!" Voices were raised against the sound of the bombardment. There were screams and sobs, desperate pleas for help, for a means of getting out of the beleaguered town, as the pitiless Borgia troops piled on cannonade upon cannonade.

Please God they do not breach the walls before our own guns have been brought into proper play, Ezio thought, and though he could hear the explosions as the sakers and falconets spat shot at the attackers, he could not yet hear the boom of the big guns he had encountered the day before, the only cannon that might truly smash the huge wooden siege towers the Borgia forces were trundling toward the city walls.

He goaded the chestnut up the ramp to the walls and leapt off as he reached the point where he had last met the drunken armorer next to the ten-foot cannon. He was—perfectly sober now—directing gunners to bring this gun to bear on a tower that the highly trained attackers were shoving slowly but surely in the direction of the ramparts. Ezio could see that its top matched the height of the crenellations at the top of the walls.

"The wretches!" he muttered. But how could anyone have predicted the speed and—even Ezio had to admit this to himself—masterly perfection of the attack?

"Fire!" yelled the grizzled master-sergeant in command of the first big gun as Ezio approached. The great cannon boomed and sprang back, but the ball was just wide, nicking a splattering of wood off a corner of the siege tower's roof.

"Try to hit the fucking towers, you fools!" yelled the sergeant.

"Sir—we need more ammunition!"

"Then go down to the stores, and make it snappy! Look! They're storming the gate!"

Other cannon bellowed and spat. Ezio was pleased to see a tranche of attackers smashed into a sea of blood and bone.

"Reload!" yelled the sergeant. "Fire again at my command!"

"Wait until the tower's closer," ordered Ezio. "Then aim for the bottom. That'll bring the whole thing down. Our crossbowmen can finish off any survivors."

"Yes, sir!"

The armorer came up. "You learn tactics fast," he said to Ezio.

"Instinct."

"Good instinct's worth a hundred men in the field," returned the armorer. "But you missed target practice this morning. No excuse for that!"

"How dare you!" said Ezio jokingly.

"Come on." The armorer grinned. "We've got another of these covering the left flank, and the commander of its gun crew has been killed. Crossbow bolt bang in his forehead. Dead before he hit the ground. You take over. I've got my work cut out for me making sure none of the guns overheat or crack. We'd be well fucked then."

"OK."

"But watch how you aim. Your girlfriend's troops are out there fighting the Borgia. Wouldn't want to take any of them out."

"What girlfriend?"

The armorer winked. "Do me a favor, Ezio! This is a very small town!"

Ezio made his way to the second big gun. A gunner was sponging it down to cool it after firing as another was muzzle-loading it with tamped-down powder and a fifty-pound iron ball. A third man prepared the slow match, lighting it at both ends so that there would be no delay if one end accidentally burned out at the moment of touch.

"Let's go," said Ezio as he came up.

"Signore!"

He scanned the field beyond the wall. The green grass was splattered with blood, and the fallen lay strewn among the wheat sheaves. He could see the yellow, black, and blue livery of Caterina's men interspersed with the Borgia tunics—and their device was a black bull, head down, in a field of golden corn. It made a very good target.

"Get some of the smaller guns to pick out those individuals. Tell them to aim for the black-and-gold," Ezio snapped. "And let's get this gun trained on the siege tower over there. It's getting too close for comfort and we must take it out!"

The gunners heaved the cannon around and dipped

the barrel so that it was aimed at the base of the approaching tower, now not fifty yards from the walls.

Ezio was directing aim when a nearby saker was hit.
It exploded, flinging red-hot bronze in every direction.
Ezio's gunner, inches from him, had his head and shoulders sliced off by shards. The man's arms fell to the floor,
and the remains of his body followed suit, spewing blood
like a fountain. The pungent smell of burned meat filled
Ezio's nostrils as he leapt to take the gunner's place.

"Keep your nerve," he yelled to the rest of the crew.
He squinted along the gunsight. "Steady now . . . and . . .
fire!"

The cannon thundered as Ezio jumped to one side and
watched as the ball smashed into the base of the tower.
Had that one shot been enough? The tower lurched
badly, seemed to steady, and then—by God!—crashed
to the earth, in slow motion it seemed, throwing some
of the men it contained clear, crushing others; and the
screams of the wounded mules that had been drawing it
forward added to the cacophony of panic and death—
the attendants of all battles. Ezio watched as Caterina's
troops moved swiftly in to wipe out the wounded and
the bemused Borgia survivors of the wreck. She herself
was at their head, her silver breastplate flashing in the
cold sunlight. Ezio saw her plunge her sword straight
through a Borgia captain's right eye and into his brain.
The man's body squirmed for a long moment, pivoted by
its point, his hands automatically and uselessly trying to
clutch the firmly held blade and pull it out in the agony
of death.

But there was no time to take pleasure in triumph. Or to rest on any laurels. Looking down over the ramparts, Ezio could see Borgia troops bringing up massive battering rams to the main gate, and at the same time he heard Caterina's warning cry. *We'll send a thousand men to Forlì to help her against this bastard Cesare,* he promised himself.

"If they get in, they'll kill us all," said a voice at his shoulder, and Ezio turned to see the old master-sergeant. He had lost his helmet and an ugly head wound seeped blood.

"We must get the people out. Now."

"Luckily some have already been able to leave. But those less able to help themselves are stranded."

"I'll deal with it," said Ezio, recalling Mario's admonition. "Take over here, Ruggiero. Look! Over there! They've got a tower right up to the ramparts! Their men are storming the wall! Get some more of our men over there before they overpower us."

"Sir!" And the sergeant was gone, yelling orders, at the head of a platoon that had swiftly gathered at his command; within seconds, he and his men were locked in hand-to-hand combat with the vicious Borgia mercenaries.

Ezio, sword in hand and slashing his way past the oncoming enemy troops, made his way down to the town. Quickly organizing a group of Caterina's men who had been forced to retreat into the town as the tide of battle turned once again in the Borgia's favor, he did his best to round up the remaining and vulnerable

townspeople and shepherd them into the relative safety
of the citadel. As he completed the task, Caterina joined
him.

"What news?" he asked her.

"Bad news," she rejoined. "They've smashed down
the main gate. They are moving into the town."

"Then we haven't a minute to lose. We must all retreat
into the citadel."

"I'll muster the rest of my men."

"Come quickly. Have you seen Mario?"

"He was fighting outside the walls."

"And the others?"

"Your mother and sister are already in the citadel.
They have been guiding the citizens through the escape
tunnel that leads to the north, beyond the walls, to
safety."

"Good. I must go to them. Join us as fast as you can.
We'll have to fall back."

"Kill them all," yelled a Borgia sergeant as he rounded
a corner at the head of a small troop of men. All held
bloodied swords aloft, and one man brandished a pike
on which he had stuck the head of a girl. Ezio's throat
went dry as he recognized the face—it was Angelina's.
With a roar, he fell on the Borgia soldiers. Six against one
was nothing to him. Slicing and stabbing, within barely
seconds he stood in the middle of a circle of maimed and
dying men—his chest heaving as he breathed hard with
the exertion.

The blood cleared from his eyes. Caterina was gone.
Wiping sweat, blood, and grime from his face, he made

his way back up to the citadel, telling the men guarding it to open only to Mario and Caterina. He climbed the inner tower and looked down over the burning town.

But apart from the crackle of the flames and the isolated moans of the wounded and the dying, things had gone ominously quiet.

NINE

But not for long. Just as Ezio was checking that the cannon on the ramparts were correctly aligned and loaded, a mighty explosion threw the citadel's massive wooden gates aside, hurling the defenders in the courtyard, below where Ezio stood on the battlements, backward and killing many.

As the smoke and dust cleared, Ezio discerned a group of people standing in the gateway. Uncle Mario appeared to be at their head, but evidently something was badly wrong. His face was grey and drained of blood. He also suddenly looked far older than his sixty-two years. His eyes locked with Ezio's as his nephew leapt down from the battlements to confront the new danger. Then,

Mario fell to his knees and from there onto his face. He struggled to rise, but a long, thin, thrusting sword—a Bilbo—projected from between his shoulder blades, and the young man behind him shoved him back into the gravel with the toe of his black boot. A trail of blood formed at the corner of the old man's mouth.

The young man was dressed in black, and a black mask partially covered his vicious face. Ezio recognized the pustules of the New Disease on the man's skin. He shuddered inwardly. There was no doubt whom he was confronting.

Flanking the man in black were two others, both in early middle age, and a beautiful blonde with cruel lips. Another man, also dressed in black, stood apart and a little to one side. He held a bloodstained falchion in his right hand. His other hand held a chain that was attached to a heavy collar around Caterina Sforza's neck. Bound and gagged, her eyes flashed unquenchable rage and defiance. Ezio's heart stopped—he couldn't believe that just this morning he'd held her once again, and now, now she'd been captured by the vile Borgia leader. How could this be happening? His eyes met hers for an instant across the courtyard, sending her a promise that she would not be a prisoner for long.

With no time to figure out all that was unfolding around him, Ezio's soldier's instinct took control. He must act now—or lose everything. He strode forward, closed his eyes, and stepped off the battlement, his ragged cape flowing out behind him—it was a leap of faith to the courtyard below. With practiced grace he landed on his feet, and he stood tall to confront his enemies, cold determination etched on his face.

The armorer staggered up, struggling with a wounded leg, and stood by Ezio. "Who are these people?" he breathed.

"Oh," said the young man in black. "We haven't introduced ourselves. How remiss of us. But of course I know you, Ezio Auditore, if only by repute. Such a pleasure. At last I shall be able to remove the biggest thorn in my side. After your dear uncle, of course."

"Step back from him, Cesare!"

One eyebrow went up and the dark eyes blazed in the handsome, flawed face. "Oh—how flattered I am that you have guessed my name correctly. But let me present my sister, Lucrezia." He turned to nuzzle the blonde in a most *un*brotherly way as she squeezed his arm and pressed her lips dangerously close to his mouth. "And my close associates: Juan Borgia, cousin, and friend; my dear French ally, General Octavien de Valois; and, last but not least, my indispensable right-hand man, Micheletto Corella. What would I do without my friends?"

"And your father's money."

"Bad joke, my friend."

As Cesare spoke, his troops moved like ghosts into the citadel. Ezio was powerless to stop them as his own men—hopelessly outnumbered—were swiftly overcome and disarmed.

"But I'm a good soldier, and part of the fun is choosing efficient support," Cesare continued. "I must admit

I didn't think you'd be quite such a pushover. But of course, you aren't getting any younger, are you?"

"I'll kill you," Ezio said evenly. "I'll wipe you and your kind from the face of the earth."

"Not today you won't," said Cesare, smiling. "And just look what I've got—courtesy of your uncle." A gloved hand delved into a pouch at his side and from it he produced—to Ezio's horror—the Apple!

"Useful gadget," said Cesare, smiling thinly. "Leo tells me he already knows quite a lot about it so I'm hoping he'll enlighten me further, which I'm sure he will if he wants to keep his head on his shoulders! Artists! Ten a penny, as I'm sure you'd agree."

Lucrezia sniggered unfeelingly at this.

Ezio looked across at his old friend but da Vinci refused to meet his gaze. On the ground, Mario stirred and groaned. Cesare pushed his face into the ground with his boot and produced a gun—it was a new design, as Ezio immediately recognized, regretting the destruction of most of his own Codex weapons at the outset of the attack.

"That's not a matchlock," said the armorer keenly.

"It's a wheel lock," said Cesare. "You're clearly no fool," he added, addressing the armorer. "It is much more predictable and efficient than the old guns. Leonardo designed it for me. Reloads fast, too. Would you like a demonstration?"

"Indeed!" the armorer replied, his professional interest overcoming any other instinct.

"By all means," said Cesare, leveling the pistol at him

and shooting him dead. "Reload, please," he continued, passing the gun to General Valois and producing its twin from his belt. "We've had so much bloodshed," he went on. "So it's distressing to reflect that a little more cleansing is still in order. Never mind. Ezio, I'd like you to take this in the spirit it's meant—from my family to yours."

Stooping slightly and placing one foot in the center of Mario's back, he drew the Bilbao sword out, letting the blood ooze forth. Mario's eyes went wide with pain as he struggled instinctively to crawl away, toward his nephew.

Cesare leaned forward and fired the pistol at point-blank range into the back of Mario's cranium, which burst apart.

"No!" shouted Ezio. In an instant the recollection of the brutal murder of his father and brothers flashed through his mind. "No!" He lunged toward Cesare, the agony of loss surging through him uncontrollably. Mario's body slumped to the ground.

As Ezio leapt forward, General Valois, having reloaded the first gun, shot him in the shoulder. Ezio staggered back, choking, and the world went black.

TEN

When Ezio came to, the tide of battle had turned again, and the attackers were chased back outside the walls of the citadel. He found himself being dragged to safety as the defenders of the *rocca*, who had retaken it, closed the broken gate with a barricade, gathered all the remaining citizens of Monteriggioni within its walls, and were now organizing their escape to the countryside beyond, for there was no knowing how long they could hold out against the determined forces of the Borgia, whose strength seemed limitless.

All this Ezio learned from the grizzled master-sergeant as he was recovering.

"Stay still, my lord."

"Where am I?"

"On a stretcher. We're taking you to the Sanctuary. The inner sanctum. No one will reach there."

"Put me down. I can walk!"

"We have to dress that wound."

Ezio, ignoring him, shouted an order at the stretcher bearers. But when he stood up, his head reeled.

"I cannot fight like this."

"Oh, God, here they come again," bellowed the sergeant as a siege tower crashed into the upper crenellations of the citadel, disgorging yet another fresh troop of Borgia soldiers.

Ezio turned to face them, his head slowly clearing from the darkness, his steely self-control overcoming the searing pain of the gunshot wound. But his shoulder was so damaged that he could not raise his sword. Assassin *condottieri* quickly surrounded him and fought off Cesare's men. They managed to beat a retreat with very few casualties, but as they made their way back into the inner vastness of the castle Claudia shouted from a doorway, eager to hear of her brother's well-being. As she stepped into the open, a Borgia captain rushed toward her—bloodied sword in his hand. Ezio looked on in horror, but recovered his composure enough to yell to his men. Two Assassin fighters ran toward Ezio's sister— only just managing to put themselves between her and the flashing blade of the Borgia murderer. Sparks shot from the contact of the three blades—both Assassins raising their own swords simultaneously to block the killing blow. Claudia stumbled to the ground—her mouth open in a silent scream. The stronger of the Assassin soldiers, the master-sergeant, pushed the enemy's sword skyward—locking the hilts at the hand guards—as the other Assassin pulled back his blade and stabbed forward into the guts of the Borgia captain. Claudia regained her composure and rose slowly to her feet. Safely in the fold of the Assassin troop, she rushed toward Ezio, ripping a strip of cotton from her skirts and pressing it to his shoulder, the white cloth quickly blooming with red from the wound.

"Shit! Don't take risks like that!" Ezio told her, thanking the sergeant as his men pushed the enemy back, hurling some from the high battlements, while others fled.

"We must get you inside the Sanctuary," cried Claudia. "Come *on!*"

Ezio allowed himself to be carried again—he had lost a lot of blood. In the meantime, the remaining citizens of the town who had not yet been able to escape crowded around them. Monteriggioni itself was deserted now—under the complete control of the Borgia force. Only the citadel remained in Assassin hands.

But now they had reached their goal—the cavernous fortified room beneath the castle below its northern wall, linked to the main building by a secret passage leading off Mario's library. But only in the nick of time. One of their men, Paganino, one of the Venetian thieves once under Antonio de Magianis's control, was in the act of closing the secret door to the stairwell as the last fugitives passed through it.

"We thought you had been killed, *Ser* Ezio!" he cried.

"They haven't got me yet," returned Ezio grimly.

"I don't know what to do. Where does this passage lead?"

"To the north, outside the walls."

"So it's true. We always thought it was a legend."

"Well, now you know better," said Ezio, looking at the man and wondering if, in the heat of the moment, he had said too much to a man he knew little of. He ordered his sergeant to close the door, but at the last moment, Paganino slipped through it, back to the main building.

"Where are you going?"

"I have to help the defenders. Don't worry, I'll lead them back this way."

"I must bolt this door behind us. If you don't come now, you are on your own."

"I'll manage, sir. I always do."

"Then go with God. I must ensure the safety of these people."

Ezio took stock of the crowd gathered in the Sanctuary. In the gloom he could make out, among the rest of the fugitives, the features of not only Claudia, but his mother. He breathed an inward sigh of relief.

"There is no time to be lost," he told them, jamming the door shut behind him with a sizable iron bar.

ELEVEN

Quickly, his mother and sister dressed and bandaged his wound properly and got him to his feet, as Ezio directed the master-sergeant to twist the hidden lever built into the statue of the Master Assassin, Leonius, which stood by the side of the giant chimneypiece at the center of the northern wall of the Sanctuary. The concealed door swung open, revealing the corridor through which the people could escape to the safety of the countryside half a mile beyond the city limits.

Claudia and Maria stood by the entrance, shepherding townsfolk through it. The master-sergeant had gone ahead with a platoon, bearing torches, to guide and protect the refugees as they made their escape.

"Hurry!" Ezio urged the citizens as they rushed into the dark maw of the tunnel. "Don't panic! Be quick but don't run! We don't want a stampede in the tunnel."

"And what of us? What of Mario?" asked his mother.

"Mario—how can I tell you this?—Mario has been killed. I want you and Claudia to make your way home to Florence."

"Mario dead?" cried Maria.

"What is there in Florence for us?" asked Claudia.

Ezio spread his hands. "Our home. Lorenzo de' Medici and his son undertook to restore the Auditore mansion to us, and they were as good as their word. Now the city is in the control of the Signoria again, and I know that Governor Soderini watches over it well. Go home. Put yourselves in the care of Paola and Annetta. I will join you as soon as I can."

"Are you sure? The news we've heard about our old house is very different. *Messer* Soderini was too late to save it. In any case, we want to stay with you. To help you!"

The last remaining townspeople were filing into the dark tunnel now. As they did so, a great hammering and the crashing of blows fell on the door that divided the Sanctuary from the outside world.

"What is that?"

"It's the Borgia troops! Make haste! Make haste!"

He ushered his family into the tunnel after the last remaining citizens, bringing up the rear with the few surviving Assassin troops.

* * *

It was a tough haul through the tunnel, and halfway along Ezio heard the crash as the Borgia men broke through the door into the Sanctuary. Soon they would be in the tunnel itself. He urged his charges forward, shouting at the stragglers to hurry. Then he heard the stamping of armed soldiers running down the tunnel behind them. The group rushed past a gateway that ended one section of the passage. Ezio grabbed at a lever on the wall beside the gateway—and just as the last of the Assassin fugitives rushed through he yanked hard, releasing the portcullis gate. As it came crashing down, the first of the pursuers caught up—only to be pinned to the floor by the heavy ironwork of the gate. His screams of agony filled the passage. Ezio had already run on— knowing that he'd bought his people precious time to make good their escape.

After what seemed like hours but could only have been minutes, the passage seemed to change incline—leveling out and then rising slightly. The air seemed less stale— they were nearly out. Just at that moment, they all heard a heavy rumbling of sustained cannon fire—the Borgia must be unleashing their firepower at the citadel, a final act of desecration. The passage shook—eddies of dust fell from the ceiling, and a sound like cracking ice could be heard, quiet at first but getting ominously louder.

"*Dio, ti prego, salvaci*—the roof is coming down!" sobbed one of the townswomen. The others began to scream—the fear of being buried alive flooding through the crowd.

Suddenly the roof of the tunnel seemed to open up and a torrent of rubble came cascading down. The fugitives rushed forward trying to escape from the falling rock, but Claudia reacted too slowly—she disappeared in a cloud of dust. Ezio wheeled around in alarm—hearing his sister scream, but unable to see her. "Claudia!" he shouted, panic in his voice.

"Ezio!" came a shout back, and as the dust cleared, Ezio's sister picked her way carefully across the debris.

"Thank God you're OK—did anything fall on you?" he asked.

"No, I'm OK. Is Mother OK?"

"I'm fine," answered Maria.

They dusted themselves down, thanking the gods that they had survived this far, and made their way along the final stretch of the escape passage. At last they broke out into the open air. Never had grass, and the earth itself, smelled sweeter.

The mouth of the tunnel was separated from the countryside by a series of rope bridges swung across ravines. It had been designed like this by Mario as part of a master escape plan. Monteriggioni itself would survive the Borgia desecration—once the Borgia had razed it, it would be of no further interest to them. Ezio would return in time and rebuild it. Once again it would be the proud stronghold of the Assassins. Of that Ezio was certain. And it would be more than that. It would be a monument to his noble uncle, so pitilessly slain, Ezio promised himself.

He had had enough of the depredations wrought on his family by pointless villainy.

Ezio planned to cut the bridges down behind them as they fled, but they were shepherding elderly and wounded stragglers, and at his back he heard the yells and footsteps of their pursuers approaching rapidly. He was scarcely able to carry anyone on his back, but he managed to haul a woman whose leg had given out onto his good shoulder and staggered forward across the first rope bridge. It swung dangerously under their weight.

"Come on!" he yelled, encouraging his rear guard, who were already engaging with the Borgia soldiers. He waited on the far side until the last of his own men had reached the safety of the rocks. His men ran from the bridge—but a couple of Borgia soldiers had also made it across. Ezio stepped across their path and, using his good arm to wield his sword, engaged the enemy. Even hampered by his wound, Ezio was more than a match for the Borgia men—his sword parried their attacks with a blur of steel, taking on both blades at once. Stepping to one side, he crouched low under a wild swing from one of the men and used his own weapon to slice at the knee joint of the man's leg armor. The man toppled—his left leg useless. The other attacker lunged down, thinking Ezio off balance, but Ezio rolled aside and the blade clanged off the rocks, sending shards of rock skittering into the ravine. The man winced as the blow vibrated along his sword, jarring the bones of his hand and arm. Ezio saw his chance and, heaving himself upright, brought his sword above his foe's lowered arm and across the man's face. The man went down—and in a single fluid movement Ezio brought his blade to bear on the ropes supporting the bridge. They severed instantly, the tension sending the ropes pinging violently backward across the ravine. The bridge concertinaed away from the rocks, and the Borgia men who had begun to cross fell screaming into the abyss below.

Turning back, on the other side Ezio saw Cesare. Next to him was Caterina, still in chains, and held by a vicious-looking Lucrezia. Juan Borgia, the deathly pale Micheletto, and the sweaty Frenchman, General Valois, stood by them. Leonardo was nowhere to be seen—but how could he have sided with such scum? Surely there must be a threat hanging over him. Ezio couldn't believe that Leo would voluntarily stoop so low.

Cesare was waving something at Ezio.

"Yours next!" he screamed in fury.

Ezio could see that it was his uncle's head.

TWELVE

There was only one place for Ezio to go now. The way forward for Cesare's troops was cut off—it'd take them days to work around the ravines and catch up with Ezio's survivors. He directed them to towns out of Borgia control, at least for the moment—to Siena, to San Gimignano, to Pisa, Lucca, Pistoia, and Florence. They'd find sanctuary there, and he had tried to impress upon his mother and sister the wisdom of returning to the safety of Florence themselves, whatever had happened to the Villa Auditore—despite the sad memories the city held, and despite the fact that both were seized with a compulsive desire to avenge Mario's death.

But Ezio was bound for Rome. Rome, he knew, would be where Cesare would go now, to regroup. It might even be that Cesare in his arrogance would think Ezio beaten, even dead on the road, like carrion. If so, then that could only be to the Assassin's advantage. But something else was haunting Ezio. With Mario dead, the Brotherhood was leaderless. Machiavelli was a powerful force within it, and at present Machiavelli did not seem to be Ezio's friend.

This was something that had to be resolved.

Along with the human survivors of the town, they had managed to bring livestock with them, and among the animals was the great chestnut warhorse Mario had loved so much.

He now mounted the steed, held for him by the old stable-master, who had managed to get out, too—though, alas, most of his horses had been captured by the Borgia.

As he reined the horse in, he took his leave of his mother and sister.

"Must you really go to Rome?" asked Maria.

"Mother, the only way to win this war is to take it to the enemy."

"But how can you possibly succeed against the forces of the Borgia?"

"I am not their only enemy. And besides, Machiavelli is already there. I must make my peace with him, and work with him."

"Cesare has the Apple," Claudia said soberly.

"We must pray that he does not master its powers," Ezio replied, though privately he felt great misgivings. Leonardo was in Cesare's pay and Cesare's power now, and Ezio was well aware of the intelligence of his former friend. If Leonardo taught Cesare the mysteries of the Apple—worse still, if Rodrigo got hold of it again . . .

He shook his head to rid himself of these thoughts. Time enough to confront the threat of the Apple when it presented itself.

"You shouldn't be riding now. Rome is miles to the south. Can't you at least give it a day or two?" asked Claudia.

"The Borgia will not rest and the evil spirit of the Templars rides within them," rejoined Ezio drily. "No one will be able to sleep easily until their power is broken."

"What if it never is?"

"We must never give up the fight. The minute we do that, we have lost."

"È vero." His sister's shoulders slumped, but then she straightened them again. "The fight must *never* be given up," she said firmly.

"Until death," said Ezio.

"Until death."

"Take care on the road."

"Take care on the road."

Ezio leaned down from the saddle to kiss his mother and his sister before wheeling the horse around and onto the road south. His head was pounding with the pain of his wound and the exertions of battle. More than this was the aching of his heart and soul at the loss of Mario and the capture of Caterina. He shuddered at the thought of her in the clutches of the evil Borgia family—he knew all too well what fate might befall her in their hands.

But Ezio also knew that if ever a person would go down fighting, she was that person. He'd have to skirt the Borgia troops but his heart told him that, now that his main objective had been achieved, to break the Assassins' stronghold, Cesare would head home.

But the most important thing was to lance the boil that was infecting Italy, and lance it soon, before it could infect the whole body of the land.

He dug his heels hard into the horse's flanks and galloped south down the dusty road.

His head was swimming with exhaustion but he willed himself to keep awake. He vowed he would not rest until he arrived in the broken-down capital of his beleaguered country. But he had miles to go before he would be able to sleep.

THIRTEEN

How stupid had he been . . . to ride for so long, wounded; and so far—only breaking the ride for the horse's sake and then impatiently flogging the poor beast on before he was properly rested. Post-horses would have been a more sensible choice, but Campione was his last link with Mario.

Now—where was he? He remembered a crumbling, dingy suburb and then, rising out of it, a once-majestic yellow stone arch, an erstwhile gateway that pierced a formerly magnificent city's walls.

Ezio's impulse had been to rejoin Machiavelli—to right the wrong he had committed by not making sure that Rodrigo Borgia, the Spaniard, was dead.

But by God, he was tired!

He lay back on the pallet. He could smell the dry straw, its odor carrying with it a hint of cow dung.

Where was he?

An image of Caterina came suddenly and strongly into his mind. He must free her! They had to be together at last!

But perhaps he should also free himself *from* her— though part of his heart still told him that this was not what he really wanted. How could he trust her? How could a simple man ever understand the subtle labyrinths of a woman's mind? And, alas, the torture of love didn't get any less acute with age.

Was she using him?

Ezio had always maintained an inner room within his heart, where he was himself alone, where he had his *sanctum sanctorum*; it was kept locked, even to his most intimate friends, to his mother (who knew of it and respected it), to his sister, and, formerly, to his late brothers and father.

Had Caterina broken in? He hadn't been able to prevent the killing of his father and brothers, and by Christ and the Cross he had done his best to protect Maria and Claudia.

Caterina could look after herself—she was a book that kept its covers closed—and yet—and yet—how he longed to read it!

"I love you!"—his heart cried out to Caterina, despite himself. The woman of his dreams at last—at last, this late in life. But his duty, he told himself, came first—and

Caterina—Caterina!—never truly showed her cards. Her brown, enigmatic eyes, her smile, the way she could twist him around her little finger. Her long, expert fingers. The closeness. The closeness. But also the keen silence of her hair, which always smelled of vanilla and roses . . .

How could he ever trust her, even when he laid his head on her breast after they had made passionate love and wanted—wanted so much—to feel secure?

No! The Brotherhood. The Brotherhood. The Brotherhood! His mission and his destiny.

I am dead, Ezio said to himself. *I am already dead inside. But I will finish what I have to do.*

The dream dissolved and his eyelids flickered open. They bestowed a view of an ample but elderly cleavage descending toward him, the chemise the woman was wearing parting like the Red Sea.

Ezio sat up rapidly in the straw he'd been lying on. His wound was properly dressed now, and the pain was so dull as to be almost negligible. As his eyes focused, they took in a small room with walls of rough-hewn stone. Calico curtains were drawn across the small windows, and in a corner an iron stove burned, the embers from its open door giving the place its only light. Then the door was shut, but whoever it was with him in the room lit the stump of a candle.

A middle-aged woman, who looked like a peasant, knelt beside him, came within the frame of his vision. Her face was kindly as she tended to his wound, rearranging the poultice and bandage.

It was sore! Ezio winced in pain.

"*Calmatevi,*" said the woman. "The pain will end soon."

"Where's my horse? Where's Campione?"

"Safe. Resting. God knows he deserves it. He was bleeding from the mouth. A good horse like that. What were you doing to him?"

The woman put down the bowl of water she was holding and stood.

"Where am I?"

"In Rome, my dear. *Messer* Machiavelli found you fainting in your saddle, your horse frothing, and brought you both here. And don't worry, he's paid me and my husband well to look after you and your horse. And a few more coins for our discretion. But you know *Messer* Machiavelli—cross him at your peril. Anyway, we've done this kind of job for your organization before."

"Did he leave me any message?"

"Oh, yes. You're to meet him as soon as you're fit at the Mausoleum of Augustus. Know where that is?"

"One of the ruins, isn't it?"

"Dead right. Not that it's much more of a ruin than most of this awful city is nowadays. To think it was once the center of the world! Look at it now—smaller than Florence, half the size of Venice. But we do have one boast." She cackled.

"And that is?"

"Only fifty thousand poor souls live in this shanty-town of a city that once was proud to call itself Rome; and *seven thousand of them* are prostitutes! That's got to be a record!" She cackled some more. "No wonder everyone's riddled with the New Disease. Don't sleep with anyone here," she added, "if you don't want to fall apart with the pox. Even cardinals have got it—and they say the Pope himself, and his son, are sufferers."

Ezio remembered Rome as if in a dream. A bizarre place now, whose ancient, rotting walls had been designed to encompass a population of one million. Now most of the area was given over to peasant farming.

He remembered, too, the ruined wasteland of what had once been the Great Forum in ancient times, where sheep and goats grazed now. People stole the ancient carved marble and porphyry stones, which lay higgledy-piggledy in the grass, to build pigsties with or to grind down for lime. And out of the desolation of slums and crooked, filthy streets, the great new buildings of Pope Sixtus IV and Pope Alexander VI rose obscenely, like wedding cakes on a table where there was nothing else to eat but stale bread.

The aggrandizement of the Church was confirmed, back at last from the papal exile at Avignon; and above all the Pope—the leading figure in the international world, outclassing not only kings, but the Holy Roman Emperor Maximilian himself—had his seat in Rome again.

And hadn't it been Pope Alexander VI who'd divided, in his great judgment, the southern continent of the New Americas, through a vertical line, between

the colonizing countries of Portugal and Spain by the
Treaty of Tordesillas in 1494, the same year the New
Disease broke out—for the first time in Italy—so badly
in Naples? They called it the French disease—*morbus
gallicus*. But everyone knew it'd come back from the
New World with Columbus's bunch of Genoese sailors.
It was an unpleasant affliction. People's faces and bodies
bubbled morphews and boils, and in the last stages their
faces were often pressed out of all recognizable shape.

And in Rome, the poor made do on barley and
bacon—when they could get bacon. And the dirty
streets harbored typhus, cholera, and the Black Death.
As for the citizens—there were the ostentatiously rich,
to be sure; but as for the rest, they looked like cowherds
and lived as badly.

What a contrast to the gilded opulence of the Vatican!
Rome, that great city, had become a rubbish heap of history. Along the filthy alleys that passed for streets, in
which feral dogs and wolves now roamed, Ezio remembered churches, which today were falling apart, rotting
refuse, deserted palaces that reminded him of the prob-
able wreck (as his prophetic soul told him) of his own
family seat in Florence.

"I must get up. I must find *Messer* Machiavelli!" said
Ezio urgently, flinging the visions from his mind.

"All in good time," replied his nurse. "He left you a
new suit of clothes. Put them on when you are ready."

Ezio stood, and as he did so his head swam; but
he shook himself to clear it. Then he donned the suit

Machiavelli had left him—new linen, and a hood of soft wool with a peak like an eagle's beak. Strong, soft gloves and boots made of Spanish leather. He dressed himself, fighting the pain the effort caused him. When he was done, the woman guided him to a balcony. Ezio realized then that he had not been in some shrunken hovel, but in the remains of what had once been a great palace. They must have been on the *piano nobile*. He drew in his breath as he looked at the desolate wreck of a city spread out below him. A rat scuttled boldly over his feet. He kicked it away.

"Ah, Roma," he said ironically.

"What's left of it," the woman repeated, cackling again.

"Thank you, Madonna. To whom do I owe . . . ?"

"I am the *Contessa* Margherita degli Campi," she said, and in the dim light Ezio could see at last the fine lines of a face once beautiful. "Or what's left of her."

"*Contessa*," Ezio said, trying to keep the sadness out of his voice, and bowed.

"The *mausoleo* is over there," she replied, smiling and pointing. "That is where you are to meet."

"I can't see it."

"In that direction. Unfortunately, you cannot see it from my *palazzo*."

Ezio squinted into the dark. "What about from the tower of that church?"

She looked at him. "Santo Stefano's? Yes. But it's a ruin. The stairs to the tower have collapsed."

Ezio braced himself. He needed to get to his meeting

place as safely and as quickly as possible. He did not want to be delayed by the beggars, tarts, and muggers who infested the streets by day and even more by night.

"That should not be a problem," he told the woman. *"Vi ringrazio di tutto quello che avete fatto per me, buona Contessa. Addio."*

"You are more than welcome," she replied with a wry smile. "But are you sure you are fit enough to go so soon? I think you should see a doctor. I'd recommend one, but I can't afford them anymore. I have cleaned and dressed your wound, but I am no expert."

"The Templars don't wait, and nor can I," he replied. "Thank you again, and goodbye."

"Go with God."

He leapt from the balcony down to the street, wincing at the impact, and darted across the square dominated by the disintegrating palace in the direction of the church. Twice he lost sight of the tower and had to double back. Three times he was accosted by leprous beggars and once confronted a wolf, which slunk away down an alley with what may have been a dead child between its jaws, but at last he was in the open space before the church. It was boarded up, and the limestone saints that adorned its portal were deformed by neglect. He didn't know whether he could trust the rotten stonework, but there was nothing for it—he had to climb.

He managed it—though he lost his footing on several occasions and once his feet fell free over an embrasure that collapsed under them, leaving him hanging by the tips of his fingers. But he was still a very strong man, and he managed to haul himself up, out of danger—and at last he was on the top of the tower, perched on its lead roof. The dome of the mausoleum glinted dully in the moonlight several blocks away. He'd go there now and wait for Machiavelli to arrive.

He adjusted his hidden-blade and his sword and dagger, and was about to make a leap of faith down to a hay wain parked in the square below when his wound shrieked and he doubled up in pain.

"The *contessa* dressed my shoulder well, but she was right—I must see a doctor," he said to himself.

Painfully he clambered down the tower to the street. He had no idea where to find a *medico*, so he first made his way to an inn, where he obtained directions in exchange for a couple of ducats; the money also bought him a beaker of filthy Sanguineus, which nevertheless assuaged his pain somewhat.

It was late by the time he reached the doctor's surgery. He had to knock several times, and hard, before there was a muffled response from within. Then the door opened a crack to reveal a fat, bearded man of about sixty, wearing thick eyeglasses. He looked the worse for wear and Ezio could smell drink on his breath. One eye seemed larger than the other.

"What do you want?" said the man.

"Are you *Dottor* Antonio?"

"And if I am . . . ?"

"I need your help."

"It's late," said the doctor, but his eyes had wandered to the wound on Ezio's shoulder, and his eyes became—cautiously—more sympathetic. "It'll cost extra."

"I am not in a position to argue."

"Good. Come in."

The doctor unchained his door and stood aside. Ezio staggered gratefully into a hallway whose beams were hung with a collection of copper pots and glass vials, dried bats and lizards, mice and snakes.

The doctor ushered him through into an inner room with a huge desk untidily covered with papers, a narrow bed in one corner, a cupboard whose open doors revealed more vials, and a leather case, also open, containing a selection of scalpels and miniature saws.

The doctor followed Ezio's eyes and barked out a short laugh. "We *medici* are just jumped-up mechanics," he said. "Lie down on the bed and I'll have a look. Before you do, it's three ducats—in advance."

Ezio handed over the money.

The doctor undressed the wound and pushed and shoved so that Ezio virtually passed out with the pain.

"Hold still!" the doctor grumbled. He poked around some more, poured some stinging liquid from a flask over the wound, dabbed at it with a cotton wad, then produced some clean bandages and bound it back firmly.

"Someone your age cannot recover from a wound like this with medicine." The doctor rummaged about in his cupboard and produced a vial of treacly looking stuff. "But here's something to dull the pain. Don't drink it all at once. It's another three ducats, by the way. And don't worry. You'll heal over time."

"Grazie, Dottore."

"Four out of five doctors would have suggested leeches, but they haven't proven effective against this sort of wound. What is it? If they weren't so rare, I'd say it was from a gunshot. Come back if you need to. Or I can recommend several good colleagues around the city."

"Do they cost as much as you do?"

Dr. Antonio sneered. "My good sir, you've got off lightly."

Ezio stomped out into the street. A light rain had begun to fall, and the streets were already turning sticky and muddy.

"'Someone your age,'" grumbled Ezio. *"Che sobbalzo!"*

He made his way back to the inn. He'd seen they had rooms for rent. He'd stay there, eat something, and make his way to the mausoleum in the morning. Then he'd just have to wait for his fellow Assassin to show up. Machiavelli might at least have left some kind of rendezvous time with the *contessa*. But Ezio was aware of Machiavelli's passion for security. He'd no doubt turn up at the appointed spot every day at regular intervals. Ezio shouldn't have too long to wait.

Ezio picked his way through the wretched streets and alleys, darting back into the darkness of doorways whenever a Borgia patrol, easily recognized by the charging black bull device on their breastplates, passed clatteringly by.

It was midnight by the time he reached the inn again. He took a swig from the vial of dark liquid. It was good. He hammered on the inn door with the pommel of his sword.

FOURTEEN

The following day, Ezio left the inn early. His wound felt stiff but the pain was duller and he was far better able to use his arm now. Before leaving, he practiced a few strokes with the hidden-blade and found he could use it without difficulty, as well as more conventional sword-and-dagger work. It was just as well he hadn't been shot in the shoulder of his sword arm.

Not being sure whether the Borgia and their Templar associates knew he had escaped the battle of Monteriggioni with his life, and noting the high number of soldiers armed with guns and dressed in the dark mulberry red and yellow livery of the Borgia, he took a round-about route to the Mausoleum of Augustus. The sun was high by the time he reached it.

There were fewer people here, and after having scouted around, assuring himself that no guards were watching the place, Ezio cautiously approached it, slipping through a ruined doorway into the gloomy interior.

As his eyes quickly accustomed themselves to the darkness, he made out a figure dressed in black, leaning against a stone outcrop, and still as a statue. He glanced to each side to ascertain that there was somewhere to duck behind before the figure noticed him, but apart from tussocks of grass among the fallen stones of the ancient Roman ruin, there was nothing. He decided on the next best thing and swiftly but silently started to move toward the deeper darkness of the mausoleum's walls.

But he was too late. Whoever it was had seen him, probably as soon as he'd entered, framed by the light from the doorway, and moved toward him. As it approached, he recognized the black-suited figure of Machiavelli, who placed a finger to his lips as he came. Beckoning him discreetly to follow, Machiavelli made his way into a deeper, darker area of the ancient Roman emperor's tomb, built almost one and a half millennia previously.

At last he stopped and turned.

"Shh," he said and, waiting, listened keenly.

"Wha—?"

"Voice down. Voice very low," admonished Machiavelli, listening still.

At last he relaxed. "All right," he continued. "There's no one."

"What do you mean?"

"Cesare Borgia has eyes everywhere." Machiavelli's look softened a little. "I am glad to see you here."

"But you left me clothes at the *contessa*'s . . ."

"She had word to watch for your arrival in Rome." Machiavelli grinned. "Oh, I knew you'd come here. Once you'd assured yourself of the safety of your mother and sister. After all, they are the last of the Auditore family."

"I don't like your tone," said Ezio, bridling slightly.

Machiavelli allowed himself a thin smile. "This is no time for tact, my dear colleague. I know the guilt you feel about your lost family, even though you are not remotely to blame for that great betrayal." He paused. "News of the attack on Monteriggioni has spread across this city. Some of us were sure that you had died there. I left the clothes with our trusted friend because I knew you better than to go and die on us at such a crucial time! Or at any rate, just in case!"

"You still have faith in me, then?"

Machiavelli shrugged. "You blundered. Once. Because fundamentally your instinct is to show mercy and trust. Those are good instincts. But now we must strike, and strike hard. Let's hope that the Templars never know that you are still alive."

"But they must already know!"

"Not necessarily. My spies tell me there was a lot of confusion."

Ezio paused for thought. "Our enemies will know soon enough that I am alive—and very much so! How many do we fight?"

"Oh, Ezio—the good news is that we have narrowed the field. We have wiped out many Templars across Italy and across many of the lands beyond its boundaries. The bad news is that the Templars and the Borgia family are now one and the same thing. And they are going to fight like a cornered lion."

"Tell me more."

"We are too isolated here. We need to lose ourselves in the crowds in the center of town. We will go to the bullfight."

"The bullfight?"

"Cesare excels as a bullfighter. After all, he is a Spaniard. In fact he's not a Spaniard, but a Catalan, and that may one day prove to be to our advantage."

"How?"

"The king and queen of Spain want to unify their country. They are from Aragon and Castile. The Catalans are a thorn in their side, though they are still a powerful nation. Come, and be cautious. We must both use the skills of blending in that Paola taught you so long ago in Venice. I hope you have not forgotten them!"

"Try me!"

They walked together through the half-ruined, once-imperial city, keeping to shadows where there was shadow, otherwise slipping in and out of crowds as fish hide in rushes. At last they reached the bullring, took seats in the more expensive and crowded shady side of it, and watched for an hour as Cesare and his many backup men dispatched three fearsome bulls. Ezio watched Cesare's fighting technique: He used the banderilleros and the picadors to break the animal down before he himself delivered the coup de grâce, after a good deal of showing off. But there was no doubting his courage and his prowess during the grim ritual of death, despite the fact that he still had four junior matadors to support him. Ezio looked over his shoulder at the box of the *presidente* of the fight: there he recognized the harsh but compellingly beautiful face of Cesare's sister, Lucrezia. Was it his imagination or had he seen her bite her lip until it bled?

At any rate, he had learned something of how Cesare would behave in the field of battle—and how far he could be trusted in any other kind of combat.

Everywhere there were Borgia guards, watching the throng, just as there had been in the streets before. And armed with those lethal-looking new guns.

"Leonardo . . ." he said involuntarily, thinking of his old friend.

Machiavelli looked at him. "Leonardo was forced to work for Cesare on pain of death—and a most painful death it would have been. It's a detail—a terrible detail, but a detail nonetheless. The point is, his heart is not with his new master, who will never have the intelligence or the facility fully to control the Apple. Or at least I hope it isn't. We must be patient. We will get it back—and we will get Leonardo back with it."

"I wish I could be so sure."

Machiavelli sighed. "Perhaps you are wise to be doubtful," he said at last.

"Spain has taken over Italy," said Ezio.

"Valencia has taken over the Vatican," Machiavelli replied. "And we can change that. We have allies in the College of Cardinals, some powerful. They aren't all lap-dogs. And Cesare, for all his vaunting, depends on his father, Rodrigo, for funds." He gave Ezio a keen look. "That is why you should have made sure of this interloping Pope."

"I didn't know."

"I'm as much to blame as you are. I should have told you. But as you said yourself, it's the present we have to deal with, not the past."

"Amen to that."

"Amen."

"But how do they afford all this?" Ezio asked, as another bull foundered and fell under Cesare's unerring and pitiless sword.

"*Papa* Alexander is a strange mixture," Machiavelli replied. "He's a great administrator and he has even done the Church some good. But the evil part of him always defeats the good. He was the Vatican's treasurer for years and found ways of amassing money—the experience has stood him in good stead. He sells cardinal's hats, creating dozens of cardinals virtually guaranteed to be on his side. He has even pardoned murderers—provided they have enough money to buy their way off the gallows."

"How does he justify that?"

"Very simple. He preaches that it is better for a sinner to live and repent, than to die and forgo such pain."

Ezio couldn't help laughing, though his laugh was a

mirthless one. His own mind went back to the celebra-
tions to mark the year 1500—the Great Year of the Half-
Millennium. True, there had been flagellants roaming
the country in expectation of the Last Judgment, and
hadn't the mad monk Savonarola, who'd briefly had control of the Apple, and whom he had himself defeated in
Florence—not been duped by that superstition?

Fifteen hundred had been a great jubilee year. Ezio
remembered that thousands of hopeful pilgrims had
made their way to the Holy See from all parts of the
world. The year had perhaps even been celebrated in
those small outposts across the far seas to the west in the
New Lands discovered by Columbus and, a few years
later, by Amerigo Vespucci, who had confirmed their
existence. Money had flowed into Rome as the faithful bought indulgences to redeem them from their sins
in anticipation of Christ returning to Earth to judge
both the quick and the dead. It had also been the time
when Cesare had set out to subjugate the city-states of
the Romagna, and when the king of France had taken
Milan, justifying his action as being the rightful heir—
the great-grandson of Gian Galeazzo Visconti.

The Pope had then made his son Cesare captain-
general of the papal forces and Gonfaloniere of the Holy
Roman Church in a great ceremony on the morning of
the fourth Sunday of Lent. Cesare was welcomed by
boys in silk gowns, and four thousand soldiers wearing his personal livery. His triumph had seemed complete: the previous year, in May, he'd married Charlotte

d'Albret, sister of John, king of Navarre, and King Louis of France—with whom the Borgia were allied—gave him the Dukedom of Valence. Having already been Cardinal of Valencia, no wonder the people gave him the nickname Valentino!

And now this viper was at the peak of his power.

How could Ezio ever defeat him?

He shared these thoughts with Machiavelli.

"In the end, we will use their own vainglory to bring them down," said Niccolò. "They have an Achilles' heel. Everyone does. I know what yours is."

"And that is?" snapped Ezio, needled.

"I do not need to tell you her name. Beware of her," rejoined Machiavelli, but then, changing the subject, he continued, "Remember the orgies?"

"They continue?"

"Indeed they do. How Rodrigo—I refuse to call him Pope anymore—loves them! And you've got to hand it to him; he's seventy years old." Machiavelli laughed wryly and then suddenly became more serious. "The Borgia will drown under the weight of their own self-indulgence."

Ezio remembered the orgies well. He had been witness to one. There'd been a dinner, attended by fifty of the best of the city's army of whores, given by the Pope in his Nero-like, overdecorated, gilded apartments. Courtesans, they liked to call themselves, but whores for all that. When the eating—or should it be called feeding?—was over, the girls danced with the servants who were in attendance, clothed at first, but later they'd shed their clothes. The candelabra that had been on the tables were set down on the marble floor, and the nobler guests threw roasted chestnuts among them. The whores were then told to crawl about the floor on all fours like cattle, buttocks high in the air, and collect the chestnuts. Then almost everyone had joined in. Ezio remembered with distaste how Rodrigo, with Cesare and Lucrezia, had looked on. At the end, prizes were given—silk cloaks, fine leather boots, from Spain of course, mulberry-and-yellow velvet caps encrusted with diamonds, rings, bracelets, brocade pouches each containing a hundred ducats, daggers, silver dildos—anything you could imagine—all awarded to those men who had had sex the maximum number of times with the crawling prostitutes. And the Borgia family, fondling each other, had been the principal judges.

The two Assassins left the bullfight and made themselves invisible in the crowds that thronged the early evening streets.

"Follow me," Machiavelli said, an edge in his voice. "Now you have had a chance to see your principal opponent at work, it would be well to purchase any equipment you are missing. And take care not to draw any undue attention to yourself."

"Do I ever?" Ezio found himself once again needled by the younger man's remarks. Machiavelli wasn't the Brotherhood's leader. After Mario's death, no one was.

And this interregnum would have to be concluded soon. "In any case, I have my blade."

"And the guards have their guns. These things Leonardo has created for them—and you know his genius cannot control itself—are fast to reload, as you've seen, and moreover they have barrels filed in a cunning way on the inside to make the shot more accurate."

"I'll find Leonardo and talk to him."

"You may have to kill him."

"He's worth more to us alive than dead. You said yourself his heart wasn't with them."

"I said that is what I hope." Machiavelli stopped. "Look. Here is money."

"Grazie," said Ezio, taking the proffered pouch.

"While you are in my debt, listen to reason."

"As soon as I hear more reason from you, I shall."

Nevertheless, Ezio left his friend and made his way to the quarter of the armorers, where he provided himself with a new breastplate, steel cuffs, and a sword and dagger of higher quality and better balance than those he already possessed. He missed above all the old Codex bracer, made of a secret metal, which had staved off so many blows that otherwise would have been fatal. But it was too late to regret it now. He'd just have to rely on his wits and his training all the more. No one, no accident, could take them from him.

He returned to Machiavelli, who was waiting for him at a low inn, their preappointed rendezvous.

He found him in a prickly mood.

"*Bene*," said Machiavelli. "Now you can survive the journey back to Firenze."

"Perhaps. But I am not going back to Florence."

"No?"

"Perhaps you should. It is where you belong. I have no home there anymore."

Machiavelli spread his hands. "It is true that your old home has indeed been destroyed. I didn't want to tell you. But surely your mother and sister are safe there now. It is a city safe from the Borgia. My master, Piero Soderini, guards it well. You can recoup there."

Ezio shuddered at having his worst fears confirmed. Then he pulled himself together and said: "I stay here. You said yourself, there will be no peace until we rise up against the entire Borgia family and the Templars who serve them."

"Such brave talk! After Monteriggioni."

"That is cheap of you, Niccolò. How could I have known that they would find me so quickly? That they would kill Mario?"

Machiavelli spoke earnestly, taking his companion by the shoulders. "Look, Ezio—whatever happens, we must prepare ourselves carefully. We must not hit out in rash anger. We are fighting *scorpioni*—worse, serpents! They can coil around your neck and bite your balls in one movement! They know nothing of right and wrong. They only know their goal! Rodrigo surrounds himself with snakes and murderers. Even his daughter, Lucrezia, has been sharpened into one of his most artful weapons, and she knows all there is to know about the art of poisoning." He paused. "But even she pales by comparison with Cesare!"

"Him again!"

"He is ambitious, ruthless, and cruel beyond—thank God!—your imagination. The laws of men mean nothing to him. He has murdered his own brother, the Duke of Gandia, to claw his way toward absolute power. He will stop at nothing!"

"I'll pluck him down."

"Only if you are not rash. He has the Apple, don't forget. Heaven help us if he really learns its powers."

Ezio's mind flashed nervously onto Leonardo. Leonardo understood the Apple only too well . . .

"He recognizes neither danger nor fatigue," Machiavelli continued. "Those who do not fall by his sword clamor to join his ranks. Already the powerful Orsini and Colonna families have been brought down to kneel at his feet, and King Louis of France stands at his side." Machiavelli paused again, thoughtful. "But at least King Louis will only remain his ally as long as he is useful to him . . ."

"You overestimate the man!"

Machiavelli appeared not to have heard him. He was lost in his own thoughts. "What does he intend to do with all that power? All that money? What drives the man? . . . That, I still do not know. But, Ezio," he added, fixing his friend with his eyes, "Cesare has indeed set his sights on all Italia, and at this rate he will have it!"

Ezio hesitated, shocked. "Is that . . . is that *admiration* I hear in your voice?"

Machiavelli's face was set. "He knows how to exercise his will. A rare virtue in the world today. And he is the kind of man who could indeed make the world bend to that will."

"What do you mean, exactly?"

"Just this: People need someone to look up to—even to adore. It may be God, or Christ, but better yet someone you can really see, not an image. Rodrigo, Cesare, even a great actor or singer, as long as they're dressed well and have faith in themselves. The rest follows quite logically." Machiavelli drank a little wine. "It's part of us, you see—it doesn't interest you or me or Leonardo; but there are people out there who have a hunger to be followed, and they are the dangerous ones." He finished his drink. "Fortunately, they can also be manipulated by people like me."

"Or destroyed by people like me."

They sat in silence for a long moment.

"Who will lead the Assassins now that Mario is dead?" asked Ezio.

"What a question! We are in disorder and there are few candidates. It's important, of course, but the choice will be made. In the meantime, come on. We have work to do."

"Shall we take horses? Half of it may be falling down, but Rome's still a big city," suggested Ezio.

"Easier said than done. As Cesare's conquests in the Romagna increase—and he controls most of it now— and the Borgia grow in power, they've taken the best areas of the city for themselves. And we're in a Borgia *rione*—district—now. We won't get horses from the stables here."

"So—the will of the Borgia is the only law here now?"

"Ezio—what are you implying? That I approve of it?"

"Don't play dumb with me, Niccolò."

"I don't play dumb with anyone. Do you have a plan?"

"We'll improvise."

They made their way toward the place where the local stables with horses for hire were located, walking down streets where, Ezio noticed, many of the shops, which should have been open in normal circumstances, had their shutters down. What was the matter here? And, sure enough, the closer they got, the more numerous and menacing were the guards in mulberry-and-yellow livery. Machiavelli, Ezio noticed, was becoming increasingly wary.

It wasn't long before a burly sergeant, at the head of a dozen or so tough-looking thugs in uniform, blocked their path.

"What's your business here, friend?" he said to Ezio.

"Time to improvise?" whispered Machiavelli.

"We want to hire some horses," Ezio replied evenly to the sergeant.

The sergeant barked out a laugh. "Not here, you won't, friend. On your way." He pointed back in the direction they'd come from.

"Isn't it allowed?"

"No."

"Why not?"

The sergeant drew his sword as the other guards followed suit. He held the point of his blade against Ezio's neck and pushed slightly, so that a drop of blood appeared. "You know what curiosity did to the cat, don't you? Now fuck off!"

With an almost imperceptible movement, Ezio swept out his hidden-blade and with it severed the tendons of the wrist holding the sword, which clattered uselessly to the ground. With a great cry the sergeant buckled over, grasping his wound. At the same time, Machiavelli leapt forward and slashed at the nearest three guards with his sword in a great sweeping motion—they all staggered back, astonished at the sudden boldness of the two men. Ezio swiftly withdrew the hidden-blade and in one fluid movement unsheathed his sword and dagger. His weapons were clear and poised just in time to cut down the first two of his own attackers, who, recovering some composure, had stepped forward to avenge their sergeant. None of the Borgia men had the skill at arms required to take on either Ezio or Machiavelli—the Assassins' training was of a wholly different class. Even so, the odds were against the two friends, heavily outnumbered as they were. However, the unexpected ferocity of their attack was enough to give them an unassailable edge. Taken almost wholly by surprise, and unused to coming off worse in any encounter, the dozen men were soon dispatched. But the commotion of the scuffle had raised the alarm, and more Borgia soldiers came, and yet more—over two dozen men, all told. Machiavelli and Ezio were nearly overwhelmed with the sheer weight of numbers, and with the effort of taking on so many enemies, at once. The flourishes of style that they were both capable of were set aside for a wholly more efficient and quick form of swordsmanship—the three-second kill, a single thrust sufficing. The two men stood their ground, grim determination set on their faces, and finally all their enemies had either fled or lay wounded, dead or dying at their feet.

"We'd better hurry," said Machiavelli, breathing hard. "Just because we've sent a few Borgia henchmen to their Maker doesn't mean we'll get access to the stables. The ordinary people remain afraid. That's why many of them won't even open their shops."

"You're right," agreed Ezio. "We need to send them a signal. Wait here!"

A fire was burning in a brazier nearby. From it, Ezio seized a brand, then leapt up the wall of the stable, where the Borgia flag, with the black bull in a golden field, flew in the light breeze. Ezio set it on fire. As it burned, one or two shop doors cautiously opened, as did the gates of the stables.

"That's better!" cried Ezio. He turned to address the small, doubtful crowd that had gathered. "Do not fear the Borgia! Do not be in thrall to them! Their days are numbered, and the hour of reckoning is at hand!"

More people came up, raising a cheer.

"They'll be back," Machivelli said.

"Yes, they will, but we've shown these people that they are not the all-powerful tyrants they took them to be!"

He leapt down from the wall into the stable yard, where Machiavelli joined him. Swiftly, they picked two sturdy mounts and had them saddled.

"We'll come back," Ezio promised the head ostler. "You might like to get this place cleaned up a bit—now that it belongs to you again, as it rightfully should."

"We will, my lord," said the man. But he still looked fearful.

"Don't worry. They won't harm you, now that you've seen them bested."

"How do you figure that, my lord?"

"They need you. They can't do without you. Just show them you won't be bullied and pushed around and they'll have to cajole you into helping them."

"They'll hang us—or worse!"

"Do you want to spend the rest of your lives under their yoke? Stand up to them. They'll have to listen to reasonable requests. Even tyrants cannot function if enough people refuse to obey them."

Machiavelli, already on his horse, took out a small black notebook and wrote in it, smiling absently to himself. Ezio swung himself into the saddle.

"I thought you said we were in a hurry," said Ezio.

"We are. I was just making a note of what you said."

"I hope I should be flattered by that."

"Oh, yes—you should be. But come on!"

"You excel at opening wounds, Ezio," Machiavelli continued as they rode. "But can you also close them?"

"I intend to heal the sickness that's at the heart of our society, not merely tinker about with the symptoms."

"Bold words! But you don't have to argue with me! We're on the same side, don't forget. I'm just putting another point of view."

"Is this a test?" Ezio was suspicious. "Well, let us talk openly, then. I believe that Rodrigo Borgia's death would not have solved our problem."

"Really?"

"Well—I mean, look at this city. Rome is the epicenter of Borgia and Templar rule. What I just said to that stableman holds true. Killing Rodrigo won't change things—cut off the head of a man, and he is dead, sure. But we are dealing with a Hydra."

"I see what you mean—like the seven-headed monster Heracles had to kill—and even then the heads grew back until he learned the trick of stopping that from happening."

"Precisely."

"So—you suggest that we appeal to the people?"

"Maybe—how else?"

"Forgive me, Ezio, but the people are fickle. Relying on them is like building on sand."

"I disagree, Niccolò. Surely our belief in humanity rests at the heart of the Assassin's Creed."

"And that's something you intend to put to the test?"

Ezio was about to reply, but at that instant a young thief ran alongside them and, with his knife, swiftly and surely cut through the leather strings that attached Ezio's money pouch to his belt.

"What the—!" Ezio shouted.

Machiavelli laughed. "He must be from your inner circle! Look at him run! You might have trained him yourself! Go! Get back what he's stolen. We need that money! I'll meet you at the Campidoglio on the Capitoline!"

Ezio wheeled his horse around and galloped off in pursuit of the thief. The man ran down alleys too narrow for the horse and Ezio had to go around, worried that he might lose his quarry but at the same time knowing—to his chagrin—that on foot the younger man could surely outrun him. It was almost as if the man had indeed had some Assassin training. But how could that be?

At last he cornered the man in a blind alley and pushed him up against the wall of the dead end with the body of his horse, pinning him there.

"Give it back," he said evenly, drawing his sword.

The man still seemed bent on escape, but when he saw how hopeless his situation was, his body slumped and, mutely, he raised the hand that held the pouch. Ezio snatched it and stowed it away safely. But in doing so he let his horse move back a fraction, and in the wink of an eye the man had scrambled up the wall with almost extraordinary speed and disappeared on the other side.

"Hey! Come back! I haven't finished with you yet!" Ezio yelled, but all he got in reply was the receding sound of running feet. Sighing, and ignoring the small crowd that had gathered, he steered the horse in the direction of the Capitoline Hill.

* * *

Dusk was falling as he rejoined Machiavelli there.

"Did you liberate your money from our friend?"

"I did."

"A small victory."

"They add up," said Ezio. "And in time, with work, we'll have a few more."

"Let's hope we make it before Cesare's gaze falls on us again and we're broken again. He damned nearly succeeded at Monteriggioni. Now, let's get on with things." He spurred his horse.

"Where are we going?"

"To the Colosseum. We have a rendezvous with a contact of mine, Vinicio."

"And?"

"I'm expecting him to have something for me. Come on!"

As they rode through the city toward the Colosseum, Machiavelli commented drily on the various new buildings erected by Pope Alexander VI during his administration.

"Look at all these façades, masquerading as government. Rodrigo is very clever in the way he keeps this place in business. It fools your friends 'the people' quite easily."

"When did you become so cynical?"

Machiavelli smiled. "I'm not being cynical at all. I'm just describing Roma as she is today! But don't worry, Ezio—perhaps I am a little too bitter, a little too negative, sometimes. All may not be lost. The good news is that we do have allies in the city. You will meet them. And the College of Cardinals is not completely under Rodrigo's thumb, much as he'd like it to be. But it is touch-and-go . . ."

"What is touch-and-go?"

"Our ultimate success."

"We can only try. Giving up is a sure way to failure."

"Who said anything about giving up?"

They rode on in silence and reached the gloomy hulk of the ruined Colosseum, a building over which, for Ezio, the remembered horrors of the games that had taken place here a thousand years ago still hung. But his attention was immediately caught by a group of Borgia guards with a papal courier. Their swords drawn, halberds pointing threateningly, and bearing flickering red torches, they were jostling a small, harassed-looking man.

"*Merda!*" said Machiavelli softly. "It's Vinicio. They've got to him first."

Silently, the two men slowed their horses, approaching the group quietly and with as much caution as they could, in order to gain the maximum element of surprise. As they neared, they picked up snatches of conversation.

"What you got there?" one guard was asking.

"Nothing."

"Attempting to steal official Vatican correspondence, eh?"

"*Perdonatemi, signore.* You must be mistaken."

"No mistake, you little thief," said another guard, prodding the man with his halberd.

"Who are you working for, *ladro*?"

"No one!"

"Good! Then no one will care what happens to you."

"I've heard enough," said Machiavelli. "We've got to save him, and get the letter he carries."

"Letter?"

"Come *on*!"

Machiavelli dug his heels into his mount's flanks—the surprised horse bolted forward, as Machiavelli tugged hard on the reins. The beast reared, forelegs kicking wildly and slamming into the temple of the nearest Borgia guard, caving his helmet into his skull. The man fell like a stone. Meanwhile, Machiavelli had swiveled himself to his right, leaning low out of his saddle—reaching down, he slashed viciously at the shoulder of the guard threatening Vinicio. The man dropped his halberd instantly and collapsed with the pain flaming through his shoulder. Ezio spurred his own steed forward—careening past two other guards and using the pommel of his sword to strike hard, fatally hard, down on the first man's head and slapping the second across the eyes with the flat of his blade. One more guard was left—distracted by the sudden attack, he didn't notice Vinicio grabbing the shaft of his halberd and suddenly felt himself yanked forward. Vinicio's dagger was waiting and pierced the man's throat. He fell with a sickly gargling sound as blood flooded into his lungs. Once again, the element of surprise gave the Assassins the edge; the Borgia soldiers were clearly not used to such effective resistance to their bullying. Vinicio wasted no time and gestured to the main thoroughfare leading from the central plaza. A courier's horse could be seen clattering from the plaza— the man standing hard in the stirrups urging his ride on.

"Give me the letter. Be quick about it!" ordered Machiavelli.

"But I haven't got it—he has," Vinicio cried, pointing toward the fleeing horse. "They got it back from me!"

"Get after him!" Machiavelli shouted to Ezio. "Whatever it costs, get that letter and bring it to me at the Terme di Diocleziano by midnight! I'll be waiting."

Ezio rode off in pursuit.

It was easier than catching the thief, this time. Ezio's horse was better than the courier's, and the man was no fighter. Ezio pulled him from the horse with ease. Ezio didn't like to kill the man, but he couldn't afford to let him go and raise the alarm. *"Requiescat in pace,"* he said softly, as he slit his throat. He put the letter, unopened, in his belt pouch and slapped the courier's horse on its rear, hoping it would find its way back to its stable. He turned his own mount and made for the ruins of the Baths of Diocletian.

It was now almost pitch-dark, except for where the occasional torch guttered in a wall-mounted sconce. To reach the baths, Ezio had to cross a sizable stretch of wasteland, and halfway across, his horse reared and neighed in fear. But then a bloodcurdling sound came to his ears, like the howling of wolves. And yet not quite the same. Possibly worse. It sounded more like human

voices imitating the animals. He spun his horse around
in the dark.

But he didn't have much time to reflect on that as
he reached the deserted baths. Machiavelli had not yet
arrived—no doubt off again on one of his mysterious
private missions in the city—but then—

From among the hillocks and tussocks of grass that
had grown over remains of the ancient Roman city, figures appeared, surrounding him. Feral-looking humans,
but hardly human in appearance at all. They stood
upright, but they had long ears, snouts, claws, and tails,
and they were covered in rough grey hair. Their eyes
seemed to glint red. Ezio drew a sharp breath—what
on earth were these devilish creatures? His eyes darted
around the ruins—he was encircled by at least a dozen of
these wolfmen. Ezio unsheathed his sword once more.
This was not turning out to be the best of days.

With wolflike snarls and howls, the creatures fell
upon him. As they came close, Ezio could see that these
were indeed men like him, but seemingly mad, like creatures in some kind of holy trance. Their weapons were
long, sharp steel talons sewn firmly into the tips of heavy
gloves, and with these they slashed at his legs and at the
horse's flanks, trying to bring him down.

He was able to keep them at bay with his sword, and,
as their disguises seemed to have no chain mail or other
protection under the wolfskins, he was able to damage
them effectively with the keen edge of his sword. He cut
one creature's arm off at the elbow and it slunk away,

wailing horribly in the darkness. The strange creatures seemed to be more aggressive than skillful—their weapons no match for the point of Ezio's flashing blade. He quickly pressed forward—splitting the skull of another and piercing the left eye of a third. Both wolfmen fell on the spot—mortally injured by Ezio's blows. By then the other wolfmen seemed to be having second thoughts about continuing their attack, some melting into the darkness or into hollows and caves formed by the overgrown ruins surrounding the baths. Ezio gave chase, gouging the thigh of one of his would-be assailants, while another fell under the hooves of the horse only to have his back broken by them. Overtaking a sixth, Ezio leaned down and, turning backward, ripped the man's stomach open so that his guts spilled onto the ground, and he stumbled over them as he fell and died.

Then all was silent.

Ezio calmed his horse and stood up in his stirrups, willing his keen eyes to penetrate the darkness and his ears to pick up signals his eyes could not see. Presently he thought he could make out the sound of labored breathing not far off, though nothing was visible. He urged his horse into a walk and softly made his way in the direction it was coming from.

It seemed to be coming from the blackness of a shallow cave, formed by the overhang of a fallen archway and festooned with creepers and weeds. Dismounting and tying his horse firmly to a tree stump, and rubbing the blade of his sword with dirt so that it would not glint and give his location away, gingerly he made his way forward. He had thought that for a brief second he had seen the flickering of a flame in the bowels of the cave.

As he inched his way forward, bats swooped over his head and out into the night. The place stank of their droppings. Unseen insects and doubtless other creatures clattered and scuttled away from him. He cursed them for the noise they made, as it seemed as loud as thunder to him, but the ambush—if there was one—still did not come.

Then he saw the flame again and heard what he could have sworn was a faint whimpering. He saw that the cave was less shallow than the fallen arch suggested, and that its corridor curved gently, and at the same time narrowed, leading into a deeper darkness. As he followed the curve, the flickers of flame he had glimpsed earlier resolved themselves into a small fire, in the light of which he could make out a hunched figure.

The air was slightly fresher here. There must be some airway in the roof that he could not see. That would be why the fire could breathe. Ezio stood stock-still and watched.

Whimpering, the creature reached out a skinny left hand, grubby and bony, and plucked at the end of an iron bar that was stuck in the fire. Its other end was red-hot, and, tremblingly, the creature drew it out and, bracing itself, applied the end to the bloody stump of its other arm, stifling a shriek as it did so, in an attempt to cauterize the wound.

The wolfman Ezio had maimed!

In the second when the wolfman's attention was exclusively bound up in his pain and the job at hand, Ezio surged forward. He was almost too late, for the creature was fast and almost got away, but Ezio's fist closed hard around its good arm. It was difficult, for the limb was slippery with grease, and the stench the creature released as it moved was all but overpowering, but Ezio held on firmly. Catching his breath, and kicking the iron bar away, Ezio said: "What the fuck are you?"

"*Uurrgh,*" was all the reply he got. Ezio slapped the man hard on the head with his other fist, still sheathed in a mailed glove. Blood spurted close to the man's left eye and he moaned in additional pain.

"What are you? Speak!"

"*Errrgh.*" The open mouth displayed a broken, greyish set of teeth and the smell that came from it made that of a drunken whore seem sweet.

"Speak!" Ezio drove the point of his sword into the stump and twisted it. He hadn't time to mess about with this wreck of a person. He was worried about his horse.

"*Aaarrgh!*" This time a cry of pain. Then a rough, almost incomprehensible voice emerged from the inarticulate grunting—speaking good Italian. "I am a follower of the Secta Luporum."

"The Sect of the Wolves? What the hell is that?"

"You will find out. What you did tonight—"

"Oh, shut up." Tightening his grip, Ezio stirred up the fire to gain more light and glanced around. He now saw that he was in a kind of domed chamber, possibly hollowed out deliberately. There was little in it but a couple of chairs and a rough table with a handful of papers on it, weighted down with a stone.

"My brothers will return soon—and then—"

Ezio dragged him to the table, pointing with his sword at the papers. "And these? What are these?"

The man looked at him and spat. Ezio placed his swordpoint close to the bloody stump again.

"No!" wailed the man. "Not again!"

"Then tell me." Ezio looked at the papers. The moment would come when he would have to put his sword down, however briefly, to pick them up. Some of the writing was in Italian, some in Latin, but there were other symbols, which looked like writing, but which he could not decipher.

Then he heard a rustling, coming from the direction he had entered from. The wolfman's eyes gleamed. "Our secrets," he said.

At the same moment two more of the creatures bounded into the room, roaring and clawing at the air with their steel claws. Ezio's prisoner wrenched himself free and would have joined them if Ezio had not slashed his head from his shoulders and sent it rolling toward his friends. He tore around to the other side of the table, seizing the papers, and hurled the table over toward his enemies.

The firelight dimmed. The fire needed stirring again. Needed more fuel. Ezio's eyes strained to pick out the two remaining wolfmen. They were like grey shadows in

the room. Ezio dropped back into the darkness, stashed
the papers in his tunic, and waited.

The wolfmen may have had the strength of the insane,
but they couldn't have been very skilled, except in the
art, perhaps, of scaring people to death. They certainly
couldn't keep quiet or move silently. Using his ears more
than his eyes, Ezio managed to circle, skirting the walls,
until he knew he was behind them when they thought
he was still somewhere in the darkness ahead of them.

There was no time to lose. He sheathed his sword,
unleashed his hidden-blade, came up as stealthily as
a real wolf behind one of them, and, holding him
firmly from behind, cut his throat. He died instantly
and silently, and Ezio eased the body just as silently to
the floor. He considered trying to capture the other,
but there was no time for interrogation. There might
be more of them, and Ezio wasn't sure he had enough
strength left to fight anymore. Ezio could sense the
other man's panic, and it was confirmed when he left
off his wolf impersonation and called anxiously into the
silent darkness, "Sandro?"

It was a simple matter then to locate him, and again
the exposed throat was Ezio's hoped-for target. But this
time the man spun around, tearing at the air in front
of him frantically with his claws. He could see Ezio,
but Ezio remembered that these creatures wore no mail
under their fancy dress. He withdrew the hidden-blade
and with his larger and less subtle dagger, which had
the advantage of a serrated edge, opened the man's
chest. The exposed heart and lungs glistened in the

dying firelight as the last wolfman fell forward, his face in the fire. The smell of burning hair and burning flesh threatened to overcome Ezio almost immediately, but he sprang back and made his way as fast as he could, fighting down panic, to the kindly air and the night again.

Once outside, he could see that the wolfmen had not touched his horse. Perhaps they had been too sure of trapping him to bother to kill it or drive it away. He untied it and realized he was trembling too much to mount. Instead he took its bridle and led it back to the Baths of Diocletian. Machiavelli had better be there and he had better be well armed. By God, if only he still had his Codex gun! Or one of those things Leonardo had fashioned for his new master. But Ezio did have the satisfaction of knowing he could still win fights by using his wits and his training—two things they couldn't deprive him of until the day they caught him and tortured him to death.

He remained fully alert on the short journey back to the baths and found himself—something that would not have happened to him as a younger man—occasionally starting at shadows. The thought of a safe arrival back at the baths brought him no comfort. What if there was another ambush awaiting him there? And what if these creatures had surprised Machiavelli? Was Machiavelli himself aware of the Secta Luporum?

Where were Machiavelli's loyalties anyway?

But he reached the dim, vast ruin, a memorial to the lost age when Italy had ruled the world, in safety. There was no sign of life that he could see, but then Machiavelli himself emerged from behind an olive tree and greeted him soberly.

"What kept you?"

"I was here before you. But then I was . . . distracted." Ezio looked at his colleague evenly.

"What do you mean?"

"Some jokers in fancy dress. Sound familiar?"

Machiavelli's gaze was keen. "Dressed as wolves?"

"So you do know about them."

"Yes."

"Then why suggest here as a meeting place?"

"Are you suggesting that I—?"

"What else am I to think?"

"Dear Ezio—" Machiavelli took a step forward. "I assure you, by the sanctity of our Creed, that I had no idea they would be here." He paused. "But you are right. I sought a meeting place remote from men, little realizing that they, too, might choose such a place."

"If they'd been tipped off."

"If you are impugning my honor—"

Ezio made an impatient gesture. "Oh, skip it," he said. "We've enough to do without quarreling with each other." In truth, Ezio knew that for the moment he would have to trust Machiavelli. And so far, he had had no reason not to. But he would play his cards closer to his chest in future. "Who are they? What are they?"

"The Sect of the Wolves. Sometimes they call themselves the Followers of Romulus."

"Shouldn't we move away from here? I managed to grab some papers of theirs and they might be back to collect."

"First, tell me if you got the letter back, and tell me quickly what else has happened to you. You look as if you have been well in the wars," said Machiavelli.

After Ezio had done so, his friend smiled. "I doubt if they will return tonight. We are two trained, armed men and it sounds as if you well and truly thrashed them. But that in itself will have incensed Cesare. You see, although there is little proof as yet, we believe that these creatures are in the Borgia's employ. They are a band of false pagans who have been terrorizing the city for months."

"To what purpose?"

Machiavelli spread his hands. "Political. Propaganda. The idea is that people will be encouraged to throw themselves under the protection of the Papacy—and in return, a certain loyalty is exacted from them."

"How convenient. But even so, shouldn't we be getting out of here now?" Ezio was suddenly and unsurprisingly tired. His very soul ached.

"They won't be back tonight. No disparagement to your prowess, Ezio, but the wolfmen aren't fighters or even killers. The Borgia use them as trusted go-betweens, but their main job is to frighten. They are poor, deluded souls whom the Borgia have brainwashed into working for them. They believe their new masters will help them rebuild ancient Rome—from its very beginnings. The founders of Rome were Romulus and Remus. They were suckled as babies by a she-wolf."

"I remember the legend."

"For the wolfmen, poor creatures, it is no legend. But they are a dangerous enough tool in the Borgia's hands." He paused briefly. "Now—the letter! And those papers you say you grabbed from the wolfmen's lair. Well done, by the way."

"If they're of any use."

"We'll see. Give me the letter."

"Here it is."

Hastily, Machiavelli broke the seal and unfolded the parchment. *"Cazzo,"* he muttered. "It's encrypted."

"What do you mean?"

"This one was supposed to be in plain text. Vinicio is—was—one of my moles among the Borgia. He told me he had it on good authority. The fool! They are transmitting information in code. Without their code sheet, we have nothing."

"Perhaps the papers I got hold of will help."

Machiavelli smiled. "By heaven, Ezio—sometimes I thank God we are on the same side. Let's have a look!"

Quickly he sifted through the pages Ezio had seized, and his troubled face cleared.

"Any good?"

"I think . . . perhaps . . ." He read some more, his brow once more furrowed. "Yes! By God, yes! I think we have it!" He clapped Ezio on the shoulder and laughed.

Ezio laughed, too. "You see? Sometimes logic is not

the only way to win a war. Luck can play a part, too. *Andiamo!* You said we had allies in the city. Come on! Bring me to them!"

"Follow me!"

FIFTEEN

"What about the horse?" Ezio asked.

"Turn her loose. She'll find her way back to her stable."

"I can't abandon her."

"You must. We are going back to the city. If we let her go there, they'll know you got back. If they find the horse out here, they'll think—with luck—that you're still wandering around this area and divert their search here."

Ezio reluctantly did as he was told, and Machiavelli led him to a concealed flight of stone steps leading underground. At the foot of them a torch was burning. This Machiavelli seized.

"Where are we?" asked Ezio.

"This leads to a system of ancient underground

tunnels that crisscross the city. Your father discovered them and they have remained the Assassins' secret ever since. We can use this route to avoid any guards who'll be out looking for us, because you may be sure that the wolfmen who escaped will raise the alarm. They're big, because they were used for transport and troops in ancient times, and well built, as everything was in those days. But many of the outlets within the city have collapsed now and are blocked. We must pick our way carefully. Stay close—it would be fatal for you to get lost down here."

For two hours they passed through a labyrinth that seemed never-ending. Ezio, as he passed, glimpsed side tunnels, blocked entranceways, strange carvings of forgotten gods over archways, and the occasional flight of steps leading upward, some leading into blackness, others, fewer, showing a glimmer of light at their heads. At last Machiavelli, who had kept up a steady but hurried pace all along, paused at one such flight.

"We're here," he announced. "I'll go first. It's almost dawn. We must be careful." He vanished up the steps.

After what seemed an age, during which the thought crossed Ezio's mind that he might have been abandoned, he heard a whispered "All clear" from Machiavelli.

Despite his fatigue, he ran up the steps, glad to be back in the fresh air. He'd had enough of tunnels and caves to last a lifetime.

He found himself emerging from a kind of big manhole into a large room, large enough to have been a warehouse of sorts once.

"Where are we?"

"On an island in the Tiber. It was used years ago as a depot. No one comes here now, except us."

"Us?"

"Our Brotherhood. It is, if you like, our hideout in Rome."

A burly, confident young man rose from a stool by a table on which lay papers and the remains of a meal and came to greet them. His tone was open and friendly.

"Niccolò! *Ben trovato!*" He turned to Ezio. "And you—you must be the famous Ezio! Welcome!" He took Ezio's hand and shook it warmly. "Fabio Orsini—at your service. I've heard a lot about you from my cousin—and old friend of yours—Bartolomeo d'Alviano."

Ezio smiled at the name. "A fine warrior," he said.

"It was Fabio who discovered this place," put in Machiavelli.

"Every convenience here," said Fabio. "And outside, so overgrown with ivy and whatnot, you wouldn't even know it existed!"

"It is good to have you on our side."

"My family has taken a few bad blows from the Borgia of late—and my one aim is to kick their stall in and restore our patrimony." He looked around doubtfully. "Of course, this may all seem a bit shabby to you, after your accommodations in Toscana."

"This is perfect."

Fabio smiled. "*Bene.* Well, now that you have arrived, you must forgive me that I must leave you—immediately."

"What are your plans?" asked Machiavelli.

Fabio's face became more serious. "I am off to begin preparations for Romagna. Today, Cesare has control of my estate and my men; but soon, I hope, we will be free again."

"*Buona fortuna!*"

"*Grazie!*"

"*Arrivederci!*"

"*Arrivederci!*"

And, with a friendly wave, Fabio was gone.

Machiavelli cleared a space on the table and spread out the encrypted letter, together with the wolfmen's decoding page. "I have to get on with this," he said. "Look—you must be exhausted—there's food and wine there, and good, clear Roman water. Refresh yourself while I work, for there is still much to be done."

"Is Fabio one of the allies of whom you spoke?"

"Indeed. And there are others. One very great indeed."

"And he is? Or is it a she?" Ezio asked, thinking, despite himself, of Caterina Sforza. He could not get her out of his mind. She was the Borgia's prisoner still. His own private priority was to free her. But was she playing games with him? He could not rid his mind of a grain of doubt. But she was a free spirit. He did not own her. Only—he did not relish the thought of being played for a fool. And he did not want to be used.

Machiavelli hesitated, as if he had already divulged too much, but then he spoke: "It is the cardinal Giuliano della Rovere. He was in competition with Rodrigo for the Papacy, and lost; but he is still a powerful man—and has powerful friends. He has potentially strong connections with the French, but bides his time—he knows that King Louis is only using the Borgia for as long as it suits him. Above all, he hates the Borgia with a deep and enduring loathing. Do you know how many Spaniards the Borgia have placed in positions of power? We are in danger of having them control Italy."

"Then he's the man for us. When can I meet him?"

"The time is not yet ripe. Eat, while I work."

Ezio was glad of the hour's respite, but found that hunger and even thirst—at least, for wine—had abandoned him. He drank some water gratefully, and toyed with a chicken leg, as he watched Machiavelli pore over the papers in front of him.

"Is it working?" he asked at one point.

"Shh!"

The sun had reached the church towers of Rome when Machiavelli put down his quill and drew toward him the spare sheet of paper on which he'd been writing.

"It's done."

Ezio waited expectantly.

"It's a directive to the wolfmen," said Machiavelli. "It states that the Borgia will provide their usual payment, and orders the wolfmen to attack—that is, to create terrifying diversions—in various parts of the city not yet under full Borgia control. The attacks are to be timed with the 'fortuitous' appearance of a Borgia priest, who will use the powers of the Church to 'banish' the attackers."

"What do you propose?"

"If you agree, Ezio, I think we should begin planning

our own assault on the Borgia. Carry on the good work you started at the stables."

Ezio hesitated. "You think we are *ready* for such an attack?"

"*Sì.*"

"I'd like to know where the Borgia are holding Caterina Sforza first. She'd be a powerful ally."

Machiavelli looked nonplussed. "If she is their prisoner, she'll be held at the Castel Sant'Angelo. They've turned it into a stronghold." He paused. "It is too bad they have control of the Apple. Oh, Ezio, how could you have let that happen?"

"You were not at Monteriggioni." It was Ezio's turn to pause, after an angry silence. "Do we *really* know what goes on with our enemies? Do we at least have an underground network here to work with?"

"Hardly. Most of our mercenaries, like Fabio, are tied up in battle with Cesare's forces. And the French still back him."

Ezio remembered the French general at Monteriggioni—Octavien.

"What have we got?" he asked.

"One solid source. We have girls working at a brothel. High-class joint, frequented by cardinals and other important Roman citizens; but there's a snag. The madam we have in place is lazy and seems rather to enjoy parties for their own sake than to further our cause by gathering information."

"What about the city's thieves?" asked Ezio, thinking about the adroit robber who'd almost cost him his purse.

"Well, *sì*; but they refuse to talk to us."

"Why?"

Machiavelli shrugged. "I have no idea."

Ezio rose. "You'd better tell me how to get out of here."

"Where are you going?"

"To make some friends!"

"May I ask what friends?"

"I think for the moment you had better leave that to me."

SIXTEEN

It was nightfall again by the time Ezio had found the headquarters of the Roman Thieves' Guild. Another long day lay behind him, a day of asking questions discreetly in taverns, getting suspicious looks and misleading answers, until, finally, word must have got around that it was all right to let him know the secret location, and a ragamuffin of a boy had led him into a run-down district through a maze of alleys and left him at a door, only to disappear immediately the way he had come.

It wasn't much to look at: a large but broken-down-looking inn, whose sign, showing a fox, either asleep or dead, hung awry; whose windows were shrouded with tattered blinds; and whose woodwork was in need of repainting. This was the same Sleeping Fox Inn that he and Mario visited a week ago.

Unusually for an inn, its door was shut fast. Ezio hammered on it. In vain.

Then he was surprised by a voice coming from behind him, speaking softly. Ezio spun around. It wasn't like him to allow himself to be approached noiselessly from behind like that. He must ensure that it didn't happen again.

Fortunately, the voice was friendly, if guarded.

"Ezio!"

The man who'd spoken stepped forward from the shelter of a tree. Ezio recognized him immediately. It was his old ally Gilberto—La Volpe, the Fox—who had led the thieves in Florence in alliance with the Assassins some time previously.

"La Volpe! What are you doing here?"

Gilberto grinned as they embraced. "Why am I not in Florence, do you mean? Well, that's simply answered. The thieves' leader here died, and they elected me. I felt like a change of air, and my old assistant, Corradin, was ready to take over back home. Besides"—he lowered his voice conspiratorially—"just at the moment, Rome presents me with a little bit more of a . . . challenge, shall we say?"

"Seems a good enough reason to me. Shall we go in?"

"Of course." La Volpe knocked at the door himself—obviously a coded knock, for the door swung open almost immediately, to reveal a spacious courtyard, with tables and benches laid out, just as you'd expect at an inn—but all still very dingy. A handful of people, men and women, bustled about, in and out of doors that led from the courtyard into the inn itself, built around it.

"Doesn't look like much, does it?" said La Volpe, ushering him to a seat and calling for wine.

"Frankly—"

"It suits our purposes. And I have plans. But what brings you here?" La Volpe held up a hand. "Wait! Don't tell me. I think I know the answer."

"You usually do."

"You want to put my thieves to work as spies for you."

"Exactly!" Ezio said, leaning forward eagerly. "Will you join me?"

La Volpe raised his beaker in a silent toast, and drank a little of the wine that had been brought, before replying, flatly: "No."

Ezio was taken aback. "What? Why not?"

"Because that would only play into Niccolò Machiavelli's hands. No, thank you. That man is a traitor to our Brotherhood."

This came as a little less of a surprise, though Ezio was very far from convinced of the truth of it. He said: "That's a very serious allegation, coming from a thief. What proof do you have?"

La Volpe looked sour. "He was an ambassador to the papal court, you know—and he traveled as a personal guest of Cesare himself."

"He did those things on our behalf!"

"Did he? I also happen to know he abandoned you just before the attack on Monteriggioni."

Ezio made a gesture of disgust. "Pure coincidence! Look, Gilberto, Machiavelli may not please all tastes, but he *is* an Assassin, *not* a traitor."

La Volpe looked at him with a set face. "I am not convinced."

At that point in their conversation, a thief—Ezio, recognizing him as the one who had cut his purse, glared at him—scuttled up and whispered in La Volpe's ear. La Volpe stood as the thief scuttled off. Ezio, sensing trouble, stood, too.

"I apologize for Benito's behavior the other day," said La Volpe. "He did not then know who you were. But he did see you riding with Machiavelli."

"To hell with Benito. What's going on?"

"Ah. Benito brought news. Machiavelli is meeting someone in Trastevere very soon. I'm going to check out what's going on. Care to accompany me?"

"Lead on."

"We'll use one of the old routes—the rooftops. It's a bit tougher here than it was in Florence. Do you think you're up to it?"

"Just lead on!"

It was hard going. The roofs of Rome were spaced farther apart than in Florence, and many were crumbling, making it harder to gain footing. More than once, Ezio sent a loose tile crashing to the ground. But there were few people about in the streets, and they moved so fast that by the time any Borgia guards could react, they

were already out of sight of them. At last they reached a
market square, its stalls closed up except for one or two
brightly lit wine booths, where a number of people were
gathered. Ezio and La Volpe paused on a roof overlooking it, concealing themselves behind chimney stacks,
and watched.

Soon afterward, Machiavelli himself walked into the
square, first glancing around carefully. Ezio watched
keenly as another man, wearing the Borgia crest on his
cloak, approached Machiavelli and discreetly handed
him what looked like a note before walking on, barely
breaking his stride. Machiavelli similarly moved on, out
of the square.

"What do you make of that?" La Volpe asked Ezio.

"I'll follow Machiavelli; you follow the other guy,"
snapped Ezio tersely.

But at that moment a brawl broke out at one of the
wine booths. They heard angry cries and saw the flash
of weapons.

"Oh, *merda!* That's some of my men. They've picked
a fight with a Borgia guard!" cried La Volpe.

Ezio glimpsed Machiavelli's retreating back as he fled
down a street that led toward the Tiber, then he was
gone. Too late to follow him now. He turned his attention back to the brawl. The Borgia guard lay prostrate
on the ground. Most of the thieves had scattered, scram-
bling up the walls to the rooftops and safety, but one of
them, a young man, scarcely more than a boy, lay groaning on the ground, his arm spurting blood from a flesh
wound.

"Help! Help! My son has been injured!" an anguished voice rang out.

"I recognize that voice," said La Volpe with a grimace. "It's Trimalchio." He looked keenly at the wounded thief. "And that's Claudio—his younger son!"

Meanwhile, Borgia guards armed with guns had appeared on the parapets of two roofs, on either side of the far wall of the market, and were taking aim.

"They're going to shoot him!" Ezio said urgently.

"Quickly then! I'll take the group to the left; you take the one to the right!"

There were three guards on each side. Moving as unobtrusively as shadows but as swiftly as panthers, Ezio and La Volpe swept around the connecting sides of the square. Ezio saw his three gunmen raise their weapons and take aim at the fallen boy. He sprinted along the spine of the roof—his feet seemingly barely touching the tiles—and with one huge leap sprang toward the three gunmen. His jump had sufficient height that he was able to crumple the middle gunman with the heel of his foot—connecting with the nape of the man's neck. In one movement, Ezio landed on his feet, crouched to absorb the impact of the landing, and then straightened his knees, arms outstretched on either side of him. The two remaining gunmen fell at that instant—a dagger piercing one man's right eye from the side, the blade pushing deep into his skull. The other gunman was felled by the needlelike point of Ezio's hidden-blade— it had punctured his ear, dark viscous liquid trickling down his neck. Ezio looked up to see that La Volpe had also felled his opponents with similar efficiency. After this minute of silent slaughter, all the guards with firearms were dead. But there was a fresh danger, as a platoon of halberdiers charged into the square—weapons lowered and rushing toward the unfortunate Claudio. The people in the wine booths shrank back.

"Claudio! Get out!" La Volpe yelled.

"I can't! Too much . . . pain . . ."

"Hang on!" Ezio, who was fractionally closer to where the boy lay, shouted. "I'm coming!"

He leapt down from the rooftops, breaking his fall on the canvas roof of one of the market stalls, and was soon by the boy's side. Quickly, he checked the wound. It looked more serious than it was.

"Get up!" he ordered.

"I can't!" Claudio was clearly in a state of panic. "They're going to kill me!"

"Look. You can walk, can't you?" The boy nodded. "Then you can also run. Pay attention. Follow me. Do exactly what I do. We've got to hide from the guards."

Ezio drew the boy to his feet and made his way to the nearest wine booth. Once there, he quickly melted into the crowd of by now very nervous drinkers and was surprised to see with what aptitude Claudio was able to do the same. They eased their way through the booth to the side nearest the wall, while on the other side some of the halberdiers started to push their way in. Just in time, they made it to an alleyway leading off the square and to safety. La Volpe and Trimalchio were waiting for them.

"We guessed you'd come this way," said La Volpe as

the father hugged his son. "Get going!" he said to them. "We've no time to lose! Get back to headquarters fast and have Teresina dress that wound. Go!"

"And you—keep out of sight for a while, *intensi?*" Ezio added to Claudio.

"Molte grazie, Messere," said the departing Trimalchio, his arm around the boy, guiding him, but also admonishing him: *"Corri!"*

"You're in trouble now," said La Volpe, once they'd reached the safety of a quiet square. "Especially after this. I've already seen posters up for you, after that business at the stables."

"None for Machiavelli?"

La Volpe shook his head. "No. But it's quite possible they didn't get a good look at him. Not many people know how handy he is with a sword."

"But you don't believe that."

La Volpe shook his head.

"What to do about the Wanted posters?"

"Don't worry. My people are already ripping them down."

"Glad some of them are more disciplined than to start picking fights for no reason with Borgia guards."

"Listen, Ezio—there's a tension in this city you haven't yet experienced."

"Really?" Ezio hadn't yet told his friend about the episode with the wolfmen.

"As for the heralds, a few ducats each should be enough to shut them up," La Volpe continued.

"Or . . . I could eliminate the witnesses."

"Needn't come to that," said La Volpe, more lightly. "You know how to 'disappear.' But be very careful, Ezio. The Borgia have many other enemies than you, but none quite so irritating. They won't rest until they have you hanging from hooks at Castel Sant'Angelo."

"Have to catch me first."

"Keep your guard up."

They returned by a circuitous route to the Thieves' Guild, where Claudio and his father had already arrived safely. Teresina was dressing the boy's wound, but once the bleeding had been stanched, it turned out to be nothing more than a deep cut into an arm muscle, hurting like hell but doing no serious harm, and Claudio himself was already much more cheerful.

"What a night," said La Volpe tiredly as they sat over a glass of Trebbiano and a plate of coarse salami.

"You're telling me. I could do with a few less of them."

"You won't get many while the fight goes on."

"Listen, Gilberto," Ezio said, "I know what we saw, but I am sure you have nothing to fear from Machiavelli. You know his methods."

La Volpe looked at him evenly. "Yes. Very devious." He paused. "But I have you to thank for saving Claudio's life. If you believe Machiavelli remains loyal to the Brotherhood, then I am inclined to trust your judgment."

"So—how do I stand with your thieves? Will you help me?"

"I told you I had plans to do something about this

place," La Volpe said thoughtfully. "Now that you and I seem to be working together again, I'd like to know what you think, too."

"Are we working together?"

La Volpe smiled. "Looks like it. But I'm still keeping an eye on your black-suited friend."

"Well, it'll do no harm. Just don't do anything rash."

La Volpe ignored that. "So tell me—what do you think we should do with this place?"

Ezio considered. "We need to make sure the Borgia stay away at all costs. Perhaps we could turn it into a proper, working inn."

"I like that idea!"

"It'll need a lot of work—repainting, reshingling, a new inn sign."

"I've got a lot of men. Under your direction . . ."

"Then I will make it so."

A month followed of respite, or at least semi-respite, for Ezio, as he busied himself with the business of renovating the thieves' headquarters, helped by many willing hands. Between them, the thieves represented a variety of skills, since many were tradesmen who'd been put out of work because they'd refused to kowtow to the Borgia. At the end of that time, the place had been transformed. The paintwork was bright; the windows were clean and carried new blinds. The roof was no longer rickety and the fresh inn sign showed a young male dog-fox, still sleeping but certainly not dead. He looked as if, the moment he awoke, he'd be capable of raiding fifty hen coops at a stroke. The double doors gleamed on new hinges and stood open, revealing an immaculate yard.

Ezio, who'd had to go on a mission to Siena during the last week of work, was delighted at the finished product when he returned. It was already up and running when he arrived.

"I've kept the name," La Volpe said. "I like it. La Volpe Addormentata. Can't think why."

"Let's hope it lulls the enemy into a sense of false security." Ezio grinned.

"At least all this activity hasn't drawn any undue attention to us. And we run it like a regular inn. We even have a casino. My own idea. And it's turned out to be a great source of income, since we ensure that the Borgia guards who patronize us now always lose!"

"And where—?" said Ezio, lowering his voice.

"Ah. Through here." La Volpe led the way to the west wing of the inn, through a door marked UFFIZI—PRIVATI, where two thieves stood guard without making it too obvious.

They passed along a corridor that led to a suite of rooms behind heavy doors. The walls were hung with maps of Rome, the desks and tables covered with neatly stacked papers at which men and women were working already, though it was only just past dawn.

"This is where our real business is done," said La Volpe.

"Looks very efficient."

"One good thing about thieves—good ones, at least,"

said La Volpe. "They're independent thinkers and they like a bit of competition, even among themselves."

"I remember."

"You'd probably be able to show them a thing or two, if you took part yourself."

"Oh, I will."

"But it wouldn't be safe for you to stay here," said La Volpe. "For you or for us. But visit me whenever you like—visit me often."

"I will." Ezio thought of his own lonely lodgings— lonely, but comfortable and very discreet. He'd have been happy nowhere else. He turned his mind to the business at hand. "Now that we are organized—the most important thing is to locate the Apple. We have to get it back."

"Va bene."

"We know the Borgia have it, but despite our best efforts, we still haven't been able to track it down. So far, at least, they seem to have made no use of it. I can only think they are still studying it, and getting nowhere."

"Have they sought . . . expert advice?"

"Oh, I'm pretty sure they will have. But he may be pretending to be less intelligent than he is. Let's hope so. Let's hope the Borgia don't become impatient with him."

La Volpe smiled. "I won't pursue you on that. But in the meantime, rest assured that we already have people scouring Rome for its location."

"They'll have hidden it well. Very well. Maybe even from one another. There's an increasingly rebellious streak in young Cesare, and his father doesn't like it."

"What are thieves for, but to sniff out well-hidden valuables?"

"*Molto bene.* And now, I must go."

"A last glass, before you do?"

"No. I have much to do now. But we will see each other again soon."

"And where shall I send my reports?"

Ezio considered. Then he said: "To the rendezvous of the Assassin Brotherhood—on Tiber Island!"

SEVENTEEN

It was high time now, Ezio decided, to look up his old friend Bartolomeo d'Alviano, Fabio Orsini's cousin. He'd fought shoulder to shoulder with the Orsini against the papal forces back in 1496 and had recently returned from mercenary service in Spain.

Bartolomeo was one of the greatest of the *condottieri*, and an old companion-in-arms of Ezio's. He was also, despite his sometimes oafish manner and a tendency to alarming fits both of anger and depression, a man of unbending loyalty and integrity. Those qualities made him one of the mainstays of the Brotherhood—those, and his adamantine hatred of the Templar sect.

But how would Ezio find him to be now? Well, he would soon know. He had learned that Bartolomeo had just returned from fighting and was at the barracks of his private army, on the outskirts of Rome. The barracks were well outside town, in the countryside to the northeast, but not far from one of the fortified watchtowers the Borgia had erected at various vantage points in and around the city; but the Borgia knew better than to tangle with Bartolomeo—at least, not until they felt powerful enough to crush him like the cockroach they considered him to be. And their power, Ezio knew, was growing daily.

He arrived at his destination soon after the hour of *pranzo*. The sun was past its peak and the day was too hot, the discomfort mitigated by a westerly breeze. Arriving at the huge gate in the high palisade that surrounded the barracks, he pounded it with his fist.

A judas set in the gate opened and Ezio sensed an eye appraising him. Then it closed and he heard a muffled and brief conversation. The judas opened again. Then there was a joyous, baritone bellow, and after much drawing of bolts, the gate was flung open. A large man, slightly younger than Ezio, stood there, his rough army clothes in slightly less than their usual disarray, with his arms held wide.

"Ezio Auditore! You old so-and-so! Come in! Come in! I'll kill you if you don't!"

"Bartolomeo!"

The two old friends embraced warmly, then walked across the barracks square toward Bartolomeo's quarters.

"Come on! Come on!" Bartolomeo said with his usual eagerness. "There's someone I want you to meet."

They'd arrived inside a long, low room, well lit from

large windows facing the inner square. It was a room that clearly served both for living and dining, and it was spacious and airy. But there was something very un-Bartolomeo-ish about it. There were clean blinds on the windows. There was an embroidered cloth spread on the table, from which the remains of any lunch had already been cleared. There were pictures on the walls. There was even a bookcase. Bianca, Bartolomeo's beloved greatsword, was nowhere to be seen. Above all, the place was unbelievably tidy.

"Wait here," said Bartolomeo, snapping his fingers at an orderly for wine and clearly in a high state of excitement. "Now just guess whom I want you to meet!"

Ezio glanced around the room again. "Well, I've met Bianca . . ."

Bartolomeo made a gesture of impatience. "No, no! She's in the map-room—it's where she lives nowadays. Guess again!"

"Well," Ezio said slyly, "could it possibly be—your wife?"

Bartolomeo looked so crestfallen that Ezio almost felt sorry for having made so accurate a deduction, not that it'd been hard, exactly. But the big man cheered up quickly and went on: "She's such a treasure. You wouldn't believe!" He turned and bellowed in the direction of the inner rooms: "Pantasilea! Pantasilea!" The orderly appeared again with a tray bearing sweetmeats, a decanter, and glasses. "Where is she?" Bartolomeo asked him.

"Have you checked behind the table?" Ezio asked, tongue in cheek.

Just then, Pantasilea herself appeared, descending a staircase that ran along the western wall of the room.

"Here she is!"

Ezio stood to greet her.

He bowed. "Auditore, Ezio."

"Baglioni, Pantasilea—now Baglioni-d'Alviano."

She was still young—in her mid to late twenties, Ezio judged. Judging by her name she was from a noble family, and her dress, though modest, was pretty and tasteful. Her face, framed in fine blond hair, was oval, her nose tip-tilted like a flower, her lips generous and humorous, as were her intelligent eyes—a deep, dark brown, which were welcoming when she looked at you and yet seemed to withhold something of herself. She was tall, reaching Bartolomeo's shoulders, and slender, with quite wide shoulders and rather narrow hips, long, slim arms, and shapely legs. Bartolomeo had clearly found a treasure. Ezio hoped he'd be able to hang on to her.

"Lieta di conoscervi," Pantasilea was saying.

"Altrettanto a Lei."

She glanced from one man to the other. "We will have time to meet properly on another occasion," she said to Ezio, with the air of a woman not leaving men to their business, but of having business of her own.

"Stay a little, *tesora mia.*"

"No, Barto, you know I have to see the clerk. He always manages to bungle the accounts somehow. And there is something wrong with the water supply. I must see to that, too." To Ezio she said, *"Ora, mi scusi, ma . . ."*

"Con piacere."

Smiling at both, she remounted the stairs and disappeared.

"What do you think?" Bartolomeo asked.

"Charmed, truly." Ezio was sincere. And he'd also noticed how his friend reined himself in, in her presence. He imagined there'd be very little barrack-room swearing around Pantasilea. He did wonder what on earth she saw in her husband, but then, he didn't know her at all.

"I think she'd do anything for me."

"Where did you meet her?"

"We'll talk about that some other time." Bartolomeo seized the decanter and two glasses and put his free arm around Ezio's shoulders. "I am very glad you've come. I've just got back from campaigning, as you must know, and as soon as I heard you were in Rome I was going to send men out to locate you—I know you like to keep your lodgings secret, and I don't blame you, especially not in this nest of vipers. But luckily, you've beaten me to it. And that's good, because I want to talk to you about the war. Let's go to the map-room."

"I know Cesare has an alliance with the French," Ezio said. "How goes the fight against them?"

"*Bene.* The companies I've left out there, who'll be campaigning under Fabio, are holding their own. And I've more men to train here."

Ezio considered this. "Machiavelli seemed to think things were . . . more difficult."

Bartolomeo shrugged. "Well, you know Machiavelli. He—"

They were interrupted by the arrival of one of

Bartolomeo's sergeants. Pantasilea was at his side. The man was in a panic. She was calm.

"*Capitano!*" said the sergeant urgently. "We need your help now. The Borgia have launched an attack."

"What? I hadn't expected that so soon! Excuse me, Ezio." To Pantasilea, Bartolomeo cried, "Throw me Bianca!"

She immediately tossed the greatsword across the room to him, and, buckling it on, Bartolomeo hurled himself out of the room, following his sergeant. Ezio made to follow, but Pantasilea held him back, grasping his arm firmly.

"Wait!" she said.

"What is it?"

She looked deeply concerned. "Ezio. Let me get straight to the point. The fight is not going well—either here or out in the Romagna. We've been attacked on both sides. The Borgia are on one flank, the French under General Valois on the other. But know this: The Borgia position is weak. If we can defeat them, we can concentrate our forces on the French front. Taking this tower would help. If someone could get around the back . . ."

Ezio inclined his head. "Then I think I know a way I can help. Your information is invaluable. *Mille grazie, Madonna d'Alviano.*"

She smiled. "It is the least a wife can do to help her husband."

EIGHTEEN

The Borgia had launched a surprise attack on the barracks, choosing the hour of the siesta to do so. Bartolomeo's men had fought them off, using traditional weapons, but as they drove them back toward the tower, Ezio could see Cesare's gunmen massing on its battlement, all armed with their new wheel locks, which they were training on the *condottieri* swarming below.

He skirted the melee, managing to avoid any confrontation with the Borgia troops. He circled and made his way around to the back of the tower. As he'd expected, everyone's attention was focused on the battle going on at the front. He clambered up the outer walls, easily finding footholds in the rough-hewn stones of which it had been built. Bartolomeo's men were armed with crossbows, and some had matchlocks, for long-range work, but they would not be able to withstand the deadly fire of the sophisticated new guns.

Ezio arrived at the top, some forty feet above the ground, in less than half a minute. He heaved himself over the rear parapet, sinews straining, and silently lowered himself to the roof of the tower. He stalked behind the musketeers, moving one quiet step after another closer to the enemy. He silently drew his dagger and also unleashed his hidden-blade. He stole up on the backs of the men and, in a sudden frenzy of movement, dispatched four gunmen with the two blades. It was only then that the Borgia sharpshooters realized that the enemy was among them. Ezio saw a man turn his loaded wheel lock toward him—the man was still some fifteen feet away, so Ezio simply launched his dagger through the air. It pirouetted three times before embedding between the man's eyes with a sickening thud. The man fell, but in doing so squeezed the trigger of his musket—luckily for Ezio the barrel had slipped away from its intended aim. The ball shot to the man's right—hitting his nearest colleague—but passing clean through his Adam's apple and embedding in the shoulder of the man behind him. Both men fell—leaving only three Borgia gunmen on the tower roof. Without pausing, Ezio leapt sideways—and with the flat of his hand slapped the nearest man across the face with such force that he toppled backward over the battlements. Ezio grabbed his weapon by the barrel as the man fell and swung the gun, butt first, into the next soldier's face. He followed his colleague over the wall with an agonized yell. The last man raised his hands in surrender—but too late—Ezio's hidden-blade had already found its way between his ribs.

Ezio grabbed another rifle and bounded down the stairs to the floor below. There were four men down here, firing through narrow slits in the thick stone walls. Ezio squeezed the trigger, holding the musket at waist height. The farthest went down with the impact of the shot—his chest exploding with red gore. Taking two strides forward, again, Ezio swung the gun like a club, barrel first this time, connecting with another man's knee. He crumpled. One of the remaining men had turned sufficiently to take a shot. Ezio rolled forward instinctively—he felt the air searing as the ball missed his cheek by only a matter of inches and embedded in the wall behind. Ezio's momentum sent him crashing into the gunman—the man lurched backward, his head crunching into the thick stone battlement. The last man had also swiveled around to tackle the unexpected threat. He looked down as Ezio was springing up from the floor, but only for an instant, as the hidden-blade skewered under the man's jaw.

The man whose knee Ezio had shattered stirred to reach for his own dagger. Ezio simply kicked the man's temple and turned, unbothered, to watch the battle unfolding down below. It was resolving itself into a rout. With no overwhelming firepower on their side anymore, the Borgia soldiers fell back fast and soon turned tail and fled, abandoning the tower to the *condottieri*.

Ezio descended the staircase to the tower's main gate,

encountering a handful of guards, who put up fierce resistance before succumbing to his sword, but no one else. Ensuring that the tower was now clear of Borgia men, he flung open the gate and went out to join Bartolomeo. The battle was over, and Pantasilea had joined her husband.

"Ezio! Well done! Together, we sent those *luridi codardi* running for the hills!"

"Yes, we did." Ezio exchanged a secret, conspiratorial smile with Pantasilea. Her sound advice had won the fight as much as anything.

"Those newfangled guns," said Bartolomeo. "We managed to capture a few, but we're still working out how to use them." He beamed. "Anyway, now that the Pope's dogs have fled, I'll be able to draw more men to the fight on our side. But first, and especially after this business, I want to reinforce our barracks."

"Good idea. But who's going to do it?"

Bartolomeo shook his head. "I'm not much good with these things. You're the one with an education, why don't you approve the plans?"

"You got some drawn up?"

"Yes! Engaged the services of a pretty brilliant young man. Florentine like you. Name of Michelangelo Buonarroti."

"I've heard of him, but I don't know him. Either way, *va bene*. In return I need to know Cesare's and Rodrigo's every move. Can some of your men shadow them for me?"

"One thing I'll soon have no shortage of is men. At least, I've enough to give you a decent workforce for the rebuilding work and a handful of skilled scouts to cover the Borgia for you."

"Excellent!" Ezio well knew that Machiavelli had spies in place, but Machiavelli tended to play his cards close to his chest, and Bartolomeo didn't. Machiavelli was a closed room; Bartolomeo was the open sky. And while Ezio didn't share La Volpe's suspicions—which he hoped he'd now allayed—there was still no harm at all in having a second string to his bow.

He spent the next month supervising the strengthening of the barracks, repairing the damage done in the attack, building taller and stronger watchtowers, and replacing the palisades with stone walls. When the work was complete, he and Bartolomeo took a tour of inspection.

"Isn't she a thing of beauty?" Bartolomeo beamed.

"Very impressive, I think."

"And the even better news is, more and more men are joining us every day. Of course, I encourage great competition between them—it's good for morale, and it's good training, too, for when they go out and fight for real." He showed Ezio a large wooden board with his crest at the top, mounted on an easel. "As you can see, this board shows the ranking of our top warriors. The better they become, the higher they move up the board."

"And where am I?"

Bartolomeo gave him a look and waved at the air above the board. "Somewhere up here, I should think!"

A *condottiero* came up to tell him that one of his best men, Gian, had begun his fight down in the parade ground.

"If you want to show off, we have sparring matches, too. Now, if you'll excuse me, I've got money on this boy!" Laughing, he took his leave.

Ezio made his way to the new, improved map-room. The natural light was better, and the room had been enlarged to accommodate broader map tables and easels. He was poring over a map of the Romagna when Pantasilea joined him.

"Where is Bartolomeo?" she asked.

"At the fight."

Pantasilea sighed. "He has such an aggressive view of the world. However, I think strategy is just as important. Don't you agree?"

"I do."

"Let me show you something."

She led the way from the room to a wide balcony overlooking an inner courtyard of the barracks. On one side of it was a sizable new dovecote, alive with birds.

"These are carrier pigeons," Pantasilea explained. "Each one, sent from Niccolò Machiavelli in the city, now brings me the name of a Borgia agent in Rome. The Borgia grew fat on the Jubilee of 1500. All that money from eager pilgrims, willing to buy themselves absolution. And those who would not pay were robbed."

Ezio looked grim.

"But your various attacks have unsettled the Borgia badly," Pantasilea continued. "Their spies comb the city, seeking out our people and exposing them where they can. Machiavelli has uncovered some of their names as well, and these, too, he is often able to send me by pigeon post. Meanwhile, Rodrigo has added even more new members to the Curia, in an attempt to maintain his balance of power among the cardinals. As you know, he has decades of experience in Vatican politics."

"Indeed he has."

"You must take these names with you when you return to the city. They will be useful to you."

"I am lost in admiration, Madonna."

"Hunt these people down, eliminate them if you can, and we will all breathe more easily for it."

"I must return to Rome without delay. And I will tell you something that makes *me* breathe more easily."

"Yes?"

"What you have just disclosed proves that Machiavelli is undoubtedly one of us." But then Ezio hesitated. "Even so . . ."

"Yes?"

"I have a similar arrangement with Bartolomeo. Give it a week, and then ask him to come to the island in the Tiber—he knows the place and I daresay you do, too—bringing me what he has gleaned about Rodrigo and Cesare."

"Do you doubt Machiavelli still?"

"No—but I am sure you'll agree that it is good to double-check *all* the information one gets, especially in times like these."

A shadow seemed to pass across her face, but then she smiled and said, "He will be there."

NINETEEN

Back in Rome, Ezio made his first port of call the brothel
Machiavelli had mentioned as being another source of
information—perhaps some of the names he was sending Pantasilea by carrier pigeon came from there. He
needed to check on how the girls collected their information, but he'd decided to go there incognito. If they
knew who he was, they might just give him the information they thought he wanted.

He arrived at the address and checked the sign: the
Rosa in Fiore. There was no doubt of it, and yet it didn't
look like the kind of place the Borgia *nomenclatura*
might normally frequent. Unless they went in for slum-
ming. It certainly wasn't a patch on Paola's establishment

in Florence, at least from the outside. But then, Paola's place had kept a pretty discreet shopfront. He knocked, dubiously, on the door.

It was opened immediately by an attractive, plump girl of about eighteen. She was wearing a tired-looking silk dress.

She flashed him a professional smile. "Welcome, stranger! Welcome to the Rosa in Fiore."

"Salve," he said, as she let him pass. The entrance hall certainly was a step up, but even so, there seemed to be an air of neglect about the place.

"And what did you have in mind for today?" the girl asked.

"Would you be kind enough to get your boss for me?"

The girl's eyes became slits. "Madonna Solari isn't in."

"I see." He paused, uncertain what to do. "Do you know where she is?"

"Out." The girl was distinctly less friendly now.

Ezio gave her his most charming smile, but he wasn't a young man anymore and he could see that it cut no ice with the girl. She thought he was an official of some sort. Damn! Well, if he wanted to get any farther in, he'd have to pretend to be a client. And if pretending to be one meant actually becoming one, well, so be it.

He'd decided on this course of action when the street door suddenly burst open and another girl burst in, her hair awry, her dress disarranged. She was distraught.

"Aiuto! Aiuto!" she cried urgently. "Madonna Solari—" She sobbed, unable to continue.

"What is it, Lucia? Pull yourself together. And what are you doing back so soon? I thought you'd gone off with Madonna and some clients."

"Those men weren't clients, Agnella! They—they said they were taking us to a place they knew down by the Tiber but there was a boat there and they started to slap us about and drew knives. They took Madonna Solari on board and chained her up."

"Lucia! *Dio mio!* How did you get away?" Agnella put an arm around her friend and guided her to a couch set along one wall. She took out a handkerchief and dabbed at a red weal that was starting to rise on Lucia's cheek.

"They let me go—sent me back with a message— they're slave traders, Agnella! They say they'll only let her go if we buy her back! Otherwise they'll kill her!"

"How much do they want?" Ezio asked.

"A thousand ducats."

"How much time do we have?"

"They'll wait an hour."

"Then we have time. Wait here! I'll get her back for you." *Cazzo*, Ezio thought. *This looks bad. I need to talk to that woman.* "Where are they?"

"There's a jetty, *Messere*. Near Isola Tiberina. Do you know the place?"

"Very well."

Ezio made haste. There was no time to get to Chigi's bank and none of its three branches was on his route, so he resorted to a moneylender, who drove a hard bargain, but made up the sum Ezio already carried to the one thousand required. Armed with this, but determined not to part with a penny of it if he could possibly avoid it, and swearing to exact the interest he'd have to pay from the bastards who'd taken the one person he most needed to talk to, he hired a horse and rode recklessly through the streets toward the Tiber, scattering the people, chickens, and dogs that cluttered the street as he did so.

He found the boat—a large one, more of a small ship—without difficulty, thank God, and, dismounting, ran to the end of the jetty at which it was moored, yelling Madonna Solari's name.

But they were prepared for him. There were two men already on deck, and they trained pistols on him. Ezio's eyes narrowed. Pistols? In the hands of cheap little villains like these?

"Don't come any closer."

Ezio backed off, but kept his finger on the release trigger of his hidden-blade.

"Brought the fuckin' money, have you?"

Ezio slowly produced the pouch that contained the thousand ducats with his other hand.

"Good. Now we'll see if the captain's in a good enough mood *not* to slit her fuckin' throat."

"The captain! Who the hell do you think you are? Bring her out! Bring her out *now!*"

The rage in Ezio's voice subdued the slave trader who'd spoken. He turned slightly and called to someone belowdecks, who must have heard the interchange anyway, since two men started to come up the companionway from below, manhandling a woman of perhaps thirty-five. The makeup she was wearing was badly smeared, by both tears and rough treatment. There were ugly bruises on her face, shoulders, and breasts, exposed where her lilac dress had been ripped apart, revealing the bodice beneath. There was blood on her dress, lower down, and she was manacled hand and foot.

"Here's the little treasure now," sneered the trader who'd first spoken.

Ezio breathed hard. This was a lonely bend of the river, but he could see Tiber Island only fifty yards distant. If only he could get word to his friends. But if they'd heard anything, they'd assume it was just a bunch of drunken sailors—God knows, there were enough of them along the riverbank. And if Ezio raised his voice or called for help, La Solari would be dead in an instant, and himself, too, unless the gunmen were bad shots, for the range was negligible.

As the woman's desperate eyes caught Ezio's, a third man, sloppily dressed in the sad remains of a naval captain's jacket, came up the ladder. He looked at Ezio, then at the bag of money.

"Throw it over," he said in a rough voice.

"Hand her over first. And take off those manacles."

"Are you fuckin' deaf? Throw. Over. The. Fuckin'. Money!"

Involuntarily, Ezio moved forward. Immediately the guns were raised threateningly, the captain drew a falchion, and the two others took a tighter grip on the woman, making her moan and wince with pain.

"Don't come any closer! We'll finish her if you do!"

Ezio stopped, but he did not retreat. He measured

the distance between where he stood and the deck with his eyes. His finger trembled over the trigger of the hidden-blade.

"I have the money—it's all here," he said, waving the bag and edging one step closer while their eyes were on it.

"Stay where you are! Don't test me. If you take one step more, she dies!"

"You won't get your money then."

"Oh, won't we? There's five of us and one of you, and I don't think you'd get a fuckin' toe on board before my friends here had shot you in the gob and in the balls."

"Hand her over first!"

"Look, you thick or what? Nobody gets near this fuckin' boat unless you want this *puttana* dead!"

"Messere! Aiutateme!" whimpered the wretched woman.

"Shut the fuck up, you bitch!" snarled one of the men holding her, hitting her across the eyes with the pommel of his dagger.

"All right!" yelled Ezio, as he saw fresh blood spurt from the woman's face. "That's enough. Let her go. Now!"

And he threw the bag of money over to the "captain." It landed at his feet.

"That's better," said the slave trader. "Now, let's just finish this business."

Before Ezio could react, he placed the blade of his sword against the side of the woman's throat and drew it across, down and deep, half severing her head from her body.

"Any objections, take it up with *Messer* Cesare," sneered the captain as the body slumped to the deck under a fountain of blood. Almost imperceptibly, he nodded to the two men with pistols.

Ezio knew what was coming next, and he was ready. With lightning speed he dodged both the bullets, and in the same instant that he threw himself into the air, he released the hidden-blade. With it he stabbed the first of the men who'd been holding the prisoner, deep in the left eye, penetrating the brain. Before the man had even fallen to the deck, Ezio, dodging a swinging blow from the captain's falchion and coming up from under, plunged the blade into the other man's belly, low down and ripping as he thrust. The blade wasn't designed for slicing, and it bent a little, tearing rather than cutting. But no matter.

Now for the gunmen. As he'd expected, they were frantically trying to reload, but panic had made them clumsy. He rapidly withdrew the blade and unsheathed his heavy dagger. The fighting was too close for him to be able to use his sword, and he needed the dagger's serrated edge and heavy blade. He sliced off the hand holding one man's gun and then jabbed the point hard into the man's side. But he hadn't time to finish the job, for the other gunman, coming from behind, clubbed him with the butt of his pistol. Luckily the blow didn't find its mark, and Ezio, shaking his head to clear it, swung around and was able to drive his dagger into the man's chest as he was attempting another blow, leaving his body vulnerable by raising his arm.

He looked around. Where was the captain?

He caught sight of him stumbling along the riverbank,

clutching the bag, from which coins were spilling. *Fool*, Ezio thought. *He should have taken the horse. Panic again.* He bounded after him, easily catching up, for the bag was heavy. He seized the captain by the hair and kicked his legs away, forcing him to kneel with his head back.

"Now for a taste of your own medicine," he said, and he did to the captain exactly what the captain had done to the woman.

Letting the body fall and leaving it to writhe, he picked up the bag and made his way back to the boat, picking up the fallen coins as he went. The wounded slave trader squirmed on the deck. Ezio ignored him and went below, ransacking the meager cabin he found there and quickly locating a small strongbox, which he wrenched open with the bloody blade of his dagger. It was full of diamonds.

"That'll do," said Ezio to himself, tucking it under his arm and running up the companionway again.

He loaded the bag of coins and the box of diamonds into the saddlebags of his horse, and added the pistols to them. Then he went back to the wounded man, nearly slipping on the blood in which the slave trader was slithering. Bending down, Ezio cut one of the man's hamstrings, keeping a hand over his mouth to stop him from howling. That should slow him up. For good.

He pressed his mouth close to the man's ear.

"If you survive," he said, "and get back to that pox-ridden louse you call your master, tell him all this was done with the compliments of Ezio Auditore. If not— *requiescat in pace*."

TWENTY

Ezio didn't return to the brothel immediately. It was late. He returned the horse, bought a sack from the ostler for a few coins, and stowed his spoils, and the money, in it. He slung it over his shoulder and made his way to the moneylender, who was surprised and disappointed to see him back to repay so soon, and gave him what he owed. Then he went to his lodgings, taking care to blend in with the evening crowds whenever he sighted Borgia guards.

Once there, he had them bring him water to bathe, undressed, and washed himself wearily, wishing that Caterina would once again appear at the door and surprise him. But this time there was no one to interrupt him so pleasantly. He changed into fresh clothes and shoved the ones he'd been wearing, ruined by the day's work, into the sack. Time to get rid of them later. He cleaned the pistols and put them in a satchel. He'd thought of keeping them, but they were heavy and unwieldy, so he decided to hand them over to Bartolomeo. Most of the diamonds would go to Bartolomeo, too, but after examining them, Ezio selected five of the best and largest and put them in his own wallet. They'd ensure that he wouldn't have to waste time scraping around after money for a while, at least.

Everything else he'd get La Volpe to send to the barracks. If you can't trust a friendly thief, whom can you trust?

He was ready to go out again. The satchel was slung over his shoulder and his hand was on the latch. But then—then he felt tired. Tired of the killing. Tired of the greed, and the grasping for power, and the misery all of that led to.

Almost tired of the fight.

He let his hand fall from the door and unslung the satchel, placing it on his bed. He locked the door and undressed once more. Then he snuffed out the candle and all but fell onto the bed. He just had time to remember to place a protecting arm around the bag before he fell asleep.

He knew the respite wouldn't be long.

At the Sleeping Fox, Ezio handed over the satchel with precise instructions. He didn't like to delegate this job, but he was needed here in Rome. The reports La Volpe's "spies" had brought in were few, but the results coincided with those Machiavelli had sent by carrier pigeon to Pantasilea, which assuaged most of Ezio's remaining misgivings about his friend; though La Volpe remained, Ezio could see, reserved. Ezio could understand it. Machiavelli could come across as remote, even cold. Although they were fellow Florentines, and Florence had no love for Rome, and especially not for the Borgia, it seemed that La Volpe, despite all the evidence to the contrary, still harbored doubts.

"Call it a gut feeling," was all he said, gruffly, when Ezio pressed the point.

There was no news of the Apple, except that it was still in the possession of the Borgia, though whether Cesare had it, or Rodrigo, was uncertain. Rodrigo well knew its potential, though to Ezio it seemed unlikely that he would confide much of what he knew to his son, given the tension between them; as for Cesare, he was the last person seen in control of it, but there was no sign that he was using it. Ezio prayed that whomever he had given it to for study—if he *had* done so—was either stumped by its mysteries or concealing them from his master.

Machiavelli was nowhere to be found. Even at the Assassins' secret headquarters on Tiber Island he had left no news. The best information Ezio could get was that he was "away," but he wasn't reported to be in Florence. The two young friends who were temporarily in Rome at the time and running the hideout—Baldassare Castiglione and Pietro Bembo—were completely reliable and already associate members of the Brotherhood, not least because one had connections with Cesare and the other with Lucrezia. It was a pity, Ezio thought, that the first had soon to return to Mantua and the other to Venice. He consoled himself with the thought they would nonetheless be useful to him in their hometowns.

Satisfied that he had done what he could on those fronts, Ezio turned his thoughts back to the Rosa in Fiore.

This time when he paid a visit to the brothel, the door was open. The place seemed airier somehow, and lighter. He'd remembered the names of the girls he'd met on his previous visit, and after having given them to the older and more sophisticated woman in the entrance hall, who, he noticed, had two well-dressed, young, polite, but tough-looking men standing guard, he was ushered through to the inner courtyard. He was told he'd find the girls there.

He found himself in a rose garden, surrounded by high, redbrick walls. A pergola, almost hidden under luxuriant pink climbing roses, ran along one of these, and in the center was a small fountain with white marble benches around it. The girls he sought were with a group of others talking to two older women whose backs were to him. But they turned at his approach.

He was about to introduce himself—he'd decided to try another tack this time—but then his jaw dropped.

"Mother! Claudia! What are you doing here?"

"Waiting for you. *Ser* Machiavelli told us we might find you here. Before he left."

"Where is he? Did you see him in Florence?"

"No."

"But what are you doing here in Rome?" he repeated dumbly. He was filled with shock and anxiety. "Has Florence been attacked?"

"No—nothing like that," said Maria. "But the rumors were true—our palazzo has been destroyed. There is nothing for us there."

"And even if it were not in ruins, I would never go back to Mario's *rocca* at Monteriggioni," put in Claudia. Ezio looked at her. He understood what a backwater that place would seem to a woman like her. He nodded. But his heart was troubled.

"So we have come here. We have taken a house in Rome," continued Maria. "Our place is with you."

Thoughts raced across Ezio's mind. In his innermost heart, though he scarcely admitted it to his conscious mind, he still felt that he might have prevented the deaths of his father and brothers. He had failed them. Maria and Claudia were all that was left of his family. Might he not fail them in the same way? He did not want them to be dependent on him.

He attracted danger. If they were near him, would he not attract danger to his mother and sister, too? He didn't want their deaths on his head. They'd have been better off in Florence, where they had friends, where their safety, in a city once again stable under the wise management of Piero Soderini, would have been ensured.

"Ezio," said Claudia, interrupting his thoughts, "we want to help."

"I sought to keep you safe by sending you to Firenze."

He tried to keep the impatience out of his voice, but he found that he was snapping as he spoke. Maria and Claudia looked shocked, and although Maria let it go quickly, Ezio could see that Claudia was wounded and offended. Had she picked up something of his thoughts?

Luckily, they were interrupted by Agnella and Lucia. "*Messere*—excuse us, but we are anxious. We have still had no news of Madonna Solari. Do you know what has become of her?"

Ezio's thoughts were still on Claudia and the expression in her eyes. But his attention switched at the question. Cesare must have done one hell of a cover-up job. But then, bodies were found in the Tiber practically every day—and some of them had been there for some time.

"She's dead," he said abruptly.

"What?" cried Lucia.

"*Merda,*" said Agnella, succinctly.

The news spread quickly among the girls.

"What do we do now?" asked one.

"Will we have to close?" asked another.

Ezio deduced the undercurrent of their anxiety. Under Madonna Solari, however inefficient Machiavelli had said she'd been, these girls had been collecting information for the Assassins. Without protection, and if, as Solari's death suggested, Cesare had his suspicions about the Rosa in Fiore, what might their fate be? On the other hand, if he had thought that Solari wasn't the *only* spy in the place, wouldn't he have made a move by now?

That was it! There was still hope.

"You cannot close," he told them. "I need your help."

"But *Messere*, without someone to run things, we are finished."

A voice near him said decisively: "I'll do it."

It was Claudia.

Ezio wheeled on her. "You do not belong *here*, sister!"

"I know how to run a business," she retorted. "I ran Uncle Mario's estates out in the sticks for *years*."

"This is quite different!"

His mother's calming voice intervened. "What alternative do you have, Ezio? You need someone fast, evidently. You know you can trust your sister."

Ezio saw the logic of this, but it would mean putting Claudia on the front line—the very place he most dreaded her being. He glared at her. She returned the look with defiance.

"You do this, Claudia, and you are on your own. You'll get no special protection from me!"

"I've done perfectly well without that for twenty years," she sneered.

"Fine," he returned icily. "Then you'd better get down to work. First of all, I want this place thoroughly cleaned up, redecorated, improved in every way. Even this garden needs a good job done on it. I want this place to be the best establishment in town. And God knows you've got competition. And I want the girls clean—this New Disease no one seems to know much about—well, it's worst of all in the ports and in the biggest cities—so we all know what that means."

"We'll see to it," replied Claudia coldly.

"You'd better. And there's another thing. While

you're at it, I want your courtesans to find the whereabouts of Caterina Sforza." He remained stone-faced.

"You can count on us."

"You're in this now, Claudia—any mistakes, they're
on your head."

"I can take care of myself, brother."

"I hope you can," growled Ezio, turning on his heel.

TWENTY-ONE

Ezio was busy for the next few weeks—consolidating the remaining forces of the Brotherhood gathered in Rome and deciding what use to make of the initial information he had gathered from them, from La Volpe, and from the early reports sent by Bartolomeo. He hardly dared hope yet that the tide against the Borgia was turning, but it may have been that he was looking at the beginning of the end. He remembered, however, the old adage about how much easier it is to handle a young lion than to approach an old, experienced one. And against his cautious optimism was the fact that Cesare's grip on the Romagna was tightening and the French held Milan. Nor had the French withdrawn their support from the papal commander. Years earlier, the Cardinal of San

Pietro in Vincula, Giuliano della Rovere, the Pope's great enemy, had tried to turn the French against the Borgia and topple Alexander from his seat, but Alexander had outwitted him. How could Ezio succeed where della Rovere had failed? But at least no one had poisoned the cardinal—he was too powerful for that—and the cardinal remained Ezio's ace in the hole.

Ezio had also decided, though this he kept to himself—that his mission should be to encourage the Brotherhood to relocate their headquarters permanently to Rome. Rome was at the center of world affairs, as it was also the center of world corruption. Where else could be better suited—especially now that Monteriggioni was no longer a viable option? He also had plans for a system of distribution of the Brotherhood's funds in response to individual Assassins' successfully completed missions. Those diamonds he'd taken from the slave traders had come in very handy, a welcome addition to the campaign fund.

One day . . .

But "one day" was still a long way off. The Brotherhood still had no new elected leader, though by common consent and by virtue of their actions, he and Machiavelli had become its temporary chiefs. But they were still only temporary. Nothing had been ratified in formal council.

And Caterina preyed on his mind.

He had left Claudia to oversee the renovation of the Rosa in Fiore without any supervision or interference. Let her sink or swim in her own overweening confidence! It'd be no fault of his if she sank. But the brothel was an important link in his network, and he admitted to himself that if he really had had absolutely no faith in her, he might have leaned on her harder in the first place. Now was the time to put her work—what she had achieved—to the test.

When he returned to the Rosa in Fiore, he was as surprised as he was pleased. Just as successful, he hoped, as his own previous transformations in the city, and at Bartolomeo's barracks, had been (though even for those he was modest and realistic enough not to take all the credit). But he hid his delight as he took in the sumptuous rooms hung with costly tapestries, the wide sofas, the soft silk cushions, and the white wines chilled with ice—an expensive luxury.

The girls looked like ladies, not whores, and judging from their manner someone had evidently taught them to be much more refined. And as for the clientele—the least he could infer was that business was booming, and though he had had his reservations about the nature of their standing before, there could be no doubt now. Looking around the central salon, he could see at least a dozen assorted cardinals and senators, as well as members of the Apostolic Camera and other officers of the Curia.

All enjoying themselves, all relaxed, and all—he hoped—unsuspecting. But the proof of the pudding would lie in the value of the information Claudia's courtesans were able to extract from this venal bunch of slobs.

He caught sight of his sister—modestly dressed, he was glad to see—talking rather (to his mind) too affectionately to Ascanio Sforza, the former vice-chancellor of the Curia and now in Rome again after his brief disgrace, trying to wheedle his way back into papal favor. When Claudia caught sight of Ezio, her expression changed. She excused herself from the cardinal and came toward him, a brittle smile on her face.

"Welcome to the Rosa in Fiore, Brother," she said.

"Indeed." He did not smile.

"As you can see, it is the most popular brothel in Rome."

"Corruption is still corruption, however well dressed it is."

She bit her lip. "We have done well. And don't forget why this place *really* exists."

"Yes," he replied. "The Brotherhood's money seems to have been well invested."

"That's not all. Come to the office."

To Ezio's surprise, he found Maria there, doing some paperwork with an accountant. Mother and son greeted each other guardedly.

"I want to show you this," said Claudia, producing a book. "Here is where I keep a list of all the skills taught to my girls."

"*Your* girls?" Ezio could not keep the sarcasm out of his voice. His sister was taking to this like a duck to water.

"Why not? Take a look." Her own manner had tightened.

Ezio leafed through the proffered book. "You are not teaching them much."

"Think you could do better?" she answered sarcastically.

"*Nessun problema,*" Ezio said unpleasantly.

Sensing trouble, Maria abandoned her accounts and came up to them. "Ezio," she said, "the Borgia make it difficult for Claudia's girls. They keep out of trouble, but it's hard to avoid suspicion. There are several things you could do to aid them . . ."

"I'll keep that in mind. You must let me have a note of them." Ezio turned his attention back to Claudia. "Anything else?"

"No." She paused, then said: "Ezio—"

"What?"

"Nothing."

Ezio turned as if to go. Then he said: "Have you found Caterina?"

"We are working on it," she replied coldly.

"I'm glad to hear it. *Bene.* Come to see me at Isola Tiberina the minute you have found out *exactly* where they are holding her." He inclined his head toward the sounds of merriment coming from the central salon. "With this lot to milk, you shouldn't find it all *that* difficult."

He left them to it.

Outside in the street, he felt like a heel about the way he'd behaved. They seemed to be doing a great job. But would Claudia be able to hold her own?

Inwardly, he shrugged. He acknowledged once again that the true source of his anger was his own anxiety about his ability to protect those whom he held most dear. He needed them, he knew, but he was aware that his fear for their safety threatened to cramp his style.

TWENTY-TWO

Ezio's long-awaited reunion with Machiavelli finally took place on Tiber Island, soon after the encounter at the brothel. Ezio was reserved at first—he didn't like any of the Brotherhood disappearing without his knowledge of where they'd gone, but he recognized in his heart that, for Machiavelli, he must make an exception. And indeed, the Brotherhood itself was an association of free-minded, free-spirited souls acting together not from coercion or obedience, but from a common concern and interest. He didn't own, or have any right to control, any of them.

Serious and determined, he shook hands with his old colleague—Machiavelli shunned the warmth of an embrace. "We must talk," he said.

"We certainly must." Machiavelli looked at him. "I gather you know about my little arrangement with Pantasilea?"

"Yes."

"Good. That woman has more sense of tactics in her little finger than her husband has in his whole body—not that he isn't the best man possible in his own field." He paused. "I've been able to secure something of great worth from one of my contacts. We now have the names of nine key Templar agents whom Cesare has recruited to terrorize Rome."

"Just tell me how I may find them."

Machiavelli considered. "I suggest looking for signs of distress within any given city district. Visit the people there. Perhaps you'll uncover citizens who can point you in the right direction."

"Did you get this information from a Borgia official?"

"Yes," said Machiavelli carefully, after a pause. "How do you know?"

Ezio, thinking of the encounter he had witnessed with La Volpe in the market square, wondered if that might not have been the initial contact. Machiavelli must have been following it up ever since.

"Lucky guess," he said. *"Grazie."*

"Look—Claudia, Bartolomeo, and La Volpe are waiting for you in the inner room here." He paused. "That *was* a lucky guess."

"Virtù, dear Niccolò, that's all," said Ezio, leading the way.

"Virtue?" said Machiavelli to himself, as he followed.

His companions in the Brotherhood stood as he entered the hideout's inner sanctum. Their faces were somber.

"*Buona sera*," Ezio said and got straight down to business. "What have you discovered?"

Bartolomeo spoke first. "We've ascertained that that *bastardo* Cesare is now at the Castel Sant'Angelo—with the Pope!"

La Volpe added, "And my spies have confirmed that the Apple has indeed been given to someone for secret study. I am working on determining his identity."

"We can't guess it?"

"Guesswork's no good. We need to know *for sure*."

"I have news of Caterina Sforza," Claudia put in. "She will be moved to the prison within the Castel next week, on Thursday toward dusk."

Ezio's heart involuntarily skipped a beat at this. But it was all good news.

"*Bene*," said Machiavelli. "So—the Castel it is. Rome will heal quickly once Cesare and Rodrigo have gone."

Ezio held up a hand. "Only if the right opportunity to assassinate them arises will I take it."

Machiavelli looked irritated. "Do not repeat your mistake in the Vault. You must kill them now."

"I'm with Niccolò," said Bartolomeo. "We shouldn't wait."

"Bartolomeo is right," agreed La Volpe.

"They must pay for Mario's death," said Claudia.

Ezio calmed them, saying, "Do not worry, my friends: they will die. You have my word."

TWENTY-THREE

On the day appointed for Caterina's transfer to Castel
Sant'Angelo, Ezio and Machiavelli joined the crowd
that had gathered in front of a fine carriage, its windows
closed with blinds, whose doors bore the Borgia crest.
Guards surrounding the carriage kept the people back,
and it was no wonder, because the mood of the people
was not unanimously enthusiastic. One of the coachmen
leapt down from his box and hastened around to open
the nearside carriage door, pulled down the steps, and
stood ready to assist the occupants down.

After a moment, the first figure emerged, in a dark blue
gown with a white bodice. Ezio recognized the beautiful
blonde with the cruel lips. He had last seen her at the
sack of Monteriggioni, but it was a face he could never

forget. Lucrezia Borgia. She stepped down to the ground, all dignity, but this was lost as she reached back into the carriage, seized hold of something—or someone—and pulled hard.

She dragged Caterina Sforza out by her hair and flung her to the ground in front of her. Bedraggled and in chains, wearing a coarse brown dress, Caterina in defeat still had greater presence and spirit than her captor would ever know. Machiavelli had to put a restraining hand on Ezio's arm as he automatically started forward. Ezio had seen enough loved ones maltreated; but this was the time for restraint. A rescue now would be doomed to failure.

Lucrezia, one foot on her prostrate victim, started to speak: "*Salve, cittadini de Roma!* Hail, citizens of Rome! Behold a sight most splendid. Caterina Sforza, the she-whore of Forlì! Too long has she defied us! Now she has, at last, been brought to heel!"

There was little reaction from the crowd at this, and in the silence Caterina raised her head and cried: "Ha! No one stoops as low as Lucrezia Borgia! Who put you up to this? Was it your brother? Or your father? Perhaps a bit of both? Perhaps at the same time, eh? After all, you all pen in the same sty!"

"*Chiudi la bocca!* Shut your mouth!" screamed Lucrezia, kicking her. "No one speaks ill of the Borgia!" She bent down, dragging Caterina up to her knees, and slapped her hard, so that she fell into the mud again. She raised her head proudly. "The same will happen to any—*any*—who dare to defy us!"

She motioned to the guards, who seized the hapless

Caterina, dragged her to her feet, and manhandled her in the direction of the Castel gates. Still, Caterina managed to cry out: "Good people of Rome! Stay strong! Your time will come! You will be free of this yoke, I swear it!"

As she disappeared, and Lucrezia got back into her carriage to follow, Machiavelli turned to Ezio. "Well, the *contessa* hasn't lost any of her spirit."

Ezio felt drained. "They are going to torture her."

"It is unfortunate that Forlì has fallen. But we will get it back. We will get Caterina back, too. But we must concentrate. You are here, now, for Cesare and Rodrigo."

"Caterina is a powerful ally, one of us, indeed. If we help her now, while she is weak, she will aid us in return."

"Perhaps. But kill Cesare and Rodrigo first."

The crowd was beginning to disperse, and, apart from the sentries at the gate, the Borgia guards withdrew into the Castel. Soon only Machiavelli and Ezio were left, standing in the shadows.

"Leave me, Niccolò," said Ezio as the shadows lengthened. "I have work to do."

He looked up at the sheer walls of the ancient, circular structure, the mausoleum of the emperor Hadrian over a thousand years earlier, now an unassailable fortress. Its few windows were high up, and its walls sheer. Connected to Saint Peter's Basilica by a fortified stone corridor, it had been the great stronghold of the popes for nearly two hundred years.

Ezio studied the walls. Nothing was completely impregnable. By the light of the torches flickering in their sconces, as night fell, his eyes began to trace the slight ridges, fissures, and imperfections that, however small, would enable him to climb. Once he'd planned his route, he leapt like a cat up to the first hand- and foot-holds, digging fingers and toes in, steadying his breath, and then, deliberately, unhurriedly, started to scale the wall, keeping wherever possible away from the light cast by the torches.

Halfway up, he came to an opening—an unglazed window in a stone frame—beneath which, on the inner side of the wall, was a walkway for guardsmen. He looked each way along it, but it was deserted. Silently, he swung himself over and looked down, on the other side of the walkway, over a railing into what he quickly saw was the stable yard. Four men were walking there, and he recognized every one of them. Cesare was holding some kind of conference with three of his chief lieutenants: the French general Octavien de Valois; Cesare's close associate Juan de Borgia Lanzol de Romaní; and a lean man in black—a lean man with a cruel, scarred face: Micheletto Corella—Cesare's right-hand man and most trusted killer.

"Forget the Pope," Cesare was saying. "You answer only to me. Rome is the pillar that holds our entire enterprise aloft. She cannot waver. Which means—neither can you!"

"What of the Vatican?" asked Octavien.

"What? That tired old men's club?" answered Cesare contemptuously. "Play along with the cardinals for now, but soon we shall have no more need of them."

With that, he went through a door leading from the stable yard, leaving the other three alone.

"Well, it looks as if he's left Rome for us to manage," said Juan after a pause.

"Then the city will be in good hands," said Micheletto evenly.

Ezio listened for a while longer but nothing more was said that he reckoned useful—nothing that he didn't already know—so he continued his climb around the outer wall, in his quest to locate Caterina's whereabouts. He saw light coming from another window, glazed this time, but open to the night air, and with an outer sill on which he could partially support himself. Doing so, he looked cautiously through the window into a candlelit corridor with plain wooden walls. Lucrezia was there, sitting on an upholstered bench, writing in a notebook; but every so often she looked up, as if she were expecting someone.

A few minutes later, Cesare came through a door at the far end of the corridor and made his way hurriedly toward his sister.

"Lucrezia," he said and kissed her. It was no fraternal kiss.

Once they had greeted one another, he took her hands from around his neck and, still holding them and looking into her eyes, said, "I hope you are treating our guest with kindness."

Lucrezia grimaced. "That mouth on her! . . . How I'd love to sew it shut."

Cesare smiled. "I rather like it open, myself."

"Oh, really?"

Ignoring her archness, he continued: "Have you talked to our father about the funds requested by my banker?"

"The Pope is at the Vatican just now, but he might need some convincing when he returns. As will his own banker. And you know how cautious Agostino Chigi is."

Cesare laughed briefly. "Well, he certainly didn't get rich by being rash." He paused. "But—that shouldn't be a problem, should it?"

Lucrezia wound her arms around her brother's neck again, nuzzling against him. "No—but . . . it gets quite lonely sometimes without you here. You and I spend so little time together these days, busy as you are with your *other* conquests."

Cesare held her to him. "Don't worry, kitten. Soon, once I have secured the throne of Italy, you are going to be my queen; and your loneliness will be a thing of the past!"

She withdrew a little and looked him in the eye. "I cannot wait."

He ran his hand through her fine blond hair. "Behave yourself while I am gone."

Then, after another lingering kiss, Cesare left his sister by the door through which he'd entered. She herself, downcast, took the opposite direction.

Where was Cesare going? Was he leaving immediately? From that leave-taking, it looked likely. Quickly, Ezio maneuvered himself around the circumference of the wall until he could take up a position that overlooked the Castel's main gate.

And not before time. As he watched, it was being

thrown open, amid cries from the guards of "Attention! The captain-general is leaving for Urbino!" And shortly afterward, on a black horse, Cesare rode forth, accompanied by a small entourage.

"*Buona fortuna, Padron Cesare!*" cried one of the officers of the watch.

Ezio watched his archenemy ride off into the night. *That was a flying visit,* he thought to himself. *And no chance to kill him at all. Niccolò will be very disappointed.*

TWENTY-FOUR

Ezio turned his attention back to the task at hand. To find Caterina. High up on the western side of the Castel he noticed a small window, set deep in the wall, from which a faint light came. He made his way to it. When he reached it, he saw that there was no sill on which he could rest, but instead there was a narrow transom projecting above the window, which he could cling to securely with one hand.

He looked into the room. It was empty, though a torch burned on one wall. It looked like a guardroom, though, so Ezio hoped he was on the right track.

Farther along on the same level there was another, similar window. Ezio made his way to it and peered through the bars, though there seemed no reason for bars. No one slim enough to escape through this window would be able to climb down a good 150 feet to the ground, and then make it across the open ground to the river and possible safety. The light was dimmer here, but Ezio could see immediately that it was a cell.

Then he drew in his breath sharply. There, still in chains, was Caterina! She sat on a rough bench against one wall, but Ezio could not see if she was also chained to it. Her head was down, and Ezio did not know if she was awake or asleep.

Whatever the case, she raised her head at a thunderous hammering on the door.

"Open up!" Ezio heard Lucrezia cry.

One of the two guards outside the door, who had both been dozing, hastened to obey. "Yes, *Altezza!* At once, *Altezza*."

Once inside the cell, and followed by one of the guards, Lucrezia wasted no time at all. From the conversation Ezio had already heard, he could guess the reason for her fury: jealousy. Lucrezia believed that Caterina and Cesare had become lovers. He could not believe that to be true. The thought of Caterina being defiled by such a monster of depravity was something his mind refused to accept.

Lucrezia rushed across the cell and pulled Caterina to her feet by her hair, bringing her face close to her prisoner's. "You bitch! How was your journey from Forlì to Rome? Did you ride in Cesare's private carriage? What did you get up to?"

Caterina looked her in the eye. "You're pathetic,

Lucrezia. Even more pathetic if you think I'd live by the same standards as you."

Enraged, Lucrezia threw her to the floor. "What did he talk about? His plans for Naples?" She paused. "Did you . . . enjoy it?"

Wiping blood from her face, Caterina said: "I really can't remember."

Her quiet insolence drove Lucrezia into a blind fury. Pushing the guard aside, she seized an iron bar used for slatting across the door and brought it down heavily across Caterina's back. "Perhaps you will remember *this!*"

Now, Caterina screamed in intense pain. Lucrezia stood back, satisfied.

"Good. That's put you in your place at last!"

She threw the iron rod onto the floor and strode out of the cell. The guard followed her and the door slammed shut. Ezio noticed that there was a grille set into it.

"Lock it, and give me the key," ordered Lucrezia from the outside.

There was a rattle and a rusty creak as the key turned, then a chain clattered as the key was handed over.

"Here it is, *Altezza*." The man's voice was trembling.

"Good. Now, if I come back and catch you asleep at your post, I'll have you flogged. One hundred lashes. Understood?"

"Yes, *Altezza*."

Ezio listened to Lucrezia's footsteps as they grew fainter. He considered. The best way to reach the cell would be from above.

He climbed up until he came to another opening,

giving on to a guard's walkway. This time, sentries were on duty, but it seemed that there were only two, patrolling together. He calculated it must take them five minutes to complete the circuit, so he waited until they had passed and then swung himself inside once again.

Crouching low, Ezio followed the guards at a distance until he came to a doorway in the wall from which a stone stairway led downward. He knew that he'd climbed into the Castel two floors above where Caterina's cell was located, and so, two flights down, he left the stairway and found himself in a corridor similar to the one in which he'd seen the encounter between Cesare and Lucrezia, only this time it was clad in stone, not wood. He doubled back in the direction of Caterina's cell, encountering no one, though passing a number of heavy doors, each with a grille, which suggested cells. As the wall curved following the line of the Castel, he heard voices ahead and recognized the Piedmontese accent of the guard who'd been talking to Lucrezia.

"This is no place for me," he was grumbling. "Did you hear the way she spoke to me? I wish I was back in fucking Torino."

Ezio edged forward. The guards were facing the door, as Caterina had appeared at the grille. She spotted Ezio behind them as he withdrew into the shadows.

"Oh, my poor back," she said to the guards. "Can you give me some water?"

There was a jug of water on the table near the door, where the two guards had been sitting earlier. One of them picked it up and brought it close to the grille.

"Anything else you require, Princess?" he asked sarcastically.

The guard from Turin sniggered.

"Come on, have a heart," said Caterina. "If you open the door, I might show you something worth your while."

The guards immediately became more formal. "No need for that, *Contessa*. We have our orders. Here."

The guard with the water jug unlatched the grille and passed the jug to Caterina through it. Then he closed the grille again.

"About time we were relieved, isn't it?" said the Piedmontese guard.

"Yes, Luigi and Stefano should have been here by now." They looked at each other.

"Do you think that bitch Lucrezia will be back anytime soon?"

"Shouldn't think so."

"Then why don't we take a look down the guardroom—see what's keeping them?"

"All right. Only take us a couple of minutes anyway."

Ezio watched as they disappeared around the curve of the wall, and then he was at the grille.

"Ezio," breathed Caterina. "What the hell are you doing here?"

"Visiting my tailor—what do you think?"

"For Christ's sake, Ezio, do you think we have time for *jokes*?"

"I'm going to get you out. Tonight."

"If you do, Cesare will hunt you down like a dog."

"I think he's already trying to do that. But his men

don't seem all that fanatical, to judge by these two. Do you know if the guards have another key?"

"I don't think so. The guards handed theirs to Lucrezia. She paid me a visit."

"I know. I saw."

"Then why didn't you do anything to stop her?"

"I was outside the window."

"Out *there*? Are you mad?"

"Just athletic. Now—if Lucrezia has the only key we know of, I'd better go and get it. Do you know where she is?"

Caterina considered. "I heard her mention that her quarters are at the very top of the Castel."

"Excellent. That key is as good as mine! Now—stay here until I get back!"

Caterina gave him a look, and glanced at her chains, and at the cell door. "Why—where do you think I *might* go?" she said with a dry smile.

TWENTY-FIVE

He was getting used to the contours of the outer walls of
the Castel Sant'Angelo by now and found that, the higher
he climbed, the easier it was to find hand- and footholds.
Clinging like a limpet, his cape billowing slightly in the
breeze, he soon found himself on a level with the highest
parapet and silently hauled himself up onto it.

The drop on the other side was slight—four feet to
a narrow brick walkway, from which stairs led down,
at occasional intervals, to a garden. A rooftop garden,
in the center of which was a stone building, one story
high, with a flat roof. It had broad windows, so the place
was no extra fortification, and the light of many candles
blazed within, disclosing opulent and tastefully decorated rooms.

The walkway was deserted, but the garden was not. On a bench under the spreading bows of a buttonwood tree, Lucrezia sat demurely, holding hands with a handsome young man whom Ezio recognized as one of Rome's leading romantic actors—Pietro Benintendi. Cesare wouldn't be too pleased if he knew about this! Ezio, a mere silhouette, crept along the walkway to a point as close to the couple as he dared, grateful for the moon, which had risen by now and provided not only light but also confusing, camouflaging pools of shade. He listened.

"I love you so, I want to sing it to the heavens," Pietro was saying ardently.

Lucrezia shushed him. "Please! You must whisper it only to yourself. If Cesare found out, who knows what he would do."

"But you are free, are you not? Of course I heard about your late husband and I am very sorry, but—"

"Quiet, you fool!" Lucrezia's hazel eyes glittered. "Do you not know that Cesare had the Duke of Bisceglie murdered?—my husband was strangled."

"What?"

"It's true."

"What happened?"

"I loved my husband. Cesare grew jealous. Alfonso was a handsome man, and Cesare was conscious of the changes the New Disease had made to his own face, though God knows they are slight. He had his men waylay Alfonso and beat him up. He thought that would act as a warning. But Alfonso was no puppet. He hit back;

while he was still recovering from Cesare's attack, he had his own men retaliate. Cesare was lucky to escape the fate of San Sebastiano! But then, cruel man!—he had Micheletto Corella go to his bedchamber, where he lay nursing his wounds, and strangle him there."

"It isn't possible." Pietro looked nervous.

"I loved my husband. Now, I make-believe to Cesare, to allay his suspicions. But he is a snake—always alert, always venomous." She looked into Pietro's eyes. "Thank God I have you to console me. Cesare has always been jealous of where I place my attentions; but that should not deter us. Besides, he has gone to Urbino to continue his campaigning. There is nothing to hinder us."

"Are you sure?"

"I will keep our secret—if you will," said Lucrezia intensely. She disengaged one hand from his and moved it to his thigh.

"Oh, Lucrezia!" sighed Pietro. "How your lips call to me!"

They kissed, delicately at first, then more and more passionately. Then Ezio shifted his position slightly and inadvertently kicked a brick loose, which fell into the garden. He froze.

Lucrezia and Pietro sprang apart.

"What was that?" she said. "No one is allowed access to my garden or my apartments without my knowledge—no one!"

Pietro was already on his feet, looking around fearfully. "I'd better go," he said hastily. "Look—I have to prepare for my rehearsal—scan my lines for the morning.

I must go!" He stooped to give Lucrezia a last kiss. "Farewell, my love!"

"Stay, Pietro—I am sure it was nothing!"

"No—it is late. I must go!"

Putting on a melancholy expression, he slipped away across the garden and vanished through a door set into the wall on the far side.

Lucrezia waited a moment, then stood and snapped her fingers. Out of the shelter of some tall shrubs growing nearby, one of her personal guardsmen emerged and bowed.

"I heard the entire exchange, *mia signora*, and can vouch for it."

Lucrezia pursed her lips. "Good. Tell Cesare. We shall see how he feels when the boot is on the other foot."

"Yes, *signora*."

Bowing again, the guard withdrew.

Left alone, Lucrezia picked a marguerite from a clump of the flowers that were growing nearby and started to pluck its petals off, one by one.

"He loves me; he loves me not; he loves me; he loves me not . . ."

Ezio slipped down the nearest staircase and made his way toward her. She had sat down again and looked up at his approach, but showed no fear and only slight surprise. Well, if she had any more guards concealed in the garden, Ezio would give them short shrift.

"Please continue. I do not mean to interrupt," Ezio said, bowing in his turn, though in his case the bow was not made without irony.

"Well, well. Ezio Auditore da Firenze." She gave him her hand to kiss. "How pleasant to meet you properly at last. I've heard so much about you, especially recently. That is, I imagine no one else can have been responsible for the little upsets we have been experiencing here in Rome?" She paused. "It's a pity Cesare is no longer here. He would have enjoyed this."

"I have no quarrel with you personally, Lucrezia. Free Caterina and I will stand down."

Her voice hardened slightly. "I'm afraid that is impossible."

Ezio spread his hands. "Then you leave me no choice!" He closed in on her, but cautiously. She had long fingernails.

"Guards!" she shrieked, turning in an instant from noblewoman to harpy, and slashing at his eyes as—just in time—he caught her wrists. Pulling a length of twine from his leather pouch he twisted her wrists behind her and tied them swiftly, before flinging her to the ground and placing one foot firmly on a fold of her dress so that she could not rise and run. Then he drew his sword and dagger and stood his ground, ready to face whatever guards came running from the direction of the apartments. Luckily for Ezio, they were lightly armed and heavily built and wore no chain mail. Though unable to change his position, for above all he could not afford to have Lucrezia cut and run—and already she was trying to bite his ankle through his boot—he ducked below the swinging blade of the first guard and hacked at the man's exposed flank. One down. The second guard was more cautious but, conscious of the now-snarling Lucrezia on the floor, stepped forward to attack Ezio. He lunged at Ezio's chest—Ezio parried upward, locking the guards of both blades, and simply swung his left hand, dagger pointing forward, at the man's head. Two down. The final man, hoping to take advantage of the fact that both of Ezio's blades were engaged, rushed forward. Ezio flicked his right arm hard—sending the blade of the second guard spiraling up toward the new foe. The final guard had to raise his sword to deflect the blow— but just too late and the flying blade nicked his biceps. He winced with pain but came forward again—sword swinging—at Ezio. Ezio had recovered his stance and deflected the attack with his dagger—freeing his sword hand to slash viciously at the man's torso. It was over. The guards lay dead around him—and Lucrezia was silent for the first time. Breathing hard, Ezio pulled his captive to her feet.

"Now come on," he said. "And don't scream. If you do, I will be forced to take your tongue."

He dragged her toward the door through which Pietro had left, found himself in a corridor, and half pushed, half dragged Lucrezia back down the tower, in the direction of the cells.

"Rescuing princesses from castles now? How romantic!" Lucrezia spat out.

"Shut up."

"I suppose you think you're achieving great things, charging around, creating havoc, killing whomever you wish."

"I said, shut up."

"But does your plan have any form? What do you think you are going to achieve? Don't you know how strong we are?"

Ezio hesitated at a staircase leading down to the next floor. "Which way?" he asked her.

She laughed, and didn't reply.

He shook her. "Which *way*?"

"To the left," she replied sullenly.

She was silent for a while, then started again. This time, Ezio let her ramble on. He was sure of where he was now. She squirmed in his grip, and he was concentrating on two things: to keep a firm hold of her and to be alert for any ambush by the Castel guards.

"Do you know what became of the remains of the Pazzi family in Florence once you'd brought them to their knees? Your dear friend Lorenzo, the so-called Magnifico, stripped them of all their possessions and threw them into prison. All of them! Even those who'd played no part in the conspiracy against him." Ezio's mind turned unwillingly to the revenge Caterina had taken against a rebellion against her in Forlì. Her measures had far exceeded Lorenzo's—indeed, made them look mild. He shook the thoughts away.

"The women were forbidden to marry and the family tombstones were erased," Lucrezia went on. "Wiped from the history books. Poof! Just like that!"

But they were not tortured and killed, thought Ezio. Well, it was possible that Caterina had felt justified in her actions at the time. Still, her cruelty had cost her some of the loyalty she had always been able to depend on before, and perhaps that was why Cesare had finally been able to take Forlì.

But she was still an important ally. That was what Ezio had to remember. That, and to suppress whatever feelings—real or imagined—he may have felt for her.

"You and your Assassin friends ignore the consequences of your actions. You are content to set things in motion but you are never willing to see them through!" Lucrezia paused for breath, and Ezio gave her a savage yank forward. But that didn't stop her. "Unlike you, Cesare will finish what he started, and bring peace to Italy. He kills for a higher purpose—again, unlike you!"

"The ignorant and the passive make easy targets," retorted Ezio.

"Say what you like," replied Lucrezia, seeing she had touched a nerve. "In any case, my words are wasted here, you *ipocrita!*"

They had all but reached the cells now. "Remember," Ezio said, drawing his dagger, "if you try to warn your guards, your tongue—"

Lucrezia breathed hard, but was silent. Watchfully, Ezio inched forward. The two new guards were seated at the table, playing cards. Throwing Lucrezia to the ground in front of him, he leapt on them and had dispatched them both before they had a moment to react. Then he spun around and charged after Lucrezia, who had got to her feet and begun to run back the way she had come, screaming for help. He caught up with her in two bounds, clapped a hand over her mouth, and pulled her to him with his other arm, swinging her around and pushing her back toward Caterina's cell. She bit and tore at the gloved hand over her mouth with her teeth at first, then, seeing she was powerless, seemed to give up and went limp.

Caterina was already at the grille, which Ezio unlatched.

"*Salute*, Lucrezia," said Caterina, smiling unpleasantly. "How I've missed you!"

"*Vai a farti fottere, troia*—Go fuck yourself, you whore!"

"Charming as always," said Caterina. "Ezio! Bring her close. I'll take the key."

She reached out as Ezio obeyed her order. He noticed that Caterina grazed Lucrezia's breasts as she reached between them and extracted the key, which hung on a black silk cord.

Caterina passed the key to Ezio, who quickly unlocked the door. The same key fitted the padlock securing the chains—Caterina had not, after all, been chained to the wall—and as Caterina divested herself of these, Ezio shoved Lucrezia into the cell.

"Guards! Guards!" screamed Lucrezia.

"Oh, shut up," said Caterina, picking up a dirty rag from the guards' table and using it to gag her enemy. Then Ezio took some more twine and bound Lucrezia's ankles, before slamming the cell door and locking it securely.

Ezio and Caterina looked at each other.

"My hero," she said drily.

Ezio ignored that. "Can you walk?"

Caterina tried, but stumbled. "I don't think I

can—the manacles they had on me must have done some damage."

Ezio sighed and lifted her into his arms. He'd have to drop her like a sack if they were surprised by guards and he needed to get to his weapons quickly.

"Which way?" she asked.

"Stables first. Then the quickest route out of here."

"Why save me, Ezio? Seriously. With Forlì taken, I am useless to you."

"You still have a family."

"It isn't your family."

Ezio kept walking. He remembered where the stables should be in relation to where they were. It was fortunate that Caterina seemed to be the only prisoner in this section. There were no other guards about. Still, he trod softly and moved quickly, but not so fast as to lumber into a trap. Every so often he stopped and listened. She was light in his arms, and, despite imprisonment, her hair still smelled of vanilla and roses, reminding him of happier times they had had together.

"Listen, Ezio—that night in Monteriggioni—when we . . . bathed together . . . I had to ensure your allegiance. To protect Forlì. It was in the Assassins' interests as much as mine, but—" She broke off. "Do you understand, Ezio?"

"If you had wanted my allegiance, all you had to do was ask for it."

"I needed you on my side."

"My loyalty and my sword arm on your side weren't

enough. You wanted to be sure of my heart as well."
Ezio walked on, shifting her weight in his arms. "But, *è
la politica*. Of course. I knew it. You need not explain."

Within him, his heart felt as if it had fallen down a bot-
tomless mineshaft. How *could* her hair still be scented?

"Caterina," he asked, his throat dry, "did they . . . ?
Did Cesare . . . ?"

She sensed, however dimly, what he felt, and smiled—
with her lips, though, he noticed, not with her eyes.
"Nothing happened. My name must still have some
small value. I was left . . . unspoiled."

They had reached the main door of the stables. It was
unguarded, but firmly closed. Ezio put Caterina down.
"Try to walk a little. You must get the strength back in
your ankles."

He looked around for a means of opening the door.
It had no bolts or handles. But there had to be a way . . .

"Try over there," said Caterina. "Isn't that a lever of
some kind?"

"Wait here," Ezio said.

"As if I had a choice!"

He made his way over to the lever, noticing as he went
a square hole in the floor with an open trapdoor above it.
To judge from the smell beneath, it must have been some
sort of grain store. And, peering down, he could make
out a large number of sacks. But boxes, too—boxes of
what looked like gunpowder.

"Hurry," said Caterina.

He took the lever in his hands and hauled on it. It was

stiff at first, but under the strain of his muscles, it gave a little and then swung over easily. At the same time, the door swung open.

But there were a couple of guards in the stables and they whirled around at the sound of the door creaking on its hinges and rushed toward it, drawing their swords.

"Ezio! *Aiuto!*"

He sped over to her, picked her up, and carried her toward the hole in the floor.

"What are you doing?!"

He held her over the hole.

"Don't you dare!"

He dropped her down, unable to resist a short snicker at her yell of panic. It wasn't far, and he had time to see her land safely on the soft sacks before turning to face the guards. The fight was short and sharp, and the guards were heavy with fatigue and had been taken by surprise. Ezio's skills with the blade were more than a match for them. However, one of them managed to get a glancing blow in, but it cut the material of Ezio's doublet and didn't reach the flesh. Ezio was tiring himself.

When it was over, Ezio reached down and hauled Caterina out again.

"*Figlio di puttana,*" she swore, dusting herself down. "Never do that to me again."

He noticed that she seemed to be walking at least a little better already.

Quickly, he selected horses for them and soon had them saddled and ready. He helped her onto one and leapt into the saddle of the other himself. An archway led

off one side of the stables and through it he could see the
main gate of the Castel. It was guarded, but it was open.
Dawn was approaching, and no doubt tradesmen from
the city were expected, to make deliveries.

"Ride like hell," Ezio told her. "Before they have time
to realize what's going on. Across the bridge and then
make for Tiber Island. You'll be safe there. Find Machiavelli. He'll be waiting for me."

"But we *both* have to get away from here!"

"I'll follow. But for now I must stay and take care of
the remaining guards, create a diversion, a delay, something."

Caterina pulled the reins of her horse in, so that it
reared. "Get back in one piece," she said. "Or I will
never forgive you!"

Ezio hoped she meant it, as he watched her kick the
horse into a gallop. She charged past the guards at the
main gate, scattering them. As soon as he saw that she was
clear, he rode his own horse back through the stables to
the grain and powder store, seizing a torch from its sconce
as he passed. This he threw into the hole, and then he
wheeled around and galloped back the way he had come,
drawing his sword.

The guards had formed a cordon and were waiting
for him, halberds raised. Ezio didn't know the horse but
he knew what he had to do; he rode straight at the line
of guards and at the last minute pulled hard on the reins
and, leaning forward in the saddle, dug his heels in. At
the same time as the horse charged forward, there was an
almighty explosion from near the stables. He was right!

It had been gunpowder! The ground shook with the explosion—and the guards instinctively ducked down. The horse, also shocked with the noise of the bang, was more determined to make good her flight. She flew into the air, clearing the line of guards as easily as she might have cleared a fence.

Leaving panic and confusion in his wake, he rode in the direction of the rising sun. His heart swelled within him. He had saved Caterina!

TWENTY-SIX

Once he was sure he had shaken off any possible pursuers, Ezio turned his horse. He was loath to lose such a good animal, but he took it to the stables where he and Machiavelli had hired horses what seemed like a lifetime ago and turned it over to the chief ostler there. The stables were neat and clean and clearly doing a thriving business, in a district that seemed to have shaken off Borgia control and, for the moment at least, maintained its independence. Then he made his way back toward Tiber Island on foot. The Assassins' secret ferry was waiting at the bank and, once on the island itself, he hastened toward the hideout.

Inside, he found that Caterina had arrived safely. She

was lying on a makeshift bed near the door, being tended by a doctor. She smiled when she saw him, and tried to sit up, but the doctor gently restrained her.

"Ezio! I am relieved to see you safe."

He took her hand and squeezed it. "Where is Machiavelli?" There was no return of his pressure, but perhaps she was still too weak.

"I don't know."

La Volpe emerged from the shadows at the end of the room. "Ezio! Good to see you again!" He embraced the younger man. "I brought your *contessa* here. As for Machiavelli . . ."

But just then the main door swung open and Machiavelli himself came in. He looked drawn.

"Where have you been?" asked La Volpe.

"Looking for Ezio—not that I am accountable to you," said Machiavelli, and Ezio was saddened to note the tension that still existed between his two friends. Machiavelli turned to Ezio and, without ceremony, asked: "What of Cesare and Rodrigo?"

"Cesare left almost immediately for Urbino. As for Rodrigo, he was at the Vatican."

"That is odd," said Machiavelli. "Rodrigo should have been in the Castel."

"Very odd indeed," La Volpe put in evenly.

If he'd noticed the dig, Machiavelli ignored it. "What a wasted opportunity," he mused. Then, recollecting himself, he said to Caterina, "Oh, no offense, *Contessa*. We are glad to see you safe."

"I take none," she said.

"Now that Cesare has gone to Urbino, we must concentrate on building our forces here."

Machiavelli raised his eyebrows. "But I thought we intended to strike now! We should go after him and cut him down where he stands."

"That would be impossible," Caterina said. "I have seen his army. It is massive. You would never reach him."

Ezio said, "I say we work here. In Rome. Here, we have already made a good start. We should continue to erode the Borgia's influence, while restoring our own. And, in fact, I want to begin immediately."

"You speak as if you were already our leader," said Machiavelli. "But the post has not been discussed, let alone ratified, by our council."

"And I say we need a leader, and we need one right away," countered La Volpe. "We have no time for councils and ratifications. We need to consolidate the Brotherhood once again, and, for my money, Ezio is the right man for the job. Machiavelli, I appeal to you—you and I are two of the most senior Assassins left. Bartolomeo is bound to agree. Let us make this decision now—keep it secret if you like—and later, we can put it to a formal vote."

Machiavelli seemed to be on the point of speech, but then let it go and simply shrugged.

"I will not fail you," Ezio said. "Gilberto, I'd like you to bring Bartolomeo and my sister, Claudia, here. There are matters to discuss. Niccolò, please come with me."

On his way out, Ezio paused by Caterina's bed. "Take care of her," he said to the doctor.

"Where are we going?" Machiavelli said, once they were back in the city center.

"There's something I want to show you."

He led the way to the nearest market square. Half of it was open for business: there was a baker; a butcher was swatting flies away from his wares; and a greengrocer had a selection of rather tired-looking produce on sale. Early as it was, it was the wine shops that were doing the best business. And, as Ezio expected, a small knot of Borgia guards were duffing up the hapless owner of a leather goods stall.

"Look," said Ezio, as they blended in with the small crowd of shoppers.

"I know what is going on," said Machiavelli.

"I know you do, Niccolò," said Ezio. "Forgive me, but you see the big picture. You understand what is to be done politically to break the Borgia, and I for one do not doubt your sincerity in this." He paused. "But we must start at a more fundamental level. The Borgia take what they want from the people with complete impunity, to maintain their power."

They watched the guards push the man to the ground, then, laughing, help themselves to what they fancied from his stall and move on. The man picked himself up, watched them go in impotent rage, and then, close to tears, began to rearrange his goods. A woman came up to comfort him, but he shook her off. Nevertheless she stayed, hovering near him, care and concern in her eyes.

"Why did you not help him?" asked Machiavelli. "Send them packing?"

"Look," said Ezio, "helping one man is good, but it will not solve the problem. They will come again, when we are not here, and they will do the same again. Look at the quality of the stuff on offer here. The vegetables are old, the meat is flyblown, and the bread, no doubt, is hard. The best goes to the Borgia. And why do you think so many people are drinking?"

Machiavelli said, "I do not know."

"Because they are in pain," Ezio replied. "They are without hope and they are oppressed. They want to blot it all out. But we can *change* that."

"How?"

"By recruiting them to our cause." He spread his arms. "These people—these are the ones who will form the backbone of our resistance to the Borgia."

"We've talked of this before," said Machiavelli sharply. "You cannot be serious."

"I'm going to start with that stallholder. To win this war, Niccolò, we need loyal soldiers—however they fight for us. We must sow the seeds of rebellion in their minds." He paused, then continued earnestly, "By recruiting those whom the bullying State has made its enemies, we arm the people who have been disarmed by the Borgia."

Machiavelli looked at his friend long and hard. "Go, then," he said. "Go, and recruit our first novices."

"Oh, I intend to," said Ezio. "And you will see that

from the group of determined men and women I gather around us, I will forge a sword capable of cutting the limbs and head from the trunk of the Borgia—and of the Templars themselves."

TWENTY-SEVEN

Ezio returned to the Assassins' center of operations on Tiber Island having done a good morning's work, discreetly converting a number of disaffected citizens to his cause.

Apart from the loyal attendants who staffed and guarded the place, it was deserted, and Ezio looked forward to a little quiet time, to think and plan; but as he approached, he found that, after all, he had a visitor. One who wanted to be quite sure that his presence would not be noted, and one who, therefore, waited until the general staff had gone about their business elsewhere in the building before he made himself known.

"Psst! Ezio! Over here!"

"Who's there?" Ezio was instantly alert, though already he thought he knew the voice. Tall bushes grew on either side of the lane that led to the hideout, and the place was known to no one outside the organization. If by any chance the secret had been penetrated . . .

"Come here!"

"Who is it?"

"It's me!"

And Leonardo da Vinci, dandified and distracted as ever, stepped out of his hiding place into the lane.

"Leo! My God!"

But then Ezio, remembering who Leonardo's new master was, checked his initial impulse, which had been to run and embrace his old friend.

His reaction registered with Leonardo, who looked a little older, to be sure, but who had lost none of his élan, or his vigorous enthusiasm. He took a step forward, but kept his head lowered. "I'm not surprised you don't show that much enthusiasm at seeing me again."

"Well, Leo, I must admit, you have disappointed me."

Leonardo spread his hands. "I knew you were behind the break-in at the Castel. It could only have been you. So—I knew you were still alive!"

"Surely your new masters would have told you that."

"They tell me nothing! I am no more than a slave to them." There was a smallest twinkle in Leonardo's eye. "But they have to trust me."

"As long as you deliver."

"I think I'm just about bright enough to stay one step ahead of them." Leonardo took another step toward

Ezio, arms half held out. "It is good to see you again, my friend."

"You have designed weapons for them—new guns we will find difficult to match."

"I know. But if you will let me explain . . ."

"And how did you find this place?"

"I can explain . . ."

Leonardo looked so contrite, and so unhappy, and he seemed so sincere, that Ezio's heart warmed, despite himself, toward his old friend. He also reflected that, after all, Leonardo had come to see him, no doubt at great personal risk; and that if he sought a rapprochement, it would be a foolish leader indeed who would turn down the friendship and the partnership of such a man.

"Come here!" cried Ezio, spreading his arms wide.

"Oh, Ezio!" Leonardo hurried forward and the two men embraced warmly.

Ezio led his friend inside and they sat down together. Ezio knew that Caterina had been moved to an inner room, where she could complete her recovery in peace and quiet, and the doctor had given orders that she was not to be disturbed. He was tempted to disobey, but there would be time enough for talk with her later. Besides, Leonardo's appearance dictated a change of priorities.

Ezio had wine and cakes brought for them.

"Tell me everything," said Ezio.

"I will explain. First of all, you must forgive me. The Borgia commandeered my services—but under duress. If I'd refused to serve them, they would have subjected me to a long and painful death. They described what they would do to me if I refused to help them. Even now I cannot think of it without trembling."

"You are perfectly safe now."

Leonardo shook his head. "No! I must go back to them. I am of far more use to you if they think I am still working for them. As it is, I have done my utmost to create the minimum possible number of new inventions to satisfy them." Ezio was about to interrupt but Leonardo held up a nervous hand. "Please—this is a kind of confession, and I'd like to complete it. Then you may judge me as you think fit."

"No one is judging you, Leonardo."

Leonardo's manner became more intense. Ignoring the refreshments, he leaned forward. "I say I work for them under duress," he went on, "but it is more than that. You know I keep out of politics. I like to keep my nose clean. But men who seek power seek me out because they know what I can do for them."

"This I do know."

"But I play along, too. I play along to stay alive. And why do I wish to stay alive? Because I have so much to *do!*" He took a breath. "I cannot tell you, Ezio, how my poor brain teems!" He made a gesture that seemed partly all-embracing and partly despairing. "There is so much to discover!"

Ezio was silent. This he also knew.

"So," Leonardo concluded. "Now you know."

"Why have you come here?"

"To make amends. I had to assure you that my heart is not with them."

"And what do they want of you?"

"Whatever they can get! War machines are the main thing. They know what I am capable of."

Leonardo produced a packet of papers, which he handed over. "Here are some of the designs I've done for them. Look! Here is an armored vehicle capable, if correctly constructed, of moving across all terrains—and the men concealed within it can fire guns—big guns—while remaining fully protected from all assaults. I call it a tank."

Ezio blanched as his eye scanned the drawings. "And is it . . . under construction?"

Leonardo looked artful. "I said 'if correctly constructed.' Unfortunately, as the design stands, the thing is only able to swivel on its own axis!"

"I see." Ezio smiled.

"And look at this."

Ezio perused a drawing of a horseman managing two horses, harnessed side by side. To their traces were attached, by long horizontal poles, in front and at the rear—where there were also wheels—rotating scythelike devices, to cut down any enemy at which the horseman rode. "A fiendish device," he said.

"Yes! But unfortunately the horseman himself is . . . fully exposed." Leonardo's eyes twinkled some more.

Ezio's smile broadened, but then faded again. "But what of the guns you have given them?"

Leonardo shrugged. "One has to throw a sop to Cerberus," he said. "I have to give them something of actual use or they will grow suspicious."

"But they are very efficient guns."

"Indeed they are—but they are not half as efficient as that little pistol I made for you once, years ago, based on the design from the Codex page. A pity, really—I had trouble reining myself in on that one!"

Ezio thought sadly of his lost Codex weapons. But he would come back to them.

"What else is in this packet of papers?"

Although they were alone, Leonardo lowered his voice. "I have copied the plans not only for the largest of the machines, but also of where they are to be used in battle." He spread his hands ironically. "Alas, that they should not be more efficient!"

Ezio looked at his old friend admiringly. This was the man who had designed a submarine for the Venetians to use against the Turkish galleys! If he had chosen not to build in defects to these designs, there would be no hope at all against the Borgia. How glad he was to have welcomed Leonardo as he had. This man was worth more than two armies.

"For God's sake, Leo, have a glass of wine at least. I know I can never reward you enough for all this."

But Leonardo waved the proffered beaker away. "There is far graver news. You know they have the Apple?"

"Of course."

"They have given it to me to study. You and I already know something of the extent of its powers. Rodrigo knows a little less, but he has more intellect than Cesare, though Cesare is the one to watch."

"How much information on the Apple have you given them?"

"As little as possible, but I have to give them something. Fortunately, Cesare seems satisfied—so far—with the limited applications I have vouchsafed him. But Rodrigo knows there is more and grows impatient." He paused. "I have considered ways of stealing it, but it is kept under close guard, and I am only allowed access to it under the strictest supervision. But I was able to use its powers to locate you. It has that facility, you know. Quite fascinating."

"And you taught them that trick?"

"Of course not! All I want is to return it to its rightful owner."

"Fear not, Leo. We will recover it. In the meantime, stall them as far as you can, and if you can, keep me posted on how much you have let them know."

"I will."

Ezio paused. "There is something else."

"Tell me."

"I have lost all the Codex weapons you once fashioned for me."

"I see."

"Except for the original hidden-blade. But the pistol, the poison-blade, the double-blade, the miraculous bracer—all these are gone."

"Hmm," said Leonardo. Then he smiled. "Well, recreating them for you may not be a problem."

"Really?" Ezio could scarcely believe it.

"The designs you let me have are still in Florence, well hidden with my old assistants Agniolo and Innocento. The Borgia will never have them. If they ever—heaven forfend!—took Florence, or even if the French did, Agni-olo has strict orders to destroy them, and even he and Innocento—not that I do not trust them absolutely—would never be able to re-create them independently of me. But I—I never forget a design. However—"

He hesitated, almost embarrassed. "You must pay me for the raw materials I will need. In advance."

Ezio was astonished. "Really? They are not paying you at il Vaticano?"

Leonardo coughed. "Very . . . very little. I suppose they think that keeping me alive is payment enough. And I am not such a fool as to think that the minute my services become . . . superfluous to requirements, they will not kill me with as little reflection as they might kill a dog."

"Hardly that," said Ezio. "They would rather you were dead than have you work for anyone else."

"Yes, I've been thinking along the same lines," said Leonardo. "And there's really nowhere to run. Not that I want to—I want to see the Borgia crushed—I'll engage myself so far in politics as to say that! But my beloved Milan is in French hands . . . " he started to muse. "Perhaps . . . later . . . when all this is over . . . I might even try my luck in France. They say it's a very civilized country . . ."

It was time to bring him back to reality. Ezio went to an ironbound chest and from it produced a leather pouch bulging with ducats. This he gave to Leonardo.

"Payment on account for the Codex weapons," he said briskly. "When can you have them ready?"

Leonardo considered. "It won't be as easy as it was

last time," he said. "I must work secretly, and alone—for I cannot wholly trust all the assistants I have working for me here." He paused. "Let me contact you again. As soon as possible, I promise." He hefted the heavy bag in his hand. "And who knows, for this much money I may even be able to throw in a couple of new weapons— my own inventions this time, of course, but effective, I think you'll find."

"Whatever you can do for us will earn my undying gratitude and my protection, wherever you are," said Ezio. He made a mental note to delegate a handful of his new recruits, as soon as they finished their training, to keep a watchful eye on Leonardo and to report back regularly on him. "Now, how shall we maintain contact?"

Leonardo said, "I've thought of that." He took out a piece of chalk and on the table between them drew a man's right hand, pointing.

"It's beautiful," said Ezio.

"Thank you—it's just a sketch of part of a painting I've been thinking of doing—of Saint John the Baptist. If I ever get around to it. Go and sit where it's pointing to."

Ezio obeyed.

"That's it," said Leonardo. "Tell your people to keep their eyes peeled. They see one of these—it'll just look like a bit of *graffito* to anyone else—tell them to let you know, and follow the direction it's pointing in. That's how we'll rendezvous."

"Splendid," said Ezio.

"Don't worry, I'll make sure you're forewarned. In

case you're thinking of charging off somewhere on some mission or other."

"Thanks."

Leonardo stood. "I must go. Otherwise I'll be missed. But first—"

"First what?"

Leonardo grinned and shook the bag of money.

"First, I'm going shopping!"

TWENTY-EIGHT

Ezio left the hideout shortly after Leonardo, to continue his recruiting work but also to keep himself busy. He was impatient to have the replacement Codex weapons back in his hands.

When, later in the day, he returned for a prearranged meeting, it was to find that Machiavelli had preceded him. Caterina was with him, sitting in a chair, her knees covered with a fur rug. As usual, Machiavelli did not stand on ceremony.

"Where have you been?" he asked.

Ezio didn't like his tone. "We all have our secrets," he replied, keeping his voice level. "And, may I ask, what have you been up to?"

Machiavelli smiled. "I've been refining our carrier

pigeon system. We can use it now to send orders to the new recruits scattered about the city."

"Excellent. Thank you, Niccolò."

They looked at each other. Machiavelli was almost ten years Ezio's junior; yet there was no doubting the independence and ambition behind those veiled eyes. Did he resent Ezio's leadership? Had he hoped it might have fallen on him? Ezio put the thought aside: no, surely the man was more of a theorist, a diplomat, a political animal. And there could be no doubt about his usefulness—or his allegiance—to the Brotherhood. If only Ezio could convince La Volpe of that, fully.

And, as if on cue, La Volpe entered the hideout, accompanied by Claudia.

"What news?" Ezio asked him, after the two had greeted one another.

"Bartolomeo sends his apologies. It seems that General Valois has had another stab at attacking the barracks."

"I see."

"They redoubled their assault. But we are holding our ground."

"Good." Ezio turned to his sister, coldly. "Claudia," he said, inclining his head.

"Brother," she rejoined, with equal frostiness.

"Please sit down, all of you," said Ezio.

Once they were settled, he continued. "I have a plan prepared for the Borgia."

"I suggest," Machiavelli put in immediately, "that we either go after their supplies or Cesare's followers."

"Thank you, Niccolò," said Ezio evenly. "*My* plan is

to attack both. If we can cut off his funds, Cesare will lose his army and return without his men. How does he get his money?"

La Volpe said, "We know that he depends for much of his money on Rodrigo, and Rodrigo's banker is Agostino Chigi. But Cesare also has his own banker, whose identity has yet to be confirmed, though we have our suspicions."

Ezio decided, for the moment, to keep his own suspicions in that direction quiet. It would be best to have them confirmed, if possible, by La Volpe's men.

"I know someone—a client of ours at the Rosa in Fiore—who owes that banker money. The senator Egidio Troche is complaining about interest rates all the time."

"Bene," said Ezio. "Then we must follow that up."

"There's something else," said Machiavelli. "We have news that they are planning to station French troops on the road that leads to Castel Sant'Angelo. Your attack must have really rattled them. And apparently Cesare is planning to return to Rome. Immediately. Quite why, so soon, is beyond me. But we'll find out. In any case, when he does arrive, he'll be so well guarded that you'll never get to him. In any case, our spies tell us that he intends to keep his return secret, at least for the moment."

"He's got something up his sleeve," said La Volpe.

"Brilliant," said Machiavelli, and the two men exchanged a look that wasn't friendly.

Ezio considered this. "Seems to be that our best course of action is to corner this French general of theirs, Octavien, and kill him. Once he's out of the way,

Bartolomeo will have the Frenchmen on the defensive, and they'll abandon their guard duty at the Castel."

Caterina spoke for the first time. "Even so, Ezio— even with those troops gone, the Papal Guard will continue to protect the bridge and the main gate."

"Ah," said La Volpe, "but there's a side entrance. Lucrezia's latest plaything, the actor Pietro Benintendi, has a key."

"Does he?" said Ezio. "I saw him with her at the Castel."

"I'll have my men find out where he is," promised La Volpe. "Shouldn't be too difficult."

Caterina smiled. "Sounds like a good idea. I'd like to help. We should be able to scare that key out of him— and he'll stop seeing Lucrezia. Anything to rob that bitch of any pleasure."

"Momentino, Contessa," said Machiavelli. "We are going to have to do without your help."

Caterina looked at him, surprised. "Why?"

"Because we are going to have to get you out of the city—maybe to Florence, until we can get Forlì back for you. Your children are already safe there." He looked around. "Ezio's rescuing you wasn't without its consequences. There are heralds all over the city proclaiming a rich reward for the *contessa*'s capture—alive or dead. And no bribe can shut them up."

There was a silence. Then Caterina rose, letting the rug fall to the floor. "Then it appears that I have outstayed my welcome," she said. "Excuse me."

"What are you talking about?" said Ezio, alarmed.

"Only that I am in danger here—"

"We will protect you!"

"And—more important—a liability to you." She was looking at Machiavelli as she spoke. "Isn't that so, Niccolò?"

Machiavelli was silent.

"I am answered," said Caterina. "I will make my preparations at once."

TWENTY-NINE

"Are you sure you are able to ride?" Ezio asked her.

"I rode from the Castel when you rescued me, didn't I?"

"Yes, but then there was no choice."

"Is there a choice now?"

Ezio was silent. It was the following morning and Ezio watched as Caterina and her two female attendants packed the few clothes and provisions Claudia had organized for her journey. She would leave the next day before dawn. A small escort of Ezio's men would ride with her part of the way, to see her safely out of Rome. Ezio had offered to join them, but this Caterina had refused. "I don't like goodbyes," she'd said. "And the more drawn out they are, the worse they are."

He watched her as she bustled about her packing. He

thought about the times they had had together, long ago in Forlì, and then about what he had fondly imagined was a reunion in Monteriggioni. The Assassins' Brotherhood seemed to have taken over his life—and left him alone.

"I wish you would stay," he said.

"Ezio, I can't. You know I can't."

"Dismiss your women."

"I have to hurry."

"Dismiss them. This won't take long."

She did so, but he could see with what reluctance, and even then she said, "Be sure to return in five minutes by the water clock."

Once they were alone, he didn't know where to begin.

"Well?" she said, more gently, and he could see that her eyes were troubled—though by what, he could not tell.

"I . . . I rescued you," he said lamely.

"You did, and I am grateful. But didn't you tell the others that you did so purely because I am still a useful ally—even with Forlì gone?"

"We'll get Forlì back."

"And then I shall go there again."

Ezio was silent again. His heart felt empty.

She came up to him and put her hands on his shoulders. "Ezio, listen. I am no use to anyone without Forlì. If I leave now, it is to seek safety—and to be with my children. Don't you want that for me?"

"Yes."

"Well, then—"

"I didn't rescue you because you're valuable to the cause."

It was her turn to be silent.

"But because—"

"Don't say it, Ezio."

"Why not?"

"Because I cannot say it back."

No weapon could have cut more deeply into him than those words. "You used me, then?"

"That sounds rather harsh."

"What other words would you wish me to use?"

"I tried to explain earlier."

"You are a ruthless woman."

"I am a woman with work to do, and a duty."

"Then whatever serves your cause, goes."

She was silent again, then said, "I've tried to explain this to you already. You must accept it." She had taken her hands from his shoulders. He could see that her mind had wandered back to her journey. She was looking at the stuff yet to be packed.

He thought, recklessly, *To hell with the Brotherhood! I know what I want! Why shouldn't I live for myself, for a change?*

"I'm coming with you," he said.

She turned to him again, her eyes serious. "Listen, Ezio. Perhaps you are making a choice, but you are making it too late. Perhaps I have done the same thing. But you are leader of the Assassins now. Don't give up the work you have started—the great work of rebuilding after the disaster at Monteriggioni. Without you, things will fall apart again, and then who will there be to save us?"

"But you never really wanted me."

He looked at her. She was still there, in the room with him, but her spirit had long gone. How long ago it had left him, he did not know—perhaps it had never really been there. Perhaps he had only hoped for it, or imagined it. At that moment, he felt that he was looking at the corpse of love, yet still he refused to believe in its death. But, as with any other death, he saw that he had no choice now but to get used to its reality.

There was a knock at the door.

"Come in," said Caterina, and her attendants returned.

Ezio left them to their packing.

The next morning he was determined to resist seeing them off, but he could not. It was cold. When he got to the appointed square, in a safe district of the city, they were already mounted, the horses restless. Perhaps, even now, at the last moment, she would relent.

But her eyes, though kind, were distant. He thought he could have borne things better if she hadn't looked at him with kindness. Kindness was almost humiliating.

All he could say was, "*Buona fortuna, Contessa*—and . . . farewell."

"Let's hope it's not 'farewell.'"

"Oh, I think it is."

She looked at him once more. "Well, then—*buona fortuna anche*, my prince; and—*Vittoria agli Assassini!*"

She wheeled her horse around, and without another word, without even a backward glance, at the head of her guardian entourage, she galloped north out of the city and out of his life. He watched them until they were mere specks in the distance, a lonely, middle-aged man who had been given a last chance at love and missed it.

"*Vittoria agli Assassini,*" murmured Ezio tonelessly to himself, as he turned and made his way back into the still-sleeping city.

THIRTY

With Cesare's return imminent, Ezio had to put his private grief aside and get on with the work Fate had given him. In his attempt to cut Cesare off from his funds, the first step was to find and neutralize Cesare's banker, and the initial lead would come from the Rosa in Fiore.

"What do you want?" Claudia couldn't have been less friendly if she'd tried.

"You spoke of a senator at the meeting."

"Yes, I did. Why?"

"You said he owed money to Cesare's banker. Is he here?"

She shrugged. "You'll probably find him on the Campidoglio. Surely you don't need my help for that."

"What does he look like?"

"Oh—let me see—average?"

"Don't play games with me, sister!"

Claudia relented slightly. "He's maybe sixty, lean, worried looking, clean shaven, grey hair, your height or a little less. Name's Egidio Troche. Stubborn type, Ezio, pessimistic, set in his ways. You'll have your work cut out trying to get around him."

"Thank you." Ezio looked at her hard. "Now—I intend to track down this 'Banker' and kill him. I've a pretty shrewd idea who he is, but I need to find out where he lives. This senator could lead me to him."

"The Banker's security's pretty tight. So would yours be, if you were in a position like his."

"You think mine isn't?"

"As if I cared."

"Listen, Claudia—if I'm tough with you, it's because I worry about you."

"Spare me!"

"You're doing well—"

"Thank you, kind sir—"

"—but I need you to organize a big job for me. Once I have neutralized this Banker, I need your girls to get his money to a place of safety."

"Just let me know when—or should I say, *if*—you succeed."

"Just—stay alert."

In a dark mood, Ezio set off for the Capitoline Hill, the administrative center of Rome. He was greeted by a busy scene. There were several senators going about their business in the broad piazza around which the government buildings were arranged, accompanied by secretaries and assistants, who carried papers in leather folders and bustled after their masters as they moved from building to building, all trying to look as busy and as important as possible. Ezio, as far as he could, blended into the melee, keeping a watchful eye out for a man answering the description Claudia had given him. As he moved through the crowd, he kept his ears pricked for any hint he might pick up about his quarry. There certainly wasn't any sign of Egidio among the senators at the moment, though he seemed to be providing his colleagues with a lively topic of conversation.

"Egidio's been asking for money again," said one.

"When doesn't he? What's it for this time?"

"Oh, some proposal to reduce the number of public executions."

"Ridiculous!"

Ezio moved on to another knot of senators and there gleaned more information. He wasn't sure, from what he heard, whether Egidio was a militant (and therefore foolish) liberal reformer or a rather ham-fisted con man.

"Egidio's petitioning for an end to the torturing of witnesses in the criminal courts," someone in the next group was saying.

"Fat chance!" replied the harassed-looking man he was talking to. "It's just a front, anyway. All he really wants the money for is to pay off his debts!"

"And he wants to get rid of exemption licenses."

"Please! Like that's going to happen! Every citizen who feels mistreated by our laws should surely be allowed to pay for an exemption from those laws! It's our duty! After all, it's our own Holy Father who brought the exemption licenses in—and he's following the example of Christ Himself—'Blessed are the merciful'!"

Another Borgia scam for making money, thought Ezio, while the other senator rejoined, "Why should we give any money to Egidio? Everyone knows what he'd do with it."

The two men laughed and went about their business.

Ezio's attention was attracted then to a small group of Borgia guards in their mulberry-and-yellow uniforms, but Ezio noticed that these had Cesare's personal crest—two red bulls, quartered with fleurs-de-lis—sewn onto their doublets. As they always spelled trouble, he made his way over to them and saw, as he approached, that they had surrounded a senator. The other senators were carrying on as if nothing out of the ordinary was happening, but Ezio could see that they left plenty of space between the guards and themselves.

The unfortunate senator answered Claudia's description perfectly.

"No more arguing," the guards' sergeant was saying.

"Your payment's fallen due," added his corporal. "A debt's a debt."

Egidio had dropped any pretense of dignity. He was pleading. "Make an exception for an old man!" he quavered. "I beg of you!"

"No," snarled the sergeant, nodding to two of his men, who seized Egidio and threw him to the ground. "The Banker has sent us to collect—and you know what that means!"

"Look—give me until tomorrow—this evening!—I'll have the money ready then!"

"Not good enough," responded the sergeant, kicking the senator hard in the stomach. He stepped back and the corporal and the two other guards set about belaboring the prostrate old man.

"That won't get you your money," said Ezio, stepping forward.

"Who are you? Friend of his?"

"I'm a concerned bystander."

"Well, you can take your concern and fuck off with it! And mind your own fucking business!"

The sergeant, as Ezio had hoped, had stepped too close. With practiced ease he slipped the catch on his hidden-blade and, raising his arm, swept it across the guard's exposed throat just above the gorget he was wearing. The other guards watched, rooted to the spot in astonishment as their leader fell to his knees, his hands futilely scrabbling at the wound to stanch the fountaining blood. Before they could react, Ezio was upon them, and, a matter of seconds later, the three of them had joined their sergeant on the Other Side, all with their throats slit. Ezio's mission left no time for swordplay—only swift, efficient killing.

The piazza had emptied as if by magic. Ezio helped the senator to his feet. There was blood on the man's clothes and he looked—and indeed was—in a state of shock. But it was shock mingled with relief.

"We'd better get out of here," Ezio said to him.

"I know a place. Follow me," Egidio replied, and he

set off with remarkable speed for an alleyway between two of the larger government buildings. They hastened down it and turned left, then down some stairs into a basement area and to a door. This the senator quickly unlocked, and he ushered Ezio into a small, dark, but comfortable-looking apartment.

"My bolt-hole," said Egidio. "Useful when you have as many creditors as I have."

"But one big one."

"My mistake was to consolidate all my debts with the Banker. I wasn't fully aware of his exact connections at the time. I should have stuck to Chigi. At least he's honest—as far as a banker can be!" Egidio paused. "But what of you? A Good Samaritan in Rome? I thought they were a dying breed."

Ezio let that go. "You are Egidio Troche, *il senatore*?"

Egidio looked startled. "Don't tell me I owe you money as well!"

"No—but you can help me. I am looking for Cesare's banker."

The senator smiled thinly. "Cesare *Borgia's* banker? Ha! And you are . . . ?"

"Let's just say I'm a friend of the family."

"Cesare has a lot of friends these days. Unfortunately, I am not one of them. So, if you'll excuse me, I have some packing to do."

"I can pay."

Egidio stopped looking nervous. "Ah! You can *pay*? *Ma che merviglia!* He fights off guards for one, *and* he offers one money! Tell me, where have you been all my life?"

"Well, I haven't descended from heaven. You help me, and I'll help you. It's as simple as that."

Egidio considered this. "We'll go to my brother's place. They've got no quarrel with him, and we can't stay here—it's too depressing, and it's far too close to my—dare I say, our?—enemies."

"Let's go, then."

"But you'll have to protect me. There'll be more of Cesare's guards out after me, and they won't be especially friendly, if you know what I mean—especially after that little show you put on in the piazza."

"Come on."

Egidio led the way out, cautiously, making sure the coast was clear before they set off by a labyrinthine route through back alleys and seedy lanes, across little *piazze*, and skirting the edges of markets. Twice they encountered pairs of guards, and twice Ezio had to fight them off—this time using his sword to full effect. It seemed that the city was on full alert for both men—and both men in flight together proved too good a bounty for the Borgia henchmen. Time was not on Ezio's side—so when the next pair of guards appeared at the other side of one small piazza, they simply had to run for it, and Ezio, unable to take to the rooftops with the senator in tow, simply had to depend on Egidio's apparently exhaustive knowledge of Rome's backstreets. But at last they reached the rear of a new, quietly splendid villa, set in its own walled courtyard, a few blocks east of Saint Peter's. Egidio let them into the courtyard through a small ironbound gate set into one of the walls, for which he produced a key.

Once inside, they both breathed more easily.

"Someone really wants you dead," said Ezio.

"Not yet—they want me to pay them first."

"Why? Once they've got their money—? And by the sound of things you're something of a milch-cow to them."

"It isn't that simple. The fact is, I've been a fool. I'm no friend of the Borgia, even if I have borrowed money from them, and recently a bit of information came my way that gave me an opportunity of doing them down—if only a little."

"And that was . . . ?"

"A few months ago, my brother Francesco, who's Cesare's chamberlain—I know, I know, don't get me started—Francesco told me a good deal about Cesare's plans for the Romagna. What he plans to do there, I mean. And that is, to create a mini-kingdom from which he intends to conquer the rest of the country and bring it to heel. As the Romagna is on the doorstep of the Venetian territories, Venice is already unhappy about Cesare's inroads there."

"So what did you do?"

Egidio spread his hands. "I wrote to the Venetian ambassador, giving him all the information I'd got from Francesco. Warning him. But one of my letters must have been intercepted."

"But won't that implicate your brother?"

"He's managed to keep himself in the clear so far."

"But what possessed you to do such a thing?"

"I had to do something. The Senate has nothing to do, really, these days, except put its imprimatur on all the

Borgia's decrees. If it didn't, it would cease to exist altogether. As it is, there's nothing to do—nothing independent. Do you know what it's like not to have *un cazzo* to do?" Egidio shook his head. "It changes a man. I admit that even I have taken to gambling, to drinking . . ."

"And whoring."

The senator looked at him. "Oh, you're good. You're very good. What was it that gave me away? The scent of perfume on my sleeve?"

Ezio smiled. "Something like that."

"Hmm. Well, anyway, as I was saying, senators used to do what senators are supposed to do—petitioning about real issues, like—oh, I don't know, where to start?—like unlawful cruelty, abandoned children, street crime, lending rates, keeping some kind of rein on Chigi and the other bankers. Now the only legislation we are allowed to draw up independently concerns stuff like the appropriate width of the sleeves of women's dresses."

"But not you. You try to raise money for false causes in order to use it to pay off your gambling debts."

"They're not false causes, my boy. As soon as we have a proper government again, and as soon as I'm on an even keel financially again, I intend to pursue them vigorously."

"And when do you think that will be?"

"We must be patient. Tyranny is unbearable, but it never lasts. It's too brittle."

"I wish I could believe that."

"Of course you've got to stand up to it. Whatever happens. You obviously do." He paused. "I'm probably—what?—ten or fifteen years older than you. I must make the most of my time. Or have you never looked at a grave and thought, 'This is the most significant thing I will ever do—die'?"

Ezio was silent.

"No," continued Egidio. "I guess not." He turned in on himself. "*Maledetto* letters! I should never have sent them to the ambassador. Now Cesare will kill me as soon as he gets a chance, debt or no debt, unless by some miracle he decides to vent his anger on someone else. God knows, he's capricious enough."

"Someone else? Like your brother?"

"I'd never forgive myself."

"Why not? You're a politician."

"We're not all bad."

"Where is your brother?"

"I've no idea. Not here, thank God. We haven't talked since he found out about the letters, and I'm enough of a liability for him. If he saw you—"

"Can we get down to business?" said Ezio.

"Of course. One good turn, and so on . . . Now, what was it you wanted again?"

"I want to know where Cesare's banker is. Where he works. Where he lives.And most of all, who he is."

Egidio was suddenly all briskness. "Right! I need to arrive with the money." He spread his hands again. "Problem is, I have none."

"I told you I'd get it for you. Just tell me how much. And where you are meeting this Banker."

"I never know until I'm actually there. I usually go to

one of three prearranged points. His associates meet me and take me to him.

"I owe ten thousand ducats."

"No problem."

"*Sul serio?*" Egidio almost beamed. "You have to stop this! You might actually give me hope!"

"Stay here. I'll return with the money at sunset."

Early in the evening, Ezio returned to an increasingly incredulous Egidio. He placed two heavy leather bags in the senator's hands.

"You came back! You actually came back!"

"You waited."

"I am a desperate man. I cannot believe you would just . . . do this."

"There is a condition."

"I knew it!"

"Listen," Ezio said. "If you survive, and I hope you will, I want you to keep an eye on what's going on politically in this city. And I want you to report everything you find to . . ." He hesitated, then said, "To Madonna Claudia, at the bordello they call the Rosa in Fiore. Especially anything you can pick up on the Borgia." Ezio smiled inwardly. "Do you know the place?"

Egidio coughed. "I . . . I have a friend who sometimes frequents it."

"Good."

"What'll you do with this information? Make the Borgia disappear?"

Ezio grinned. "I'm just . . . recruiting you."

The senator looked at the bags of money. "I hate to give this to them." He fell into a thoughtful silence, then said, "My brother has watched my back because we're family. I hate the *pezzo di merda*, but he is still my brother."

"He works for Cesare."

Egidio pulled himself together. "*Va bene.* They sent me word of the meeting place this afternoon while you were gone. The timing's perfect. They're impatient for their money, so the meeting's for tonight. I sweated blood, you know, when I told their messenger that I'd be sure to have their money ready for them." He paused again. "We should go soon. What will you do? Follow me?"

"It wouldn't look good if you didn't seem to be alone."

Egidio nodded. "Good. Just time for a glass of wine before we set off. Join me?"

"No."

"Well, I certainly need one."

THIRTY-ONE

Ezio followed the senator through another maze of streets, though these, leading closer to the Tiber, were also more familiar to him, and he passed monuments, squares, and fountains familiar to him, as well as building works—for the Borgia spent lavishly on *palazzi* and theaters and even galleries in quest of their own self-aggrandizement. At last Egidio halted in an attractive square formed by large private houses on two sides and a row of expensive shops on a third. On the fourth was a well-tended little park that sloped down toward the river. This was Egidio's destination. He selected a stone bench and took up a position by it in the gathering gloom, looking left and right, but apparently unruffled.

Ezio admired his poise—and it was also useful. Any sign of nervousness might have put the Banker's minions on their guard.

Ezio took up a position by a cedar tree and waited. He didn't have to wait long. Minutes after Egidio's arrival, a tall man dressed in a livery he did not recognize came up to him. A badge on his shoulder showed, on one half of the crest, a red bull in a golden field, and on the other, broad black and gold horizontal stripes. Ezio was none the wiser for this.

"Good evening, Egidio," the newcomer said. "It seems that you are ready to die like a gentleman!"

"That's hardly friendly of you, *Capitano*," replied Egidio. "Seeing that I have the money."

The man raised an eyebrow. "Really? Well, that makes all the difference. The Banker will be most pleased. You came alone, I trust?"

"Do you see anyone else here?"

"Just follow me, *furbacchione*."

They moved off, retracing their steps eastward, and crossed the Tiber. Ezio followed them at a discreet distance, but staying within earshot.

"Is there any news of my brother, *Capitano*?" asked Egidio as they walked.

"I can only tell you that Duke Cesare wishes very much to interview him. As soon as he returns from the Romagna, that is."

"He's all right, I hope."

"If he has nothing to hide, he has nothing to fear."

They continued in silence, and at the Church of Santa

Maria sopra Minerva, turned north, in the direction of the Pantheon.

"What'll happen to my money?" said Egidio. Ezio realized that he was pumping the captain for Ezio's benefit. Clever man.

"*Your* money?" The captain snickered. "I hope all the interest's there."

"It is."

"It had better be."

"Well?"

"The Banker likes to be generous to his friends. He treats them well. He can afford to."

"Treat you well, does he?"

"I like to think so."

"How generous he is," observed Egidio, with such heavy sarcasm that even the captain caught it.

"What did you say?" he asked threateningly, breaking his stride.

"Oh—nothing."

"Come on—we're there."

The great bulk of the Pantheon rose out of the gloom in its cramped piazza. The tall Corinthian portico of the fifteen-hundred-year-old building, constructed as a temple to all the Roman gods but long since consecrated as a church, towered above them. In its shadow three men were waiting. Two were dressed similarly to the captain. The third was in civilian dress, a tall but dry and withered-looking man, whose fine robes sat ill on him. They greeted the captain, and the civilian nodded coldly at Egidio.

"Luigi! Luigi Torcelli!" said Egidio loudly, for Ezio's benefit. "It's good to see you again. Still the Banker's agent, I see. Thought you'd have been promoted by now. Desk job and all that."

"Shut up," said the withered man.

"He's got the money," said the captain.

Torcelli's eyes glittered. "Well, well! That *will* put my master in a good mood. He's having a rather special party this evening, so I'm delivering your payment to him personally, at his palazzo. And I must hurry. Time is money. So give it here!"

Egidio clearly hated to comply, but the two underling guards leveled their halberds at him and he handed the bags over. *"Oof!"* he said. "It's heavy. Glad to get shot of them!"

"Shut up," snapped the agent once again. To the guards he said, "Hold him here until I get back."

With that, he disappeared inside the cavernous, deserted church, closing its mighty, heavy doors firmly behind him.

Ezio needed to follow him, but there was no way he'd get through those doors, and anyway, first he had to get past the guards undetected. But Egidio must have guessed this, for he started up a line of banter with the uniforms, irritating them, but, above all, distracting them.

"Well, why not release me? I've paid up," he said indignantly.

"What if you've sold us short?" replied the captain. "The money has to be counted first. You must see that."

"What? Ten thousand ducats? It'll take all night!"

"It has to be done."

"If Luigi's late, he'll get the stick. I can imagine the kind of man the Banker must be!"

"Shut *up*."

"You people certainly have a very limited vocabulary. Look, think of poor old Torcelli—if he doesn't show up with the money soon, the Banker probably won't let him join in the fun. *Does* he let his lackeys join in the fun?"

The captain cuffed the senator impatiently on the head, and Egidio fell silent, still grinning. He'd seen Ezio slip past and begin to climb the façade of the building in the direction of the dome behind it.

Once on the roof of the circular edifice, which the classical frontage partially concealed, Ezio made his way toward the round opening—the oculus—he knew was at its center. It would be a test of all his climbing skills, but once inside, he would find the agent and put the next phase of the plan, which was rapidly forming in his mind, into operation. The agent was about his size, though far less muscular, and his flowing robes would hide Ezio's physique—if all went well.

The trickiest part would be lowering himself through the aperture at the dome's apex and then finding some way of descending from there. But he'd been to the church before and knew that censers, hanging far below, were suspended by chains from this very roof. If he could reach one of them . . . if it would take his weight . . .

Well, there was no other way. Ezio knew full well that even he couldn't climb, flylike, across the inner curve of a dome, coffered though it was, 140 feet above the cold grey flagstones of the floor.

He hung over the edge of the oculus and peered into the gloom beneath. A pinpoint of light far below showed where the agent was, seated on a bench that ran around the edge of the wall. He'd have the money next to him and be counting it by candlelight. Next, Ezio looked around for the chains. None was within reach, but if he could just . . .

He changed his position and lowered his legs over the edge of the circular opening, gripping it with both hands. It was a huge risk, but the chains looked solid and old, and far heavier than he'd thought. He looked at their fixtures in the ceiling, and as far as he could see they were set fast in the solid stone.

Well, there was nothing for it. Pushing hard with his hands, he threw himself forward and sideways into the void.

For a moment it seemed to him that he was suspended in the air, that the air even held him up, as water does a swimmer. But then he started to fall.

His arms flailed forward and he willed his body toward the nearest chain. And caught it! The links slipped under his gloves and he slid several feet before he was able to get a firm grip, but then he found himself swaying gently in the darkness. He listened. He had heard no sound, and it was too dark for the agent to see the chain swinging, from far below where he sat. Ezio looked toward the light. It still burned steadily and there were no calls of alarm.

Steadily, he lowered himself, down and down, until he was near the floor, perhaps twenty feet above it. He was quite close to the agent and could see his silhouette as he hunched over the money bags, the gold coins glinting in the the candlelight. Ezio could hear the man muttering and the gentle, rhythmic click of an abacus.

Suddenly, though, there was an awful, tearing sound from above. The fixture of the chain in the roof could bear the strain of the extra weight no longer and had ripped loose. Ezio let go of the chain as it went slack in his hands and threw himself forward, toward the candle. As he sailed through the air, he heard a startled "Who's there?" from the agent, and a seemingly unending rattle as 140 feet of chain fell snaking to the floor. Ezio thanked God the church doors were closed: their thickness would deaden any sound from within.

Ezio fell upon the agent with his full weight, knocking the breath out of him. Both men sprawled on the floor, the agent spread-eagled beneath Ezio.

He wriggled free, but Ezio had him by the arm.

"Who are you? Christ protect me!" said the agent, terrified.

"I am sorry, friend," said Ezio, releasing the hidden-blade.

"What? No! No!" the agent jabbered. "Look, take the money! It's yours! It's *yours!*"

Ezio adjusted his grip and drew the man close.

"Get away from me!"

"Requiescat in pace," said Ezio.

Leaving the body on the floor, Ezio quickly stripped the agent of his outer robes and put them on over his own, drawing a scarf over his lower face and tipping the agent's hat down low. The robes were a little snug on him, but it was not a noticeably bad fit. Then he finished transferring the money from the bags into the metal box the agent had brought for the purpose, where much of it was already neatly stacked. To it he added the account book, and, abandoning the abacus and the leather bags, he tucked the heavy box under his arm and made for the door. He had heard enough of the agent's manner of speech to be able to emulate it tolerably, he hoped. Anyway, he'd have to chance it.

As he approached the door, it opened and the captain called through it, "Everything going well in there?"

"Just done."

"Well, hurry up, Luigi, or we'll be late."

Ezio emerged into the portico.

"The count is complete?"

Ezio nodded.

"Va bene," said the captain. Then, turning to the men who held Egidio, he crisply ordered: "Kill him."

"Wait!" said Ezio.

"What?"

"Don't kill him."

The captain looked surprised. "But that's . . . that's hardly usual procedure, is it, Luigi? Besides, do you know what this guy's *done*?"

"I have my orders. From the Banker himself. This man is to be spared."

"May I ask why?"

"Do you question the commands of the Banker?"

The captain shrugged and nodded to the guards, who let go their hold of the senator.

"Lucky you," he said to Egidio, who had the sense not to glance at Ezio before hastening off, without another word.

The captain turned to Ezio. "OK, Luigi. Lead the way."

Ezio hesitated. He was stumped, as he had no idea where to go. He hefted the box. "This is heavy. Have the guards carry it between them."

"Certainly."

He passed the box over but still didn't move.

The guards waited.

"*Ser* Luigi," said the captain after a few moments, "with respect, we must get this to the Banker on time. Of course, I am not questioning your authority . . . but should we not get going?"

What was the point of buying time to think? Ezio knew he'd have to work on a hunch. It was likely that the Banker would live somewhere in the vicinity either of the Castel Sant'Angelo or of the Vatican. But which? He plumped for the Castel Sant'Angelo and started off in a westerly direction. His security detail looked at one another, but followed him. Even so, he sensed their disquiet, and indeed, after they had gone a little way, he heard the two guardsmen whispering:

"Is this some kind of test?"

"Not sure."

"Perhaps we're too early?"

"Maybe we're taking a roundabout route deliberately—for some reason."

Finally the captain tapped him on the shoulder and said: "Luigi—are you all right?"

"Of course I am!"

"Then—again with respect—why are you taking us toward the Tiber?"

"Security reasons."

"Ah—I did wonder. Normally we just go straight there."

"This is a particularly important consignment," said Ezio, hoping it was. But the captain didn't bat an eyelid.

While they had stopped to talk, one of the guards muttered to the other, "Load of rubbish, if you ask me. This kind of arsing about makes me wish I were still a blacksmith."

"I'm starving. I want to go home," muttered the other. "Stuff the security. It's only a couple of blocks north of here."

Hearing this, Ezio breathed a sigh of relief, for his mind had flashed on the location of the palazzo of the other banker, Agostino Chigi, who dealt with the Pope's affairs. That was a little to the northeast of where they were now. It stood to reason that Cesare's banker's place would not be far away—in the financial district. What a fool he'd been not to think of that before. But it had been another busy day.

"We've made enough of a detour," he said decisively. "We'll take a direct route from here."

He set off toward the Palazzo Chigi and was reassured by the sense of relief he got from his companions. After a while, the captain even decided to take the lead. They adopted a brisk pace and very soon reached a district of clean, broad streets. The large and well-lit marble edifice they then headed for had different guards on duty at the foot of its entrance steps and in front of the imposing double front door at their head.

Evidently, Ezio's party was expected.

"Not before time," said the leader of the new guards, who clearly outranked the captain. Turning to Ezio, he added, "Hand over the box to my men, Luigi. I'll see the Banker gets it. But you'd better come, too. There's someone here who wants to talk to you." He looked around. "Where's Senator Troche?"

"Dealt with as ordered," said Ezio quickly, before anyone else could answer.

"Good," replied the guard leader gruffly.

Ezio followed the box, now in the hands of the new guards, up the steps. Behind him, the captain made to follow.

"Not you," said the guard leader.

"We can't go in?"

"Not tonight. You and your men are to join the patrol here. And you might send one of them to fetch another detachment. We're on full security. Orders of Duke Cesare."

"Porco puttana," growled one of Ezio's guards, the former blacksmith, to his mate.

Ezio pricked up his ears. *Cesare? He's here?*—he thought to himself, his mind racing, and he went through the open doors into an entrance hall ablaze with light and, luckily, thronged with people.

The captain and the guard leader were still arguing

about the extra patrol duty when a detachment of papal city police came up to them on the double. They were out of breath, and concern showed on their faces.

"What is it, Sergeant?" the guard leader said to their commander.

"*Perdone, Colonnello*—but we've just been on the beat near the Pantheon—the doors were open—"

"And?"

"And so we investigated. I sent some men in—"

"Spit it out, man!"

"We found *Messer* Torcelli, sir. Murdered."

"Luigi?" The guard leader turned to look up at the front door, through which Ezio had just disappeared. "Nonsense. He arrived here a few minutes ago. With the money. Must be some mistake."

THIRTY-TWO

Ezio, after having quickly and discreetly divested himself of Luigi's outer garments and hidden them behind a column, made his way through the crowd of richly attired guests, many of them wearing masks, keeping a close eye on the guards with the box of money. He drew nearer to them as they approached an attendant in fine livery, to whom they handed it.

"For the Banker," said one of the guards.

The attendant nodded and, carrying the box with ease, turned to make his way toward the back of the hall. Ezio was about to follow when he was joined by three girls, who brushed against him. Their dress was as opulent as that of the other guests, but their décolletage left little to the imagination. With a shock both of surprise and pleasure, Ezio recognized them as courtesans from the Rosa in Fiore. He'd obviously underestimated his sister. No wonder she was so furious with him.

"We'll take over from here, Ezio," said one of the girls.

"It wouldn't do for you to get too close," said a second. "But keep us in sight."

They swanned off after the attendant and caught up with him; one of the girls engaged him in conversation.

"Hi, there," she said.

"Hello," replied the man guardedly. But it wasn't much fun, being at such a party and yet having to be on duty.

"Mind if I walk with you? All these people! Hard to get through them with any speed."

"Sure. I mean—I don't mind if you want to keep me company."

"I've never been here before."

"Where did you come from?"

"Trastevere." She shuddered theatrically. "Have to pass some of the old ruins to get here. They make me nervous."

"You're safe here."

"With you, you mean?"

The attendant smiled. "I could protect you—if the need arose."

"I bet you could." She looked at the box. "My, what a fine chest you have there."

"It isn't mine."

"Oh—but you are holding it in those strong arms of yours. What muscles you must have!"

"Want to touch them?"

"My goodness! But what would I tell the priest in Confession?"

By now they had arrived at an ironbound door flanked by two guards. Ezio watched as one of them knocked. A moment later, the door was opened and a figure in the red robes of a cardinal appeared in the entrance, with an attendant similarly dressed to the first.

"Here is the money you were expecting, Your Eminence," said the first attendant, handing the box to the second.

Ezio drew in his breath, his suspicions confirmed. The Banker was none other than Juan Borgia the Elder, Archbishop of Monreale and Cardinal-Priest of Santa Susanna. The selfsame man he had seen in Cesare's company at Monteriggioni and in the stable yard at the Castel Sant'Angelo!

"Good," said the Banker. Black eyes glittered in a sallow face. He was eyeing the girl, who still stood close to the first attendant. "I'll take her, too, I think."

He grabbed her by the arm and pulled her to him. He looked levelly at the first attendant. "As for you—you are dismissed."

"Onoratissima!" said the girl willingly, snuggling up to the Banker as the attendant tried to control the expression on his face. The second attendant disappeared into the room beyond the door and it closed behind him as the Banker led the girl back into the party.

The first attendant watched them go, then gave a resigned sigh. He started to leave, but then stopped, patting himself down. "My coin purse! What's happened to it?" he muttered, then he looked in the direction the Banker had gone with the girl. They were surrounded by laughing guests, among whom agile servants moved with silver trays loaded with food and drink. "Oh, shit!" he said to himself and made his way back toward the front doors. As he passed through them, the doors closed behind him. Evidently all the guests had arrived. Ezio watched him go and thought, *If they continue to treat people like that, I should have no trouble at all in mustering all the new recruits I need.*

Ezio turned and pushed his way through to a position close to the Banker. At that point a herald appeared on a gallery and a trumpeter blew a short fanfare to make silence for him.

"*Eminenze, Signore, Signori,*" announced the herald. "Our esteemed lord, and guest of honor, the Duke of Valence and Romagna, Captain-General of the Papal Forze Armate, Prince of Andria and Venafro, Count of Dyois, and Lord of Piombino, Camerino, and Urbino— His Grace *Messer* Cesare Borgia—is about to honor us with an address in the great inner chamber!"

"Come on, my dear—you shall sit near me," the Banker said to the courtesan from the Rosa in Fiore, his bony hand snaking around her buttocks. Joining the press of people that now moved obediently through the double doors leading to the inner chamber, Ezio followed. He noticed that the other two girls were not far away, but now they sensibly ignored him. He wondered how many other allies his sister had managed to infiltrate into this gathering. If she succeeded in all he had asked her to do, he would have to do more than eat humble pie, but he also felt proud and reassured.

He took a seat on an aisle near the middle of the assembly. Papal guards lined the edges of the room, and another row stood in front of the dais that had been erected at one end of it. Once everyone had settled, the women fanning themselves, for the room was hot, a familiar figure in black strode onto the dais. He was accompanied, Ezio noticed, by his father; but Rodrigo simply took a seat behind him. To his relief, Lucrezia was nowhere to be seen, though she must have been released from her cell by now.

"Welcome, my friends," said Cesare, smiling a little. "I know we all have a long night ahead of us . . ." And he paused for the laughter and scattered applause . . . "But I will not detain you long . . . My friends, I am honored that the Cardinal-Priest of Santa Susanna has gone to so much trouble to help me celebrate my recent victories . . ."

Applause.

". . . And what better way shall I have to mark them than by joining in the brotherhood of Man? Soon, soon we will gather here again for an even greater gala, for then we shall be celebrating a united Italy. Then, then, my friends, the feasting and the revelry will last not one night, or two, or even five, six, or seven—but we shall spend *forty* days and nights in celebration!"

Ezio saw the Pope stiffen at this, but Rodrigo said nothing, did not interrupt. The speech, as Cesare had promised, was a short one, amounting to a list of the new city-states brought under his sway and a vague outline of his plans for future conquests. When it was over, amid loud shouts of approval and applause, Cesare turned to go, but his way was blocked by Rodrigo, clearly struggling to suppress his fury. Ezio made his way forward to listen to the terse conversation that had started, sotto voce, between father and son. As for the other revelers, they had begun to drift back to the main hall, their minds already on the pleasures of the party ahead.

"We did not agree to conquer all Italy," Rodrigo was saying, his voice full of spite.

"But, *caro padre*, if your brilliant captain-general says we can do it, why not rejoice, and let it happen?"

"You risk ruining everything! You risk upsetting the delicate balance of power we have worked so hard to maintain!"

Cesare's lip curled. "I appreciate all that you have done for me, of course, *caro padre*. But do not forget that I control the army now, and that means that I am the one who makes the decisions." He paused to let his words sink in. "Don't look so glum! Enjoy yourself!"

With that, Cesare walked off the dais and through a curtained door to one side. Rodrigo watched him go for a moment, then, muttering to himself, followed.

Strut as much as you like for now, Cesare, thought Ezio. *But I'll pluck you down. In the meantime, your Banker must pay the price for his involvement with you.*

Putting on the air of any other party guest, he sauntered in the direction the others had gone. During the speech, the main hall had been transformed—beds and couches were placed around it under heavy canopies, and the floor had been covered with damask cushions and thick Persian rugs. Servants still passed among the guests, providing wine, but the guests had now become more interested in one another. All over the room, men and women were shedding their clothes, in pairs, threesomes, foursomes, and more. The smell of sweat rose with the heat.

Several women and not a few men, some not yet engaged in the fun and games, gave Ezio the eye, but few paid any serious attention to him as he made his way, using the columns of the room as cover, toward the Banker, who had now shed his biretta, his magnificent *ferraiolo*, and his cassock to reveal a spindly figure in a white cotton shirt and woolen long johns. He and the courtesan were half sitting, half lying on a canopied couch set in an alcove, more or less hidden from the view of the rest of the guests. Ezio drew near.

"And are you having a pleasant evening, my dear?" the Banker was saying, his gnarled hands fiddling clumsily with the stays of her dress.

"Yes, *Eminenza*. Indeed I am. There is so much to look at!"

"Oh, good. I spared no expense, you know." His lips slobbered over her neck. He bit and sucked, moving her hand lower.

"I can tell," she replied, her eyes meeting Ezio's over the Banker's shoulder and warning him to stay back—for the moment.

"Yes, sweetheart—the finer things in life make power so rewarding. If I see an apple growing on a tree, I simply pluck it. No one can stop me."

"Well," said the girl, "I suppose is does depend a bit on whose tree it is."

The Banker cackled. "You don't seem to understand, my dear—*all* the trees are owned—by me!"

"Not mine, dearie!"

The Banker drew back a little, and when he spoke again, frost had crept into his voice. "On the contrary, *tesora*; I saw you steal my attendant's purse. I believe I've earned a free ride for your penance. In fact, I'm taking a free ride that'll last all night long!"

"Free?" Ezio hoped the girl wasn't pushing her luck. He glanced around the room. The few guards were stationed around its perimeter at intervals of perhaps fifteen feet. None was near. The Banker, on his own ground, was clearly sure of himself. Maybe too sure.

"That's what I said," replied the Banker, the ghost of menace in his tone. Then a new thought struck him. "Do you have a sister, by any chance?"

"No—but I have a daughter."

The Banker considered this. "Three hundred ducats?"

"Seven."

"You drive a hard bargain, but—done! A pleasure doing business with you."

THIRTY-THREE

The evening wore on. Ezio listened to the voices around him—"Do it again!" "No, no—you're hurting me!" "No, you can't do that. I won't allow it!"—and all the sounds of pain and pleasure—the pain real, the pleasure simulated.

The Banker was not running out of steam, unfortunately, and lost patience with his fumbling and started to tear the girl's dress off her. She still implored Ezio with her eyes to hold his ground. "I can handle this!" she seemed to be saying to him.

He looked around the room again. Some of the servants and most of the guards had been inveigled by the guests to join in the fun. He noticed people wielding wooden and ivory dildos and little black whips.

Soon . . .

"Come here, my dear," the Banker was saying, pushing the girl back down onto the couch and managing to straddle her, pushing himself into her. Then his hands closed around her neck and he started to strangle her. Choking, she struggled, then fainted.

"Oh, yes! That's nice!" he gasped, the veins in his neck bulging. His fingers tightened around the girl's neck. "This should increase your pleasure. It certainly increases mine!" A minute later he had finished and lay heavily on her body, slipping on their sweat, catching his breath.

He had not killed the girl. Ezio could see the rise and fall of her chest.

The Banker clawed his way to his feet, leaving her prostrate form half on and half off the couch.

He snapped out an order to a pair of servants, still on duty nearby: "Get rid of her!"

As the Banker moved toward the main orgy, Ezio and the servants watched him go. As soon as he was at a safe distance, and otherwise occupied, the servants lifted the girl gently onto the couch, placed a carafe of water near her, and covered her with a fur rug. One of them noticed Ezio. Ezio put a finger to his lips. The man smiled and nodded. At least there was some good in this fetid hellhole.

Ezio shadowed the Banker as he pulled up his long johns and moved from group to group, muttering his appreciation like a connoisseur in an art gallery.

"Oh, *bellissima*," he would say from time to time,

stopping to watch. Then he made for the ironbound door he'd originally appeared from and knocked on it. It was opened from within by the second attendant, who'd almost certainly been spending all that time verifying the new accounts.

Ezio didn't give them a chance to close the door behind them. He leapt forward and his impetus pushed both men back inside. Ezio closed the door and faced them. The attendant, a little man, now in his shirt-sleeves, burbled and fell to his knees, a dark stain flowering between his legs. Then he fainted. The Banker drew himself up.

"You!" he said. "*Assassino!* But not for much longer." His arm snaked out to a bellpull, but Ezio was quicker. The hidden-blade sprang out and slashed through the fingers of the hand the Banker was extending. The Banker snatched his maimed hand back as three fingers scattered onto the carpet. "Stay back!" he screamed. "Kill me and it'll do no good! Cesare will never let you live! But—"

"Yes?"

The man's face became sly. "If you spare me . . ."

Ezio smiled. The Banker understood. He nursed his ruined hand.

"Well," he said, though tears of pain and rage were starting in his eyes, "at least I have lived. The things I have seen, felt, tasted. I regret none of them. I do not regret a moment of my life."

"You have played with the trinkets power brings. A man of real strength would be contemptuous of such things."

"I gave the people what they wanted!"

"You delude yourself."

"Spare me!"

"Your own debt is due, *Eminenza*. Unearned pleasure only consumes itself."

The Banker fell to his knees, mumbling half-remembered prayers.

Ezio raised the hidden-blade.

"Requiescat in pace," he said.

He left the door open when he departed. The orgy had declined into sleepy, smelly groping. One or two of the guests, supported by servants, were vomiting. Another pair of servants was carrying out a corpse—it had all evidently been too much for someone's heart. There was no one left on guard.

"We are ready," said a voice at his elbow. He turned to see Claudia. Around her, around the room, a dozen girls detached and disentangled themselves and stood. Among them, dressed again and looking shaken but otherwise determined, was the girl the Banker had molested so vilely. The servants who had helped her stood by her. More recruits.

"Get out of here," said Claudia. "We'll recover the money. With interest."

"Can you—?"

"Just—just this once, trust me, Ezio."

THIRTY-FOUR

Though his mind remained full of misgivings about leaving his sister in charge, Ezio admitted to himself that he had, after all, asked her to do this job for him. A lot hung on it, but he had better do as she'd said, and trust her.

It was cold in the small hours of the new day, and he pulled his hood up as he slipped past the dozing guards posted outside the Banker's palazzo, where the torches had burned low and the house itself, no longer so brilliantly lit from within, seemed grey, old, and tired. He toyed with the idea of going after Rodrigo, whom he hadn't seen since his furious departure from the dais after Cesare's speech—and Cesare himself had clearly not chosen to stay at the party—but he put the notion to one side. He wasn't going to storm the Vatican single-handed, and he was tired.

He returned to Tiber Island to clean up and refresh himself, but he didn't linger over it. He had to find out, as soon as possible, how Claudia had fared. Only then would he be able truly to relax.

The sun was appearing over the horizon, turning the rooftops of Rome gold as he skimmed over them in the direction of the Rosa in Fiore. From his vantage point, he saw a number of Borgia patrols running about the city, in a state of high excitement and agitation, but the brothel was well hidden, and its location was a respected secret among its clients—they certainly wouldn't want to be answerable to Cesare if he got wind of it—so Ezio was not surprised to find no mulberry-and-yellow uniforms in its vicinity. He dropped down to a street not far away and walked—trying not to hurry—toward the bordello.

As he approached, he tensed. Outside, there were signs of a struggle, and the pavement was stained with blood. Drawing his sword, and with a pounding heart, he made his way through the door, which he found ajar.

The furniture in the reception room had been over-turned and the place was a mess. Broken vases lay on the floor, and the pictures on the walls—tasteful illustrations of the juicier episodes in Boccaccio—were askew. But that was not all. The bodies of three dead Borgia guards lay in the entrance, and there was blood everywhere. He was making his way forward when one of the courtesans—the selfsame girl who had suffered so much at the hands of the Banker—came to greet him. Her dress and hands were covered in blood, but her eyes were shining.

"Oh, Ezio—! Thank God you're here!"

"What's happened?" His thoughts flew to his mother and sister.

"We got away all right—but the Borgia guards must have followed us all the way back here—"

"What's *happened*?!"

"They tried to trap us inside—to ambush us."

"Where are Claudia and Maria?"

The girl was crying now. "Follow me—"

She preceded him in the direction of the inner courtyard of the Rosa in Fiore. Ezio followed, still in great trepidation, but he noticed that the girl was unarmed and, despite her distress, led the way without fear. What kind of massacre—? Had the guards killed everyone except her—and how had she escaped?—and left, taking the money with them?

The girl pushed open the door leading to the courtyard. An appalling sight greeted his eyes—but it was not the one he had expected.

There were dead Borgia guards everywhere, and those that were not dead were badly wounded or dying. In their midst, by the fountain, stood Claudia, her dress drenched in blood, with a rondel dagger in one hand and a stiletto in the other. Most of the girls whom Ezio had seen at the Banker's palazzo stood near her, similarly armed. To one side, protected by three of the girls, was Maria, and behind her, stacked against the wall, was not one, but seven metal boxes of the same type that Ezio had delivered to the Banker.

Claudia was still on guard, as were the other women, expecting another wave of the attack.

"Ezio!" she said.

"Yes," he replied, but he was looking at the carnage.

"How did you come here?"

"Over the rooftops, from Tiber Island."

"Did you see any more of them?"

"Plenty, but they were running around in circles. None near here."

His sister relaxed slightly. "Good. Then we must get the street outside cleaned up and the door closed. Then we must do something about this mess."

"Did you—lose anyone?"

"Two—Lucia and Agnella. We have already laid them on their beds. They died bravely."

She wasn't even trembling.

"Are you all right?" asked Ezio hesitantly.

"Perfectly," she replied, composed. "We'll need help disposing of this lot. Can you drum up some of your recruits to help? We left our new friends the servants behind at the palazzo, so that they can put anybody who asks off the scent."

"Did any of this patrol escape?"

Claudia looked grim. She hadn't yet lowered either of her weapons. "Not one. No news will get back to Cesare."

Ezio was silent for a moment. Nothing could be heard but the splashing of the fountain and the song of the morning birds.

"How long ago?"

She half smiled. "You just missed the party."

He smiled back. "No need for me. My sister knows how to wield a knife."

"And I'm ready to do it again."

"You speak like a true Auditore. Forgive me."

"You needed to test me."

"I wanted to protect you."

"As you see, I can take care of myself."

"I do see."

Claudia dropped her daggers. She made a gesture toward the treasure chests. "Enough interest for you?"

"I see that you can totally outplay me, and I am lost in admiration."

"Good!"

Then they did what they'd really been wanting to do for the last five minutes: They flung themselves into each other's arms.

"Excellent," said Maria, joining them. "It's good to see you've both come to your senses—at last!"

THIRTY-FIVE

"Ezio!"

Ezio hadn't expected to hear the familiar voice again so soon. A pessimistic part of him had not expected to hear it again at all. Nevertheless, he'd been pleased to get the note left for him at Tiber Island bidding him to this rendezvous, which he was keeping on his way to the Sleeping Fox, the headquarters of La Volpe's Thieves' Guild in Rome.

He looked around, but there was no one to be seen. The streets were empty, even of Borgia uniforms, for he was already in a district reclaimed by La Volpe's men.

"Leonardo?"

"Over here!" The voice came from a darkened doorway.

Ezio walked across to it and Leonardo dragged him into the shadows.

"Were you followed?"

"No."

"Thank God. I've been sweating blood."

"Were you?"

"No—my friend *Messer* Salai watches my back. I'd trust him with my life."

"Your friend?"

"We're very close."

"Be careful, Leo—you have a soft heart where young men are concerned and that could be a chink in your armor."

"I may be softhearted but I'm not a fool. Now, come on."

Leonardo pulled Ezio out of the doorway after having first looked up and down the street. A few yards to the right, he ducked down an alleyway, which snaked between windowless buildings and featureless walls for a furlong or so, when it became part of a crossroads with three other alleys. Leonardo took the one on the left, and after another few yards arrived at a low, narrow door, painted dark green. This he unlocked. Both men had to squeeze through the entrance, but once inside, Ezio found himself in a large, vaulted hall. Natural light bathed the place through windows placed high in the walls, and Ezio's eyes scanned the usual trestle tables, cluttered and crowded with all manner of stuff, the drawings pinned to the walls, the easels, the animal skeletons, the dusty books, the maps—rare and precious, like all maps—the Assassins' own collection at Monteriggioni had been invaluable, but the Borgia in their ignorance had destroyed the map-room there with cannonades, and so had no use of them themselves— the pencils, pens, brushes, paints, piles of papers . . . in short, the typical and familiar, and somehow comforting, clutter of Leonardo's studios wherever Ezio had encountered them.

"This is my own place," said Leonardo proudly. "As far as possible from my official workshop near Castel Sant'Angelo. No one comes here but me. And Salai, of course."

"Don't they keep tabs on you?"

"They did for a while, but I'm good at ingratiation when it suits me and they swallowed the act whole. I rent this place from the Cardinal of San Pietro in Vincoli. He knows how to keep a secret and he's no friend of the Borgia—"

"And there's no harm in taking out a little insurance for the future?"

"Ezio, my friend, nothing—but nothing—gets past you! Now, to business. I don't know if there's anything I can offer you—there must be a bottle of wine somewhere."

"Leave it—don't worry. Just tell me why you sent for me."

Leonardo went over to one of the trestle tables on the right-hand side of the hall and rummaged underneath it. He produced a long, leather-bound, wooden case, which he placed on the tabletop.

"Here we are!" With a flourish, he opened it.

The case was lined in purple velvet—"Salai's idea, bless him!" explained Leonardo—and contained perfect copies of Ezio's lost Codex weapons: there was the bracer for protecting the left forearm, the little retractable pistol, the double-bladed dagger, and the poison-blade.

"The bracer was the biggest problem," continued Leonardo. "Very hard to get a match for that extraordinary metal. But from what you told me of the accident in which you lost the originals, it might have survived. If you could get it back . . . ?"

"If it did survive, it'll be buried under several tons of rubble," said Ezio. "It might as well be at the bottom of the sea." He slipped the bracer on. It felt a little heavier than the first, but it looked as if it would serve—and very well. "I don't know how to thank you," he said.

"That's easy," replied Leonardo. "With money! But these are not all." He delved under the table again and brought out another case, larger than the first. "These are new and may come in handy from time to time."

He opened the lid to reveal a lightweight crossbow with a set of bolts; a set of darts; and a mailed leather glove.

"The darts are poisoned," said Leonardo, "so don't ever touch the points with your bare hands. If you can retrieve them from your—ahem—target, you'll find they are reusable up to a dozen times."

"And the glove?"

Leonardo smiled. "I'm rather proud of that. It'll enable you to climb on any surface with ease. Almost as good as becoming a gecko!" He paused, troubled. "We haven't actually tested it on glass, but I doubt if you'll ever encounter a surface *that* smooth." He paused. "The crossbow's just a crossbow, but it's very compact and light. What makes it special is that it's just as powerful as those heavy things that are now being superseded by my wheel locks—forgive me—and of course the advantage it has over a gun is that it's more or less silent."

"I can't carry these with me now."

Leonardo shrugged. "No problem. We'll deliver them. To Tiber Island?"

Ezio considered. "No. There's a bordello called the Rosa in Fiore. It's in the *rione* Montium et Biberatice, near the old forum with the column."

"We'll find it."

"Leave them there with my sister, Claudia. May I?" Ezio took a sheet of paper and scribbled something on it. "Give this to her. I've sketched its location, as it's hard to find. I'll get the money to you as soon as possible."

"Five thousand ducats."

"*How* much?"

"Not cheap, these things . . ."

Ezio pursed his lips. "Fine." He took back the note and wrote an additional line. "We have recently come into some new and . . . unexpected funds. My sister will pay you. And listen, Leo—I have to trust you. Not a word to anyone else."

"Even Salai?"

"Salai, if you have to. But if the brothel's location is discovered by the Borgia, I will kill Salai, and I will kill you, my friend."

Leonardo smiled. "I know these are very troubled times, my dear—but when—when—have I *ever* let you down?"

Content with that, Ezio took leave of his friend and continued on his way to the Sleeping Fox. He was running late, but the meeting with Leonardo had been more than worth it.

He went through the courtyard, pleased to see that business still seemed to be booming, and was about to announce himself to the thieves standing guard on either side of the door marked UFFIZI when La Volpe himself appeared, apparently out of nowhere—but he was good at that.

"*Buon giorno*, Ezio!"

"*Ciao*, Gilberto!"

"I'm glad you've come. What is it you want?"

"Let's sit somewhere quiet."

"In the *uffizi*?"

"Let's stay here. What I have to say is for your ears alone."

"That's good, for I have something to say to you, too, which should stay between us—for now."

They settled down at a table in an otherwise empty bar inside the inn, away from the gamblers and drinkers.

"It's time to pay a visit to Lucrezia's lover, Pietro," said Ezio.

"Good. I've already got men out looking for him."

"*Molto bene*; but a working actor shouldn't be that hard to find, and this one's famous."

La Volpe shook his head. "He's famous enough to have minders of his own. And we think he may have gone to ground because he's frightened of Cesare."

"That makes sense. Well, do your best. Now, what is it you have on your mind?"

La Volpe wrestled with himself for a moment, then said, "It's delicate . . . Ezio, if I may . . ."

"What is it?"

"Someone has warned Rodrigo to stay away from the Castel Sant'Angelo."

"And you think that someone is . . . Machiavelli?"

La Volpe was silent.

"Do you have proof?" Ezio pressed him.

"No, but—"

"I know that Machiavelli is eating you up, but listen, Gilberto, we must not be split apart by mere suspicion."

At that moment, the door banged open and they were interrupted by the arrival of a wounded thief, who staggered into the room. "Bad news!" he cried. "The Borgia know the whereabouts of our spies!"

"Who told them?" thundered La Volpe, rising.

"Maestro Machiavelli was asking about our search for the actor, Pietro, earlier today."

La Volpe's hand tightened into a fist. "Ezio?" he said quietly.

"They've got four of our men under guard," said the thief. "I was lucky to get away!"

"Where?"

"Not far from here—near Santa Maria del Orto."

"Come on!" La Volpe yelled to Ezio.

Within minutes, La Volpe's men had readied two horses, and the two Assassins rode out of the stables of the Sleeping Fox at breakneck speed.

"I still do not believe Machiavelli has turned traitor," insisted Ezio as they rode.

"He went quiet for a bit, to allay our doubts," La Volpe hurled back. "But look at the facts: first the attack on Monteriggioni, then the business at the Castel Sant'Angelo, and now this! He is behind it all!"

"Just ride! Ride like the devil! We may still be in time to save them!"

They galloped helter-skelter through the narrow streets, reining in and thrusting forward as they strove to avoid injuring people and smashing down market booths in their headlong career. Citizens and chickens alike scattered in their path, but when Borgia guards tried to block their way, halberds raised, they simply rode them down.

They reached the place the wounded thief had indicated within seven minutes and saw the mulberry-and-yellow uniforms preparing to pack the four captured thieves onto a covered wagon, hitting them with the pommels of their swords and taunting them as they did so. In a moment, Ezio and La Volpe were upon them like avenging Furies. Swords drawn, they steered their mounts skillfully among the guards, cutting them off from their prisoners and dispersing them about the square in front of the church. Grasping his sword firmly in his right hand, La Volpe let go of his reins with his left, and, holding on with his thighs, wheeled toward the wagon, seized the driver's whip from him, and struck hard at the flanks of the horses in the shafts. They reared and neighed and then stampeded off, as the wagoner strove in vain to control them. Hurling the whip aside and almost falling, La Volpe grabbed his reins again and swung his horse around to join Ezio, who was surrounded by five guards stabbing at his horse's chest and quarters with their halberds. Flailing them with his sword, La Volpe gave Ezio enough time to break free of the trap and slice open the midriff of the closest guard. Turning the horse in a tight circle, he swiped with his sword again and neatly severed the head from the body of another. Meanwhile, La Volpe had dispatched the last of the guards with any fight left in them—the rest either lay wounded or had fled.

"Run, you swine," La Volpe yelled at his men. "Back to base! Now! We'll join you there!"

The four thieves pulled themselves together and darted down the main street out of the square, ducking and diving through the small crowd that had gathered to watch the fight. Ezio and La Volpe rode after them, shepherding them, making sure they all got back in one piece.

They made their way into the Sleeping Fox by a secret side entrance and had soon all assembled in the bar, now with a Closed sign on its door. La Volpe ordered beer for his men but did not wait for it to arrive before he started his interrogation.

"What were you able to find out?"

"Boss, there's a plan to kill the actor this evening. Cesare is sending his 'butcher' to see to it."

"Who's that?" asked Ezio.

"You've seen him," replied La Volpe. "Micheletto Corella. No one could ever forget a face like that."

Indeed, Ezio's inner eye flashed on the man he'd seen at Cesare's right hand at Monteriggioni, and again in the stables of the Castel Sant'Angelo. A cruel, battered face, which looked much older than its owner's age warranted, with hideous scars near his mouth that gave him the appearance of wearing a permanent, sardonic grin. Micheletto Corella. Originally *Miguel de* Corella.

Corella—did that region of Navarre, which produced such good wine, really also produce this torturer and murderer?

"Can kill a person one hundred and fifty different ways," La Volpe was saying. "But his preferred method is strangulation." He paused. "He's certainly the most accomplished murderer in Rome. No one escapes him."

"Let's hope tonight will be the first time," said Ezio.

"Where this evening? Do you know?" La Volpe was asking the thieves.

"Pietro's performing in a religious play this evening. He's been rehearsing at a secret location."

"He must be scared. And?"

"He's playing Christ." One of the other thieves snickered at this. La Volpe glared. "He's to be suspended from a cross," continued the man who'd been talking. "Micheletto will come at him with a spear—pierce his side—only it won't be make-believe."

"Do you know where Pietro is?"

The thief shook his head. "I cannot tell you that. We

couldn't find out. But we do know that Micheletto will wait at the old baths of the emperor Trajan."

"The Terme di Traiano?"

"Yes. We think the plan is this: Micheletto intends to disguise his men in costumes, and he'll make the killing look like an accident."

"But where's the performance taking place?"

"We don't know. But it can't be far from where Micheletto will be waiting for his men to gather."

"I'll go there and shadow him," Ezio decided. "He'll lead me to Lucrezia's lover."

"Anything else?" La Volpe asked his men.

They shook their heads. A serving-man came in then, bringing a tray with beer, bread, and salami, and the thieves fell on it gratefully. La Volpe drew Ezio to one side.

"Ezio, I am sorry, but I am convinced that Machiavelli has betrayed us." He held up a hand. "Whatever you say will not convince me otherwise. I know we would both wish to deny it, but the truth is now clear. In my opinion, we should do . . . what needs to be done." He paused. "And if you don't, I will."

"I see."

"And there's another thing, Ezio. God knows I'm loyal, but I also have the welfare of my men to consider. Until this thing is settled, I'm not putting them at risk—at *unnecessary* risk—anymore."

"You have your priorities, Gilberto, and I have mine."

Ezio left, to prepare himself for his evening's work. Borrowing a horse from La Volpe, he made his way straight to the Rosa in Fiore. Claudia greeted him.

"You've had a delivery," she said.

"Already?"

"Two men, both very dapper. One quite young and a bit shifty looking, but handsome in a pretty sort of way. The other, maybe fifty—a few years older than you, anyway. Of course I remembered him—your old friend Leonardo—but he was quite formal. Gave me this note. And I paid him."

"That was quick."

Claudia smiled. "He said he thought you might appreciate an *express* delivery."

Ezio smiled back. It would be good to encounter tonight's bunch—and he imagined Micheletto's men would be trained to a very high standard of villainy— armed with a few of his old friends, the Codex weapons. But he'd need backup, too—from La Volpe's attitude, he knew he couldn't depend on the loan of a contingent of thieves.

His thoughts turned to his own militia of new recruits. It was time to put a few of them through their paces.

THIRTY-SIX

Unknown to Ezio, *Messer* Corella had one other small piece of business to conclude for his boss, before the main event of the evening. But it was still quite early.

He stood silently on a deserted dock by the Tiber. A few barges and two ships rode at anchor, gently moving with the river's flow. The ships' grubby furled sails rippled slightly in the wind. Several guards wearing Cesare's insignia were coming toward them, half hauling, half carrying a blindfolded man between them. At their head was Cesare himself.

Micheletto recognized the man, without surprise, as Francesco Troche.

"Please," Francesco was whimpering, "I have done nothing wrong."

"Franceso, my dear friend," said Cesare, "the facts are plain: Your told your brother about my plans in the Romagna, and he contacted the Venetian ambassador. Not can absterge the blame for that from you."

"It was an accident. I am still your servant and your ally."

"Are you demanding that I discount your actions and rely on mere friendship?"

"I am asking . . . not demanding."

"My dear Francesco, in order to unite Italy I must have every institution under my control. You know what higher organization we serve—the Order of Templars, of which I am now head."

"I thought—your father . . ."

"And if the Church does not fall into line," continued Cesare firmly, "I will eliminate it entirely."

"But you know that I really work for you, not the Pope."

"Ah, but do I, Troche? There's only one way I can be unconditionally sure of that now."

"Surely you can't intend to kill me. Your most loyal friend?"

Cesare smiled. "Of course not."

He snapped his fingers. Noiselessly, Micheletto approached from behind Francesco's back.

"You are—you are letting me go?" Relief flooded into Troche's voice. "Thank you, Cesare. Thank you from my heart. You will not regret—"

But his words were cut short as Micheletto, a thin cord twisted between his hands, leaned forward and bound it tightly around Troche's neck. Cesare watched for a moment, but even before Francesco was fully killed, he turned to the captain of the guard and said, "Have you got the costumes for the play ready?"

"Yes, sir!"

"Then give them to Micheletto—when he's finished."

"Yes, sir!"

"Lucrezia is mine, and mine alone. I didn't think she was that important to me, but when I got that message in Urbino, from one of her own men, that that wretched toad of an actor had been pawing her, slobbering over her, I came back immediately! Can you understand a passion like that, Captain?"

"Yes, sir!"

"You're a fool. Have you done, Micheletto?"

"*Messere*, the man is dead."

"Then weigh him down with stones and dump him in the Tiber."

"I obey, Cesare."

The captain had given orders to his men, and four of them had gone to fetch two large wicker hampers, which they now carried between them.

"Here are the costumes for your men. Make doubly sure the work is done correctly."

"Indeed, *Messere*."

Cesare stalked off, leaving his subordinate to make the arrangements. Motioning the guards to follow him, Micheletto led the way toward the Baths of Trajan.

Ezio and his band of recruits were already there, hidden in the shelter of a ruined portico. He had noticed

a number of men in black already foregathered, and
he watched them closely as Micheletto appeared. The
guards put the costume skips down and Micheletto
motioned them to depart. The shadows were deep, and
Ezio nodded to his own men to prepare themselves. He
had strapped the bracer to his left forearm and the poison-
blade to his right.

Micheletto's men formed a line, and as each man came
up to his leader, he was handed a costume—uniforms
copying those worn by Roman legionaries at the time
of Christ. Ezio noticed that Micheletto himself wore the
costume of a centurion.

As each man stepped away to don his costume, Ezio
stood ready. Silently, he extended the concealed poison-
blade that Leonardo had just recrafted for him. The
unsuspecting thugs went down without a whisper. Then
his own recruits put on the theatrical clothes and pulled
Micheletto's henchmen's bodies out of sight.

Absorbed in his work, Micheletto was unaware, once
it was complete, that the men he now commanded were
not his own. He led them, with Ezio close behind, in the
direction of the Colosseum.

A stage had been erected in the ruins of the old Roman
amphitheater where, since the time of the emperor Titus,
gladiators had fought each other to the death, *bestiarii*
had dispatched wild animals in the tens of thousands,
and Christians had been thrown to the lions. It was a
gloomy place, but the gloom was dispersed somewhat by
the hundreds of flickering torches that illuminated the
stage, and the audience, ranged on benches on a wooden

grandstand, were absorbed in watching a play on the subject of Christ's Passion.

"I seek Pietro Benintendi," Micheletto said to the doorkeeper, showing him a warrant.

"He acts onstage, *signore*," replied the doorkeeper. "But one of my men will take you to where you may wait for him."

Micheletto turned to his companions. "Don't forget," he told them. "I will be wearing this black cloak with the white star on its shoulder. Cover my back, and wait for your cue, which will be Pontius Pilate's order to the Centurion to strike."

I must get to Pietro before he does, thought Ezio, tagging along at the back of the group as the men followed their leader into the Colosseum.

Onstage, three crosses had been erected. He watched as his recruits disposed themselves according to Micheletto's orders and saw Micheletto himself take his place in the wings.

The play was reaching its climax:

"My God, my God, why hast Thou forsaken me?" cried Pietro from the cross.

"Hark," said one of the actors playing the Pharisees. "How he crieth upon Elijah to deliver him!"

One, dressed as a Roman legionary, dipped a sponge in vinegar and placed it on the tip of his spear. "Wait and see whether Elijah dare come here or not."

"My thirst is great; my thirst is great," cried Pietro.

The soldier raised the sponge to Pietro's lips.

"Yea, thou shalt drink no more," said another Pharisee.

Pietro raised his head. "Mighty God in Majesty," he declaimed. "To work Thy Will I shall never cease. My spirit I betake to Thee; receive it, O Lord, into Thy hands." Pietro gave a great sigh. *"Consummatum est!"*

His head dropped. Christ had "died."

On his cue, Micheletto then strode onto the stage. His centurion's uniform glittered under the thrown-back black cloak. Ezio, watching, wondered what had become of the actor originally playing the Centurion, but imagined that he'd met a fate similar to that of most of Micheletto's victims.

"Lords, I say unto you," Micheletto recited boldly, "this was indeed the Son of God the Father Almighty. I know it must be so. I know by the manner of His cry that He has fulfilled the prophecy, and the godhead is revealed in Him!"

"Centurion," said the actor playing Caiaphas, "as God gives me speed, thy folly is great indeed. Thou dost not understand! When thou seest his heart bleed, then we shall see what thou wilt say. Longinus! Take this spear into thy hand."

Caiaphas handed a wooden spear to the actor playing the Roman legionary Longinus, a large man with flowing locks, clearly a favorite of the audience and doubtless, thought Ezio, a bitter rival of Pietro's.

"Take this spear and take good heed," added one of the Pharisees for good measure. "Thou must pierce the side of Jesus Nazarenus that we shall know he is truly dead."

"I will do as thou biddest me," declaimed Longinus,

out front. "But on your heads be it. Whatever the conse-
quence, I wash my hands of it."

He then made a great show of stabbing Jesus' side
with the prop spear, and, as the blood and water spilled
forth from a hidden sac concealed in Pietro's loincloth,
so Longinus began his big speech. Ezio could see the
beady glint in the "dead" Jesus' eyes as Pietro watched
him jealously.

"High King of Heaven, I see Thee here. Let water be
thrown onto my hands and onto my spear, and let my
eyes be bathed, too, that I may see Thee more clearly!"
He made a dramatic pause. "Alas, alack, and woe is me!
What is this deed that I have done? I think that I have
slain a man, sooth to say; but what manner of man I
know not. Lord God in Heaven, I cry Thee mercy—for
it was my body which guided my hand, not my soul."
Allowing himself another pause for a round of applause,
he plowed on: "Lord Jesus, much have I heard spoken of
Thee—that Thou hast healed, through Thy pity, both the
sick and the blind. And let Thy Name be praised!—Thou
hast healed me this day of my own blindness—my blindness of spirit. Henceforward, Lord, Thy follower will I
be. And in three days Thou shalt rise again to rule and
judge us all!"

The actor who was playing Joseph of Arimathea, the
wealthy Jewish leader who donated his own tomb—
which had already been built—for the housing of Christ's
body, then spoke: "Ah, Lord God, what heart had Thou
to allow them to slay this man that I see here dead, and
hanging from a cross—a man who ne'er did aught amiss?

For surely, God's own Son is He. Therefore, in the tomb that is made for me, therein shall His body buried be—for He is King of Bliss!"

Nicodemus, Joseph's colleague in the Sanhedrin and a fellow sympathizer, added his voice. "*Ser* Joseph, I say surely, this is God's Son Almighty. Let us request His body of Pontius Pilate, and nobly buried He shall be. And I will help thee to take Him down devotedly."

Joseph then turned to the actor playing Pilate and spoke again. "*Ser* Pilate, I ask of thee a special boon to grant me as thou may. This prophet that is dead today—allow me of His body custody!"

During this, Ezio had slipped backstage. Micheletto has taken up a position very near the central cross. He rummaged swiftly through a costume skip and found a rabbinical robe, which he hurriedly put on. He'd have to get onstage himself. Entering from backstage left, he managed to slip close to, and behind, Micheletto, without anyone's noticing or the action skipping a beat.

"Joseph, if indeed Jesus Nazarenus is dead, as the Centurion must confirm, I will not deny you custody." Turning to Micheletto, Pilate spoke again. "Centurion! Is Jesus dead?"

"Ay, *Ser* Governor," said Micheletto flatly, and Ezio noticed him draw a stiletto from under his cloak. Ezio had replaced his poison-blade, now exhausted of venom, with his trusty hidden-blade, and with it he now pierced Micheletto's side, holding him upright and maneuvering him offstage, in the direction he had come. Once backstage, he laid the man down.

Micheletto fixed him with a glittering look. "Hah!" he said. "You cannot save Pietro. The vinegar on the sponge was poisoned. As I promised Cesare, I made doubly sure." He fought for breath. "You had better finish me."

"I did not come here to kill you—you helped your master rise and you will fall with him—you don't need me—you are the agent of your own destruction! If you live, well, a dog always returns to its master, and you will lead me to my real quarry."

Ezio had no time for more. He had to save Pietro!

As he rushed back onstage, he saw a scene of chaos. Pietro was writhing on the cross and vomiting. He'd turned the color of a peeled almond. The audience was in uproar.

"What's going on? What's happening?" cried Longinus, as the other actors scattered.

"Cut him down!" Ezio yelled to his recruits. Some threw keenly aimed daggers to slice through the ropes that bound Pietro to the cross, while others stood ready to catch him. Yet others were fighting back the Borgia guards who had appeared from nowhere and were now storming the stage.

"This wasn't in the script!" gurgled Pietro as he fell into the arms of the recruits.

"Will he die?" asked Longinus hopefully. One rival less is always good news in a tough profession.

"Hold off the guards!" shouted Ezio, leading the recruits off the stage and carrying Pietro in his arms across a shallow pool of water in the middle of the Colosseum, disturbing dozens of drinking pigeons, which flew up and away in alarm. The very last glimmer from the setting sun bathed Ezio and Pietro in a dull red light.

Ezio had trained his recruits well, and those bringing up the rear guard successfully fought off the pursuing Borgia guards as the rest made their way out of the Colosseum and into the network of streets to the north of it. Ezio led the way to the house of a doctor of his acquaintance. He hammered on the door and, having been granted reluctant admission, had Pietro laid on a table covered with a palliasse in the doctor's consulting room, from whose beams a baffling number of different dried herbs hung in organized bunches, giving the room a pungent smell. On shelves, unidentifiable or unmentionable objects and creatures and parts of creatures floated in glass bottles filled with cloudy liquid.

Ezio ordered his men outside, to keep watch. He wondered what any passersby might think if they saw a bunch of Roman soldiers. They'd probably think they were seeing ghosts, and run a mile. He himself had shed his Pharisee outfit at the first opportunity.

"Who are you?" murmured Pietro. Ezio was concerned to see that the actor's lips had turned blue.

"Your savior," said Ezio. To the doctor he said, "He's been poisoned, *Dottor* Brunelleschi."

The doctor examined the actor quickly, shining a light into his eyes. "From the pallor, it looks like they used canterella. Poison of choice for our dear masters, the Borgia." To Pietro, he said, "Lie still."

"Feel sleepy," said Pietro.

"Lie still! Has he been sick?" Brunelleschi asked Ezio.

"Yes."

"Good." The doctor bustled about, mixing a number of fluids from bottles of variously colored glass with practiced ease and pouring the mixture into a vial. This he handed to Pietro, propping his head up.

"Drink this."

"Hurry up," said Ezio urgently.

"Just give him a moment."

Ezio watched anxiously. After what seemed an age, the actor sat up.

"I think I feel slightly better," he said.

"Miracolo!" said Ezio in relief.

"Not really," said the doctor. "He can't have had much, and for my sins I've had quite a bit of experience with canterella victims—it's enabled me to develop this pretty effective antidote. Now," he continued judiciously, "I'll apply some leeches. They will lead to a full recovery. You can rest here, my boy, and very soon you'll be as right as rain." He bustled some more and produced a glass jar full of black, wriggling creatures. He scooped out a handful.

"I cannot thank you enough," said Pietro to Ezio. "I—"

"You *can* thank me enough," replied Ezio briskly. "The key to the little gate you use for your trysts at the Castel Sant'Angelo with Lucrezia. Give it to me. Now!"

Misgiving appeared on Pietro's face. "What are you talking about? I'm simply a poor actor, a victim of circumstance—I—"

"Listen, Pietro: Cesare knows about you and Lucrezia."

Now misgiving was replaced by fear. "Oh, God!"

"But I can help you. If you give me the key."

Mutely, Pietro delved into his loincloth and handed it over. "I always keep it with me," he said.

"Wise of you," said Ezio, pocketing the key. It was reassuring to have it, for it would guarantee him access to the Castel whenever he had need of it. "My men will fetch your clothes and get you to a place of safety. I'll detail a couple to keep watch over you. Just keep out of sight for a while."

"But . . . my public!" wailed the actor.

"They'll have to make do with Longinus until it's safe for you to put your head above the parapet again." Ezio grinned. "I shouldn't worry. He isn't a patch on you."

"Oh, do you really think so?"

"No question."

"Ouch!" said Pietro, as the first leech went on.

In the wink of an eye, Ezio had disappeared outside, and there gave the necessary orders to his men. "Get out of those costumes as soon as you can," he added. "The Baths of Trajan aren't far. With any luck, your street clothes will still be where you left them."

He departed on his own, but he hadn't gone far when he noticed a figure skulking in the shadows. As soon as the man felt Ezio's eyes on him, he cut and ran. But not before Ezio had recognized Paganino, the thief who'd been determined to stay behind at the sack of Monteriggioni.

"Hey!" Ezio shouted, giving chase. *"Un momento!"*

The thief certainly knew his way around these streets. Ducking and diving, he was so adroit that Ezio all but lost him in the pursuit and more than once had to leap to the rooftops to scan the streets below in order to locate the man again. Leonardo's magical glove came in surprisingly handy at such times, he found.

At last he managed to get ahead of his prey and cut off his line of escape. The thief went for his dagger, an ugly-looking *cinquedea*, but Ezio quickly wrested it out of his hand and it clattered harmlessly to the pavement.

"Why did you run?" asked Ezio, pinioning the man. Then he noticed a letter protruding from the man's leather belt pouch. The seal was unmistakable: It was that of Pope Alexander VI—Rodrigo—the Spaniard!

Ezio let out a long breath as a series of suspicions fell into place. Paganino had long ago been with Antonio de Magianis's Thieves' Guild in Venice. He must have been offered enough money by the Borgia to persuade him to switch sides and had infiltrated La Volpe's group here—the Borgia had had a mole at the heart of the Assassins' organization all along.

Here was the traitor—not Machiavelli at all!

But while Ezio's attention was distracted, the thief wrenched himself free and, in a flash, seized his fallen weapon. His desperate eyes met Ezio's.

"Long live the Borgia!" he cried and thrust the *cinquedea* firmly into his own breast.

Ezio looked down at the fallen man as he thrashed about in his death agonies. *Well, better this death than a slow one at the hands of his masters*—Ezio well knew the price exacted by the Borgia for failure. He stuffed the letter into his doublet and made off. *Merda,* he thought to himself, *I was right! And now I have to stop La Volpe before he gets to Machiavelli!*

THIRTY-SEVEN

As Ezio made his way across the city, he was accosted by Saraghina, one of the girls from the Rosa in Fiore.

"You must come quickly," she said. "Your mother wants to see you urgently."

Ezio bit his lip. There should be time. "Hurry," he said.

Once at the bordello, he found Maria waiting for him. Her face betrayed her anxiety.

"Ezio," she said, "thank you for coming to see me."

"I have to be quick, Mother."

"There's something amiss."

"Tell me."

"The old proprietor of this establishment—"

"Madonna Solari?"

"Yes." Maria collected herself. "It turns out that she

was a cheat and a liar. We've discovered that she was playing *il doppio gioco*. She had close ties with the Vatican. Worse—several of those still employed here may still be—"

"Don't worry, *Madre*. I'll root them out. I'll send my most trusted recruits to interview the girls. Under Claudia's direction, they will soon get at the truth."

"Thank you, Ezio."

"We will ensure that only girls loyal to us remain here. As for the rest—" The expression on Ezio's face was harsh.

"I have other news."

"Yes?"

"We have word that ambassadors from King Ferdinand of Spain and from the Holy Roman Emperor, Maximilian, have arrived in Rome. It seems they seek an alliance with Cesare."

"Are you sure, Mother? What need have they of him?"

"I don't know, *figlio mio*."

Ezio's jaw was set. "We had better be safe rather than sorry. Ask Claudia to investigate for me. I give her a full mandate to give orders to the recruits I will send."

"You trust her for this?"

"Mother, after the business with the Banker, I would trust the two of you with my life. I am ashamed not to have done so before—but it was only my anxiety for your safety that—"

Maria held up a hand. "You do not need to explain. And there is nothing to forgive. We are all friends again now. That is what matters."

"And Cesare's days are numbered. Even if the ambassadors gain his support, they will soon find it is worthless."

"I hope your confidence is well-founded."

"Believe me, Mother, it is. Or will be—if I can save Machiavelli from La Volpe's misguided suspicion!"

THIRTY-EIGHT

Borrowing a horse from the stables he had liberated, Ezio rode posthaste to the Sleeping Fox. It was crucial that he get there before anything happened to Machiavelli. Lose him, and he'd lose the best brains in the Brotherhood.

Although the hour was not that late, he was alarmed to see that the inn was closed. He had his own key and let himself in through the wicket gate.

The scene that met his eyes told him that he had arrived not a moment too soon. The members of the Thieves' Guild were all present. La Volpe and his principal lieutenants stood together, busily discussing something that appeared to be of great importance and it looked as though judgment had been reached, since

La Volpe, a baleful look on his face, was approaching Machiavelli with a businesslike basilard in his right hand. Machiavelli, for his part, looked unconcerned, seemingly without any idea about what was happening.

"Stop!" shouted Ezio, bursting in on the scene and catching his breath after his headlong ride.

All eyes turned to him, while La Volpe stood rooted to the spot.

"Stay your hand, Gilberto!" commanded Ezio. "I have discovered the real traitor!"

"What?" said La Volpe, shocked, against a background of excited murmuring from his people.

"He is—was—none other than one of your own men—Paganino! He was present at the attack on Monteriggioni, and now I see his mischief in many of our recent misfortunes."

"Are you sure of this?"

"He himself revealed his guilt."

La Volpe's brow darkened. He sheathed his dagger. "Where is he now?" he growled.

"Where no one can touch him anymore."

"Dead?"

"By his own hand. He was carrying this letter." Ezio held the sealed parchment aloft.

Ezio passed the letter to La Volpe, and Machiavelli came up as the thieves' leader broke the seal and opened the paper.

"My God!" said La Volpe, scanning the words.

"Let me see," said Machiavelli.

"Of course," La Volpe said, crestfallen.

But Machiavelli was scanning the letter. "It's from Rodrigo to Cesare. Details of our plans for the French general, Octavien—among other things."

"One of my own men!"

"This is good news," Machiavelli said to Ezio. "We can substitute this letter with another. Containing false information—put them off the scent . . ."

"Good news indeed," replied Ezio, but his tone was cold. "Gilberto, you should have listened to me."

"I am once again in your debt, Ezio," said La Volpe, humbly.

Ezio allowed himself a smile. "What debt can there be amongst friends who trust—who must trust—one another?"

Before La Volpe could reply, Machiavelli put in, "And congratulations, by the way. I gather you resurrected Christ three days early!"

Ezio laughed, thinking of his rescue of Pietro. How did Machiavelli find out about things so *fast*?

La Volpe looked around at the men and women of the Guild gathered around them. "Well, what are you staring at?" he said. "We're losing business here!"

Later, after Machiavelli had left to deal with the intercepted letter, La Volpe drew Ezio aside. "I am glad you are here," he said, "and not just for preventing me from making a total fool of myself."

"More than that," said Ezio lightly. "Do you know what I would have done to you, if you had killed Niccolò?"

La Volpe grunted. "Ezio . . ." he said.

Ezio clapped him on the back. "But all's well. No more quarrels. Within the Brotherhood, we cannot afford them! Now—what is it you wanted to say to me? Do you have need of my assistance?"

"I do. The Guild is strong, but many of my men are young and untried in any real test. Look at that kid who nicked your purse. Look at young Claudio."

"And your point is . . . ?"

"I was coming to that. The thieves in Rome generally are also young men and women. Skilled in their trade, sure, but *young*. Prone to rivalries. Damaging rivalries."

"Are you speaking of another gang?"

"Yes. One in particular that may pose a threat. I need reinforcements to deal with them."

"My recruits?"

La Volpe was silent, then said, "I know I refused you help when my suspicions of Niccolò were at their height, but now . . ."

"Who are they?"

"They call themselves the Cento Occhi—the One Hundred Eyes. They are creatures of Cesare Borgia, and they cause us significant trouble."

"Where is their base?"

"My spies have located it."

"Where?"

"Just a moment. They are angry, and they are spoiling for a fight."

"Then we must surprise them."

"Bene!"

"But we must be prepared for retaliation."

"We will strike first. Then they will have no opportunity for retaliation!" La Volpe, now more and more his old self, rubbed his hands in anticipation. "The main thing is to take out their leaders. They alone have direct contact with the Borgia. Remove them, and we will have as good as beheaded the Cento Occhi."

"And you really need my help for this?"

"You broke the power of the wolfmen."

"Without your help."

"I know."

"The man who helped me break the wolfmen was—"

"I *know!*"

"Listen, Gilberto. We will combine forces and do this together—have no fear of that. Then, I presume your Guild will be the dominant cartel in Rome."

"That is true," agreed La Volpe reluctantly.

"If I help you in this," said Ezio slowly, "there is a condition."

"Yes?"

"That you shall not again threaten the unity of the Brotherhood. For that is what you almost did."

La Volpe bowed his head. "I am schooled," he said meekly.

"Whether we succeed in this venture of yours—or fail."

"Whether we succeed or fail," agreed La Volpe. "But we won't."

"Won't what?"

La Volpe gave his friend a Mephisthophelean grin. "Fail," he said.

THIRTY-NINE

Having detailed a group of his growing militia of new recruits to help La Volpe in his efforts against the Cento Occhi, Ezio made his way back to his lodgings. He was exhausted and fell into a deep sleep.

When he awoke, he refilled the poison-blade's inner vial with the venom especially prepared by Leonardo and checked and cleaned the retractable pistol, the double-blade, and the new crossbow and poison darts.

His work was interrupted by a messenger from Bartolomeo, bidding him come to the mercenaries' barracks as quickly as possible. Sensing trouble, and worried about it, for he had hoped that Bartolomeo and his *condottieri* had the French well in check, Ezio packed the Codex weapons he judged he might need into a saddlebag and made his way with all speed to the stables, where he rented his favorite horse and set off. It was a fine day, and the road was more or less dry, since rain had held off for about a week. The countryside even seemed a little dusty as he rode through it, taking care to choose a route obscure enough not to be monitored by Borgia troops, and often taking shortcuts through woods and across fields where cows raised their heads idly from their grazing to watch him pass.

It was afternoon by the time he reached the barracks, and all seemed quiet. He noticed that, since their renovation, the ramparts and walls had taken a slight bruising from French cannonades, but the damage wasn't serious, and a handful of men were busy on scaffolding or slung in baskets from the battlements, repairing the gouges and cracks the cannonballs had made.

He dismounted and handed the bridle to an ostler who came running up, wiping the little flecks of foam gently from his horse's mouth—he hadn't ridden her hard—and patting her muzzle before making his way, unannounced, across the parade ground in the direction of Bartolomeo's quarters.

His mind was on his next step, now that Cesare's banker had been removed, and he was considering what counteraction his enemy might take to ensure that there was no cessation in his supply of funds, so he was surprised suddenly to find himself with his nose to the tip of Bianca, Bartolomeo's greatsword.

"Who goes there?" bellowed Bartolomeo.

"*Salve* to you, too," rejoined Ezio.

Bartolomeo gave vent to a huge belly laugh. "Got you!"

"Teach me to be on my toes."

"Actually"—Bartolomeo gave a theatrical wink—"I was expecting my wife!"

"Well, well."

Bartolomeo lowered his sword and embraced Ezio. When he released him from the bear hug, his expression was more serious.

"I'm glad you've come, Ezio."

"What's the matter?"

"Look!"

Ezio followed his friend's gaze to where a platoon of wounded mercenaries was entering the parade ground.

"The French *puttane* have got us under pressure again," said Bartolomeo, answering Ezio's unspoken question.

"I thought you'd barked the shins of their general—what's his name?"

"Octavien de Valois. Thinks he's some kind of descendant of the noble house of Valois. Some wretch's spawn of a bastard, if you ask me."

Bartolomeo spat as another contingent of wounded men appeared.

"Looks serious," said Ezio.

"King Louis must have sent reinforcements to back Cesare up. Since we gave Valois such a fuckin' bashing." Bartolomeo scratched his beard. "I suppose I should be flattered."

"How bad is it?"

"They've got their fuckin' tower back," said Bartolomeo grumpily.

"We'll get it back. Where's Valois now?"

"You're right!" Bartolomeo ignored the question. "Of course we'll get it back! We'll have the scoundrels in retreat before you could say *fottere!* It's only a matter of time."

Just then, a bullet whizzed past their ears and embedded itself in the wall behind them.

"It was so quiet when I rode up," said Ezio. He looked at the sky. The sun had gone behind large clouds that had suddenly rolled across the sky.

"*Seemed* so quiet, you mean. They're sneaky bastards, the French. But I'll have Valois by the throat soon enough, mark my word." He turned to yell an order to a sergeant who'd come running up. "Close the gates! Get those men off the outer walls! *Move!*"

Men ran hither and thither, manning the battlements, priming the cannon.

"Don't worry, friend," said the big *condottiero*. "I've got the situation well in hand."

At that moment, a larger cannonball crashed into the ramparts nearest the two men, sending dust and shards of stone flying in all directions.

"They seem to be getting closer!" yelled Ezio.

Bartolomeo's men fired a salvo from the barracks' main cannon by way of reply—the walls seemed to shake with the report from the great guns. But the response from the French artillery was just as ferocious—the thunder of twoscore guns tore at the air—this time the balls found their marks more cleanly. Bartolomeo's men were still desperately trying to restore defensive order. Another huge salvo from the French rocked the walls of the barracks—but this time the French seemed to be focusing their fire on the main gate. Two of the gate-keepers fell dead—caught up in the bombardment.

"Close the fuckin' gates!" roared Bartolomeo.

The well-trained soldiers under Bartolomeo's command rushed forward to repel the sortie of French troops that, without any warning, had appeared at the main entrance of the barracks. It seemed that the calm was well and truly before the storm—the French had clearly been holding back for this surprise attack, and unfortunately, thought Ezio to himself, they had certainly managed to gain the upper hand on that front. Bartolomeo's fortress had been caught unprepared for this attack.

Bartolomeo jumped down from the battlements and ran toward the gate at full tilt. Whirling Bianca, he towered above the Frenchmen, and the great broadsword sliced viciously into their ranks. The French soldiers seemed to halt in trepidation at Bartolomeo's arrival. Meanwhile, Ezio directed the musketeers to cover those men who strove to push the gates closed before the enemy could gain a surer foothold within the barracks. The Assassin troops rallied with the presence of their leader and succeeded in pushing the gates closed. But seconds later there was an almighty crash—and the wooden bar that held the great gates shut bowed ominously. The French had succeeded in maneuvering a battering ram to the main gates while the defenders' attention was focused on those French soldiers who'd pushed through.

"We should have built a fuckin' moat!" yelled Bartolomeo.

"There wasn't time for that!"

Ezio shouted at the musketeers to divert their fire outside the walls at the gathering French forces. Bartolomeo leapt up the ramparts and stood next to Ezio— he stopped at the scene unfolding—French troops had appeared as if from nowhere, and in great numbers.

"We're surrounded by them!" cursed Bartolomeo, without exaggeration.

Behind them, one of the minor gates caved in with a crash and splintering of timber, and before any of the defenders could do anything to prevent it, a large unit of French infantry stormed in, swords drawn and seemingly willing to fight to the death. This sudden infiltration succeeded in cutting Bartolomeo's quarters off from the Italians.

"Oh, my God, what are they up to now?" shouted Bartolomeo. The Assassin soldiers were better trained than the French, and usually more resolved to their cause—but the sheer weight of numbers and the suddenness of the attack had caught them unawares. It was all they could do to hold the line—and slowly try to move the French squadron back. The air was thick with the chaos of close-quarter hand-to-hand combat. The space was so crowded that in places the battle seemed to have turned to a straightforward fistfight—where there was no longer room to wield weapons.

The atmosphere was also hot and claustrophobic with the brewing storm—the gods seemed to be frowning on the scene, great storm clouds oppressing the sky overhead. The dust of the parade-ground floor rose up like a mist, and the day, which had been so fine, turned dark. Soon afterward, the rain began to fall in torrents. The pitched battle turned into a confused rout, in which the two opposing forces could barely see what they were doing. The ground turned to mud—the fighting turned more desperate and more chaotic.

But then, as if the enemy had achieved some purpose, the French trumpets sounded a retreat, and Valois' men withdrew as swiftly as they had arrived.

It took a while to restore order, and Bartolomeo's first concern was for the carpenters to replace the shattered gate with a new one. Naturally they had one ready-built, in case of just such an eventuality, but it would take an hour to install it. Meanwhile, he led Ezio in the direction of his quarters.

"What the hell were they after?" he asked no one in particular. "My maps? They're precious, those maps!"

But he was interrupted by another French fanfare. With Ezio close behind, he ran up one of the stairways leading to a high rampart above the main gate. There, on the scrubby, cypress-scattered plain that confronted

the barracks, a short distance away, sat the Général Duc
Octavien de Valois himself, on horseback, surrounded by
a knot of his officers and infantry. Two of the infantrymen were holding a prisoner, whose body was obscured
by a sack thrown over the head.

"*Bonjour, Général d'Alviano,*" the Frenchman called
out smarmily, looking up at Bartolomeo. "*Êtes-vous prêt
à vous rendre?*—Are you ready to surrender?"

"Why don't you come a little closer and say that, you
crummy little Frog?"

"Tut, tut, *mon général.* You really ought to learn
French. That might help mask your barbaric sensibilities,
mais franchement, je m'en doute." Smilingly, he looked
around at his officers, who tittered appreciatively.

"Perhaps you *could* teach me," Bartolomeo hollered
back. "And I would instruct *you* in fighting, since you
seem to do so little of it—at least, fair and square, like a
gentleman should!"

Valois smiled thinly. "Hm. Well, *cher ami*, as amus-
ing as this little parley has been, I see I must repeat my
request: I'd like your unconditional surrender by sunrise."

"Come and get it! My Lady Bianca will whisper it in
your ear!"

"Ah! I believe another lady might object to that."

He nodded to his infantrymen, who pulled the sack
off their prisoner. It was Pantasilea!

"*Il mio marito vi ammazzerà tutti,*" she spluttered
defiantly, spitting out bits of hemp and dust. "My husband will murder you all!"

It took Bartolomeo a moment to recover from the shock. Ezio grasped his arm, while his men looked at one another, aghast.

"I'll kill you, *fotutto francese!*" he screamed.

"Dear me, calm down," sneered Valois. "For your wife's sake. And rest assured that no Frenchman would ever harm a woman—unnecessarily." His tone became more businesslike. "But even a dunderhead like you can imagine, I think, what will happen if you do not accede to my terms." He kicked his horse's flanks and prepared to turn away. "Come to my headquarters at dawn. Unarmed. And bone up on a little French. Soon, all Italy will be speaking it!"

He raised his hand. The infantrymen threw Pantasilea across the back of one of the officers' horses and the whole party cantered off, the infantry trotting in its wake.

"I'll get you, you *pezzo di merda figlio di puttana!*" Bartolomeo shouted impotently after them. "That whoreson piece of shit," he muttered to Ezio. Then he charged off.

"Where are you going?" Ezio yelled after him.

"To get her back!"

"Bartolomeo! Wait!"

But Bartolomeo plowed on, and by the time Ezio caught up with him, he was in the saddle, ordering the gates to be opened.

"You can't do this alone!" pleaded Ezio.

"I'm not alone," replied the *condottiero*, patting Bianca, which hung at his side. "Come with me if you wish! But you'll have to hurry!" He spurred his horse and headed for the now-open gates.

Ezio didn't even watch him go. He shouted brisk orders to Bartolomeo's captain of cavalry. Within minutes, he, Ezio, and a mounted unit of *condottieri* were galloping out of the barracks in hot pursuit of their leader.

FORTY

General Valois' headquarters was situated within the ruins of the fortified ancient Roman barracks of the old emperors' personal brigade—the Praetorian Guard. It was located in the eighteenth *rione*, on the northeastern edge of Rome, now outside the shrunken city Rome had become, for in its heyday Rome had boasted one million inhabitants, a vast city, the greatest in the world by far, fifteen hundred years earlier.

Ezio and his troops caught up with Bartolomeo on the road and now they were gathered together on a small rise near the French base camp. They'd attempted an attack, but their bullets had bounced uselessly off the strong modern walls Valois had had built on top of the old ones. Now they had moved out of range of the responding hail of gunfire that had been the French response to their foray. All Bartolomeo could do—and was doing—was hurl imprecations at his enemies.

"You cowards! What, steal a man's wife and then go and hide inside a fortress? Hah! Nothing hangs between your thighs—do you hear me? *Nothing! Vous n'avez même pas une couille entre vous tous!* There! That good enough French for you, you *bastardi*? In fact, I don't think you have any balls at all."

The French fired a cannon. They were within range of that. The shot hammered into the ground a few feet from where they were standing.

"Listen, Barto," said Ezio. "Calm down. You'll be no good to her dead. Look—let's regroup, and then we'll storm the gates, just like we did at the Arsenal that time in Venice when we were chasing down Silvio Barbarigo."

"Won't work," said Bartolomeo glumly. "The entrance is thicker with Frenchmen than the streets of Paris."

"Then we'll climb the battlements."

"They can't be scaled. And even if *you* could, you'd be so outnumbered, even *you* wouldn't be able to hold out." He brooded. "Pantasilea would know what to do." He brooded some more, and Ezio could see that his friend was becoming positively despondent. "Maybe this is the end," he continued gloomily. "I'll just have to do what he says—enter their camp at dawn, bearing propitiatory gifts, and just hope the sod spares her life. Wretched coward!"

But Ezio had been thinking. Now he snapped his fingers excitedly. "*Perché non ci ho pensato prima?*—Why didn't I think of it before!"

"What? Did I say something?"

Ezio's eyes were shining. "Back to your barracks!"

"What?"

"Call your men back to barracks. I'll explain there. Come on!"

"This had better be good," said Bartolomeo. To his men he gave the order: "Fall back!"

It was nighttime by the time they got back. Once the horses had been stabled and the men stood down, Ezio and Bartolomeo went to the map-room and sat down in conference.

"So, what's this plan of yours?"

Ezio unrolled a map that showed the Castra Praetoria and its surroundings in detail. He pointed inside the fortress.

"Once inside, your men can overpower the camp's patrols, am I correct?"

"Yes, but—"

"Especially if they are taken completely by surprise?"

"*Ma certo*. The element of surprise is always—"

"Then we need to get hold of a lot of French uniforms. And their armor. Fast. At dawn, we'll walk right in, bold as brass; but there's no time to lose."

Comprehension dawned on Bartolomeo's rugged face—comprehension, and hope: "Hah! You crafty old scoundrel! Ezio Auditore, you truly are a man after my own heart! And thinking worthy of my Pantasilea herself! *Magnifico!*"

"Give me a few men. I'm going to make a sortie to their tower now, get in, and fetch what we need."

"I'll give you all the men you need—they can strip the uniforms from the dead French troops."

"Good."

"And Ezio—"

"Yes?"

"Be sure to kill them as cleanly as possible. We don't want uniforms covered in blood."

"They won't feel a thing," said Ezio, a steely look in his eyes. "Trust me."

As Bartolomeo was detailing men for the job at hand, Ezio collected his saddlebag, and from it he selected the poison-blade.

They rode silently up to the Borgia Tower, which the French commanded, their horses' hooves muffled with sacking. Dismounting a short way off, Ezio bade his men wait while he scaled the outer wall with the skill of a denizen of the distant Alps and the grace and cunning of a cat. A scratch from the poison-blade was enough to kill, and the overconfident French had not posted many guards—those that there were, he took completely unawares and they were dead before they even knew what had happened to them. Once the guards were out of the way, Ezio opened the main gate, which groaned on its hinges, making Ezio's heart race. He paused to listen, but the garrison slept on. Without a sound, his men ran into the tower, entered the garrison, and overcame its inmates with barely a struggle. Collecting the uniforms took a little longer, but within an hour they were back at the barracks—mission accomplished!

"Bit of blood on this one," grumbled Bartolomeo, sifting through their booty.

"Exception. The only man who was truly on his toes. Had to finish him the conventional way, with my sword," said Ezio as the men detailed for the operation they had at hand changed into the French gear.

Bartolomeo said, "Well, you'd better bring me a suit of their perverted mail, too."

"You're not wearing one," said Ezio as he put on a French lieutenant's uniform himself.

"What?"

"Of course you aren't! The plan is that you gave yourself up to us. We are a French patrol, bringing you to the Général Duc de Valois."

"Of course." Bartolomeo thought hard. "Then what?"

"Barto, you can't have been paying attention. *Then* your men *attack*—on my signal."

"*Bene!*" Bartolomeo beamed. "Get a move on!" he said to those of his men who hadn't yet completed dressing. "I can smell the dawn already, and it's a long ride."

The men formed up. They rode hard through the night, but left their horses at a little distance from the French base camp, in the charge of their squires. Before leaving them, Ezio first checked Leonardo's little Codex pistol, its design now improved in order to enable him to fire more than one shot before reloading, and discreetly strapped it to his arm. He and his group of "French" soldiers then proceeded on foot in the direction of the Castra Praetoria.

"Valois thinks Cesare will allow the French to rule Italy," explained Bartolomeo as he and Ezio marched side by side. Ezio was playing the part of the senior officer of the patrol and would hand Bartolomeo over himself. "Silly fool! He's so blinded by the trickle of royalty in his blood that he can't see the plan of the battlefield— blasted little inbred runt that he is!" He paused. "But you know and I know that, whatever the French may think, Cesare intends to be the first king of a united Italy himself!"

"Unless we stop him."

"Yes," Bartolomeo reflected. "You know, brilliant though your plan is, personally I don't like using this kind of trick. I believe in a fair fight—and may the best man win!"

"Cesare and Valois may have different styles, Barto, but they both fight dirty, and we have no choice but to fight fire with fire."

"*Hmph!* 'There will come a day when men no longer cheat each other. And on that day we shall see what mankind is truly capable of,'" he quoted.

"I've heard that somewhere before."

"You should have! It's something your father once wrote."

"*Psst!*"

They had drawn close to the French encampment,

and up ahead Ezio could see figures moving about—French perimeter guards.

"What'll we do?" asked Bartolomeo, sotto voce.

"I'll kill them. There aren't many of them. But we must do this noiselessly and without fuss."

"Got enough poison left in that gadget of yours?"

"This lot are alert and they're quite widely spaced apart. If I kill one and I'm noticed, I may not be able to prevent some getting back and raising the alarm."

"Why kill them at all? We're in French uniforms. Well, you lot are."

"They ask questions. If we make an entrance with you in chains . . ."

"Chains?!"

"Shh! If we make an entrance, Valois will be so tickled it won't occur to him to ask where we sprang from. At least, I hope it won't."

"That chicken-brain? No worries! But how are we going to get rid of them? We can hardly shoot them. The gunfire would be as good as a fanfare."

"I'm going to shoot them with this," said Ezio, producing Leonardo's adapted compact, quick-load crossbow. "I've counted. There are five of them. I have six bolts. The light's still a bit dim for me to aim properly from here. I'll have to get a bit closer. Just you hang on here with the rest."

Ezio slipped forward until he was within twenty paces or so of the nearest French sentry. Cranking back the string, he placed the first bolt in the groove and, lifting the tiller to his shoulder, took a quick bead on the man's

breast and fired. There was a muted snap and a hiss, and
the man crumpled to the ground instantly, like a puppet
whose strings had been cut. But Ezio was already on his
way through the bracken to his next victim—the twang
of the crossbow was barely audible. The small bolt hit
the man's throat and he made a small, strangulated, gargling sound before his knees gave way under him. Five
minutes later, it was all over. He'd used all six bolts, since
he'd missed on the first shot at his last man, making him
lose his resolve momentarily, but he'd reloaded and fired
successfully before the soldier had had time to react to
the strange, dull noise he'd heard.

He had no more ammunition for the bow now, but he
gave a silent thanks to Leonardo. He knew this weapon
would prove more than useful on another occasion. Ezio
quietly hauled the fallen French soldiers to some sparse
cover—hoping it'd be enough to hide them from anyone
who happened to pass by. As he did so, he retrieved the
bolts he could—recalling Leonardo's advice. Stowing
the crossbow, he made his way back to Bartolomeo.

"All done?" the big man asked him.

"All done."

"Valois next," Bartolomeo vowed. "I'll make him
squeal like a stuck pig."

The sky was lightening, and dawn, clad in a russet
mantle, was walking over the dew on the distant hills to
the east.

"We'd better get going," said Bartolomeo.

"Come on, then," replied Ezio, clapping manacles
on his friend's wrists before he could object. "Don't

worry—they're fakes. Spring-loaded. Just make a sudden tight fist and they'll drop off. But for God's sake, wait for my signal. And by the way, the 'guard' just to your left will stay close to you. He's got Bianca under his cloak. All you have to do is reach across and . . ." Ezio's voice took on a warning note, "But *at my signal!*"

"Aye, aye, sir." Bartolomeo smiled.

At the head of his men, Bartolomeo two paces behind him with a special escort of four, Ezio marched boldly in the direction of the main gate of the French headquarters. The rising sun glittered on their chain mail and breastplates.

"Halte-là!" ordered a sergeant-commander at the gate. He was backed up by a dozen heavily armed sentries, but his eyes had already taken in the uniforms of his fellow soldiers. *"Déclarez-vous!"*

"Je suis le Lieutenant Guillemot, et j'emmène le Général d'Alviano ici présent à Son Excellence le Général Duc Monsieur de Valois. Le Général d'Alviano s'est rendu, seul et sans armes, selon les exigences de Monsieur le Duc," said Ezio fluently, causing Bartolomeo behind him to raise an eyebrow.

"Well, Lieutenant Guillemot, the general will be pleased to see General d'Alviano, and that he's come to his senses," said the captain of the guard, who had hurried up to take charge. "But there's something—just a trace—about your accent that I cannot place. Tell me, what part of France are you from?"

Ezio drew a breath. "Montréal," he replied firmly.

"Open the gates," the captain of the guard said to his sergeant.

"Open the gates!" shouted the sergeant.

Within seconds, Ezio was leading his men into the heart of the French headquarters. He fell back a step so as to have Bartolomeo, and the "prisoner's" escort, at his side.

"I'll kill the lot of them," muttered Bartolomeo. "And eat their kidneys fried for breakfast. By the way, I didn't know you spoke French."

"Picked it up in Florence," Ezio replied casually. "Couple of girls there I knew." He was quietly glad his accent had passed muster.

"You rogue! Still, that's where they say the best place is to learn a language."

"What—Florence?"

"No, you fool—*bed!*"

"Shut up."

"You sure these manacles are fakes?"

"Not *yet*, Barto. Be patient! And shut *up!*"

"It's taking all my patience. What are they saying?"

"I'll tell you later."

And it was just as well that Bartolomeo's French was limited to a few words, thought Ezio, as he listened to the jibes being hurled at his friend: *"Chien d'Italien"*—Italian dog; *"Prosterne-toi devant tes supérieurs"*—Bow down before your betters; *"Regarde-le, comme il a honte de ce qu'il est devenu!"*—Look at him, how ashamed of himself he is at his own downfall!

But the ordeal was soon over. They had arrived at the

foot of the broad stairway that led up to the entrance of the French general's quarters. Valois himself stood at the head of a bunch of officers, his prisoner, Pantasilea, at his side. Her hands were tied behind her back, and she wore loose manacles on her ankles, which would allow her to walk, but only in small steps. At the sight of her, Bartolomeo could not resist an angry growl. Ezio kicked him.

Valois held up his hand. "No need for violence, Lieutenant, though I do congratulate you on your zeal." He turned his attention to Bartolomeo. "My dear general, it seems that you have seen the light."

"Enough of your crap!" snarled Bartolomeo. "Release my wife! And get these cuffs off me!"

"Oh, dear," said Valois. "Such high-handedness, and from someone born with absolutely nothing to his name."

Ezio was about to give the signal when Bartolomeo retorted to Valois, raising his voice: "My name is worth its currency. Unlike yours, which is counterfeit!"

The surrounding troops fell silent.

"How dare you?" said Valois, white with rage.

"You think that commanding an army in itself grants you status—nobility? True nobility of spirit comes from fighting alongside your men, not by kidnapping a woman to cheat your way out of a battle. Why don't you release my wife?!"

"You savages never learn," said Valois malevolently, and producing a pistol, he cocked it and pointed it at Pantasilea's head.

Ezio knew he had to act fast. He took out a pistol and

fired one shot into the air. At the same time, Bartolomeo, who'd been dying for the moment, bunched his
fists and the manacles flew off.

Pandemonium followed. The disguised *condottieri*
with Ezio immediately attacked the startled French soldiers, and Bartolomeo, seizing Bianca from the "guard"
still on his left, bounded up the stairway. But Valois was
too quick for him. Keeping a tight hold on Pantasilea, he
backed into his quarters, slamming the door behind him.

"Ezio!" implored Bartolomeo. "You have to save my
wife! Only you can! That place is built like a strongbox!"

Ezio nodded and tried to give his friend a reassuring
smile. He scanned the building from where he stood. It
was not large, but it was a massive new structure, built
by French military architects and designed to be impregnable. There was nothing for it but to try to gain entry
from the rooftops, where no one would be expecting an
assault, and where, therefore, the weak points might be.
Might be.

Well, there was nothing for it but to try. Ezio leapt up
the stairs and, taking advantage of the melee, which was
taking up everyone else's attention, he looked for a place
where he might best climb. Suddenly, a dozen Frenchmen started after him, keen swords flashing in the early
morning sun, but in a flash Bartolomeo was standing
between him and them, flourishing Bianca menacingly.

The walls were designed to be unassailable, but there
were enough nooks and crannies in them for Ezio to be
able to plot a route with his eyes, and within a couple
of moments he was on the roof. It was flat and made of

wood overlaid with tile. There were five French sentries stationed up there. They challenged him, as he sprang over the parapet, demanding a password. He could not give one, and they ran toward him, halberds lowered. It was lucky they were not armed with muskets or pistols. Ezio shot the first one, then drew his sword and gave battle to the other four, who put up a desperate struggle, surrounding him and jabbing mercilessly with the points of their weapons. One slashed his sleeve open, nicking his elbow and drawing blood, but then the blade slid harmlessly off the metal bracer on his left forearm.

Using the bracer and his sword, he was able to defend himself against the increasingly frenetic blows. Ezio's skill with his blade was offset by having to tackle four opponents at once. But thoughts of Bartolomeo's beloved wife spurred him on—he knew, simply, that he could not fail, he must not fail. The tide of the fight turned in his favor—he ducked under two swords that were slashing toward his head, and engaged another with his bracer—leaving him free to smash aside the fourth man's blade. The maneuver gave him the opening—and a lethal slash across the man's jaw felled him. Three to go. Ezio stepped forward toward the nearest French-man, inside his guard—it threw the man, giving him no room to wield his sword. Ezio flicked his hidden-blade forward and into the man's abdomen. Two left—both looking more nervous. It took just a couple of minutes to defeat the two French guards—who no longer had the advantage of numbers. Their swordplay was simply not up to challenging Ezio's mastery of the blade. Breathing heavily and leaning on his sword for a moment, Ezio stood in the midst of another five vanquished foes.

The roof gave way in its center to a large square opening. After reloading his pistol, Ezio approached this cautiously. As he'd expected, he found himself looking down into a courtyard, undecorated and bare of any plants or chairs and tables, though there were two or three stone benches arranged around a dry fountain and pool.

As he looked over the edge a shot cracked out and a bullet zinged past his left ear. He drew back a little. He didn't know how many pistols Valois had. If only one, he calculated that it would take his man perhaps ten seconds to reload. He regretted the crossbow, but there was nothing to be done about that. Tucked into the back of his belt were five of the poison darts. But he'd have to be at fairly close range to use them, and he didn't want to do anything that might endanger Pantasilea.

"Don't come any nearer!" yelled Valois from below. "I'll kill her if you do!"

Ezio hovered near the edge of the roof, looking down into the courtyard; but his line of vision was limited by the rim of the roof, and he could see no one down there. But he could sense the panic in Valois' voice.

"Who are you?" the general called. "Who sent you? Rodrigo? Tell him it was all Cesare's plan!"

"You'd better tell me all you know, if you want to get back to Burgundy in one piece!"

"If I tell you, will you let me go?"

"We'll see. The woman must not be harmed. Come out where I can see you," commanded Ezio.

Below him, Valois stepped warily out from the colonnade that surrounded the courtyard and took up a position near the dead fountain. He had tied Pantasilea's hands behind her back, and he held her by a bridle attached to a halter around her neck. She had been crying, Ezio could see, but was silent now, and trying to keep her head held high. The look she was giving Valois was so withering that, had it been a weapon, it would have eclipsed all the Codex armaments put together.

How many men had he down there with him, kept hidden? But the sound of his voice was fearful. It suggested to Ezio that the general had run out of options, and that he was cornered.

"Cesare has been bribing the cardinals, to get them away from the Pope and onto his side. Once he had subdued the rest of the country for Rome, I was supposed to march on the capital and seize the Vatican, with anyone else who opposed the captain-general's will."

Valois was waving his pistol around wildly. As he turned, Ezio saw that he had two more stuck in his belt.

"It wasn't my idea," continued Valois. "I am above such scheming." A trace of his old vanity was creeping back into his voice. Ezio wondered if he'd allowed the man too much latitude. He moved into view and leapt boldly down into the courtyard, landing in a pantherlike crouch.

"Stay back!" screamed Valois. "Or I'll—"

"Harm one hair of her head and my archers above will fill you fuller of arrows than San Sebastiano," Ezio hissed. "So—you noble little soul—what was in it for you?"

"As I am of the House of Valois, Cesare will give me Italy. I will rule here, as befits my birthright."

Ezio almost laughed. Bartolomeo had not been exaggerating—rather, the opposite—when he'd called this popinjay a chicken-brain! But he still had Pantasilea; and he was still dangerous.

"Good. Now, let the woman go."

"Get me out first. Then I'll let her go."

"No."

"I have King Louis's ear. Ask for what you want in France and it shall be yours. An estate, perhaps? A title?"

"Those things I already have. Here. And you are never going to rule over them."

"The Borgia try to overturn the natural order," wheedled Valois, changing tack. "I intend to set it right again. Royal blood should rule—not the foul, tainted stuff that runs in their veins." He paused. "I know you are not a barbarian, like them."

"Neither you, nor Cesare, nor the Pope, nor anyone who does not have peace and justice on his side, will ever rule Italy while I have life in my body," said Ezio, moving slowly forward.

Fear seemed to have frozen the French general to the spot. The hand that again now held the pistol to Pantasilea's temple trembled, and he did not retreat. Evidently they were alone in his quarters, unless the only other occupants were servants who'd had the sense to hide. They could hear a steady, heavy noise, as of deliberate, slow blows being struck, and the outer doors of the quarters vibrated. Bartolomeo must have routed the French and brought up battering rams.

"Please . . ." quavered the general, all his urbanity gone. "I will kill her." He glanced up to the opening in the roof, trying to catch a glimpse of Ezio's imaginary archers, not even reflecting, as Ezio had feared he might when he'd first mentioned them—the first thing that'd come into his head—that such soldiery had been all but superseded in modern warfare, though the bow was still far quicker to reload than the pistol or musket.

Ezio took another step forward.

"I'll give you anything you want—there's money here, plenty of it, it's to pay my men with, but you may have it all! And I—I—I will do anything you want of me!" His voice was pleading now, and the man himself cut such a pathetic figure that Ezio could hardly bridle his contempt. This man actually saw himself as king of Italy!

It hardly seemed worth killing him.

Ezio was close to him now. The two men looked each other in the eye. Ezio slowly took first the pistol and then the bridle out of the general's nerveless hands. With a whimper of relief, Pantasilea hobbled back out of the way, watching the scene with wide eyes.

"I—I only wanted respect," said the general faintly.

"But real respect is earned," said Ezio. "Not inherited, or purchased. And it cannot be gained by force. *Oderint dum metuant* must be one of the stupidest sayings ever coined. No wonder Caligula adopted it: 'Let them hate, as long as they fear.' And no wonder our modern Caligula lives by it. And you serve him."

"I serve my king, Louis XII!" Valois looked crest-fallen. "But perhaps you are right. I see that now." Hope sparked in his eyes. "I need more time . . ."

Ezio sighed. "Alas, friend. You have run out of that." He drew his sword as Valois, understanding, and acting with dignity at last, knelt and lowered his head.

"Requiescat in pace," said Ezio.

With a mighty crash, the outer doors of the quarters splintered and fell open, revealing Bartolomeo, dusty and bloody but uninjured, standing at the head of a troop of his men. He rushed up to his wife and hugged her so tightly that he knocked the breath out of her, before busying himself about getting the halter off her neck, but his fingers were so nervous and clumsy that Ezio had to do it for him. He cut the manacles from her feet with two mighty blows of Bianca and, calmer, fiddled free the cords that bound her wrists.

"Oh, Pantasilea, my dove, my heart, my own! Don't you ever dare disappear like that again! I was lost without you!"

"No, you weren't! You rescued me!"

"Ah." Bartolomeo looked embarrassed. "No. Not I—it was Ezio! He came up with a—"

"Madonna, I am glad you are safe," interrupted Ezio.

"My dear Ezio, how can I thank you? You saved me!"

"I was but an instrument—just a part of your hus-band's brilliant plan."

Bartolomeo looked at Ezio with an expression of con-fusion and gratitude on his face.

"My prince!" said Pantasilea, embracing her husband. "My hero!"

Bartolomeo blushed and, winking at Ezio, said, "Well, if I'm your prince, I'd better earn that title. Mind you, it wasn't *all* my idea, you know—"

As they turned to go, Pantasilea brushed by Ezio and whispered, "Thank you."

FORTY-ONE

A few days later, after Bartolomeo had rounded up the remains of Valois' dispirited army, Ezio fell in with La Volpe, both on their way to a convocation Ezio had ordered of the Brotherhood at the Assassins' hideaway on Tiber Island.

"How do things stand here in Rome now?" was Ezio's first question.

"Very good, Ezio. With the French army in disarray, Cesare has lost important support. Your sister, Claudia, tells us that the Spanish and the Holy Roman ambassadors have left hurriedly for home, and my men have routed the Cento Occhi."

"There is still much to do."

They arrived at their destination and found the rest

of their companions already gathered in the inner room of the hideout. A fire blazed on a hearth in the middle of the floor.

After they had greeted each other and taken their places, Machiavelli stood and intoned in Arabic:

"*Laa shay'a waqi'un moutlaq bale kouloun moumkine*: The Wisdom of our Creed is revealed through these words. We work in the Dark, to serve the Light. We are Assassins."

Ezio stood in turn and addressed his sister. "Claudia. We dedicate our lives to protecting the freedom of humanity. Mario Auditore and our father, Giovanni, his brother, once stood at a fire similar to this one, engaged in the same task. Now, I offer the choice to you: of joining us."

He extended his hand and she placed hers in his. Machiavelli withdrew from the fire the familiar branding iron ending in two small semicircles like the letter *C*, which could be brought together by means of a lever in the handle.

"Everything is permitted. Nothing is true," he said gravely. And the others—Bartolomeo, La Volpe, and Ezio—repeated the words after him.

Just as Antonio de Magianis had once done to Ezio, so Machiavelli now solemnly applied the branding iron to Claudia's ring finger and closed the clamp, so that the mark of a ring was burned there forever.

Claudia winced, but did not cry out. Machiavelli removed the iron and put it safely to one side.

"Welcome to our Order—our Brotherhood," he told Claudia formally.

"Sisterhood, too?" she asked, rubbing a soothing

ointment onto her branded finger from a little vial Bartolomeo had proffered her.

Machiavelli smiled. "If you like."

All eyes were on him as he now turned to Ezio.

"We have not seen eye to eye on many issues," he began.

"Niccolò—" Ezio interrupted, but Machiavelli held up a hand to stay him.

"But ever since the epiphany in the Vault under the Sistine Chapel, and even before then, you have proven again and again that you were exactly what our Order needed. You have led the charge against the Templars, carried our *gonfalon* proud and high, and steadily rebuilt our Brotherhood after what it suffered after the debacle at Monteriggioni." He looked around. "The moment has come, my friends, to appoint Ezio formally to the position he already occupies by common consent—that of our leader. I present to you Ezio Auditore di Firenze—the Grand Master of our Order." He turned to Ezio. "My friend, from henceforth you will be known as *il Mentore*—the guardian of our Brotherhood and of our secrets."

Ezio's head swam with emotion, though still a part of him wanted to wrench itself away from this life in which the great task demanded every waking hour and allowed few even for sleep. Still, he stepped forward and austerely repeated the words central to the Creed:

"Where other men are limited by morality and law, we must, in quest of our sacred goals, always remember: Everything is permitted. Nothing is true. Nothing is true. Everything is permitted."

The others repeated the formula after him.

"And now it is time," said Machiavelli, "for our newest member to take her Leap of Faith."

They made their way to the Church of Santa Maria in Cosmedin and climbed its bell tower. Carefully guided by Bartolomeo and La Volpe, Claudia fearlessly threw herself into the void just as the golden orb of the sun broke free of the eastern horizon and caught the folds of her silver dress in its light and turned them golden, too. Ezio watched her land safely and walk with Bartolomeo and La Volpe in the direction of a nearby colonnade. Now, Machiavelli and Ezio were left alone. Just as Machiavelli was about to make his Leap, Ezio stopped him.

"Why the sudden change of heart, Niccolò?"

Machiavelli smiled. "What change of heart? I have always stood by you. I have always been loyal to the cause. My fault is independent thinking. That is what caused the doubts in your mind—and Gilberto's. Now we are free of all that unpleasantness. I never sought the leadership. I am . . . more of an observer. Now, let us take our Leap of Faith together, as friends and as fellow warriors of the Creed!"

He held out his hand and, also smiling, Ezio took it in a firm grasp. Then they threw themselves off the roof of the campanile together.

Scarcely had they landed and rejoined their companions than a courier rode up. Breathless, he announced, "Maestro Machiavelli, Cesare has returned to Rome alone from his latest foray in the Romagna. He rides for the Castel Sant'Angelo."

"*Grazie*, Alberto," said Machiavelli, as the courier wheeled his horse around and sped back the way he had come.

"Well?" Ezio asked him.

Machiavelli showed his palms. "The decision is now yours, not mine."

"Niccolò, you had better not stop telling me what you think. I now seek the opinion of my most trusted adviser."

Machiavelli smiled. "In this case you know my opinion already. It hasn't changed. The Borgia must be eradicated. Go and kill them, *Mentore*. Finish the job you have started."

"Good advice."

"I know." Machiavelli looked at him appraisingly.

"What is it?" Ezio asked.

"I had been thinking of writing a book about Cesare's methods. Now I think I will balance it with an examination of yours."

"If you're writing a book about me," said Ezio, "better make it a short one!"

FORTY-TWO

Ezio arrived at the Castel Sant'Angelo to find that a crowd had gathered on the opposite bank of the Tiber. Blending in with the gathered masses, he made his way to the front and saw that the French troops guarding the bridge that led to the Castel, and the Castel itself, were in total disarray. Some soldiers were already packing up their equipment, while officers and others moved frantically among them, issuing orders to unpack again. Some of the orders were contradictory, and here and there fights had broken out as a result. The Italian crowd was watching, Ezio noted, with quiet pleasure. Though he carried his own clothes in a satchel slung over his shoulder, he had taken the precaution of once again donning the French uniform he had saved from the attack on the

Castra Praetoria, and he now shed the cloak he'd been wearing to cover it and walked quickly onto the bridge. No one paid him any attention, but as he passed among the French troops, he gleaned useful snippets of conversation.

"When are we expecting the attack from d'Alviano and his mercenaries?"

"They say he's on his way now."

"Then why are we packing? Are we retreating?"

"I hope so! *Tout cela, c'est rien qu'un tas de merde.*"

A private spotted Ezio. "Sir! Sir! What are our orders?"

"I'm on my way to see," replied Ezio.

"Sir!"

"What is it?"

"Who's in charge now, sir? Now that General Valois is dead?"

"No doubt the king is sending a replacement."

"Is it true, sir—that he died valorously in battle?"

Ezio smiled to himself. "Of course it's true. At the head of his men."

He moved on, toward the Castel itself.

Once within, he found his way up to the ramparts and from this vantage point looked down to the courtyard, where he spotted Cesare himself, talking to a captain of the Papal Guard posted at the door of the inner citadel.

"I need to see the Pope!" Cesare was saying, urgently. "I need to see my father *now!*"

"Of course, Your Grace. You will find His Holiness in his private apartments at the top of the Castel."

"Then get out of my way, you fool!" Cesare thrust

past the hapless captain as the latter gave hasty orders for a wicket gate in the main door to be opened to admit him. Ezio watched for a moment, then made his way around the circumference of the Castel until he came to the place where the secret gate was located. He dropped to the ground and let himself through the gate with Pietro's key.

Once inside, he looked around warily, then, seeing no one, he dived down a stairway in the direction of the cells from which, an age ago, it seemed, he'd rescued Caterina Sforza. Finding a quiet spot, he swiftly shed the French lieutenant's uniform and changed back into his own clothes, which were designed for the work he had to do. He checked his weapons quickly, strapping on the bracer and the poison-blade and confirming that he had a supply of poison darts safely stowed in his belt. Then, hugging the walls, he made off in the direction of the stairway that led to the top of the Castel. But these were guarded and he had to send three guards to their Maker before he could proceed.

At last he arrived at the garden where he had watched Lucrezia and her lover keep their tryst. In daylight he could see that her apartments were part of a complex. Larger and even grander ones stood beyond, and he guessed these to be the Pope's. But as he was making in that direction he was interrupted by a conversation coming from within Lucrezia's rooms. He made his way stealthily to the open window where the voices were coming from and listened. He could just see Lucrezia, apparently none the worse for wear after her ordeal in the cells, talking to the same attendant he'd seen her entrust with the information about her affair with Pietro, which he had passed on to her jealous brother—with evident success, to judge by Cesare's fast return to Rome.

"I don't understand it," Lucrezia was saying irritably. "I ordered a fresh batch of cantarella only last night. Toffana was to have delivered it to me personally by noon. Did you see her? What's going on?"

"I'm terribly sorry, *mia signora*, but I've just heard that the Pope intercepted the delivery. He's taken it all for himself."

"That old bastard. Where is he?"

"In his rooms. Madonna. There's a meeting—"

"A meeting? With whom?"

The attendant hesitated. "With Cesare, Madonna."

Lucrezia took this in, then said, half to herself: "That's strange. My father didn't tell me Cesare was back here again."

Deep in thought, she left the room.

Alone, the attendant started to tidy up, rearranging tables and chairs while muttering under his breath.

Ezio waited a moment to see if there would be any more information useful to him, but all the attendant said was, "That woman gives me so much trouble . . . Why didn't I stay in the stables, where I was well off? Call this a promotion?! I put my head on the block every time I run an errand. *And* I have to taste her food before she does, every time she sits down to a bloody meal." He paused for a moment.

"What a family!" he added.

FORTY-THREE

But Ezio had left before he could hear those last words. He slipped through the garden toward the Pope's apartments and, since the single entrance was heavily guarded and he did not want to draw attention to himself—it wouldn't be long before the bodies of the guards he'd killed downstairs were discovered—he found a place where he could climb to one of the principal windows of the building unobtrusively. His hunch that this would be a window giving on to the Pope's principal chamber paid off, and it had a broad external sill on one end of which he could perch out of sight. Using the blade of his dagger, he was able to pry a sidelight open a fraction, so that he could hear anything that might be said.

Rodrigo—Pope Alexander VI—was alone in the room, standing by a table on which sat a large silver bowl full of red and yellow apples, whose position he adjusted nervously just as the door opened and Cesare entered, unannounced. He was clearly angry, and without any preamble he launched into a bitter diatribe.

"What the hell is going on?" he began.

"I don't know what you mean," replied his father, with reserve.

"Oh, yes, you do! My funds have been cut off, and my troops dispersed."

"Ah. Well, you know that after your banker's tragic . . . demise, Agostino Chigi took over all his affairs . . ."

Cesare laughed mirthlessly. "*Your* banker! I might have known! And my men?"

"Financial difficulties strike all of us from time to time, my boy, even those of us with armies and over-weening ambition."

"Are you going to get Chigi to release money for me or not?"

"No."

"We'll see about that!" Angrily, Cesare snatched an apple from the bowl. Ezio saw that the Pope was watching his son carefully.

"Chigi won't help you," said the Pope levelly. "And he's too powerful for even you to bend to your will."

"In that case," said Cesare, sneering, "I'll use the Piece of Eden to get what I want. It will render your help unnecessary." He bit into the apple with a mean smile.

"That has been made abundantly clear to me already," said the Pope drily. "By the way, I suppose you are aware that General Valois is dead?"

Cesare's smile disappeared in a flash. "No. I have only just returned to Rome." His tone became threatening. "Did you—?"

The Pope spread his hands. "What possible reason could I have had to kill him? Or was he plotting against me, perhaps, with my own, dear, brilliant, *treacherous* captain-general?"

Cesare took another bite of the apple. "I do not have to stand for this!" he snarled as he chewed.

"If you must know, the Assassins murdered him."

Cesare swallowed, his eyes wide. Then his face went dark with fury. "Why did you not stop them?"

"As if I could! It was your decision to attack Monteriggioni, not mine. It's high time you took responsibility for your misdeeds—if it's not too late."

"My *actions*, you mean," replied Cesare proudly. "Despite the constant interference of failures like you!"

The younger man turned to go, but the Pope hurried around the table to block his way to the door.

"You're not going anywhere," Rodrigo growled. "And you are deluded. *I* have the Piece of Eden."

"Liar! Get out of my way, you old fool!"

The Pope shook his head sadly. "I gave you everything I could—and yet it was never enough."

At that instant, Ezio saw Lucrezia burst into the room, her eyes wild.

"Cesare!" she shrieked. "Be careful! He intends to poison you!"

Cesare froze. He looked at the apple in his hand, spitting out the chunk he had just bitten out, his expression a mask. Rodrigo's own expression changed from one of triumph to one of fear. He backed away from his son, putting the table between them.

"Poison me?" said Cesare, his eyes boring into his father's.

"You would not listen to reason!" stammered the Pope.

Cesare smiled as he advanced, very deliberately, on Rodrigo, saying, "Father. Dear Father. Do you not see? I control everything. *All* of it. If I want to live, despite your efforts, I shall live. And if there is anything—*anything*—I want, I take it!" He came close to the Pope and seized him by the collar, raising the poisoned apple in his hand. "For example, if I want you to die, you *die!*"

Pulling his father close he shoved the apple into his open mouth before he had time to close it, and, grabbing him by the head and jaw, forced his lips together and held them shut. Rodrigo struggled and choked on the apple, unable to breathe. He fell to the floor in agony and his two children coldly watched him die.

Cesare wasted no time; kneeling, he searched his dead father's robes. There was nothing. He stood and bore down on his sister, who shrank from him.

"You—you must seek help. The poison is in you, too," she cried.

"Not enough," he barked hoarsely. "And do you

think I am really such a fool as not to have taken a pro-
phylactic antidote before coming here? I know what a
devious old shit our father was, and how he'd react if he
thought for a moment the real power was slipping away
in my direction. Now, he said he had the Piece of Eden."

"He—he—was telling the truth."

Cesare slapped her. "Why was I not told?"

"You were away . . . he had it moved . . . he feared the
Assassins might . . ."

Cesare slapped her again. "You plotted with him!"

"No! No! I thought he had sent messengers to tell
you—"

"Liar!"

"I am telling the truth. I really thought you knew, or
at least had been informed, of what he'd done."

Cesare slapped her again, harder this time, so that she
lost her balance and fell.

"Cesare!" she said as she struggled for breath, panic
and fear in her eyes now. "Are you mad? I am Lucrezia!
Your sister! Your friend! Your lover! Your queen!" And,
rising, she put her hands timidly to his cheeks, to stroke
them. His response was to grab her around the throat
and shake her, as a terrier shakes a ferret.

"You're nothing but a bitch!" He brought his face close
to hers, thrusting it at her aggressively. "Now tell me," he
continued, his voice dangerously low. "Where. Is. It?"

Disbelief showed in her voice when she replied, gag-
ging as she struggled to speak at all, "You . . . never
loved me?"

His response was to let go of her throat and hit her again, this time close to the eye, with a closed fist.

"Where is the Apple? *The Apple!*" he screamed. "Tell me!"

She spat in his face and he grasped her arm and threw her to the floor, kicking her hard as he repeated his question, over and over again. Ezio tensed, forcing himself not to intervene though he was appalled at what he was witnessing. But he had to know the answer.

"All right! All right!" she said at last in a broken voice.

He pulled her to her feet and she placed her lips close to his ear, whispering, to Ezio's fury.

Satisfied, Cesare pushed her away. "Smart decision, little sister." She tried to cling to him but he pushed her away with a gesture of disgust and strode from the room.

As soon as he had gone, Ezio smashed through the window and landed close to Lucrezia, who, all the spirit apparently drained from her, slumped against the wall. Ezio quickly knelt by Rodrigo's inert body and felt for his pulse.

There was none.

"*Requiescat in pace,*" whispered Ezio, rising again and confronting Lucrezia. Looking at him she smiled bitterly, a little of the fire back in her eyes at the sight of him.

"You were there? All the time?"

Ezio nodded.

"Good," she said. "I know where the bastard is going."

"Tell me."

"With pleasure. Saint Peter's. The pavilion in the courtyard . . ."

"Thank you, Madonna."

"Ezio—"

"Yes?"

"Be careful."

FORTY-FOUR

Ezio raced along the Passetto di Borgo, a passageway
that ran through the *rione* of Borgo and connected the
Castel Sant'Angelo with the Vatican. He wished he'd
been able to bring some of his men with him, or had had
time to find a horse, but urgency lent his feet wings, and
any guards he encountered were swiftly thrown aside in
his headlong rush.

Once in the Vatican itself, he made his way to the
pavilion in the courtyard Lucrezia had indicated. With
Rodrigo gone, there was a fair chance that there'd be a
new Pope on whom the Borgia could have no influence,
since the College of Cardinals, apart from those members who'd been well and truly bought, were fed up and
disgusted at being pushed around by this foreign family.

But he had to stop Cesare now, before he could get hold of the Apple and use its power, however dimly he might understand it, to regain all the ground he had lost.

Now was the time to strike his enemy down for good—and it was now or never.

Ezio reached the courtyard and found it deserted. He noticed that at its center, instead of a fountain, stood a large sandstone sculpture of a pinecone, in a stone cup, on a plinth. It stood perhaps ten feet high. He scanned the rest of the sunlit courtyard, but it was plain and bare, with a dusty white floor that burned his eyes with its brightness. There wasn't even a colonnade, and the walls of the surrounding buildings had no decoration, though there were rows of narrow windows high up, and at ground level, one plain door on each side, all of which were closed. An unusually austere place.

He looked again at the pinecone and approached it. Peering closely, he could just discern a narrow gap between the dome of the cone and its body, running around the whole circumference. Climbing up the plinth, he found he was able to steady himself by gripping with his toes, and, holding on with one hand, he ran the other around the rim of the cone where the gap was, feeling carefully for any imperfection, which might possibly disclose a hidden trigger or button.

There! He'd found it. Gently he pressed it, and the top of the cone sprang open on hitherto hidden bronze hinges, firmly screwed into the soft stone and strengthened with cement. In the center of the hollow space that was now revealed, he saw a dark green leather bag. He fumbled at its drawstring with his hand, and the faint glow he saw within its depths confirmed his hopes: He had found the Apple!

His heart was in his mouth as he carefully lifted the bag free—he knew the Borgia, and there was no guarantee that it might not be booby-trapped, but he had to take that risk.

But where the hell was Cesare? The man had had a good few minutes' start on him and had doubtless got here on horseback.

"I'll take that," cried a cold, cruel voice behind him. Bag in hand, Ezio dropped lightly to the ground and turned to confront Cesare, who had just burst through the southern wall door, followed by a troop of his personal guardsmen, who fanned out around the courtyard, surrounding Ezio.

Of course, Ezio thought, he didn't reckon on competition. He had wasted time collecting backup.

"Beat you to it," he taunted Cesare.

"It won't do you any good, Ezio Auditore. You've been a thorn in my side too long. But it ends here. Now. My sword will take your life."

He drew a modern schiavona with a basket hilt and took a step toward Ezio. But then, suddenly, he turned grey and clasped his stomach, dropping his sword as his knees buckled. Not a strong enough antidote, evidently, thought Ezio, breathing a sigh of relief.

"Guards!" croaked Cesare, struggling to stay on his feet.

There were ten of them, five armed with muskets.

Ezio ~~ducked and dived~~ as they fired at him, the balls
from their muskets cannoning into the floor and walls
as Ezio skittered into cover behind a pillar. Whisking
out the poison darts from his belt one by one, he sprang
from his cover—close enough to the musketeers to hurl
the darts. Cesare's men weren't expecting a ranged
assault—they looked in bewildered surprise when Ezio
launched the darts. The first three found their marks
with polished ease—within seconds three guards were
down—the poison was beautifully quick in its fatal
effect. One of the musketeers, regaining a moment's
composure, hurled his weapon like a club—Ezio ducked,
and the weapon went spiraling over his head. He quickly
loosed the next two darts, and the musketeers were all
down. Ezio had no time to retrieve his darts as Leonardo
had advised. The five other guards, swordsmen, after
recovering from their initial shock—for they'd assumed
that their companions with the guns would have made
short work of the Assassin—closed in quickly, wielding
heavy falchions. Ezio, almost dancing among them as he
avoided their clumsy blows—the swords were too heavy
for fast work or much maneuverability—released the
newly recrafted poison-blade and drew his own sword.
Knowing he didn't have much time to engage these men
before Cesare made a move, Ezio's fighting technique
was more sparse and efficient than usual—he preferred
to lock each opponent's blade with his own sword and
call into effect his poison-blade to finish the job. The
first two fell without a whisper—at which point the
remaining three decided their best attack was all at once.

Ezio pulled back five quick paces, extending his sword up full and high, and charged forward at the nearest of the three oncoming guards. As he drew into range, Ezio skidded to his knees—sliding across the ground, under the blade of the baffled guard. The poison-blade nicked the man's thigh—but only as Ezio was skidding past, barreling toward the remaining guards, his sword slashing at the tendons of their lower legs. Both men shrieked as Ezio's blade tore through, and the men fell, their legs useless.

Cesare had been watching all this in quiet disbelief; but as Ezio had careened across toward these last three guards, Cesare had decided not to wait for the rest of the fight. He recovered himself enough to turn and flee.

Hemmed in by the guards and unable to follow, Ezio had watched him go out of the corner of his eye.

But he still had the Apple. And he remembered enough of its power—how could he forget?—to use it, after the melee was over, to guide him back through the Vatican by a different route from that by which he'd come—reckoning as he did that Cesare would have wasted no time in securing the Passetto di Borgo. Glowing from within the leather bag, the Apple indicated on its surface a way through the high, painted halls and chambers of the offices of the Vatican toward the Sistine Chapel, and thence by a southward-leading corridor into Saint Peter's itself. Its power was such that passing monks and priests within the Vatican turned away from Ezio, avoiding him, and papal guards remained rigidly at their posts.

Ezio wondered how soon the news of the Pope's death would filter down through the hierarchy of the Vatican to these people. The confusion that would follow in its wake would need a strong hand to control, and he prayed that Cesare would not have the opportunity to take advantage of any uncertainty to stake his own claim, if not to the Papacy itself, for that was out of even his reach, then at least by influencing the election in order to place a new Pope, friendly to his ambitions, on Saint Peter's throne.

Passing young Michelangelo's brilliant new sculpture of the Pietà on his left, Ezio left the basilica and blended into the crowds milling about in the rather shabby old square that lay in front of the east entrance.

FORTY-FIVE

By the time he had reached the Assassins' hideout on Tiber Island, church bells had begun to ring out all over Rome. They were sounding the death knell.

He found his friends waiting for him.

"Rodrigo is dead," he announced.

"We guessed as much from the bells," said Machiavelli. "Magnificent work!"

"It was not by my hand—but Cesare's."

It took a moment for this to sink in. Then Machiavelli spoke again. "And what of Cesare?"

"He lives—though the Pope tried to poison him."

"The serpent is biting its own tail," said La Volpe.

"Then the day is saved!" cried Claudia.

"No!" said Machiavelli. "If he's freed himself of the restraint of his father, Cesare may yet regain the ground he has lost. We must not allow him to assemble his remaining supporters. The coming weeks will be critical!"

"With your aid I will hunt him down," said Ezio firmly.

"Niccolò is right—we must act fast," La Volpe put in. "Do you hear those trumpets? They are a summons to the Borgia forces to gather."

"Do you also know where?" asked Bartolomeo.

"It's likely that they'll rally their troops in the piazza in front of Cesare's palace in Trastevere."

"My men will patrol the city," said Bartolomeo, "but we'd need a full army to do it properly."

Ezio carefully produced the Apple from its bag. It glowed dully. "We have one," he said. "Or at least, something as good."

"Do you know what to do?" asked Machiavelli.

"I remember enough from when Leonardo experimented with it long ago in Venice," replied Ezio. He held the strange artifact aloft and, concentrating, tried to project his thoughts at it.

There was no response for several minutes, and he was about to give up, when, slowly at first, and then with increasing energy, the Apple began to glow more and more brightly, until the light emanating from it made them cover their eyes.

"Stand back!" bawled Bartolomeo, as Claudia gasped in alarm, and even La Volpe started back.

"No," said Machiavelli. "Science—but something

out of our reach." He looked at Ezio. "If only Leonardo were here!"

"As long as it serves our purpose," said Ezio.

"Look!" said La Volpe. "It's showing us the campanile of Santa Maria in Trastevere! That's where Cesare must be!"

"You were right!" cried Bartolomeo. "But look at the number of troops he still seems to have!"

"I'm going. Now," said Ezio, as the projected scene faded and the Apple became inert.

"We're coming with you."

"No!" Ezio held up a hand. "Claudia—I want you to go back to the Rosa in Fiore. Get your girls to find out all they can about Cesare's plans. And mobilize our recruits. Gilberto, please get your thieves to fan out all over the city and bring word of any Templar chapters that may be reorganizing. Our enemies are fighting for their very lives! Bartolomeo, organize your men and have them ready to move at a moment's notice."

He turned to Machiavelli. "Niccolò. Get over to the Vatican. The College of Cardinals will be going into conclave soon, to elect a new Pope."

"Indeed. And Cesare will certainly try to use what influence he has left to elevate a candidate favorable to him to the papal throne—or at least someone he can manipulate."

"But Cardinal della Rovere wields great authority now. And he is the Borgia's implacable enemy, as you know. If only—"

"I will go and talk to the cardinal camerlengo. The election may be long and drawn out."

"We must take every advantage we can of the inter-regnum. Thank you, Niccolò."

"How will you manage on your own, Ezio?"

"I'm not on my own," said Ezio, gently replacing the Apple in its bag. "I'm taking this with me."

"Just as long as you know how to keep it under control," said Bartolomeo mistrustfully. "Ask me, it's a creation straight out of Beelzebub's workshop."

"In the wrong hands, perhaps. But as long as we have it—"

"Then don't let it out of your grasp, let alone your sight!"

They broke up then, each hastening away to attend to the duties Ezio had assigned them. Ezio himself crossed to the west bank of the river and sprinted the short distance to the church La Volpe had recognized in the vision accorded them by the Apple.

The scene had changed by the time he reached it, though he saw units of soldiers in Cesare's livery making their way out of the square in organized groups as if under orders. These were disciplined men who understood that failure would spell their ruin.

There was no sign of Cesare, but Ezio knew that he must still be sick from the effects of the poison. His rallying call to the troops must have taken it out of him. There was only one place he'd think of retreating to—his own fortified palazzo, not far off. Ezio set off in its direction.

He joined a group of Borgia attendants, whom he recognized from Cesare's crest, which they wore on the shoulders of their cloaks, and blended in with them, though they were too agitated to have noticed him even if he hadn't been using the secret skill that rendered him as good as invisible. Using them as cover, he slipped through the palazzo's gates, which opened quickly for them and then, just as quickly, clanged shut again behind.

He slipped into the shadows of the courtyard's colonnade and glided along the perimeter of the inner walls, stopping to peer in at each unshuttered window. Then, ahead, he saw a door with two guards posted outside it. He looked around. The rest of the courtyard was deserted. He approached silently, releasing his hidden-blade, and fell upon the guards before they knew what was happening. One, he killed instantly. The other managed to get a blow in that would have severed his left hand from his arm had it not been for his bracer, and while the man was recovering from his astonishment at what looked like witchcraft, Ezio plunged the blade into the base of his throat, and he fell like a sack to the ground.

The door was unlocked and its hinges, when Ezio warily tried them, well oiled. Noiselessly, he slid into the room.

It was large and gloomy. Ezio took refuge behind an arras near the door, set there to exclude drafts, and watched the men seated around a large oak table at its center. The table was spread with papers and illuminated by candles in two iron candelabra. At its head sat Cesare, his personal doctor, Gaspar Torella, at his side. His face was grey, and he was sweating prodigiously. He was glaring at his officers.

"You must hunt them down!" he was saying, grasping the arms of his chair tightly in an effort to stay upright.

"They are everywhere and nowhere at once!" declared one, bolder than the rest, helplessly.

"I don't care how you do it—just do it!"

"We cannot, *signore*—without your guidance. The Assassins have regrouped. With the French gone, or in disarray, our own forces are scarcely able to match them. They have spies everywhere—our own network is no longer able to root them out! And Ezio Auditore has turned vast numbers of the citizenry to his cause."

"I am ill, *idioti!* I depend on your initiative!" Cesare sighed, falling back in his chair. "I was damned nearly killed! But I still have teeth!"

"Sir—"

"Just hold them at bay, if that's the best you can do!" Cesare paused to catch his breath, and Dr. Torella mopped the man's brow with a lint cloth soaked in vinegar or some other strong-smelling astringent, muttering soothingly to his patient as he did so. "Soon," Cesare continued. "Soon, Micheletto will reach Rome with my own forces from Romagna and the north, and then you will see how quickly the Assassins will crumble into dust!"

Ezio stepped forth and revealed the bag containing the Apple. "You delude yourself, Cesare!" he said in a loud voice. A voice of true authority.

Cesare started from his chair, fear in his eyes. "You! How many lives do you have, Ezio? But this time you will surely die! Call the guard! Now!" he bellowed at his officers as he allowed his doctor to hurry him from the room to safety through an inner door.

Lightning fast, one of the officers made for the door to raise the alarm. The others drew pistols and leveled them at Ezio, who just as swiftly withdrew the Apple from its bag and held it aloft, concentrating hard and pulling the hood of his tunic down low to shield his eyes.

The Apple began to pulsate and glow, and the glow turned to an incandescence that gave out no heat but was as bright as the sun. The room turned white.

"What sorcery is this?" shouted one of the officers, firing wildly. By chance his ball hit the Apple, but it had no more effect on it than a handful of dust.

"Truly, this man has God Himself on his side!" another bawled, vainly trying to shield his eyes and staggering blindly in what he thought was the direction of the door.

The light increased. The officers blundered up against the table, covering their eyes with their hands.

"What's happening?"

"How is this possible?"

"Do not smite me, Lord!"

"I cannot *see!*"

His lips pressed together in concentration, Ezio continued to project his will through the Apple, but even he dared not look up from under the protecting peak of his cowl. He had to judge the moment to cease. When he did so, a wave of exhaustion hit him as the Apple, invisible within its own light, suddenly, with no after-glow, went dead. There was no sound in the room. Cautiously, Ezio lifted his hood and saw that the room was as before. The candles on the table cast a pool of light at the center of the gloom. They burned on, almost reassuringly, as if nothing had happened. Their flames were steady, as there was not the hint of a breeze.

The tapestry on the arras was bleached of all its color.

All the officers lay dead around the table, save the one who had first been making for the door, and he was slumped against it, his hand still on the latch. Ezio went over to him. He had to move him aside in order to leave.

As he rolled the man over, he inadvertently looked into his eyes.

He wished he hadn't—it was a sight he would never forget.

"*Requiescat in pace,*" said Ezio, acknowledging the chill realization that the Apple indeed had powers that, if unleashed beyond check, could control the minds of men; could open up undreamed-of possibilities, and worlds.

And wreak destruction so terrible as to be beyond the power of imagination itself.

FORTY-SIX

The conclave was undecided. Despite the efforts of Cardinal della Rovere to outwit him, Cesare clearly still had enough clout to hold him in check. Fear, or self-interest, kept the cardinals wavering. Machiavelli guessed what they were trying to do—they would find a candidate to elect who would, perhaps, not last long, but who would be acceptable to all parties. An interim Pope—a caretaker, until the balance of power resolved itself.

Bearing this in mind, Ezio was pleased when, after weeks of deadlock, Claudia brought news to Tiber Island.

"The Cardinal of Rouen, a Frenchman, Georges d'Amboise, has revealed under . . . duress . . . that Cesare has planned a meeting with Templar loyalists in the countryside, outside Rome. The cardinal himself attends."

"When is it?"

"Tonight."

"Where?"

"The location is to be kept secret until the last minute."

"Then I will go to the cardinal's residence and follow him when he leaves."

"They have elected a new Pope," said Machiavelli, coming in hurriedly. "Your pet French cardinal, Claudia, will take the news to Cesare tonight. In fact, a small delegation of them, still friendly to the Borgia, is going with him."

"Who is the new Pope?" asked Ezio.

Machiavelli smiled. "It is as I thought," he said. "Cardinal Piccolomini. Not an old man, he's sixty-four, but he's in poor health. He's chosen to be known as Pius III."

"Whom does he support?"

"We don't know yet, but all the foreign ambassadors put pressure on Cesare to leave Rome during the election. Della Rovere is furious, but he knows how to wait."

Ezio spent the rest of the day in consultation with Bartolomeo, and between them they put together a combined force of recruits and *condottieri* strong enough for any battle that might ensue with Cesare.

"Turns out just as well you didn't kill Cesare back at his palazzo," said Bartolomeo. "This way, he'll draw all his supporters to him and we can smash the fuckin' guts out of 'em." He looked at Ezio. "Got to hand it to you, my friend. You might almost have planned it this way."

Ezio smiled. He went back to his lodgings, where he strapped on his pistol and put the double-blade into the wallet on his belt.

With a small group of handpicked men, Ezio made up the advance guard, leaving the rest to follow some way behind. When the Cardinal of Rouen rode out in the late afternoon with his fellows and their entourage, Ezio and his horsemen followed at a safe distance. They did not have a long ride, as they expected, and the cardinal stopped at a large country estate whose mansion was set behind fortified walls near the shores of Lake Bracciano.

Ezio, alone, scaled the walls and shadowed the delegation of cardinals as it made its way to the great hall of the mansion, blending in with the Borgia's hundred or so leading officers, though there were many other people present, from other lands, whom Ezio did not recognize but knew must be members of the Templar Order. Cesare, fully recovered now, stood on a raised dais in the center of the crowded hall. Torches flickered in their sconces on the stone walls, making shadows leap and giving the congress more the air of a witches' coven than a gathering of military forces.

Outside, Borgia soldiers were drawn up in numbers that surprised Ezio, who had not forgotten Cesare's remark about Micheletto bringing his remaining troops out of the provinces to back him up. He was worried that even with Bartolomeo's men and his own recruits, who had drawn up a couple of hundred yards from the mansion, they might find their match in this assembly. But it was too late now.

Ezio watched as a pathway was made between the serried ranks in the hall to allow the cardinals to approach the dais.

"Join me! And I will take back Rome for us!" Cesare was declaiming as the Cardinal of Rouen, their spokesman, made his appearance with his fellow prelates. Seeing them, Cesare broke off.

"What news of the conclave?" he demanded.

The Cardinal of Rouen hesitated. "Good news—and bad," he said.

"Spit it out!"

"We have elected Piccolomini."

Cesare considered this. "Well, at least it isn't that fisherman's son, della Rovere!" Then he turned on the cardinal. "But it's still not the man I wanted! I wanted a puppet! Piccolomini may have one foot in the grave, but he can still do me a lot of damage. I paid for your appointment! Is this how you thank me?"

"Della Rovere is a powerful foe!" The cardinal hesitated again. "And Rome is not what it once was. Borgia money has become tainted!"

Cesare looked at him coldly. "You will regret this decision," he said frostily.

The cardinal bowed his head and turned to go, but as he did so, he spotted Ezio, who had made his way forward in order to see more clearly.

"It's the Assassin!" he yelled. "His sister put me to the question! That's how he got here! Run! He'll kill us all!"

The cardinals, as one man, took to their heels amid a general panic. Ezio followed them and, once outside, fired his pistol. The sound carried to his advance guard, posted just outside the walls, and they in turn fired muskets as signal to Bartolomeo to attack. They arrived just as the gates in the walls were opened to allow the fleeing cardinals to depart. The defenders had no time to close them before being overpowered by the advance guard, who managed to hold the gate until Bartolomeo, whirling Bianca above his head and roaring his war cry, came up with the main Assassin force. Ezio fired his second shot into the belly of a Borgia guard who came screaming up, flailing a wicked-looking mace, but he had no time to reload. In any case, for close fighting, the double-blade was the perfect weapon. Finding an alcove in the wall, he took shelter in it and, with practiced hands, exchanged the pistol for the blade. Then he rushed back into the hall, looking for Cesare.

The battle in the mansion and the area within its encircling walls was short and bloody. The Borgia and Templar troops were unprepared for an attack of this magnitude, and they were trapped within the walls. They fought hard, and many a *condottiero* and Assassin recruit lay dead by the time it was over. The Assassins had the advantage of being already mounted, and few of the Borgia faction could get to their own horses before they were cut down.

It was late by the time the dust had settled. Ezio, bleeding from a flesh wound in his chest, had laid about him so furiously with the double-blade that it had sliced through his own glove and cut his hand deeply. Around him lay a host of bodies, half, perhaps, of the assembly—those who had not been able to flee and ride off south, into the night.

But Cesare was not among them. Cesare, too, had fled.

FORTY-SEVEN

Much occurred in the weeks that followed. The Assassins sought Cesare frantically, but in vain. He did not return to Rome, and indeed Rome *seemed* purged of all Borgia and Templar influence, though Ezio and his companions remained on the alert, knowing that as long as the enemy lived, there was danger. They suspected there were still pockets of die-hard loyalists, just waiting for the signal.

And the Vatican was rocked once more. Pius III was a bookish and deeply religious man. After a reign of only twenty-six days, his already frail health succumbed to the extra pressures and responsibilities the Papacy placed on it, and, in October, he died. But he had not, as Ezio had feared, proved to be a puppet of the Borgia. Rather, during the short span of his supremacy, he set in motion reforms within the College of Cardinals that swept away all the corruption and sensuality fomented by his predecessor. There would be no more selling of cardinalates for money, and no more accepting of payments in order to let well-off murderers escape the gallows. Alexander VI's pragmatic doctrine, "Let them live in order to repent," no longer held currency.

And he had issued a warrant throughout the Papal States for the arrest of Cesare Borgia.

His successor was elected immediately and by an overwhelming majority. Only three cardinals opposed him, and one of them was Georges d'Amboise, the Cardinal of Rouen, who vainly hoped to gain the triple tiara for the French. Following the check in his career caused by the election of Pius, Giuliano della Rovere, Cardinal of San Pietro in Vincoli, had wasted no time in consolidating his supporters and assuring himself of the Papacy at the next opportunity, which he knew would come soon.

Julius II, as he styled himself, was tough man of sixty, still vigorous, as much in his arms and loins as in his brain. He was a man of great energy, as Ezio would soon learn, a political intriguer and a warrior, and proud of his humble origins as the descendant of fishermen—for had not Saint Peter himself been a fisherman?

But the Borgia threat still cast its shadow.

"If only Cesare would show himself," growled Bartolomeo as he and Ezio sat in conference in the map-room of his barracks.

"He will. But only when he's ready."

"My spies tell me that he plans to gather his best men to attack Rome through one of its principal gates."

Ezio considered this. "If Cesare's coming from the north, as seems almost certain, he'll try to get in by the gate near the Castra Praetoria. He might even try to retake the Castra itself. It's in a strong strategic position."

"You're probably right."

Ezio stood. "Gather the Assassins. We'll face Cesare together."

"And if we cannot?"

"That's fine talk from you, Barto! If we can't, I will face him alone."

They parted company, arranging to meet in Rome later in the day. If there was going to be an attack, the Holy City would be ready for it.

And Ezio's hunch proved right. He'd told Bartolomeo to summon the others to a church piazza near the Castra. All of them arrived, and they made their way to the northern gate, already heavily defended, as Julius II had shown himself perfectly happy to accept Ezio's advice. But the sight that met their eyes, a couple of hundred yards' distant, was a sobering one. There was Cesare, on a pale horse, surrounded by a group of officers wearing the uniform of his own private army, and behind him was at least a battalion of his own troops.

Even at that distance, Ezio's keen ears could pick out Cesare's bombast—the odd thing was, why did anyone fall for it? At least, why do so still?

"All of Italy shall be united, and you will rule at my side!" Cesare was proclaiming. Then he turned and spotted Ezio and his fellow Assassins ranged along the ramparts of the gate.

He rode a little closer, though not close enough to be within crossbow or musket range. But he was alone.

"Come to watch my triumph?" he shouted up at them. "Don't worry. This isn't all my strength. Soon, Micheletto will arrive with my armies! But you will all be dead by then! I have enough men to deal with you!"

Ezio looked at him; then, turning, he looked down at the mass of papal troops, Assassin recruits, and *condottieri* ranged beneath him on the inside of the gate. He raised a hand, and the gatekeepers drew back the wooden staves that kept the gates shut. They stood ready to open them at his next signal. Ezio kept his hand raised.

"My men will never fail me!" cried Cesare. "They know what awaits them if they do! Soon—*soon!*—you will pass from this Earth, and my dominions will return to me!"

Ezio thought, *The New Disease has affected the balance of his mind.* He let his hand drop. Below him, the gates swung open and the Roman forces streamed out, cavalry first, infantry running behind. Desperately, Cesare yanked at his reins, forcing the bit hard into his horse's mouth, and wheeled. But the violence of his maneuver made his mount stumble, and he was quickly overtaken. As for his battalion, it broke and ran at the sight of the oncoming Roman brigades.

Well, well, thought Ezio. *My question is answered. These men were prepared to fight for money, but not from loyalty. And you can't buy loyalty.*

"Kill the Assassins!" yelled Cesare frantically. "Uphold

the honor of the Borgia!" But it was all in vain. He himself was surrounded.

"Throw down your arms, Cesare," Ezio called to him.

"Never!"

"This is not your city anymore. You are no longer captain-general. The Orsini and the Colonna families are on the side of the new Pope, and when some of them paid lip service to you, that was all it was—lip service. They were only waiting for the chance to get back the cities and estates you stole from them."

A small deputation rode out through the gates now. Six knights in black armor, one of them bearing Julius II's crest—a sturdy oak tree—on a pennant. At their head, on a dapple-grey palfrey—the very opposite of a warhorse— rode an elegantly dressed man whom Ezio instantly recognized as Fabio Orsini. He led his men straight up to the still-proud Cesare.

Silence fell.

"Cesare Borgia, called Valentino, sometime Cardinal of Valencia and Duke of Valence," Orsini proclaimed, and Ezio could see the triumphant twinkle in his eye. "By order of His Holiness, Pope Julius II, I arrest you for the crimes of murder, betrayal, and incest!"

The six knights fell in next to Cesare, two on each side, one before and one behind. The reins of his horse were taken from him and he was tied to the saddle.

"No, no, no, *no!*" bawled Cesare. "This is not how it ends!"

One of the knights flicked at Cesare's horse's rump, and it started forward at a trot.

"This is *not* how it ends!" Cesare yelled defiantly. "Chains will not hold me!" His voice rose to a scream. "I will not die by the hand of man!"

Everybody heard him, but nobody was listening.

"Come on, you," said Orsini crisply.

FORTY-EIGHT

"I was wondering what had happened to you," Ezio said. "Then I saw the chalked drawing of the pointing hand. So I knew you were signaling me, which is why I sent you a message. And now—here you are! I thought you might have slipped away to France."

"Not me—not yet!" said Leonardo, brushing some dust off a chair at the Assassins' Tiber Island hideaway before he sat down. Sunlight streamed in through the high windows.

"I'm glad of it. Even gladder that you didn't get caught in the dragnet for any last Borgia supporters that the new Pope's organized."

"Well, you can't keep a good man down," replied Leonardo. He was as finely dressed as ever and didn't appear to have been affected by recent events at all. "Pope Julius isn't a fool—he knows who'd be useful to him and who wouldn't, never mind what they'd done in the past."

"As long as they were truly repentant."

"As you say," Leonardo answered drily.

"And are you prepared to be useful to me?"

"Haven't I always been?" Leonardo smiled. "But is there anything to worry about, now that Cesare's under lock and key? Only a matter of time before they take him out and burn him at the stake. Look at the list of arraignments! It's as long as your arm!"

"Maybe you're right."

"Of course, the world wouldn't *be* the world, without trouble," said Leonardo, going off on another tack. "It's all very well that Cesare's been brought down, but I've lost a valuable patron, and I see they're thinking of bringing that young whippersnapper Michelangelo here from Florence. I ask you! All he can do is knock out sculptures."

"Pretty good architect, too, from what I hear. And not a bad painter."

Leonardo gave him a black look. "You know that pointing finger I drew? One day, soon I hope, it's going to be at the center of a portrait. Of a man. John the Baptist. Pointing toward heaven. Now *that* will be a painting!"

"I didn't say he was as good a painter as you," added Ezio quickly. "And as for being an inventor . . ."

"He should stick to what he knows best, if you ask me."

"Leo—are you jealous?"

"Me? Never!"

It was time to bring Leonardo back to the problem that was bothering Ezio, the reason he'd responded to the signal by seeking out his old friend and getting him to come over. He just hoped he could trust him, but he knew Leonardo well enough to know what made him tick.

"Your former employer . . ." he began.

"Cesare?"

"Yes. I didn't like the way he said, 'Chains will not hold me.'"

"Come on, Ezio. He's in the deepest dungeon of the Castel Sant'Angelo. How the mighty are fallen, eh?"

"He still has friends."

"A few misguided creatures may still think he has a future, but since Micheletto and his armies don't seem to have materialized, I can't see that there's any real danger."

"Even if Micheletto failed to keep the remains of Cesare's forces together, and I admit that seems likely, since none of our spies out in the countryside have reported any troop movements at all—"

"Look, Ezio, when the news reached them of della Rovere's elevation to the Papacy and then, on top of that, Cesare's arrest, the old Borgia army probably scattered like ants from a nest when you pour boiling water into it."

"I won't rest easy until I know Cesare is dead."

"Well, there is a way to find out."

Ezio looked at Leonardo. "The Apple, do you mean?"

"Where is it?"

"Here."

"Then get it, let's consult it."

Ezio hesitated. "No. It's too powerful. I must hide it forever from mankind."

"What, a valuable thing like that?" Leonardo shook his head.

"You said yourself, many years ago, that it should never be allowed to fall into the wrong hands."

"Well, then, all we have to do is keep it out of the wrong hands."

"There is no guarantee that we can always do that."

Leonardo looked serious. "Look, Ezio—if you ever do decide to bury it somewhere, promise me one thing."

"Yes?"

"Well, two things. First, hang on to it for as long as you need it. You need to have all you can on your side if your goal is finally to eradicate the Borgia and the Templars forever. But when you've done, and you do hide it from the world, then think of it as a seed that you plant. Leave some kind of clue as to its whereabouts for such as may be able to find it. Future generations—perhaps future Assassins—may have need of the Apple's power— to use it on the side of Good."

"And if it fell into the hands of another Cesare?"

"Back on Cesare, I see. Listen, why not put yourself out of your misery and see if the Apple can offer you any guidance?"

Ezio wrestled with himself for a few moments longer, then said, "All right. I agree."

He disappeared for a moment and then returned, holding a square box, lead-covered and closed with a massive lock. He took a key, tied to a silver chain around his neck, from within his tunic and opened the box. There, on a bed of green velvet, lay the Apple. It looked drab and grey, as it always did when inert, the size of a small melon and a texture that was curiously soft and pliant, like human skin.

"Ask it," urged Leonardo, his eyes keen as he saw the Apple again. Ezio knew his friend was fighting down a desire to grab the thing and run, and he understood how great the temptation was for the polymath, whose thirst for knowledge at times almost overwhelmed him and never let him rest.

He held the thing up and closed his eyes, concentrating his thoughts, formulating the questions. The Apple began to glow almost at once. Then it began to throw images onto the wall.

They came fast and did not last long, but Ezio—and Ezio alone—saw Cesare break from his prison and make his escape from Rome. That was all, until the inchoate images on the wall coalesced to show a busy seaport, the water shining and glittering beneath a southern sun, and a fleet in the harbor. The vision dissolved, and then there was a view of a distant castle, or perhaps a fortified hill town, far away, as Ezio somehow knew, and, judging from the landscape and the heat of the sun, certainly not in the Papal States of Italy. The architecture, too, looked foreign, but neither Ezio nor Leonardo could place it. Then Ezio saw Mario's citadel at Monteriggioni, and the picture moved and shifted to take him to Mario's private, secret study—the Sanctuary—where the Codex pages had been assembled. The concealed door to it was closed, and on the outside of it Ezio could see arcane figures and letters written. Then it was as if he were an eagle flying, flying over the ruins of the Assassins' former stronghold. Then, abruptly, the Apple went dead, and the only light in the room was once again provided by the calm sunlight.

"He will escape! I have to go!" Ezio dropped the Apple back into its box and stood so abruptly that he knocked his chair over.

"What about your friends?"

"The Brotherhood must stand, with or without me. That is how I have built it." Taking it from its box again, Ezio placed the Apple in its leather bag. "Forgive me, Leo—I have no time to waste." He already had his hidden-blade and his bracer strapped on. He packed the pistol and some ammunition in his belt wallet.

"Stop. You must think. You must plan."

"My plan is to finish Cesare. I should have done it long ago."

Leonardo spread his hands. "I see that I cannot stop you. But I have no plans to leave Rome, and you know where my studio is."

"I have a gift for you," said Ezio. There was a small strongbox on the table between them. Ezio laid a hand on it. "Here."

Leonardo rose. "If this is goodbye, then keep your money. I do not want it."

Ezio smiled. "Of course it isn't goodbye, and of course you want it. You need it, for your work. Take it.

Think of *me* as your patron, if you like, until you find a better one."

The two men hugged each other.

"We will see each other again," said Ezio. "You have my word. *Buona fortuna*, my oldest friend."

What the Apple had predicted could not be emended, for the Apple showed the future as it would be, and no man or woman could alter that, any more than he or she could change the past.

As Ezio approached the Castel Sant'Angelo, he could see papal guards, the new ones who wore the livery of Julius II, running out of the ancient fortress and dispersing in organized bands across the river and down the surrounding streets. Bells and trumpets rang out a warning. Ezio knew what had happened, even before a breathless captain he stopped told him:

"Cesare's escaped!"

"When?"

"The guards were being changed. About half an hour ago." Half an hour! Exactly the time when the Apple had shown it happening!

"Do you know how?"

"Unless he can walk through walls, we have no idea. But it looks as if he had friends on the inside."

"Who? Lucrezia?"

"No. She hasn't stirred from her apartments since all this blew up. But the Pope's had her under house arrest since he took power. We've arrested two guards who used to work for the Borgia. One's a former blacksmith. He might have been able to jimmy the lock, though there's no sign of damage to the cell door, so they probably just used the key. If they're guilty."

"Is Lucrezia giving any trouble?"

"Strangely, not. She seems . . . resigned to her fate."

"Don't trust her! Whatever you do, don't be lulled into a sense of false security by her manner. When she's quiet, she's at her most dangerous."

"She's being guarded by Swiss mercenaries. They're hard as rocks."

"Good."

Ezio thought hard. If Cesare had any friends left in Rome, and evidently he had, they'd get him out of the city as fast as they could. But the gates would already have been sealed, and from what he had already seen, Cesare, bereft of the Apple and unskilled in the Assassins' techniques, would not be able to escape the dragnets and cordons being set up all over Rome.

That left one possibility.

The river!

The Tiber flowed into Rome from the north and left it to the west, where it flowed into the sea only a few miles away, at Ostia. Ezio remembered the slave traders he had killed: they had been in Cesare's pay. They would not have been the only ones! Get him on a boat, or a small seagoing ship, disguised as a mariner or simply concealed under a tarpaulin among the cargo. It wouldn't take long for a ship under sail or oars, going with the current, to reach the Tyrrhenian Sea, and from there—well, that depended on what Cesare's plans were. The thing was to catch him before he could put them into effect!

He made his way by the quickest route down to the midtown docks, those closest to the Castel. The quays were chockablock with boats and ships of all shapes and sizes. It would be like looking for a needle in a haystack. Half an hour. He'd barely have had time to cast off yet, and the tide was only just rising.

Ezio had the Apple with him. Finding a quiet spot, he crouched down and, without hesitation this time, drew it out. There was nowhere here for it to project its images, but he felt that, if he trusted it, it would find another way of communicating with him. He held it as close to him as he dared and closed his eyes, willing it to respond to his question.

It did not glow, but he could feel it grow warm through his gloves, and it began to pulse. As it did, strange sounds came from it—or they were sounds within his head, he wasn't sure which. Then a woman's voice, oddly familiar though he could not place it, and seemingly far distant, said softly but clearly, "The small caravel with red sails at Pier Six."

Ezio ran down to the quay. It took him a little time, pushing his way through a throng of busy, cursing mariners, to locate Pier Six, and when he did so, the boat that answered the Apple's description was just casting off. It, too, seemed familiar. Its decks were stacked with several sacks and boxes of cargo—boxes large enough to conceal a man, and on deck Ezio recognized, with a shock, the seaman he had left virtually for dead after his abortive rescue of Madonna Solari. The man was limping badly as he approached one of the boxes and, with a mate, shifted its position. Ezio noticed that the box had holes bored along each side near the top. He ducked behind a rowboat, raised on trestles for repainting, to keep out of sight, as the sailor he had lamed turned to look back toward the quay, scanning it, perhaps to check for pursuers.

He watched helplessly for a moment as the caravel pushed out into midstream, raising one of its sails to catch the stiff breeze out there. Even on horseback, he couldn't follow the little ship along the river's bank, since the path was often blocked or interrupted by buildings that came right up to the water. He had to find a boat for himself.

He made his way back to the quay and walked hastily along it. The crew of a shallop had just finished unloading, and the boat itself was still rigged. Ezio approached the men.

"I need to hire your boat," he said urgently.

"We've just put in."

"I'll pay handsomely." Ezio delved into his purse and showed a handful of gold ducats.

"We've got to get the cargo seen to first," said one crew member.

"Where d'you want to go?" asked another.

"Downstream," said Ezio. "And I need to go now."

"See to the cargo," said a newcomer, approaching.

"I'll take the *signore*. Jacopo, you come with me. Won't take more than the two of us to sail it."

Ezio turned to thank the newcomer and recognized, with a shock, Claudio, the young thief he'd rescued from the Borgia guards.

Claudio smiled at him. "One way of thanking you, *Messere*, for saving my life. And keep your money, by the way."

"What are you doing here?"

"I wasn't cut out for thievery," said Claudio. "La Volpe saw that. I've always been a good sailor, so he lent me the money to buy this boat. I'm the master. Do a good trade, between here and Ostia."

"We need to hurry. Cesare Borgia's escaped!"

Claudio turned and barked out an order to his mate. Jacopo sprang aboard and began to prepare the sails. Then he and Ezio embarked, and the rest of the crew cast them off.

The shallop, free of its cargo, felt light in the water. Once they reached midstream, Claudio put on as much sail as he could. Soon, the caravel, more heavily laden, ceased to be a speck in the distance.

"That what we're after?" asked Claudio.

"Yes, please God," replied Ezio.

"Better get your head down," said Claudio. "We're well-known on this stretch, but if they see you, they'll know what's up. I know that craft. Run by an odd bunch. Don't socialize."

"Do you know how many crew?"

"Five, usually. Maybe fewer. But don't worry. I

haven't forgotten what La Volpe taught me—still comes in handy, sometimes—and Jacopo here knows how to use a blackjack."

Ezio sank beneath the low gunwale, raising his head from time to time just enough to check the closing distance between them and their objective.

But the caravel was a faster vessel than the shallop, and Ostia was in sight before Claudio could draw alongside. He boldly hailed the caravel.

"You look pretty heavily laden," he called. "What you got on board—gold bullion?"

"None of your business," the master of the caravel snarled back from his place near the wheel. "And back off. You're crowding my water."

"Sorry, mate," said Claudio, as Jacopo brought the shallop right alongside, bumping the caravel's fenders. Then he cried to Ezio, *"Now!"*

Ezio leapt from his hiding place across the narrow gap dividing the two ships. Recognizing him, the lame sailor, with a strangled roar, lunged at him with a billhook, but it caught on Ezio's bracer, and Ezio was able to pull him close enough to finish him with a deep thrust of the hidden-blade into his side. But while he was so engaged, he failed to notice another crewman stealing up on him from behind, brandishing a cutlass. He turned in momentary alarm, unable to avoid the descending blade, when a shot rang out and the man arched his back, letting his cutlass fall to the deck before crashing overboard himself.

"Look out!" yelled Jacopo, who was holding the

shallop close alongside the caravel as the master of the other boat strove to get clear. A third seaman had emerged from below and was using a crowbar to pry open the upright crate with the holes along its top sides, while a fourth was crouching at his side, covering him with a wheel-lock pistol. No ordinary sailor would have access to such a gun, thought Ezio, remembering the battle with the slave traders. Claudio leapt from the shallop onto the caravel's deck and threw himself on the man with the crowbar, while Ezio darted forward and skewered the wrist of the hand holding the gun with his hidden-blade. It fired harmlessly into the deck and the man retreated, whimpering, holding his wrist, trying to stop the blood pulsing out of the antibrachial vein.

The master, seeing his men routed, pulled a pistol himself and fired it at Ezio, but the caravel lurched in the current at the crucial moment and the shot went wide, though not wide enough, as the ball sliced a nick in Ezio's right ear, which bled heavily. Shaking his head, Ezio leveled his gun at the master and shot him through the forehead.

"Quick!" he said to Claudio. "You take the wheel of this thing and I'll deal with our friend here."

Claudio nodded and ran to bring the caravel under control. Feeling the blood from his ear soak his collar, he twisted his opponent's wrist fiercely to make him lose his grip on the crowbar. Then he brought his knee hard into the man's groin, seized his collar, and half dragged, half kicked him to the gunwale, where he tossed him overboard.

In the silence that followed the fight, furious and confused shouts and imprecations could be heard coming from the crate.

"I will kill you for this. I will twist my sword in your gut and give you more pain than you could ever dream was possible."

"I hope you're comfortable, Cesare," said Ezio. "But if you're not, don't worry. Once we get to Ostia, we'll arrange something a little more civilized for your return trip."

"It's not fair," said Jacopo from the shallop. "I didn't get a chance to use my blackjack once!"

PART II

Everything is permitted. Nothing is true.

—DOGMA SICARII, I,I.

FORTY-NINE

It was late in the spring of the year of Our Lord 1504. The Pope tore open the letter a courier had just brought him, scanned it, and then banged a meaty fist down on his desk in triumph. The other hand held up the letter, from which heavy seals dangled.

"God bless King Ferdinand and Queen Isabella of Aragon and Castile!" he cried.

"Good news, Your Holiness?" asked Ezio, seated in a chair across from him.

Julius II smiled darkly. "Yes! Cesare Borgia has been safely delivered into one of their strongest and most remote *rocche*!"

"Where?"

"Ah—that's classified information—even to you. I can't take any chances with Cesare."

Ezio bit his lip. Had Julius guessed what he'd do if he knew the location?

Julius continued reassuringly, "Don't look so downcast, dear Ezio. I can tell you this: It's a massive fortress, lost in the plains of central northeastern Spain, and totally impregnable."

Ezio knew that Julius had had his reasons for not having Cesare burned at the stake—thus making a possible martyr of him—and he acknowledged that this was the next best thing. But still Cesare's words haunted him— *Chains will never hold me.* Ezio felt in his heart that the only thing that would hold Cesare—and securely—was Death. But he smiled his congratulations.

"They've got him in a cell at the top of the central keep, in a tower one hundred forty feet high," Julius continued. "We don't have anything more to worry about, as far as he's concerned." The Pope looked at Ezio keenly. "What I've just told you is *also* classified information, by the way, so don't go getting any ideas. In any event, at a word from me, they'll switch the location, just in case anyone goes looking for him, and I get wind of it."

Ezio let it go and changed tack. "And Lucrezia? Do we have any news from Ferrara?"

"Well, her third marriage seems to be doing her good, though I must admit I was worried at first. The d'Este family are such a bunch of snobs that I thought the old duke would never accept her as a suitable wife for his son. Marrying a Borgia! Talk about marrying beneath you! To them, it'd be a bit like you getting hitched to your scullery maid!" The Pope laughed heartily. "But she's settled down. Not a peep out of her. Taken to exchanging love letters and even poems with her old friend Pietro Bembo—all aboveboard, of course." Here Julius winked broadly. "But basically a good and faithful wife—she even goes to church and embroiders tapestries. And of course there's no question of her coming back to Rome—*ever!* She'll end her days in Ferrara, and she should be thankful she's got away with her head still on her shoulders. So, all in all, I think it's safe to say that we've got that flock of Catalan perverts out of our hair for good."

Ezio wondered if the Vatican spy ring was as well-informed about the Templars as it was about the Borgia. Cesare had been their leader and continued to be so, even in prison. But he kept his counsel.

He had to admit that the affairs of Italy had seen worse days than these. A strong Pope, who'd had the sense to retain Agostino Chigi as his banker; and the French on the back foot. King Louis hadn't left Italy, but he had at least withdrawn to the north, and seemed content to dig in there. In addition, the French king had ceded Naples to King Ferdinand of Aragon.

"I hope so, Your Holiness."

Julius looked at Ezio keenly. "Listen, Ezio, I'm not a fool, so don't take me for one! Why do you think I brought you in as my counselor? I know there are still Borgia loyalist pockets in the countryside, and even a few diehards left in the city. But I have *other* enemies than the Borgia to worry about these days."

"The Borgia could still pose a threat."

"I don't think so."

"And what are you doing about your other enemies?"

"I'm reforming the Papal Guard. Have you seen what good soldiers the Swiss are? Best mercenaries of the lot! And since they got independence from the Holy Roman Empire and Maximilian five or six years ago, they've been putting themselves out to hire. They're totally loyal and not very emotional—such a change from our own dear fellow countrymen. I'm thinking of getting a brigade of them put together as my personal bodyguard. I'll arm them with the usual halberds and stuff, but I'm also issuing them Leonardo's muskets." He paused. "All I need is a name for them." He looked at Ezio quizzically. "Any ideas?"

"How about the Swiss Guard?" suggested Ezio, who was a little tired.

The Pope considered this. "Well, it's not startlingly original, Ezio. Frankly, I rather favored the Julian Guard—but one doesn't like to sound too egotistical." He grinned. "All right! I'll use what you propose! It'll do for the time being, at any rate."

They were interrupted by the sound of hammering and other building works, coming from above their heads, and in other parts of the Vatican.

"Wretched builders!" commented the Pope. "Still, it has to be done." He crossed the room to a bellpull. "I'll get someone to go and shut them up until we've finished. Sometimes I think builders are the greatest destructive force Man has yet invented."

An attendant arrived at once and the Pope gave him his orders. Minutes later, amid muffled swearing, tools were downed, noisily.

"What are you having done?" asked Ezio, knowing that architecture vied with warfare as the Pope's greatest passion.

"I'm having all the Borgia apartments and offices boarded up," replied Julius. "Far too sumptuous. More worthy of a Nero than the leader of the Church. And I'm razing all their buildings on the roof of the Castel Sant'Angelo. Turning it into one big garden. Might stick a little summerhouse up there, though."

"Good idea," said Ezio, smiling to himself. The summerhouse would doubtless be a real pleasure dome, fit, if not for a king, at least for trysts with one or another of the Pope's lovers—female or male. But the Pope's private life didn't concern Ezio. What mattered was that he was a good man and a staunch ally. And compared with Rodrigo, his corruptions were about as significant as a child's tantrum. Furthermore, he'd steadily continued the moral reforms of Pius III, his predecessor.

"I'm having the Sistine Chapel done up as well," continued the Pope. "It's so *dull!* So I've commissioned that bright young artist from Florence, Michelangelo what's-his-name, to paint some frescoes on the ceiling. Lots of religious scenes, you know the kind of thing. I'd thought of asking Leonardo, but his head's so full of ideas that he scarcely ever finishes a big painting. Pity. I rather liked that portrait he did of Francesco del Giocondo's wife . . ."

Julius interrupted himself and looked at Ezio. "But you didn't come here to talk about my interest in modern art."

"No."

"Are you *sure* you're not taking the threat of a Borgia revival too seriously?"

"I think we *should* take it seriously."

"Look—my army has regained most of the Romagna for the Vatican. There's no army left for the Borgia to fight with."

"Cesare is still alive! With him as a figurehead—"

"I hope you're not questioning my judgment, Ezio! You know my reasons for sparing his life. In any case, where he is now, he's as good as buried alive."

"Micheletto is still at large."

"*Pah!* Without Cesare, Micheletto is nothing."

"Micheletto knows Spain well."

"He's nothing, I tell you."

"He knows Spain. He was born in Valencia. He's a bastard nephew of Rodrigo!"

The Pope, who, despite his years, was a large and vigorous man still in the prime of life, had been pacing the room during this last exchange. Now he returned to the desk, placed his large hands on it, and leaned threateningly over Ezio. His manner was convincing.

"You are letting your worst fears run away with you," he said. "We don't even know whether Micheletto is still alive or not."

"I think we should find out, once and for all."

The Pope pondered Ezio's point and relaxed slightly, sitting down again. He tapped the heavy signet ring on his left hand with the index finger of his right.

"What do you want to do?" he asked heavily. "Don't expect any resources from me. The budget's over-stretched as it is."

"The first thing is to locate and destroy any last die-hards in the city of Rome itself. We may find someone who knows something about Micheletto—his where-abouts or his fate. Then—"

"Then?"

"Then, if he is still alive—"

"You'll destroy him?"

"Yes." But Ezio thought: *Unless he turns out to be more useful to me alive.*

Julius sat back. "I am impressed by your determina-tion, Ezio. It almost frightens me. And I am glad I am not myself an enemy of the Assassins."

Ezio looked up sharply. "You know about the Broth-erhood?"

The Pope made a tent of his fingers. "I always needed to know who the enemies of my enemy were. But your secret is safe with me. As I told you, I am not a fool."

FIFTY

"Your instinct is right. I will guide you and guard you. But I do not belong to you and soon you must let me go. And I have no power over he who controls me. I must obey the will of the Master of the Apple."

Ezio, alone in his secret lodgings, was holding the Apple in his hands as he tried to use it to help him locate his quarry in Rome, when the mysterious voice had come to him again. This time he could not tell if the voice was male or female, and he could not even tell whether it came from the Apple or from somewhere in his own mind.

Your instinct is right. But also: *I have no power over he who controls me.* Why then had the Apple only shown him hazy images of Micheletto—just enough to tell him that Cesare's henchman was still alive? And it could not—or would not—pinpoint Cesare's location. At least for now.

He suddenly realized something his inner self had always known: that he should not abuse the object's power by overusing it, that he should not become dependent on the Apple. Ezio knew that it was his own will that had blurred the answers he sought. He must not be slothful. He must fend for himself. One day he would have to again, anyway.

He thought of Leonardo. What could that man not do, if he had the Apple? And Leonardo, the best of men, nevertheless invented weapons of destruction as easily as he produced sublime paintings. Might the Apple have the power not only to help mankind, but to corrupt it? In Rodrigo's or Cesare's hands, had either of those two ever been able to master it, it could have become the instrument not of salvation, but destruction!

Power is a potent drug. Ezio did not want to fall victim to it.

He looked at the Apple again. It seemed inert in his hands now. But as he placed it back in its box, he found he could hardly bear to close the lid. What paths could it not open up for him?!

No! He must bury it. He must learn to live by the code without it. But not yet!

He had always sensed in his heart that Micheletto lived. Now he knew it for a fact. And while he lived, he would do his utmost to free his evil master—Cesare!

Ezio had not told Pope Julius his full plan. He

intended to seek out Cesare and kill him, or die in the attempt.

It was the only way.

He would use the Apple next only when he had to. He had to keep his own instincts and powers of deduction sharp, against the day when the Apple would no longer be in his possession. He would hunt down the Borgia diehards in Rome without it. Only if he failed— within three days—to unearth them, would he resort to its power again. He still had his friends—the girls of the Rosa in Fiore, La Volpe's thieves, his fellow Assassins— and with their help, how could he fail?

And he knew that the Apple would—in ways he could not fully comprehend—help him, as long as he respected its potential. Perhaps that was its secret. Perhaps no one could ever fully master it—except a member of the race of ancient Adepts who had left the world in trust to humanity, to make or break it, as their will elected.

He closed the lid and locked the box.

Ezio summoned a meeting of the Brotherhood on Tiber Island that night.

"My friends," he started, "I know how hard we have striven, and I believe that victory may be in sight, but there is still work to do."

The others, all except Machiavelli, looked at each other in surprise.

"But Cesare is muzzled!" cried La Volpe. "For good!"

"And we have a new Pope who has always been an enemy of the Borgia," added Claudia.

"And the French are driven back!" put in Bartolomeo. "The countryside is secure. And the Romagna is back in papal hands!"

Ezio held out a hand to quiet them. "We all know that a victory is not a victory until it is absolute."

"And Cesare may indeed be muzzled, but he lives," said Machiavelli quietly. "And Micheletto—"

"Exactly!" Ezio said. "And as long as there are pockets of Borgia diehards, both here and in the Papal States, there is still seed from which a Borgia revival may grow."

"You are too cautious, Ezio! We have won!" cried Bartolomeo.

"Barto, you know as well as I do that a handful of city-states in the Romagna remain loyal to Cesare. They are strongly fortified."

"Then I'll go and sort them out!"

"They will keep. Caterina Sforza's army is not strong enough to attack them from Forlì, but I have sent messengers requesting her to keep a close watch on them. I have a more pressing job for you." *Oh, God,* thought Ezio, *why does my heart still skip a beat when I mention her name?*

"Which is . . . ?"

"I want you to take a force to Ostia and keep a sharp eye on the port. I want to know about any suspicious ships coming into, and, especially, leaving the harbor. I want you to have messengers on horseback ready to bring news to me here the instant you have anything to report."

Bartolomeo snorted. "Sentry duty! Hardly the sort of work for a man of action like me!"

"You will get as much action as you need when the time is ripe to move against the rebel city-states I've mentioned. In the meantime, they live in hope, waiting for a signal. Let them live in hope; it'll keep them quiet. Our job is to snuff that hope out! Forever! Then, if they don't listen to reason, they still won't put up half the fight they would now."

Machiavelli smiled. "I agree with Ezio," he said.

"Well, all right. If you insist," Bartolomeo replied grumpily.

"Pantasilea will enjoy the sea air, after her ordeal."

Bartolomeo brightened. "I hadn't thought of that!"

"Good." Ezio turned to his sister. "Claudia. I imagine the change of regime hasn't affected business at the Rosa in Fiore too badly, has it?"

Claudia grinned. "It's funny how even princes of the Church find it so hard to keep the devil between their loins in abeyance. However many cold baths they say they take!"

"Tell your girls to keep their ears to the ground. Julius has the College of Cardinals firmly under his control, but he still has plenty of enemies with ambitions of their own, and some of them might just be mad enough to think that if they could set Cesare at liberty again, they could use him as a means of furthering their own ends. And keep an eye on Johann Burchard."

"What—Rodrigo's master of ceremonies? Surely he's

harmless enough. He hated having to organize all those orgies! Isn't he just a functionary?"

"Nevertheless—anything you hear—especially if it leads to diehard factions still at large here—let me know."

"It'll be easier, now that we no longer have Borgia guards breathing down our necks every minute of the day."

Ezio smiled a little absently. "I have another question to ask. I have been too busy to visit, and it troubles me, but—how is Mother?"

Claudia's face clouded. "She keeps the accounts, but, Ezio, I fear she is failing. She seldom goes out. She speaks more and more often of Father, and of Federico and Petruccio."

Ezio fell silent for a moment, thinking of his lost father, Giovanni, and his brothers. "I will come when I can," he said. "Give her my love; ask her to forgive my neglect."

"She understands the work you have to do. She knows that you do it not only for the good of us all, but for the sake of our departed kinsmen."

"The destruction of those who killed them shall be their monument," said Ezio, his voice hard.

"And what of my people?" asked La Volpe.

"Gilberto, your people are vital to me. All my recruits remain loyal, but they see that life returns to normal, and most of them long to return also to the lives they led before we persuaded them to join us in the struggle to throw off the Borgia yoke. They retain their skills, but they are not sworn members of our Brotherhood, and I cannot expect them to bear that other yoke we bear—for it is a yoke that only Death will relieve us of."

"I understand."

"I know the men and women under your command are city bred. Some country air will make a change."

"How do you mean?" asked La Volpe suspiciously.

"Send your best people into the towns and villages around Rome. There will be no need to go further out than Viterbo, Terni, L'Aquila, Avezzano, and Nettuno. I doubt if, beyond the rough circle around Rome that those towns define, we'd find much. There can't be many diehards left, and those there are will want to be within striking distance of Rome."

"They'll be hard to find."

"You must try. You know yourself how even a small force in the right place can do untold damage."

"I'll send out my best thieves. Disguise them as peddlers."

"Report anything you find back to me—especially news of Micheletto."

"Do you really think he's still out there somewhere? Mightn't he have got back to Spain, or at least the Kingdom of Naples? If he isn't dead already."

"I am convinced he is still alive."

La Volpe shrugged. "That's good enough for me."

When the others had gone, Machiavelli turned to Ezio and said, "What about me?"

"You and I will work together."

"Nothing would give me greater pleasure; but before we go into details, I have a question."

"Go ahead."

"Why not use the Apple?"

Ezio, sighing, explained as best he could.

When he'd finished, Machiavelli looked at him, took out his little black notebook, and wrote in it at length. Then he stood up, crossed the room, and sat down next to Ezio, squeezing his shoulder affectionately as he did so. Any such gesture from Machiavelli was as rare as chickens' teeth.

"Let's get down to business," he said.

"This is what I have in mind," said Ezio.

"Tell me."

"There are women in this city who may help us. We must seek them out and talk to them."

"Well, you picked the right man for the job. I am a diplomat."

Gaining access to the first woman Ezio had in mind was easy—Pope Julius had seen to that. But getting her to talk wasn't.

She received them in a sumptuous parlor on the *piano nobile* of her large house, whose windows (on four sides) provided sublime vistas of the once-great city, now part crumbling, but also part magnificent, since the last few Popes had poured money into self-aggrandizement.

"I don't see how I can help you," she said after listening to them, but Ezio noticed that she didn't meet their eyes.

"If there are pockets of diehards in the city, we need to know about them, *Altezza*, and we need your help," said Machiavelli. "If we find out later that you have held out on us . . ."

"Don't threaten me, young man," retorted Vannozza. "*Dio mio!* Do you know how long ago it is since Rodrigo and I were lovers? Well over twenty years!"

"Perhaps your children . . . ?" asked Ezio.

She smiled grimly. "I expect you are wondering how a woman like me could have produced such a brood," she said. "But I tell you there is very little Cattanei blood in them. Well, in Lucrezia, perhaps; but Cesare . . ." She broke off, and Ezio could see the pain in her eyes.

"Do you know where he is?"

"I know no more than you do. And I don't care to. It's years since I've even seen him, though we lived in the same city. He is as one dead to me."

Clearly the Pope was being very careful to keep Cesare's whereabouts secret. "Perhaps your daughter knows?"

"If I don't, why should she? She lives in Ferrara now. You could go and ask her, but it's a long way north, and the Holy Father has forbidden her ever to return to Rome."

"Do you see her?" asked Machiavelli.

Vannozza sighed. "As I said, Ferrara's a long way north. I don't care to travel much these days."

She looked around the room, glancing at the servants who stood near the door, and occasionally at the water clock. She'd offered them no refreshment and seemed eager for them to go. She constantly kneaded her hands together. An unhappy woman, and ill at ease, but whether that was because she was concealing something, or because she was being forced to talk of people she'd clearly rather not talk about, Ezio could not say.

"I have—or, rather, *had*—eight grandchildren," she said unexpectedly. Ezio and Machiavelli knew that Lucrezia had had several children by her various husbands, but few had survived childhood. People said that Lucrezia had never taken pregnancy very seriously, and indeed she had had a habit of partying and dancing right up to the moment of her accouchement. Had that alienated her from her mother? Cesare had a daughter, Louise, who was a child of four.

"Do you see any of them?" asked Machiavelli.

"No. Louise is still in Rome, I think, but her mother has made sure that she's much more French than Italian."

She rose then, and the servants, as if on cue, opened the room's ornate double doors.

"I wish I could be of more assistance . . ."

"We thank you for your time," said Machiavelli drily.

"There are other people you might like to talk to," said Vannozza.

"We intend to visit the *Princesse* d'Albret."

Vannozza pressed her lips together. *"Buona fortuna,"* she said, without conviction. "You'd better hurry, too. I hear she's making preparations to leave for France. Perhaps, if I'm lucky, she'll come and say goodbye."

Ezio and Machiavelli had risen, too, and made their farewells.

Once outside in the street, Machiavelli said, "I think we'll have to use the Apple, Ezio."

"Not yet."

"Have it your own way, but I think you're a fool. Let's go and see the princess. Lucky we can both speak French."

"Charlotte d'Albret won't be leaving for France today. I've got men watching her palazzo, in any case. No, there's someone else I want to see first. I'm surprised Vannozza didn't mention her."

"Who?"

"Giulia Farnese."

"Doesn't she live in Carbognano these days?"

"My spies tell me she's in town. We have to take advantage of that."

"What makes you think we'll get any more out of her than we got out of Vannozza?"

Ezio smiled. "Giulia was Rodrigo's last mistress. He was passionate about her!"

"I remember when the French captured her. He was beside himself. And then the French foolishly ransomed her for three thousand ducats. He'd have paid twenty times that amount to get her back. And he'd probably have struck any kind of deal they wanted. But I guess that's what happens when your mistress is well over forty years younger than you are. You get besotted."

"Didn't stop him from dumping her when she turned twenty-five."

"Yes. Too old for him by then! But let's hurry."

They made their way north through the narrow streets in the direction of the Quirinale.

On the way, Machiavelli noticed that Ezio was looking increasingly uneasy.

"What's the matter?" he asked.

"Have you not noticed anything?"

"What?"

"Don't look around!" Ezio was terse.

"No."

"Then I think we're being followed—by a woman."

"Since when?"

"Since we left Vannozza's palazzo."

"One of her people?"

"Perhaps."

"Alone?"

"Think so."

"Then we'd better shake her."

Impatient though they were to get on, they slowed their pace, looking in shop windows, even pausing at a wine booth. There, over the rim of his beaker, Ezio caught sight of a tall, athletically built blond woman dressed in a good but unassuming dark green robe of some lightweight material. She'd be able to move fast in clothes like that if the need arose.

"I've got her," he said.

They both scanned the wall of the building against which the booth was erected. It was a new place, constructed in the fashionably rusticated style of large roughened slabs of stone separated by sunken joints. At intervals, iron rings for tethering horses had been set into the wall.

It was perfect.

They made their way to the back of the booth but there was no way out there.

"We'll have to be quick," said Machiavelli.

"Watch me!" replied Ezio, putting his beaker down on a table near the entrance. A few seconds later he was halfway up the wall, with Machiavelli close behind. Bystanders gaped as the two men, their capes fluttering in the breeze, disappeared over the rooftops, leaping across alleyways and streets, and sending tiles skittering down, to smash on the cobbles or flop in the mud of unmade lanes as the people below ducked or jumped out of the way.

Even if she'd been able to, the woman couldn't climb vertical walls, however conveniently easy they were, in a long skirt, but Ezio saw that her dress had a carefully disguised slit to the thigh on one side, enabling her to run, and she was tearing through the streets after them, thrusting aside anyone who got in her way. Whoever she was, she was well trained.

But at last they lost her. Breathing hard, they came to a halt on the roof of San Niccolò de Portiis and lay down flat, keenly scanning the streets below. There seemed to be no one unduly suspicious among the various citizens in the streets, though Ezio thought he recognized two of La Volpe's thieves working the crowd, using sharp little knives to cut purses. Presumably two not selected to go out into the surrounding countryside, but he'd have to ask Gilberto about it later.

"Let's go down," suggested Machiavelli.

"No—it's easier to stay out of sight up here and we haven't far to go."

"She didn't seem to have much trouble following us.

Lucky for us there was that roof with a high wall around it, where we could change direction without her noticing."

Ezio nodded. Whoever she was, she'd be reporting back by now. He wished she were on his side. As things stood, they'd have to get to the large apartment Giulia kept in Rome fast, and then out of the Quirinale district. Maybe he should detail a couple of his recruits to watch their backs on any future forays. The Borgia diehards were lying low under the new Pope's tough regime—but only to lull the authorities into a false sense of security.

Giulia's first husband, Orsino Orsini, had been happy to wink at the affair his nineteen-year-old wife had embarked on with the sixty-two-year-old Rodrigo Borgia. She had a daughter, Laura, but no one knew if she was the child of Orsino or Rodrigo. Rodrigo, despite being a Valencian by birth, had risen through the Church until he came to control the Vatican's purse strings, and he had shown his gratitude to his delicious young mistress by installing her in a brand-new house (which she'd long since been obliged to quit) conveniently close to the Vatican, and by making her brother, Alessandro, a cardinal. The other cardinals called him "the Cardinal of the Skirts" behind his back, and of course never in Rodrigo's presence. Giulia they called "the Bride of Christ."

Ezio and Machiavelli dropped to the ground in the piazza that Giulia's apartment block fronted. A couple of papal guards stood nearby. Otherwise the square was deserted. The guards' tunics bore, on their shoulders, the crest of the della Rovere family—a massive oak tree, root and branch, now surmounted by the papal triple tiara and the keys of Saint Peter. But Ezio recognized the men. Six months earlier, they'd been in mulberry-and-yellow livery. Now, times had changed. They saluted him. He acknowledged them.

"Fuckers," said Machiavelli under his breath.

"A man's got to work," said Ezio. "I'm surprised that you, of all people, can take issue with such a bagatelle."

"Come on!"

They'd arrived without due notice and it took some trouble to convince the Farnese attendants—six blue fleurs-de-lis ranged on a yellow background on their capes—to admit them, but, as Ezio knew, Signora Farnese was at home. She received them in a room that was half as gaudy but twice as tasteful as La Vannozza's. At thirty, she had more than retained the beauty of her youth and the intelligence that informed it. Immediately, though they were unexpected guests, she had Moscato and *panpepati e mielati* served for them.

But she knew nothing, and it was clear that she was innocent of any Borgia taint, despite her previous close-ness to that execrable family (as Machiavelli called them). Machiavelli saw that she had moved on, and when he and Ezio asked her about her once-close friendship with Lucrezia, all she could say was, "What I saw of her was her good side. I think she fell too much under the bullying sway of her father and her brother. I thank God she is rid of them." She paused. "If only she had met Pietro Bembo earlier. Those two were soul mates. He might have taken her to Venice and saved her from her dark side."

"Do you see her still?"

"Alas, Ferrara is so far to the north, and I have my hands full, running Carbognano. Even friendships die, Ezio Auditore."

An image of Caterina Sforza blew into his mind before he had a chance to extinguish it. Ah, God! How the thought of her caught at his heart still!

It was late afternoon by the time they left. They kept a close eye out for anyone shadowing them, but there was nobody.

"We must use the Apple," said Machiavelli again.

"This is but the first day of three. We must learn to trust ourselves, and our own intelligence, and not lean on what has been vouchsafed us."

"The matter is pressing."

"One more appointment today, Niccolò. Then, perhaps, we shall see."

The *Princesse* d'Albret, *Dâme* de Châlus, Duchess of Valence, was, according to the gatekeepers of her opulent villa in the Pinciano district, not at home. But Ezio and Machiavelli, impatient and tired, pushed past anyway and encountered Charlotte in her *piano nobile*, engrossed in packing. Huge chests full of costly linen and books and jewelry stood about the half-empty room. In a corner, the confused little four-year-old Louise, Cesare's only legitimate heir, played with a wooden doll.

"You are damned impertinent," said the cold-looking blonde who confronted them, her dark brown eyes flashing fire.

"We have the imprimatur of the Pope himself," lied Ezio. "Here is his warrant." He held up a blank parchment, from which impressive-looking seals hung.

"Bastards," said the woman coolly. "If you think I know where Cesare is imprisoned, you are fools. I never want to see him again, and I pray that none of his *sang maudit* has passed into the veins of my innocent little daughter."

"We also seek Micheletto," said Machiavelli implacably.

"That Catalan peasant," she spat. "How should I know?"

"Your husband told you how he might escape, if taken," suggested Machiavelli. "He depended on you."

"Do you think so? I don't! Perhaps Cesare confided in one of his dozens of mistresses. Perhaps the one that gave him the *malattia venerea*?"

"Do you—?"

"I never touched him, since the first pustules appeared, and he at least had the decency to keep away from me and wallow in the gutter with his whores afterward. And father eleven brats by them. At least I am clean, and my daughter, too. As you see, I am getting out of here. France is a far better country than this wretched hellhole. I'm going back to La Motte-Feuilly."

"Not to Navarre?" asked Machiavelli slyly.

"I see you are trying to trick me!" She turned her cold, bony face toward them. Ezio noticed that her beauty was marred—or enhanced—by a dimple in the middle of her chin. "I do not choose to go to that province merely because my brother married the heiress to the throne and thereby became king."

"Does your brother remain faithful to Cesare?" asked Ezio.

"I doubt it. Why don't you stop wasting my time, and go and ask him?"

"Navarre is far away."

"Exactly. Which is why I wish you and your saturnine friend were on your way there. And now, it is late and I have work to do. Please leave."

"A wasted day," commented Machiavelli as they took to the streets again, the shadows lengthening.

"I don't think so. We know that none of those closest to Cesare are harboring or protecting him." Ezio paused. "All the most important women in his life hated him, and even Giulia had no time for Rodrigo."

Machiavelli grimaced. "Imagine being fucked by a man old enough to be your grandfather."

"Well, she didn't do too badly out of it."

"We still don't know where Cesare *is*. Use the Apple!"

"No. Not yet. We must stand on our own feet."

"Well," sighed Machiavelli, "at least God gave us good minds."

At that moment, one of Machiavelli's spies came running up, a small, bald man with alert eyes, out of breath, his face wild.

"Bruno?" said Machiavelli, surprised and concerned.

"Maestro," panted the man. "Thank God I've found you."

"What is it?"

"The Borgia diehards! They sent someone to follow you and Maestro Ezio—"

"And?"

"Sure that you were out of the way, they have taken Claudia!"

"My sister! Sweet Jesus—how?" gasped Ezio.

"She was in the square outside Saint Peter's—you know those rickety wooden colonnades the Pope wants to tear down?"

"Get on with it!"

"They took her—she was organizing her girls, getting them to infiltrate—"

"Where is she now?"

"They have a hideout in the Prati—just to the east of the Vatican. That's where they've taken her." Bruno quickly gave them the details of where Claudia was being held prisoner.

Ezio looked at Machiavelli.

"Let's go!" he said.

"At least we've found out where they are," said Machiavelli, drily as ever, as the two of them bounded up to the rooftops again; from there they ran and leapt across Rome, until they came to the Tiber, where they crossed on the Ponte della Rovere, and made haste again toward their goal.

The place Machiavelli's spy, Bruno, had indicated was a ramshackle villa just north of the Prati district market. But its crumbling stucco belied a brand-new ironbound front door, and the grilles on the windows were new, too, and freshly painted.

Before Machiavelli could stop him, Ezio had gone up to the door and hammered on it.

The judas set into it opened and a beady eye regarded them. And, to their amazement, the door swung smoothly back on well-oiled hinges.

They found themselves in a nondescript courtyard. There was no one about. Whoever had opened the door—and closed it firmly behind them—had disappeared. There were doors on three sides of the yard. The one opposite the entrance was open. Above it was a tattered banner—bearing a black bull in a golden field.

"Trapped," said Machiavelli succinctly. "What weapons do you have?"

Ezio had his trusty hidden-blade, his sword, and his dagger. Machiavelli carried a light sword and a stiletto.

"Come in, gentlemen—you are most welcome," said a disembodied voice from a window overlooking the courtyard somewhere high up in the wall above the open door. "I think we have something to trade with."

"The Pope knows where we are," retorted Machiavelli loudly. "You are lost. Give yourselves up! The cause you serve is dead!"

A hollow laugh was his rejoinder. "Is it indeed? I think not. But come in. We knew you'd take the bait. Bruno has been working for us for a year now."

"Bruno?"

"Treachery runs in families, and dear Bruno's is no exception. All Bruno wanted was a little more cash than you were giving him. He's worth it. He managed to inveigle Claudia here, in the hope of meeting one of the

English cardinals—they sit on the fence, as the English always do, and Claudia hoped to swing him to your side, and get a little information out of him. Unfortunately, Cardinal Shakeshaft met with a terrible accident—he was run over by a carriage and died on the spot. But your sister, Ezio, is still alive, just, and I am sure she is longing to see you."

"*Calma,*" said Machiavelli as the two men looked at each other. Ezio's blood boiled. He'd spent a day trying to trace the diehards only to find himself led straight to them.

He dug his fingernails into his palms.

"Where is she, *bastardi*?" he yelled.

"Come in."

Cautiously, the two Assassins approached the dark entrance.

There was a dimly lit hall, in whose center, on a plinth, was a bust of Pope Alexander VI, the coarse features—the hooked nose, the weak chin, the fat lips—done to the life. There was no other furniture, and again there were three doors leading off the three walls facing the entrance, only that facing the entrance open. Ezio and Machiavelli made for it and, passing the door, found themselves in another bleak room. There was a table, on which various rusty surgical instruments were arrayed, glittering under the light of a single candle, on a stained cloth. Next to it was a chair, and on it Claudia was seated, half undressed and bound, her hands in her lap, her face and breasts bruised, a gag in her mouth.

Three men detached themselves from the shadows

that obscured the back wall. Ezio and Machiavelli were aware of others, too, men and women, behind them and on either side. Those they could see in the darkling light wore the now-grubby mulberry-and-yellow of the former holders of power.

All were heavily armed.

Claudia's eyes spoke to Ezio's. She managed to wrestle her branded finger free enough to show him. She had not given in, despite the torture. She was a true Assassin. Why had he ever doubted her?

"We know how you feel about your family," said a gaunt man of perhaps fifty summers whom Ezio did not recognize. He seemed to be the leader of these Borgia supporters. "You let your father and brothers die. Your mother we need not bother about; she is dying anyway. But you can still save your sister. If you wish. She's already well struck in years and doesn't even have any children, so perhaps you won't bother."

Ezio controlled himself. "What do you want?"

"In exchange? I want you to leave Rome. Why don't you go back to Monteriggioni and build the place up again? Do some farming. Leave the power game to those who understand it."

Ezio spat.

"Oh, dear," said the thin man. He seized Claudia by the hair and, producing a small knife, cut her left breast.

Claudia screamed.

"She's damaged goods at the moment, but I'm sure she'll recover under your tender care."

"I'll take her back and then I'll kill you. Slowly."

"Ezio Auditore! I gave you a chance. But you threaten me—and you are in no position to threaten. If there's any killing to be done, it'll be by me. Forget Monteriggioni—a sophisticated lady like Madonna Claudia would doubtless hate it there anyway—your destiny is here—to die in this room."

The men and women on each side closed in, drawing swords.

"Told you—trapped," said Machiavelli.

"At least we've found the bastards," replied Ezio, as each man looked the other in the eye. "Here!" He passed a handful of poison darts to his companion. "Make them work!"

"You didn't tell me you came prepared."

"You didn't ask."

"I did."

"Shut up."

Ezio fell into a crouch as the diehards advanced. Their leader held the thin knife to Claudia's throat.

"Let's go!"

As one, they drew their swords. And with their free hand they threw the poison darts with deadly aim.

The Borgia supporters toppled on either side, as Machiavelli closed in and sliced and slashed with his sword and dagger, pushing against the diehards who tried to crush him—in vain—by force of numbers.

Ezio had one goal—to kill the thin man before he could rip open Claudia's throat. He leapt forward and seized the man by the throat, but his adversary was as slippery as an eel and wrenched himself to one side, without letting go of his victim.

Ezio wrestled him to the floor at last and, grasping the man's right hand with his left, forced the point of the thin knife the man was holding close to his throat. Its point touched the jugular vein.

"Have mercy," babbled the diehard leader. "I served a cause I thought was true."

"How much mercy would you have shown my sister?" asked Ezio. "You filth! You are finished."

There was no need to release the hidden-blade. "I told you it would be a slow death," said Ezio, drawing the knife down to the man's groin. "But I am going to be merciful." He slid the knife back up and sliced the man's throat open. Blood bubbled in the man's mouth. *"Bastardo!"* he gurgled. "You will die by Micheletto's hand!"

"Requiescat in pace," said Ezio, letting the man's head fall, though for once he spoke the words without much conviction.

The other diehards lay dead or dying about them as Machiavelli and Ezio hastened to untie the harsh cords that bound Claudia.

She had been badly beaten, but the diehards had at least drawn the line at leaving her honor intact.

"Oh, Ezio!"

"Are you all right?"

"I hope so."

"Come on. We must get out of here."

"Gently."

"Of course."

Ezio took his sister in his arms and, followed by a somber Machiavelli, walked out into the dying light of day.

"Well," said Machiavelli, "at least we have confirmation that Micheletto is still alive."

FIFTY-ONE

"We've found Micheletto," said La Volpe.

"Where?" Ezio's voice was urgent.

"He's holed up in Zagarolo, just to the east of here."

"Let's get him, then."

"Not so fast. He's got contingents from the Romagna towns still loyal to Cesare. He'll put up a fight."

"Let him!"

"We'll have to organize."

"Then let's do it! Now!"

Ezio, with Machiavelli and La Volpe, summoned a meeting on Tiber Island that night. Bartolomeo was still in Ostia, watching the port, and Claudia was resting up at the Rosa in Fiore, tended by her ailing mother, after her terrible ordeal, but there were enough thieves and recruits to muster a force of one hundred men and women able to bear arms. There was no need of other *condottieri* to back them up.

"He's encamped in an old gladiatorial school, and he's got maybe two hundred fifty men with him."

"What does he intend to do?"

"No idea. Break out, head for safety in the north with the French, who knows?"

"Whatever his plans are, let's nip them in the bud."

By early dawn, Ezio had gathered a mounted force. They rode out the short distance to Zagarolo and surrounded Micheletto's encampment by sunrise. Ezio bore his crossbow on one arm, over the bracer, and on the other, his poison-blade. There would be no quarter given, though he wanted to take Micheletto alive.

The defenders put up a fierce fight but, in the end, Ezio's forces were victorious, scattering the diehards under Micheletto's command like chaff.

Among the wounded, dead, and dying, Micheletto stood proud, defiant to the last.

"We take you, Micheletto Corella, as our prisoner," said Machiavelli. "No more shall you infect our nation with your putrid schemes."

"Chains will never hold me," snarled Micheletto. "Any more than they will hold my master."

They took him in chains to Florence, where he took up residence in the Signoria, in the very cell where Ezio's father, Giovanni, spent his last hours. There, the governor of the city, Piero Soderini, together with his friend and adviser Amerigo Vespucci, and Machiavelli, interrogated him and put him to the torture, but they could get nothing out of him and so, for the moment, left him to rot. His day as a killer seemed done.

Ezio, for his part, returned to Rome.

"I know you are a Florentine at heart, Niccolò," he told his friend at their parting. "But I shall miss you."

"I am also an Assassin," replied Machiavelli. "And my first loyalty will always be to the Brotherhood. You will let me know when you next have need of me and I will come to you without delay. Besides," he added darkly, "I haven't given up all hope of squeezing information out of this vile man."

"I wish you luck," said Ezio.

But he wasn't so sure they'd break him. Micheletto was indeed an evil man; but he was also very strong willed.

FIFTY-TWO

"Ezio, you must put Micheletto out of your mind,"
Leonardo told him, as they sat in the former's studio in
Rome. "Rome is at peace. This Pope is strong. He has
subdued the Romagna. He is a soldier as much as he's
a man of God and perhaps under him all Italy will find
peace at last. And although Spain controls the south,
Ferdinand and Isabella are our friends."

Ezio knew that Leonardo was happy in his work.
Pope Julius had employed him as a military engineer and
he was tinkering with a host of new projects, though he
sometimes pined for his beloved Milan, still in French
hands, and talked in his more depressed moments of
going to Amboise, where he had been offered all the

facilities he needed whenever he wanted them. He frequently said he might go, when he had finished Julius's commissions.

And as for the Romagna, Ezio's thoughts turned often to Caterina Sforza, whom he still loved. The letter he'd received from her told him that she was now involved with someone else, the Florentine ambassador. Ezio knew her life remained in turmoil and that, despite Julius's support, she'd been dismissed from her city by her own populace on account of her former cruelties in putting down their rebellion when they rose up against her late and intractable second husband, Giacomo Feo, and that she was now growing old in retirement in Florence. His letters in reply to her were at first angry, then remonstrative, then pleading; but she replied to none of them, and he knew that she had used him and that he would never see her again.

Thus it was with relationships between men and women. The lucky ones last; but too often when they end, they end for good, and deep intimacy is replaced by a desert.

He was hurt and humiliated, but he didn't have time to deal with his misery. His work in Rome consolidating the Brotherhood and above all holding it in readiness kept him busy.

"I believe that as long as Micheletto lives, he will do his best to escape, free Cesare Borgia, and help him rebuild his forces."

Leonardo was having his own problems with his

feckless boyfriend, Salai, and barely listened to his old friend. "No one has ever escaped from the prison in Florence," he said. "Not from those cells."

"Why don't they kill him?"

"They still think they might get something out of him, though personally I doubt it," said Leonardo. "But in any case, the Borgia are finished. You should rest. Why don't you take your poor sister and return to Monteriggioni?"

"She has grown to love Rome and would never return to such a small place now, and in any case the Brotherhood's new home is here."

This was another sadness in Ezio's life. After an illness, his mother, Maria, had died; Claudia, after her abduction by the Borgia diehards, had given up the Rosa in Fiore. It was now controlled by Julius's own spy network, using different girls, and La Volpe negotiated with his colleague Antonio in Venice to send Rosa, now older and statelier but no less fiery than she had been when Ezio had known her in La Serenissima, to Rome to run it.

And there was the problem of the Apple.

So much had changed. When Ezio was summoned to the Vatican for another interview with the Pope, he was unprepared for what he was to hear.

"I'm intrigued by this device you've got," said Julius, coming as always straight to the point.

"What do you mean, Your Holiness?"

The Pope smiled. "Don't prevaricate with me, my dear Ezio. I have my own sources and they tell me you have something you call the Apple, which you found under the Sistine Chapel some years ago. It seems to have great power."

Ezio's brain raced. How had Julius found out about it? Had Leonardo told him? Leonardo could be curiously innocent at times, and he had wanted a new patron very badly. "It was vouchsafed to me, in a manner I find hard to explain to you, by a force from an antique world to help us. And it has, but I fear its potential. I cannot think that the hands of Man are ready for such a thing, but it is known as a Piece of Eden. There are other Pieces, some lost to us, and others perhaps left hidden."

"Sounds very useful. What does it do?"

"It has the ability to control men's thoughts and desires. But that is not all: It is able to reveal things undreamed of."

Julius pondered this. "It sounds as if it might be very useful to me. Very useful indeed. But it could also be turned against me in the wrong hands."

"It is what the Borgia were misusing to try to gain total ascendancy. Luckily, Leonardo, to whom they gave it to research, kept its darkest secrets from them."

The Pope paused once again in thought. "Then I think it better if we leave it in your care," he said at last. "If it was vouchsafed to you by such a power as you describe, it would be rash to take it away from you." He paused again. "But it seems to me that, after all, when you feel that you have no further use for it, you should hide it in a safe place, and maybe, if you wish, leave some kind of clue for any worthy successor—who knows, possibly some descendant of yours—who perhaps alone will be able to understand it, so that it may once more have a true use in the world, in future generations. But I do somehow believe this, Ezio Auditore, and perhaps I am truly being guided by God, that in our time no one but you should have custody of it; for perhaps there is some unique quality, some unique sense that enables you to withstand any irresponsible use of it."

Ezio bowed and said nothing; but in his heart he acknowledged Julius's wisdom, and he couldn't have agreed more with his judgment.

"By the way," Julius said, "I don't care for Leonardo's boyfriend—what's his name? Salai? Seems very shifty to me. I wouldn't trust him, and it's a pity Leo seems to. But apart from that one little weakness, the man is a genius. Do you know, he's developing some kind of lightweight, bulletproof armor for me? Don't know where he gets his ideas from."

Ezio thought of the bracer Leonardo had managed to re-create for him and smiled to himself. Well, why not? But now he could guess the source of the Pope's information about the Apple, and he knew Julius had revealed it deliberately. Fortunately Salai was more of a fool than a knave, but he'd have to be watched and, if necessary, removed.

After all, he knew what the nickname Salai meant— *little Satan*.

FIFTY-THREE

Ezio made his way back to Leonardo's studio soon afterward, but he failed to find Salai at home, and Leonardo was almost shamefaced about him. He'd sent him into the country and no amount of persuasion would get him to reveal where. This would have to be a problem for La Volpe and his Thieves' Guild to deal with, but it was clear that Leonardo was embarrassed. Perhaps he would learn to keep his mouth shut in front of the boy in the future, for he knew that Ezio could place Leonardo himself in trouble. But fortunately Leonardo was still more of a help than a hindrance, and a good friend, as Ezio made very clear to him. But if there were any more breaches of security—well, no one was indispensable.

Leonardo was eager to make it up to Ezio, apparently.

"I've been thinking about Cesare," he said, with his usual eagerness.

"Oh?"

"In fact, I'm very glad you've come. I've found someone I think you should meet."

"Does he know where Cesare is?" asked Ezio.

If he did, thought Ezio, Micheletto would cease to matter. If he didn't, Ezio might even consider letting Micheletto escape from his prison—for Ezio knew the Signoria well—and using the man to lead him to his master. A dangerous plan, he knew, but he wasn't going to use the Apple . . .

But in the last resort, he would *have* to use the Apple again; but it disturbed him increasingly. Ezio had been having strange dreams, of countries and buildings and technology that couldn't possibly exist . . .

Then he remembered that vision of the castle, the remote castle in a foreign land. That was at least a recognizable building of his own time. But where could it be?

Leonardo brought him back from his musings.

"I don't know if he knows where Cesare is. But he's called Gaspar Torella, and he was Cesare's personal physician. He's got some ideas I think are interesting. Shall we go and see him?"

"Any lead is a good one."

Dottor Torella received them in a spacious surgery on the Aventine, whose ceiling was hung with herbs but also with strange creatures—dried bats, the little corpses of desiccated toads, and a small crocodile. He was wizened, and a little bent in the shoulders, but he was younger than he looked, his movements were quick, almost lizardlike, and his eyes behind his spectacles were bright. He was also another Spanish expatriate, but he was reputed to be brilliant and Pope Julius had spared him—he was, after all, a scientist with no interest in politics.

What he was interested in, and talked about at length, was the New Disease.

"You know, both my former master and his father, Rodrigo, had it. It's very ugly indeed in its final stages, and I believe it affects the mind and may have left both Cesare and the former Pope affected in the brain. Neither had any sense of proportion, and it may still be strong in Cesare—wherever they've put him."

"Do you have any idea?"

"My guess is somewhere as far away as possible, and in a place he could never escape from."

Ezio sighed. So much was surely obvious.

"I have called the disease the *morbus gallicus*—the French disease," Dr. Torella plunged on enthusiastically. "Even the present Pope has it in the first stage and I am treating him. It's an epidemic, of course. We think it came from Columbus's sailors and probably Vespucci's, too, when they came back from the New World—they brought it with them."

"Why call it the French disease, then?" asked Leonardo.

"Well, I certainly don't want to insult the Italians, and the Portuguese and the Spanish are our friends. But it broke out first among French soldiers in Naples. It starts with lesions on the genitals and it can deform the hands, the back, and the face, indeed the whole head. I'm treating it with mercury, to be drunk or rubbed on the skin, but I don't think I've found a cure."

"That is certainly interesting," said Ezio. "But will it kill Cesare?"

"I don't know."

"Then I must still find him."

"Fascinating," said Leonardo, excited by yet a new discovery.

"There is something else I've been working on," said Torella, "which I think is even more interesting."

"What is it?" asked his fellow scientist.

"It's this: that people's memories can be passed down—preserved—from generation to generation *in the bloodline*. Rather like some diseases. I'd like to think I'd find a cure for my *morbus gallicus*; but I feel it may be with us for centuries."

"What makes you say that?" said Ezio, strangely disturbed by the man's remark about memories being passed on through many years.

"Because I believe it's transmitted, in the first instance, through sex—and we'd all die out if we had to do without that."

Ezio grew impatient. "Thank you for your time," he said.

"Don't mention it," replied Torella. "And by the way, if you really want to find my former master, I think you could do worse than looking in Spain."

"In Spain? Where in Spain?"

The doctor spread his hands. "I'm a Spaniard; so is Cesare. Why not send him home? It's just a hunch. I'm sorry I can't be more specific."

Ezio thought, *It'll be like looking for a needle in a haystack . . . But it may be a start.*

FIFTY-FOUR

Ezio no longer kept the location of his lodgings secret.
But only a few knew where they were. One of them was
Machiavelli.

Ezio was awakened by him at four in the morning. A
deliberate, urgent knocking at the door.

"Niccolò! What are you doing here?" Ezio was
instantly alert, like a cat.

"I have been a fool."

"What's happened? You were working in Florence!
You can't be back so soon." But Ezio already knew
something grave had happened.

"I have been a fool," said Machiavelli.

"What's going on?"

"In my arrogance, I kept Micheletto alive." Machia-velli sighed. "In a secure cell, to question him."

"You'd better tell me what's going on."

"He has escaped! On the eve of his execution!"

"From that place? How?"

"Over the roof. Borgia diehards climbed to it in the night and killed the guards. They lowered a rope. The priest who confessed him was a Borgia sympathizer—he is being burned at the stake today—and smuggled a file into his cell. He sawed through just one bar on the window. He's a big man, but it was enough for him to squeeze out and climb up. You know how strong he is. By the time the alarm was raised, he was nowhere to be found in the city."

"Then we must seek him out, and"—Ezio paused, suddenly seeing an advantage even in this adversity—"having found him, see where he runs. He may yet lead us to Cesare. He is insanely loyal, and without Cesare's support his own power is worthless."

"I have light cavalry scouring the countryside even now, trying to hunt him down."

"But there are certainly small pockets of Borgia die-hards—like those who rescued him—willing to shelter him."

"I think he's in Rome. That's why I've come here."

"Why Rome?"

"We have been too complacent. There are Borgia sup-porters here, too. He will use them to make for Ostia, and try to get a ship there."

"Bartolomeo is in Ostia. He's fed up, but no one will escape him and his *condottieri* there. I'll send a rider to alert him."

"But where will Micheletto go?"

"Where else but Valencia—his hometown."

"Ezio—we must be sure. We must use the Apple, now, this minute, to see if we can locate him."

FIFTY-FIVE

Ezio turned and, in the bedroom of his lodgings, out of sight of Machiavelli, drew the Apple from its secret hiding place and brought the box that contained it back to his principal chamber.

Carefully he drew it out of its container with gloved hands and placed it on the table there.

He concentrated. The Apple began, very slowly at first, to glow, and then its light brightened until the room was filled with a cold illumination. Next, images, dim at first and indistinct, flickered onto the wall and resolved themselves into something the Apple had shown Ezio before—the strange, remote castle in a brown, barren landscape, very old, with a massive outer barbican, four main towers, and an impregnable-looking square keep at its center.

"Where is that *rocca*? What is the Apple telling us?"

"It could be anywhere," said Machiavelli. "From the landscape, Syria perhaps?"

"Or," said Ezio as, with a sudden rush of excitement, he remembered Dr. Torella's words, "Spain."

"Micheletto can't be in Spain."

"I am certain he plans to go there!"

"Even so, we don't know where this place is. There are many, many castles in Spain, and many similar to this one. Consult the Apple again."

But when Ezio once more consulted the Apple, the image remained unchanged: a solidly built castle on a hill, a good three hundred years old, surrounded by a little town. The image was monochrome. All the houses, the fortress, and the countryside were an almost uniform brown. There was only one spot of color, a bright flag on a pole on the very top of the keep.

Ezio squinted at it.

A white flag with a red, ragged cross in the form of an *X*.

His excitement mounted. "The military standard of King Ferdinand and Queen Isabella—of Spain!"

"Yes," said Machiavelli. "Good. Now we know what country. But we still don't know where it *is*. Or why we're being shown it. Is Micheletto on his way there? Ask the Apple again."

But the vision faded, to be replaced by a fortified hill town, from whose fort a white flag crisscrossed with red chains, their links filled with yellow, which Ezio recognized as the flag of Navarre. And then a third and final picture: a massive, wealthy seaport, with ships drawn up on a glittering sea and an army gathering. But no clue about the exact location of any of these places.

FIFTY-SIX

Everyone was in place. Couriers rode daily between the points where the Brotherhood had set up bases. Bartolomeo was beginning to enjoy Ostia, and Pantasilea loved it. Antonio de Magianis still held down the fort in Venice. Claudia had returned for the time being to Florence to stay with her old friend Paola, who kept an expensive house of pleasure on which the Rosa in Fiore had been modeled, and La Volpe and Rosa watched over Rome.

It was time for Machiavelli and Ezio to go hunting.

FIFTY-SEVEN

"Leo, we need your help," Ezio said, coming straight to the point as soon as his friend had, slightly reluctantly, allowed them into his studio.

"You weren't very pleased with me last time we met."

"Salai shouldn't have told anyone about the Apple."

"I told him in confidence."

Machiavelli gave a sharp laugh. "In confidence?!"

"He got drunk in a wine booth and blurted it out to impress. Most of the people around him didn't know what he was talking about but there was an agent of Pope Julius within earshot. He is very contrite."

"Where is he now?" asked Ezio.

Leonardo squared his shoulders. "If you want my help, I want payment."

"What kind of payment?"

"I want you to leave him alone. He means a lot to me; he is young, with time he will improve."

"He's a little sewer rat," said Machiavelli.

"Do you want my help or don't you?"

Ezio and Machiavelli looked at each other.

"All right, Leo—but keep him under a very close rein or by God we'll show no mercy next time."

"All right. Now, what do you want me to do?"

"We are having problems with the Apple. It seems not as acute as it was. Could there be something wrong with it mechanically?" asked Machiavelli.

Leonardo stroked his beard. "You have it with you?"

Ezio produced the box. "Here." He took it out and placed it carefully on Leonardo's large worktable.

Leonardo examined it with equal care. "I don't know what this thing really is," he conceded finally. "It's dangerous, it's a mystery, and it's very, very powerful. And yet only Ezio seems able fully to control it. God knows, when it was in my power in the old days under Cesare, I tried. But I only partially succeeded." He paused. "No, I don't think the word 'mechanical' actually describes this thing. If I weren't more of a scientist than an artist, I'd say this thing had a mind of its own."

Ezio remembered the voice that had come from the Apple. What if Leonardo were unconsciously telling the precise truth?

"Micheletto is on the run," said Ezio urgently. "We need to locate him, and fast. We need to pick up his trail before it's too late!"

"What do you think he's planning?"

"Ezio has convinced me that Micheletto has decided to go—we are almost certain—to Spain and there locate and liberate his master Cesare. They will then attempt to return to power. We will stop them," said Machiavelli.

"And the Apple?"

"Shows an image of a castle, somewhere in Spain, it must be; it flies the Spanish flag, but doesn't, or won't, or can't give its location. We also saw an image of a town flying the Navarrese flag. And a seaport with an army gathering to embark there. But the Apple gave us nothing on Micheletto at all," said Ezio.

"Well," said Leonardo, "Cesare can't have jinxed it because no one's that clever, so it must—how can I put this?—have *decided* not to be helpful."

"But why would it do that?"

"Why don't we ask it?"

Ezio once again concentrated, and this time a most divine music, sweet and high, came to his ears. "Can you hear it?" he asked.

"Hear what?" replied the others.

Through the music came the voice he had heard before: "Ezio Auditore, you have done well. But I have more than played my part in your career and you must now return me. Take me to a vault you will find under the Capitoline, and leave me there to be found by future members of your Brotherhood. But be quick! You must then ride posthaste to Naples, where Micheletto is embarking for Valencia! This knowledge is my last gift to you. You have more than enough power of your own now to have no further need of me. But I will lie in the ground until future generations do have need of me. So you must leave a sign to indicate my burial place. Farewell, Mentor of the Brotherhood! Farewell! Farewell!"

The Apple ceased to glow and looked dead, like an old leather-bound ball.

Swiftly, Ezio told his friends what had been imparted to him.

"Naples? Why Naples?" Leonardo asked.

"Because it's in Spanish territory. We have no jurisdiction there."

"And because he knows—somehow—that Bartolomeo is policing Ostia," said Ezio. "But we must make all speed. Come!"

Dusk was falling as Machiavelli and Ezio carried the Apple in its box down into the catacombs below the Colosseum and, passing through the dreadful gloomy rooms of the remains of Nero's Golden House, carried torches before them as they made their way through a maze of tunnels under the old Roman Forum to a spot near the church of San Nicola in Carcere, where they found a secret door within the crypt. Behind it was a small, vaulted room, in the center of which stood a plinth. On this they placed the Apple in its box and withdrew. Once closed, the door ceased as if by magic to be visible even to them, but they knew where it was and near it drew the sacred, secret symbols that only a member of the Brotherhood would understand. The same symbols they inscribed at regular intervals along their way back, and again at the mouth of the entrance near the Colosseum from which they emerged.

Then, after meeting Leonardo again, who had insisted on joining them, they rode hard to Ostia, where they took a ship for the long coastal journey south to Naples. They arrived on Midsummer Day, 1505—Ezio's forty-sixth birthday.

They didn't go into the teeming, hilly town, but remained among the fortified docks, splitting up to search among the sailors, tradesmen, and travelers busy about their fishing smacks, their shallops, and their caravels, carracks, and cogs, visiting the taverns and brothels, and all in frantic haste, for no one, Spanish, Italian, or Arab, seemed to have an answer to their question:

"Have you seen a big man, with huge hands, scars on his face, thin, seeking passage to Valencia?"

After an hour of this, they regrouped on the main quay.

"He's going to Valencia. He must be!" said Ezio through gritted teeth.

"But if he isn't?" put in Leonardo. "And we charter a ship and sail to Valencia anyway—we might lose days and even weeks, and so lose Micheletto altogether."

"You're right."

"The Apple didn't lie to you. He was—or, if we're lucky—*is* here. We just have to find somebody who knows for sure."

A whore sidled up. "We're not interested," snapped Machiavelli.

She grinned. She was a pretty blond woman, tall and slim, with dark brown eyes, long, shapely legs, small breasts, broad shoulders, and narrow hips, maybe forty years old. "But you *are* interested in Micheletto Corella."

Ezio swung around on her. She looked so like Caterina that for a moment his head swam. "What do you know?"

She snapped back with all the hardness of a whore: "What's it worth to you?" Then came the professional smile again. "I'm Camilla, by the way."

"Ten ducats."

"Twenty."

"Twenty! You'd earn less than that in a week on your back!" snarled Machiavelli.

"Charmer! Do you want the information or not? I can see you're in a hurry."

"Fifteen, then," said Ezio, pulling out his purse.

"That's better, *tesoro*."

"Information first," said Machiavelli as Camilla held out her hand for the money.

"Half first."

Ezio handed over eight ducats.

"Generous with it," said the woman. "All right. Micheletto was here last night. He spent it with me, and I've never earned my money harder. He was drunk, he abused me, he half strangled me while we were fucking, and he ran off at dawn without paying. Pistol in his belt, sword, ugly-looking dagger. Smelled pretty bad, too, but I know he had money because I guessed what he'd do and took my fee out of his purse when he finally fell asleep. Of course the bouncers from the brothel followed him, though I think they were a little scared, and kept their distance a bit."

"And?" said Machiavelli. "None of this is of any use to us so far."

"But they kept him in sight. He must have chartered a ship the night before because he went straight to a carrack called the *Marea di Alba*, and it sailed on the dawn tide."

"Describe him," said Ezio.

"Big, huge hands—I had them around my neck so I should know—broken nose, scarred face; some of the scars seemed to make him look like he had a permanent grin. Didn't talk much."

"How do you know his name?"

"I asked, just to make conversation, and he told me," she answered, simply.

"And where was he going?"

"One of the bouncers knew one of the seamen, and asked him, as they were casting off."

"Where?"

"Valencia."

Valencia. Micheletto was going back to his birthplace—also the hometown of a family called Borgia.

Ezio handed her twelve more ducats. "I'll remember you," he said. "If we find you're lying, you'll regret it."

It was already midday. It took them another hour to find a fast caravel available for charter and agree on the price. Another two hours were needed to victual and prepare the ship. Then they had to wait for the next tide. A caravel is a faster ship than a carrack. Even so, it was early evening before the sails were raised. And the sea was choppy and the wind against them.

"Happy birthday," said Leonardo to Ezio.

FIFTY-EIGHT

The Fates were against them. Their ship sailed well, but the sea remained rough and they encountered squalls that took the sails aback. The hoped-for chance of catching up with Micheletto at sea was long gone when, five days later, their battered caravel put into port at Valencia.

It was a prosperous and booming place, but none of the three—Ezio, Leonardo, or Machiavelli—was familiar with it. The recently built Silk Exchange vied in grandeur with the bell tower, the Torres de Quart, and the Palau de la Generalitat. It was a powerful Catalan city, one of the most important trading cities in the Mediterranean Sea.

But it was also confusing, and teeming with Valencianos, who mingled in the busy streets with Italians,

Dutch, English, and Arabs—the languages heard in the streets created a very Babel.

Fortunately the *Marea di Alba* was still moored near to where the caravel docked, and the two captains were friends.

"*Ciao*, Alberto!"

"*Ciao*, Filin!"

"Bad voyage?" said Alberto, a stout man of thirty, as he stood on the poop deck of his vessel supervising the loading of a mixed cargo of silk, and rare and expensive coffee for the return journey.

"*Brutissimo.*"

"So I see from the state of your ship. But there'll be a good sea and a fair wind for the next week, so I'm hurrying back as soon as I can."

"I won't be so lucky. When did you get in?"

"Two days ago."

Ezio stepped up. "And your passenger?"

Alberto spat. "*Che tipo brutto*—but he paid well."

"Where is he now?"

"Gone! I know he was in the town, asking questions, but he's well-known here, and he has many friends, believe it or not." Alberto spat again. "Not of the best sort, either."

"I'm beginning to wish I hadn't come," whispered Leonardo. "One thing I am not is a man of violence."

"Where has he gone, do you know?"

"He was staying at the Lobo Solitario; you could ask there."

They disembarked and made straight for the Lone

Wolf Inn, after Alberto had given them directions and added darkly, "But it is not a place for gentlemen."

"What makes you think we are gentlemen?" said Machiavelli.

Alberto shrugged.

Ezio scanned the busy quay. Out of the corner of his eye he saw three or four shady characters eyeing them. He checked his bracer and his hidden-blade. The pistol and the poison-blade were in his satchel. He slung his bag over his shoulder, leaving his arms free for his sword and dagger. Noticing this, Machiavelli did the same. Leonardo looked askance.

They made their way into the town, remaining on the alert. But the shady characters had disappeared.

"Shall we stay at the same place as our quarry?" suggested Ezio. "It's the best place to be to find out where he is."

The inn was located in a narrow street of tall tenements that twisted away from one of the main thoroughfares. It was a low, dark building, in contrast to the sparkling newness of most of the rest of the town. The dark wooden door was open, giving on to a dark interior. Ezio entered first, Leonardo, reluctantly, last.

They had reached the center of the vestibule, in which furniture and a long, low counter could only just be made out, when the door behind them banged shut. Ten men who had been lurking in the shadows, their eyes already accustomed to the dark, now pounced, flinging themselves on their victims with guttural cries. Ezio and Machiavelli immediately threw down their bags and in one movement Machiavelli drew his sword and dagger and closed with his first assailant. The glint of blades flashed in the semidarkness of the room. It was big enough for there to be plenty of space to move, and this helped both sides.

"Leonardo!" shouted Ezio. "Get behind the counter! And catch this!"

He threw his sword to Leonardo, who caught it, dropped it, and picked it up again in the space of a second. Ezio unleashed the hidden-blade as one of the men fell on him, stabbing him with it in the side and penetrating his guts. The man stumbled, clutching his belly, blood bubbling between his hands. Meanwhile, Machiavelli strode forward, holding his sword aloft. Quick as a flash he had thrust his sword into the throat of his first man, while simultaneously slicing into the groin of a second man with his other blade. The man fell to the floor with an anguished roar and fumbled vainly at his wound, twitching with agony. Machiavelli closed in and, glancing briefly at his victim, kicked out viciously, silencing the man in an instant.

The other men drew back for a moment, surprised that their ambush had not already achieved its purpose, and at the alacrity of their intended victims. But then they renewed their attack with redoubled vigor. There was a cry from Machiavelli as he was cut in his sword arm from behind, but in a moment Ezio was upon his friend's assailant, plunging his dagger straight into the man's face.

The next thing Ezio knew was that a big man, who

smelled of prison straw and stale sweat, had crept up behind him and thrown a garrote over his head and around his neck. He choked and dropped his dagger, raising his hand to tear at the rope being tightened on his windpipe. Machiavelli leapt over and stabbed at the big man, cutting into him and causing him to cry out in sudden pain, but Machiavelli had missed his true aim and the man thrust him away. But he had lost his grip on the garrote, and Ezio was able to spring free.

The light was too dim to make out the black-cloaked forms of the surviving attackers but the failure of their immediate assault seemed temporarily to have unnerved them.

"Get them!" an unpleasant, guttural voice said. "We are still five against three!"

"Sancho dieron en el pecho!" shouted another, as Ezio smashed his heavy dagger into the sternum of a flabby creature who had tried to close with him, splitting it as neatly as he would have split a chicken breast. "We are four against three. *Nos replegamos!"*

"*No!*" ordered the first man who had spoken. "*Aguantels mentres que m'escapi!*"

The man had spoken in Catalan. The big man who had tried to strangle him. The man who still had the stink of prison clinging to him. Micheletto!

Moments later, the door to the street was flung open and slammed shut again as Micheletto made his escape, momentarily silhouetted in the streetlight. Ezio rushed after him, but he was confronted by one of the three surviving attackers, who blocked his path, holding a scimitar aloft to bring down on him to split his head in two. He was too close to the man to wield either of his weapons in time, so he threw himself to the side, out of the way. As he rolled to momentary safety, the scimitar came swinging down, but the man had struck so violently, expecting the sword's path to be interrupted by its victim's body, that it continued its path and buried itself in the man's own genitals. With a howl, he dropped the sword and fell to the ground, clutching his smashed manhood in an attempt to stop the fountaining blood and writhing in agony.

The last two men almost struggled with each other to reach the door in order to escape, and one succeeded; but the second, somehow already wounded in the fight, was tripped by Machiavelli and crashed to the ground as Leonardo threw himself across his body to prevent his rising. When it was clear he would not, Leonardo stood clear and Ezio knelt and turned him over, pressing the point of the hidden-blade into his nostril.

"I am Ezio Auditore, Mentor of the Assassins," he said. "Tell me where your master is bound and I will show you mercy."

"Never!" croaked the man.

Ezio pressed the point of the blade in farther. Its razor-sharp edges began slowly to slit the man's nose.

"Tell me!"

"All right! He is going to the Castillo de La Mota."

"What is there?"

"That is where Cesare is held prisoner."

Ezio pushed the blade.

"Have mercy! I speak the truth! But you will never succeed in thwarting us! The Borgia will still return to power and rule all Italy with an iron fist! They will swarm into the south and throw the filthy Spanish monarchy out! And then they will destroy the kingdoms of Aragon and Castile and rule them, too!"

"How do you know where Cesare is? It is a dark secret known only to Pope Julius and his council, and to King Ferdinand and his!"

"Do you not think we have spies of our own? Even in the Vatican? They are good, these spies. This time, better than yours!"

With a sudden movement, the man brought up his right arm. In it was a small knife, which he aimed at Ezio's heart. Ezio just had time to block the blow with his left arm, and the knife skittered harmlessly off the bracer and away onto the floor.

"Long live the Royal House of Borgia!" the man cried.

"Requiescat in pace," said Ezio.

"Welcome to Valencia," Leonardo muttered.

FIFTY-NINE

The Lone Wolf Inn was deserted but there were beds of a sort and as it was late by the time Ezio and his companions had recovered from the bloody tussle with Micheletto's diehards, they had no choice but to spend the night there. They did find wine, water, and food—bread, onions, and some salami—and even Leonardo was too hungry to refuse it.

The following morning, Ezio rose early, eager to find horses for the journey ahead of them. Their ship's captain, Filin, was at the docks seeing to the refitting of his battered ship, and he knew of the remote Castle of La Mota and gave them directions, as far as he could, as to how to find it. But it would be a long and arduous journey of many days. Filin also helped organize their horses but preparations still took another forty-eight hours, since they had to provision themselves as well. The journey would take them northwest across the brown sierras of central Spain. There were no maps, so they traveled from one town or village to another, using the list of names Filin had given them.

They passed out of Valencia and after several days' hard riding on their first set of horses—Leonardo complaining bitterly—passed into the beautiful mountain country around the tiny hill town of Cuenca. Then down again onto the flat plain of Madrid, and through the royal city itself, where the bandits who tried to rob them soon found themselves dead on the road, and so north to Segovia on its hill, dominated by its Alcazar, where they spent the night as the guests of the seneschal of Queen Isabella of Castile.

Then on again through open country—attacked and almost robbed by a gang of Moorish highwaymen who had somehow slipped through the fingers of King Ferdinand and survived in the open country for twelve years. Ferdinand, king of Aragon, Sicily, Naples, and Valencia, founder of the Spanish Inquisition and scourge of the Jews—to dire effect on his nation's economy—through his Grand Inquisitor, Tomás de Torquemada; but who through marriage to his equally ugly wife, Isabella, united Aragon and Castile and started to make Spain a single nation.

Ferdinand had ambitions on Navarre. Ezio wondered how far the bigoted king's designs would have an impact on that country, where Cesare had such close family ties, being the brother-in-law of its French king.

Fighting weariness, they rode on, praying that they would be in time to thwart Micheletto's plan.

But, despite all the haste they made, he had had a good start on them.

SIXTY

Micheletto and his small band of diehards reined in their horses and stood up in their stirrups to look at the Castle of La Mota. It dominated the small town of Medina del Campo, and had been built to protect it from the Moors.

Micheletto had good eyesight, and even from that distance he could see the red scarf that Cesare had hung from his cell window. The window was high, high in the central tower, the topmost window, in fact. No need for bars on such a window—that was something to be thankful for, at least—because no one had ever escaped from this place. You could see why. The walls had been made by the skilled masons of the eleventh century and the stone blocks were so skillfully laid that the surface was as smooth as glass.

Good that they had devised this plan of the red scarf; otherwise it might have hard to find his master Cesare. The go-between, a La Mota sergeant of the guard, who'd been recruited to the Borgia cause in Valencia some time earlier, was perfect: once bribed, perfectly dependable.

But getting Cesare out was going to be difficult. His cell door was permanently watched by two of a troop of Swiss Guards on loan from Pope Julius, all totally inflexible and incorruptible. So getting Cesare out the easy way was impossible.

Micheletto measured the height of the central tower with his eyes. Once inside the place, they'd have to scale an impossible wall to a cell about 140 feet up. So, that was out.

Micheletto considered the problem. He was a practical man, but his specialty was killing, not solving problems by any other means. His thoughts led him to reflect on the main tool of his trade: rope.

"Let's ride a little closer," he said to his companions. They'd all dressed not in their customary black, but in hunting outfits, so as to arouse little or no suspicion. He had ten men with him. Each of them carried, as part of their standard equipment, a length of rope.

"We don't want to get too close," said his lieutenant. "The guards on the ramparts will see us."

"And what will they see? A hunting party coming to Medina to revictual. Don't worry, Giacomo."

That remark had given Micheletto the germ of an idea. He went on, "We'll ride right up to the town."

It was about half an hour's ride. During it, Micheletto

was more than usually silent, his battered brow deeply furrowed. Then, as they approached the walls of the city, his face cleared.

"Rein in," he said.

They did so. Micheletto looked them over. The youngest, a man of eighteen, Luca, had no hair on his chin, and a tip-tilted nose. He was already a hardened killer, but his face had the innocence of a cherub.

"Get out your ropes and measure them."

They obeyed. Each rope measured twelve feet. One hundred twenty feet, tied securely together. Add Micheletto's own and you had 130 feet. Cesare would have to drop the last ten feet or so, but that would be nothing to him.

Next problem: getting the rope to Cesare. For that they'd have to contact their recruit, the sergeant of the guard, Juan. That wouldn't be too hard. They knew Juan's movements and hours of duty. That would be Luca's job, since, as an innocent-looking young man, he'd attract little attention. The rest of his band, though dressed like hunters, looked like the men they were: hardened thugs. As for himself . . . And Juan's palm would have to be greased, but Micheletto always carried a contingency fund of 250 ducats. A tenth of that should do it. For the whole job.

Juan could gain access to Cesare's cell and deliver the rope. The Swiss guards wouldn't suspect him. Micheletto might even fake a letter with an official-looking seal on it, to be delivered to Cesare, as cover.

But the outer barbican was massive. Once Cesare was at the foot of the central tower, he'd still have to cross the inner courtyards and get out—somehow—through the only gate.

One good thing. La Mota's main function these days was to guard its single prisoner. Its original purpose had been to ward off attacks from the Moors, but that threat had been removed long since. The massive place was, in every sense other than guarding Cesare, redundant, and he knew from Juan that it was a fairly cushy posting.

If Juan could . . . They must take changes of clothes to Cesare from time to time . . . If Juan could organize delivery of a change of clothes and fix up a rendezvous once Cesare was out . . .

It might work. He could think of no other way, apart from fighting their way in and getting Cesare out by force.

"Luca," he said finally, "I have a job for you."

It turned out that Juan wanted fifty ducats for the whole job, and Micheletto beat him down to forty, but didn't waste time with too much bartering. It took Luca three trips to and fro to set the whole thing up, but finally he reported back:

"It's arranged. He's going to take the rope and a guardsman's uniform to Cesare, accompanying the man who takes him his evening meal at six o'clock. The postern gate will be guarded by Juan, who's going to take the midnight-to-six gate-watch. It's a five-minute walk from the castle to the town . . ."

* * *

Cesare Borgia's left leg hurt from the lesions of the New
Disease, but not much, a dull ache, making him limp
slightly. At two o'clock in the morning, already changed
into the uniform, he tied one end of the rope firmly to
the central mullion of the window of his cell and carefully let the length of the rest of it out into the night.
When it was all paid out, he slung his good leg over the
windowsill, hauled the other one after it, and took a firm
grip on the rope. Sweating despite the coolness of the
night, he descended hand over hand until his ankles felt
the end of the rope. He dropped the last ten feet, and
felt the pain in his left leg when he landed, but he shook
it off and limped across the deserted inner courtyard and
through the outer one, where there were guards who
were sleepy and paid him no attention, recognizing him
as one of their own.

At the gate he was challenged. His heart went to his
mouth. But then Juan came up.

"It's all right. I'll take him to the guardhouse."

What was going on? So near and yet so far!

"Don't worry," said Juan under his breath.

The guardhouse was occupied by two sleeping
guards. Juan kicked one of them into life.

"Wake up, Domingo. This man has a warrant for
town. They forgot to order more straw for the stables
and they need it before they ride out for the dawn patrol.
Take him back to the gate, explain to the guards there,
and let him out."

"Yes, sir!"

Out he went through the postern, which was then firmly locked behind him, and limped through the moonlight and the sweet night air to the town. What joy to feel the night around him, and the air, after so long. He'd been confined in this dump for more than a year. But he was free now; he was still only thirty; he'd get it all back. And he'd take such vengeance on his enemies, especially the Assassin Brotherhood, that Caterina Sforza's purges at Forlì would make her look like a nursemaid.

He heard and smelled the horses at the appointed rendezvous. Thank God for Micheletto. Then he saw them. They were all there, in the shadows of the church wall. They had a fine black beast ready for him. Micheletto dismounted and helped him to the saddle.

"Welcome back, *Eccellenza*," he said. "And now, we must hurry. That bastard *Assassino*, Ezio Auditore, is on our heels."

Cesare was silent. He was thinking about the slowest death he could devise for the Assassin.

"I've put matters in hand already at Valencia," continued Micheletto.

"Good."

They rode off into the night, heading southeast.

SIXTY-ONE

"He's *escaped*?" Ezio had ridden the last miles to La Mota without sparing himself, his companions, or their horses, with an ever-deepening sense of apprehension. "*How*?"

"It was carefully planned, *signore*," said the hapless lieutenant of the castle, a plumpish man of sixty with a very red nose. "We are holding an official inquiry."

"And what have you come up with?"

"As yet . . ."

But Ezio wasn't listening. He was looking around at the Castle of La Mota. It was exactly as the Apple had depicted it. And the thought led him to remember another vision it had vouchsafed him: the gathering army at a seaport . . . The seaport had been Valencia!

His mind raced frantically.

He could only think of getting back to the coast as fast as possible!

"Get me fresh horses!" he yelled.

"But, *signore* . . ."

Machiavelli and Leonardo looked at each other.

"Ezio! Whatever the urgency, we must rest, at least for a day," said Machiavelli.

"A week." Leonardo groaned.

As matters turned out, they were delayed, since Leonardo fell ill. He was exhausted, and he missed Italy badly. Ezio was almost tempted to abandon him, but Machiavelli counseled restraint:

"He is your old friend. And they cannot gather an army and a fleet in less than two months."

Ezio relented.

Events were to prove him right.

And to prove Leonardo invaluable.

SIXTY-TWO

Ezio and his companions were back in Valencia within a month. They found the city in a state of uproar. Machiavelli had underestimated the speed with which things could happen in such a wealthy town.

Men had been secretly mustering and now, just outside Valencia, there was a huge camp of soldiers, maybe one thousand men. The Borgia were offering mercenaries good wages, and word had got around fast. Budding soldiers were coming in from as far away as Barcelona and Madrid, and from all over the provinces of Murcia and La Mancha. And Borgia money ensured that a fleet of perhaps fifteen ships, quickly run-up troopships with half a dozen small warships to protect them, was in the process of being built.

"Well, we don't need the Apple to tell us what our old friend Cesare is planning," said Machiavelli.

"That's true. He doesn't need a vast army to take Naples, and once he's established a bridgehead there, he'll recruit many more men to his cause. His plan is to conquer the Kingdom of Naples, and all Italy."

"What are Ferdinand and Isabella doing about this?" asked Machiavelli.

"They'll be getting a force together to crush it. We'll enlist their aid."

"Take too long. Their army has to march from Madrid. The garrison here must have been put out of action. But you can see that Cesare's in a hurry," rejoined Machiavelli.

"Might not even be necessary," put in Leonardo musingly.

"What do you mean?"

"Bombs."

"Bombs?" asked Machiavelli.

"Quite little bombs—but effective enough to, say, wreck ships or disperse a camp."

"Well, if they'll do that for us . . ." said Ezio. "What do you need to make them?"

"Sulfur, charcoal, and potassium nitrate. And steel. Thinnish steel. Flexible. And I'll need a small studio and a furnace."

It took them a while, but fortunately for them, Captain Alberto's ship, the *Marea di Alba*, was tied up at its usual quay. He greeted them with a friendly wave.

"Hello again!" he said. "The people who aren't

gentlemen. I don't suppose you heard about the fracas at the Lone Wolf shortly after you arrived?"

Ezio told him what they needed.

"Hm. I do know a man here who has the facilities, and he might be able to put ticks on your shopping list."

"When do you return to Italy?" asked Leonardo.

"I've brought over a cargo of grappa, and I'm taking back silk again. Maybe two, three days. Why?"

"I'll tell you later."

"Can you get what we need arranged quickly?" asked Ezio, who suddenly had a sense of foreboding. But he couldn't blame Leonardo for wanting to leave.

"Certainly!"

Alberto was as good as his word, and within a few hours everything had been arranged and Leonardo settled down to work.

"How long will it take you?" asked Machiavelli.

"Two days, since I don't have any assistants. I've enough material here to make twenty, maybe twenty-one, bombs. That's ten each."

"*Seven* each," said Ezio.

"No, my friend, ten each—one lot for you, and one for Niccolò here. You can count me out."

Two days later, the bombs were ready. Each was about the shape and size of a grapefruit, encased in steel and fitted with a catch at the top.

"How do they work?"

Leonardo smiled proudly. "You flip this little catch—actually, it's more of a lever—you count to three, and you throw it at your target. Each of these is enough to kill twenty men and, if you hit it in the right place, to disable a ship completely, even sink it." He mused. "It's a pity there isn't time to build a submarine."

"A what?"

"Never mind. Just throw it after a count of three. Don't hold on to it any longer, or you'll be blown to pieces yourself!" He rose. "And now, goodbye, and good luck."

"What?"

Leonardo smiled ruefully. "I've had quite enough of Spain and I've booked a passage with Alberto. He sails on this afternoon's tide. I'll see you back in Rome—if you make it."

Ezio and Machiavelli looked at each other. Then each solemnly embraced Leonardo.

"Thank you, my dear friend," said Ezio.

"Don't mention it."

"Thank God you didn't build these things for Cesare," said Machiavelli.

After Leonardo had gone, they carefully packed the bombs, of which there were exactly ten each, into linen bags, which they slung around their shoulders.

"You take the mercenaries' encampment; I'll take the port," said Ezio.

Machiavelli nodded grimly.

"When we've done the job, we'll meet at the corner of the street where the Lone Wolf is," said Ezio. "I reckon the Lone Wolf is where Cesare will have his center of operations. There'll be chaos and he'll go there to regroup with his inner circle. We'll try to corner them before they can make their escape—again."

"For once I'll back your hunch." Machiavelli grinned. "Cesare is so vainglorious he won't have thought to change the Borgia diehards' hideout. And it's more discreet than a palazzo."

"Good luck, friend."

"We'll both need it."

They shook hands and parted on their separate missions.

Ezio decided to go for the troopships first. Blending in with the crowd, he made his way down to the port and, once on the quay, selected his first target. He took out the first bomb, fighting down the insidious doubt that it might not work, and, aware that he'd have to work very fast, flipped its catch, counted to three, and flung it.

He was working at close range and his aim had a deadly accuracy. The bomb landed with a clatter in the belly of the ship. For a few moments, nothing happened, and Ezio cursed inwardly. What if the plan had failed?

But then there was an almighty explosion, the ship's mast cracked and fell, and splintered wood was tossed high in the air everywhere.

Amid the chaos that followed, Ezio darted along the quay, selecting likely ships and throwing his bombs. In several cases, the first explosion was followed by a mightier one—some of the troopships were evidently already laden with casks of gunpowder. In one case, an exploding ship carrying gunpowder destroyed its two neighbors.

One by one, Ezio wrecked twelve ships, but the chaos and panic were of great value. And in the distance he could hear explosions, and the shouts and screams that followed them, as Machiavelli did his work.

As he made his way to their rendezvous, he hoped his friend had survived.

All Valencia was in uproar, but pushing his way against the flow of the crowd, Ezio made the appointed spot in ten minutes. Machiavelli wasn't there, but Ezio didn't have long to wait. Looking a bit shabby, and with a blackened face, his fellow Assassin soon came running up.

"May God reward Leonardo da Vinci," he said.

"Success?"

"I have never seen such pandemonium," replied Machiavelli. "The survivors are running away out of town as fast as they can. I think most of them will prefer the plow to the sword after this."

"Good! But we still have work to do."

They made their way down the narrow street and arrived at the door of the Lone Wolf. It was closed. Silently as cats, they climbed to the roof. It was a one-story building, bigger than it appeared from the front, and near the top of the slant of the roof there was a skylight. It was open. They approached it and cautiously looked over the edge.

It was a different room from the one in which they had been ambushed. Two men were down below. Micheletto stood at a table. Facing him, seated, was Cesare Borgia. His once-handsome face, now lacerated by the New Disease, was white with fury.

"They have destroyed my plans! Those damned

Assassins! Why did you not destroy them? Why did you fail me?"

"*Eccellenza*, I—" Micheletto looked like a whipped dog.

"I must make good my escape. I'll go to Viana. Once I'm there, I'll be in Navarre, just across the border. Let them try to recapture me then! I'm not waiting here for Ferdinand's men to come and haul me back to La Mota. My brother-in-law is king of Navarre and he will surely help me."

"*I* will help you, as I have always helped you. Only let me come with you."

Cesare's cruel lips curled. "You got me out of La Mota, sure. You built up my hopes. But now look where you have got me!"

"Master, all my men are dead—I have done what I could."

"And failed!"

Micheletto went white. "Is this my reward? For all my years of faithful service?"

"You dog, get out of my sight. I discard you! Go and find some gutter to die in."

With a cry of rage, Micheletto hurled himself at Cesare, his huge strangler's hands flexed to close on his former master's throat. But they never got there. With lightning speed, Cesare had whipped out one of the two pistols he had in his belt and fired, at point-blank range.

Micheletto's face was destroyed beyond all recognition. The rest of the body crashed over the table. Cesare sprang back, out of his chair, to avoid being covered in blood.

Ezio had drawn back, to be invisible but not out of

earshot. He was preparing to leap from the roof and grab Cesare as he came out through the front door of the inn. But Machiavelli had craned forward the better to witness this dreadful showdown. Now, he inadvertently kicked a tile loose, and the noise alerted Cesare.

Cesare looked up swiftly, drawing his second pistol at the same time. Machiavelli didn't have time to draw back before Cesare fired, shooting Machiavelli through the shoulder and smashing his collarbone. Then Cesare fled.

Ezio thought of pursuit, but only for an instant, and he had heard that Cesare intended to go to Viana. Well, he would follow him there. But not before he had seen to his wounded friend.

Machiavelli was groaning, apologies of all things, as Ezio managed to haul him off the roof. At least he could walk, but the wound was bad.

Once they had got to the main thoroughfare, Ezio accosted a passerby, having to stop the man by force since the chaos was still raging around them.

"I need a doctor," he said urgently. "Where can I find one?"

"Many people need a doctor!" replied the man.

Ezio shook him. "My friend is badly wounded. Where can I find a doctor? Now!"

"Let go of me! You could try *el médico* Acosta. His rooms are just down the street. There's a sign outside."

Ezio grabbed the near-fainting Machiavelli and supported him. He took his scarf from his tunic and with it stanched the wound as best he could. Niccolò was losing a lot of blood.

The minute he saw the wound, Acosta had Machiavelli sit in a chair. He took a bottle of alcohol and some swabs and carefully dressed it.

"The ball went right through the shoulder," he explained in broken Italian. "So at least I won't have to dig it out. And it's a clean wound. But as for the collarbone, I'll have to reset it. I hope you're not planning on traveling any time soon."

Ezio and Machiavelli exchanged a glance.

"I have been a fool again," said Machiavelli, forcing a grin.

"Shut up, Niccolò."

"Go on. Get after him. I'll manage."

"He can stay here with me. I have a small annex that needs a patient," said Acosta. "And when he's healed, I'll send him after you."

"How long?"

"Perhaps two weeks, maybe more."

"I'll see you in Rome," said Machiavelli.

"All right," replied Ezio. "Take care of yourself, my friend."

"Kill him for me," said Machiavelli. "Though at least he spared us the trouble of Micheletto."

PART III

We have reached the last era in prophetic song. Time has conceived, and the great sequence of the ages starts afresh. Justice, the virgin, comes back to dwell with us, and the rule of Saturn is restored. The Firstborn of the New Age is already on his way from high heaven down to earth.

—VIRGIL, *ECLOGUES*, IV

SIXTY-THREE

Ezio once again traveled across Spain on a long, lonely journey, almost due north to Viana. He arrived there in the month of March. The city that he saw, a mile or so distant, looked exactly like the one in the vision accorded him by the Apple, with strong walls and a well-fortified citadel at its center, but there was a difference.

Even before he crossed the border into Navarre, Ezio's practiced eye told him that the city was under siege. When he came to a village, most of the locals just shook their heads dumbly when he questioned them, but when he sought out the priest, with whom he was able to converse in Latin, he learned the whole picture.

"You may know that our king and queen have designs

on Navarre. It's a rich land, and they want to incorporate it into ours."

"So they want to take Viana?"

"They've already taken it! It's occupied by the Count of Lerin on their behalf."

"And the besiegers?"

"They are Navarrese forces. I think they will be the victors."

"What makes you say that?"

"Because they are under the command of the brother-in-law of the king of Navarre, and he is an experienced general."

Ezio's heart beat faster, but he still needed confirmation: "His name?"

"He's very famous, apparently. The Duke of Valence, Cesare Borgia. They say he once commanded the army of the Pope himself. But the Spanish troops are brave. They have taken the fight out to the enemy, and there have been bloody battles in the fields outside the town. I would not go any farther in that direction, my son; there lies only devastation and blood."

Ezio thanked him and spurred his horse forward.

He arrived at the scene to find a pitched battle going on right in front of him, as a fog grew around them. In its midst Cesare Borgia was taking a stand, hacking down any foe who came at him. And suddenly Ezio himself had to fight another horseman—a Navarrese, with his crest of a red shield crisscrossed with yellow chains. They cut and slashed at each other with their swords until finally Ezio was able to split the man's right shoulder down to the chest, and he fell, without a cry, to be finished off by Spanish infantrymen.

Cesare was on foot, and Ezio decided that it would be easier to get close to him undetected if he were also on foot, so he dismounted and ran through the fray toward him.

At last he stood face-to-face with his deadly foe. Cesare's face was streaked with blood and dust, and strained with exertion, but when he saw Ezio his expression took on a new determination.

"Assassin! How did you find me?"

"My thirst to avenge Mario Auditore led me to you."

They sliced at each other with their swords until Ezio managed to knock Cesare's out of his hand. Then, sheathing his own, he flung himself on the Borgia, putting his hands around his throat. But Cesare had learned a few things from Micheletto about the art of strangling and managed to free himself by thrusting Ezio's arms away. Ezio unleashed the hidden-blade, but once again Cesare managed to defend himself successfully, as the battle raged about them.

But then the Spanish trumpets sounded the retreat. Triumphant, Cesare yelled to the nearest Navarrese troops: "Kill him! Kill the Assassin! Tear the *maldito bastardo* into pieces!"

But the fog had increased, and Cesare melted into it. The Navarrese soldiers closed in on Ezio. He fought them off hard and long. They left him for dead.

Later, Ezio came to, to find himself in the middle of the battlefield. He was lying on his back. He had to push a corpse off him before he could sit up.

The battlefield lay under a cloudy, bloodred sky. In the distance the sun burned angrily. Dust hung in the air over a wide, unmade road, littered with the dead.

Ezio saw a crow standing on a corpse's chin, pecking hungrily at his eye. A riderless horse stampeded by, driven mad by the smell of blood. Broken banners snapped in the breeze.

Groaning with the effort, he stood up and, painfully at first, walked through the field of the dead. He found that he had lost his sword and dagger, though the hiddenblade and the bracer had not been found and looted.

His first job was to replace his weapons. Near him, he noticed a peasant sifting through the battlefield, looting. The peasant looked at him.

"Help yourself," he said. "There's more than enough to go around."

Ezio looked for fallen officers and knights, as they would be better armed, but in every case someone had got there before him. At last he found a dead captain with a fine sword and a dagger similar to his own. These he took gratefully.

He made his way off the battlefield. He had to find a horse. It would be quicker to get around that way.

He was in luck. Not half a mile from the edge of the battlefield, well away from the Navarrese camp, he came across a warhorse, its back bloodstained, but not with its own blood, and fully saddled and bridled, grazing in a green field. Talking to it gently, he mounted it. It kicked a little at first, but he soothed it quickly and, turning it, rode back the way he had come.

Back at the battlefield, he encountered more peasants gleaning what they could from the bodies. He passed them, galloping up a hill toward the sound of a renewed fight. As the crest of the hill revealed a level plain below it, Ezio saw that he was now much closer to the town. Battle had been rejoined and it was taking place on the plain, close to the battlemented walls of the town, from where cannon fire issued.

SIXTY-FOUR

Ezio steered his horse to one side of the battle, through some olive groves, but there he encountered a patrol of Navarrese troops. Before he had time to wheel around, they had fired their muskets at him, missing him, but cutting his horse down from under him.

He managed to escape among the trees, and, continuing on foot, taking care to avoid the Spanish troops who seemed to be prowling all around, he suddenly overheard snatches of conversation. Creeping closer, he came to a clearing in which he saw one Spanish soldier lying wounded on the ground while another did his best to comfort him.

"Por favor," said the wounded man. "My legs. Why won't the bleeding stop?"

"*Compadre*, I have done all I can for you. Now you must trust in God."

"Oh, Pablo, I'm afraid! *Mis piernas! Mis piernas!*"

"Quiet now, Miguel. Think of all the money we'll get when we've won the battle. And the booty!"

"Who is this old man we are fighting for?"

"Who? *El Conde de Lerin?*"

"Yes. We are fighting for him, aren't we?"

"Yes, my friend. He serves our king and queen, and we serve him. So we fight."

"Pablo, the only thing I think I'm fighting for now is my life."

A patrol arrived on the other side of the clearing.

"Keep moving," said its sergeant. "We must outflank them."

"My friend is wounded," said Pablo. "He cannot move."

"Then leave him. Come on."

"Give me a few more minutes."

"Very well. We head north. Follow us. And be sure no Navarrese sees you."

"Will we know when we have outflanked them?"

"There will be gunfire. We'll cut them down where they least expect it. Use the trees for cover."

"Just a moment, sir."

"What is it?"

"I will follow now."

"Immediately?"

"Yes, sir. My comrade, Miguel, is dead."

* * *

Once they had gone, Ezio waited for a few minutes, then made his way north, before veering east, in the direction he knew Viana lay. He left the olive groves and saw that he had passed the field of battle and was now skirting it on its northern side. He wondered what had become of the Spanish soldiers, for there was no sign of any successful outflanking movement. And the battle seemed to be going to the Navarrese.

On his way lay a shattered village. He avoided it, as he could see Spanish snipers concealed behind some of the charred and broken walls, using long-muzzled wheel locks to fire on any Navarrese troops at the edge of the battle.

He came across a soldier, his tunic so bloodstained that Ezio could not tell what side he was on, sitting with his back to a stray olive tree and hugging himself in agony, his whole body shaking, his gun abandoned on the ground.

Reaching the outskirts of the town, among the settlements crouched beneath its bastions, Ezio saw, just ahead of him, his quarry. Cesare was with a Navarrese sergeant and he was clearly assessing the best way of breaching or undermining Viana's massive walls.

The Spanish who had taken Viana had been confident enough to allow some of their camp followers to settle in the houses here. But they were evidently not now powerful enough to protect them.

Suddenly, a woman came out of one of the cottages and ran toward them, screaming and blocking their path.

"Ayúdenme!" she cried. "Help me! My son! My son is wounded!"

The sergeant went up to the woman and, seizing her by the hair, dragged her out of Cesare's way.

"Ayúdenme!" she yelled.

"Shut her up, will you?" said Cesare, surveying her coldly.

The sergeant drew his dagger and slit the woman's throat.

SIXTY-FIVE

As Ezio shadowed Cesare, he witnessed further scenes of brutality dealt out by the Navarrese troops on the hated Spanish interlopers.

He saw a young woman being roughly manhandled by a Navarrese trooper.

"Leave me in peace!" she cried.

"Be a good girl," the soldier told her brutally. "I will not hurt you! In fact, you might even enjoy it, you fucking Spanish whore."

Farther along, a man, a cook by the look of him, stood in despair as two soldiers held him and forced him to watch two others set fire to his house.

Worse, a man—doubtless a wounded Spanish soldier who had had his legs amputated—had been kicked out of his cart by another pair of Navarrese squaddies. They stood there laughing as he desperately tried to drag himself away from them along a footpath.

"Run! Run!" said one.

"Can't you go any faster?" added his comrade.

The battle had obviously gone to the Navarrese, because Ezio could see them bringing siege towers up to the walls of the city. Somewhere behind him, a Spanish preacher was intoning to a despairing congregation:

"You have brought this on yourselves through sin. This is how the Lord punishes you. Ours is a just God and this is His justice. Praise the Lord! Thank you, God, for teaching us to be humble. To see our punishment for what it is, a call to spirituality. The Lord giveth and the Lord taketh away. So is the Truth written. Amen!"

Ezio saw that several siege towers were now against the walls. Navarrese troops were swarming up them and there was fierce fighting on the battlements already.

If Cesare were anywhere, it would be at the head of his men, for he was as ferocious and fearless as he was cruel.

The only way into the city is up one of the towers, thought Ezio. The one nearest him had just been pushed up to the wall and, running, Ezio joined the men rushing up it, blending in with them, though there was scarcely any need, for amid all the roaring and bellowing of the pumped-up besiegers, who scented victory at last, he would not have been noticed.

But the defenders were in greater readiness now,

and they were pouring that mixture of pitch and oil they called Greek fire down onto the enemy below. The screams of burning men came up to those already on the tower, Ezio among them, and the rush upward, away from the flames, which had already taken the base of the tower, became frantic. Around him, Ezio saw men push their fellows out of the way in order to save themselves. Some soldiers fell from the tower, howling, into the flames below.

Ezio knew he had to get to the top before the flames caught up with him. Reaching it, he gave a great Leap of Faith onto the battlements just as the fire, seconds behind him, reached it, too, and the blazing tower collapsed, causing murderous chaos beneath.

There was fierce fighting on the ramparts of the walls, but already hundreds of Navarrese soldiers had got down into the town itself, and the Spanish trumpets were sounding the retreat into the citadel at the center of Viana. The town was as good as retaken for Navarre.

Cesare would be in triumph. His wealthy brother-in-law would reward him richly. No! Ezio would not allow that to happen.

Running along the high wall, ducking and diving among the fighting soldiery, the Navarrese soldiers cutting down the Spanish troops who had been left behind in the retreat to fend for themselves, Ezio located Cesare, cutting his way through enemy troops as a child uses a stick to smash through tall grass. Cesare was impatient to take the citadel as well, and, once clear of the men who had attempted to block his way, he sped down a stairway on the inner wall and through the town, Ezio only seconds behind him.

Ahead of them, the citadel had already opened its doors. All the fight had gone out of the Spanish, and the Count of Lerin was ready to parlay. But Cesare was not a man to parlay.

"Kill them! Kill them all!" he shouted to his troops. With superhuman speed, he ran into the citadel and up the narrow stone staircases within it, cutting down anyone who got in his way.

Ezio still kept pace with him. At last they reached the topmost battlements of the citadel. There was no one there but Cesare, who cut down the flagpole bearing the Spanish flag. Then he turned. There was but one way out, and there stood Ezio, blocking it.

"There is nowhere for you to run, Cesare," said Ezio. "This is the time to pay your debts."

"Come on then, Ezio!" snarled Cesare. "You brought down my family. Let's see how you settle *your* debts."

Such was their impatient fury, they closed with each other immediately, man-to-man, using only their fists as weapons.

Cesare got the first blows in and started to cry out in triumph. "No matter what you do, I will conquer all, but first I will kill you and everyone you hold dear. As for me, I cannot die. *Fortuna* will not fail me!"

"Your hour is come, Cesare," Ezio replied, slowly getting the upper hand. He drew his sword.

Cesare loosed his own blade in response—and the two men began to fight in earnest. Ezio swung his blade viciously toward his foe's head, the blade sweeping a lethal flat arc through the air. Cesare was shocked by the speed of the attack but managed to raise his own blade in a clumsy parry, his arm shuddering with the impact. Ezio's sword bounced away. Cesare thrust with his own attack—his balance and focus regained. The men circled on the parapet—flicking the tips of their swords in swift bursts of exchanged swordplay. Ezio stepped a quick one, two forward—leading Cesare's blade off to the right and then twisting his wrist forward, aiming the point of his sword toward Cesare's exposed left flank. Cesare was too quick again – and slapped Ezio's sword aside. He used the opening to flick his sword at Ezio—who responded by raising his wrist and using the bracer to deflect the blow. Both men stepped back, wary once again. Cesare's skill as swordsman was clearly not hampered by the onset of the French disease.

"*Pah!* Old man! Your generation is finished. It is my turn now. And I shall not wait any longer. Your antiquated systems, your rules and hierarchies—all must go."

Both men were tiring now. They confronted each other, panting.

Ezio replied, "Your new ones will bring tyranny and misery to all."

"I know what is best for the people of Italy, not a bunch of old men who wasted their energy fighting to get to the top years ago."

"Your mistakes are worse than theirs."

"I do not *make* mistakes. I am the Enlightened One!"

"Enlightenment comes through years of thought, not through blind conviction."

"Ezio Auditore—your time has come!"

Cesare drew his sword and swung an unexpected, cowardly blow at Ezio with it, but Ezio was just quick enough to parry, carry through, and, catching Cesare off balance, seize his wrist and wrench the sword from his grip. It clattered to the flagstones.

They were on the edge of the battlements. Far below, Navarrese troops were beginning to celebrate. But there was no looting, for they had regained a town that was their own.

Cesare went for his dagger, but Ezio slashed at his opponent's wrist with his sword, cutting into it and disabling it. Cesare staggered back.

"The throne was mine!" he said, like a child who has lost a toy.

"Wanting something does not give you the right to have it."

"What do you know? Have you never wanted something that much?"

"A true leader empowers the people he rules."

"I can still lead mankind into a new world!"

Ezio saw that Cesare was standing inches from the edge. "May your name be blotted out," he said, raising his sword. *"Requiescat in pace."*

"You cannot kill me! No man can murder me!"

"Then I will leave you in the hands of Fate," replied Ezio.

Dropping his sword, Ezio seized Cesare Borgia and threw him off the battlements, to plunge down to the cobblestones one hundred feet below.

SIXTY-SIX

It was Midsummer Day again—Ezio's forty-eighth birthday. Ezio, Machiavelli, and Leonardo were gathered in the newly refurbished Tiber Island headquarters, now a proud building for all to see.

"Very small birthday party," commented Leonardo. "Now, if you had let me design something for you, a real pageant . . ."

"Save that for two years' time." Ezio smiled. "But we have invited you for another reason."

"Which is . . . ?" asked Leonardo, full of curiosity.

Machiavelli, easing a slightly crooked, but fully healed, shoulder, said, "Leo, we want to extend an invitation to you."

"Another one?"

"We want you to join us," said Ezio solemnly. "To become a fellow member of the Brotherhood of the Assassins."

Leonardo smiled gravely. "So—my bombs were a success!" He was silent for a moment, then said, "Gentlemen, I thank you, and you know that I respect your goals and will support them as long as I live; and the secrets of the Assassins I will never disclose to anyone." He paused. "But I tread a different path, and it is a solitary one. So forgive me."

"Your support is almost as valuable as your becoming one of us. But can't we persuade you, old friend?"

"No, Ezio. Besides, I am leaving."

"Leaving? Where are you going?"

"I shall return to Milan, and then I am going to Amboise."

"To France?"

"They say it is a noble country. It is there I choose to end my days."

Ezio spread his hands. "Then we must let you go, old friend." He paused. "This, then, is a parting of the ways."

"How so?" asked Leonardo.

"I am returning to Florence," replied Machiavelli. "My work there is far from done." He winked at Ezio. "And I still have that book to write."

"What will you call it?"

Machiavelli looked levelly at Ezio. "*The Prince*," he replied.

"Send Claudia back to me."

"I will. She misses Rome, and you know she'll support

you as long as you continue your work as Mentor of the Brotherhood."

Machiavelli glanced at the water clock.

"It is time."

The three men rose as one and embraced each other solemnly.

"Goodbye."

"Goodbye."

"Goodbye."

LIST OF CHARACTERS

Mario Auditore: Ezio's uncle and head of the
  Brotherhood of the Assassins
Ezio Auditore: Assassin
Maria Auditore: Ezio's mother
Claudia Auditore: Ezio's sister
Angelina Ceresa: friend of Claudia's
Federico: Mario's stable-master
Annetta: Auditore family housekeeper
Paola: Assassin, sister of Annetta
Ruggiero: master-sergeant in Mario Auditore's guards

Niccolò di Bernardo dei Machiavelli: Assassin,
  philosopher and writer, 1469–1527
Leonardo da Vinci: artist, scientist, sculptor, etc.,
  1452–1519
Antonio: Assassin
Fabio Orsini: Assassin

Bartolomeo d'Alviano: Italian captain and Assassin, 1455–1515

Pantasilea Baglioni: Bartolomeo's wife

Baldassare Castiglione: Associate Assassin

Pietro Bembo: Associate Assassin

Teodora: Assassin

Gilberto the Fox, la Volpe: Assassin and head of the Thieves' Guild

Benito: member of the Thieves' Guild

Trimalchio: member of the Thieves' Guild

Claudio: thief and son of Trimalchio

Paganino: thief at the sacking of Monteriggioni

Madonna Solari: brothel keeper and Assassin accomplice

Agnella: prostitute from the Rosa in Fiore

Lucia: prostitute from the Rosa in Fiore

Saraghina: prostitute from the Rosa in Fiore

Margherita degli Campi: Roman aristocrat and Assassin sympathizer

Jacopo: sailor

Camilla: Naples prostitute

Filin: ship's captain

Captain Alberto: captain of the *Marea di Alba*

Acosta: Valencian doctor

Count of Lerin: Spanish count, 1430–1508

Caterina Sforza: the Countess of Forlì, daughter of Galeazzo, 1463–1509

Lorenzo de' Medici, "Lorenzo the Magnificent": Italian statesman, 1449–92

Piero Soderini: governor of Florence, 1450–1522

Amerigo Vespucci: friend and advisor to Soderini, 1454–1512

Rodrigo Borgia: Pope Alexander VI, 1451–1503

Cesare Borgia: son of Rodrigo, 1476–1507

Lucrezia Borgia: daughter of Rodrigo, 1480–1519

Vannozza Cattanei: mother of Cesare and Lucrezia Borgia, 1442–1518

Giulia Farnese: Rodrigo's mistress, 1474–1524

Princesse Charlotte d'Albret: wife of Cesare, 1480–1514

Juan Borgia: Archbishop of Monreale and Cesare's banker, 1476–97

Général Duc Octavien de Valois: French general and Borgia ally

Michelotto da Corella: Cesare's right-hand man

Luca: Michelotto's diehard

Agostino Chigi: Pope Alexander's banker, 1466–1520

Luigi Torcelli: Cesare's banker's agent

Toffana: Lucrezia's servant

Gaspar Torella: Cesare's personal doctor

Johann Burchard: Pope Alexander VI's master of ceremonies

Juan: Guard at La Mota

Egidio Troche: Roman senator

Francesco Troche: Egidio's brother and Cesare's chamberlain

Michelangelo Buonarotti: artist, sculptor, etc.,
    1475–1564

Vinicio: Machiavelli's contact

Giuliano della Rovere: Pope Julius II, formerly cardinal
    of San Pietro in Vincoli, 1443–1513

Ascanio Sforza: cardinal, uncle of Caterina, 1455–1505

Agniolo and Innocento: assistants to Leonardo da Vinci

Pietro Benintendi: Roman actor

Dottore Brunelleschi: Roman doctor

Georges d'Amboise: the cardinal of Rouen, 1460–1510

Pope Pius III: formerly Cardinal Piccolomini, 1439–1503

Bruno: a spy

GLOSSARY OF ITALIAN, FRENCH, AND LATIN TERMS

Aiutateme! Help me!
Aiuto! Help!
albergo hotel
Altezza Highness
altrettanto a lei also to you
Andiamo! Let's go!
arrivederci goodbye
Assassini Assassins
Ayúdenme! Help me!

bastardo, bastardi bastard/s
bellissima very beautiful
bene good, well
bestiarii gladiators
birbante rascal, rogue
brutissimo most horrible, ugliest
buona fortuna good luck
buona questa good one
buona sera good evening
buon giorno good morning

calma/calmatevi   calm down
campanile   bell tower
campione   champion
Capisci?   Do you understand?
capitano   captain
caro padre   dear father
cazzo   prick, shit
Che cosa fate qui?   What are you doing here?
Che diavolo?   What the devil?
cher ami   dear friend
che tipo brutto   what a brute
Chiudi la bocca!   Shut your mouth!
Come usciamo di qui?   How do we get out of here?
Commendatore   Commander
compadre   comrade
condottieri   mercenaries
con piacere   with pleasure
Consummatum est!   It is finished!
contessa   countess
Corri!   Run!
Cosa diavolo aspetti?   What the devil are you
   waiting for?
Curia   the Roman law courts

déclarez-vous   declare yourself
diavolo   devil
dio mio   my god
dio, ti prego, salvaci   Lord, I beg you, save us
dottore   doctor

Eccellenza   Excellence
el médico   the doctor
Eminenze   Eminence
è vero   it's true

figlio di puttana   son of a whore
figlio mio   my son
Firenze   Florence
forze armate   armed forces
fottere   fuck
fotutto Francese   fucking Frenchman
fratellino   little brother
furbacchione   cunning old devil

gonfalon   banner
graffito   graffiti
grazie   thank you

Halte-la!   Stop there!

idioti   idiots
il Magnifico   the Magnificent
Insieme per la vittoria!   Together for victory!
intesi   certainly, understood
ipocrita   hypocrite

ladro   thief
lieta di conoscervi   pleased to meet you
luridi codardi   filthy cowards

Ma attenzione!   But be careful!
ma certo   but of course
Ma che merviglia!   But what a marvel!
Madonna   my lady
madre   mother
maestro   master
mais franchement, je m'en doute   but frankly, I doubt it
malattia venerea   venereal illness
maldito bastardo   damned bastard

maledetto   cursed

mausoleo   mausoleum

medico   doctor

merda   shit

messer/e   sir

mille grazie   a thousand thank yous

miracolo   miraculous

mis piernas   my legs

molte grazie   thank you very much

molto bene   very good

momentino   one moment

morbus gallicus   French disease

nessun problema   no problem

nomenclatura   influential

Nos replegamos!   Fall back!

onoratissima   most honored one

ora, mi scusi, ma   excuse me

padrone   father

palazzo   palace

panpepati e mielati   pepper and honey breads

Papa   Pope

perdonatemi   forgive me

perdone, Colonnello   sorry, Colonel

perfetto   perfect

pezzo di merda   piece of shit

piano nobile   the principal floor of a large house

piazze   squares

pollo ripieno   stuffed chicken

porco   pig

por favor   please

pranzo   lunch

presidente president
puttana whore

requiescat in pace rest in peace
rione district
rocca fortress

salute (to your) health
salve hello
sang maudit blood curses
scorpioni scorpions
Senatore Senator
ser sir
sì yes
signora lady
signore sir
Signoria governing authority
Sul serio? Seriously?

tesora, tesoro sweetheart, treasure
Torna qui, maledetto cavallo! Come here, damned horse!

un momento one moment

va bene all right
vero true
Vi ringrazio di tutto quello che avete fatto per me, buona Contessa. Addio. I thank you for all you have done for me, good Countess. Goodbye.
virtù virtue
Vittoria agli Assassini! Victory to the Assassins!
La Volpe Addormentata The Sleeping Fox

zio uncle